THE CROWN OF THE IUTES

The Song of Octa
Book Three

JAMES CALBRAITH

FLYING SQUID

Published December 2021 by Flying Squid

Visit James Calbraith's official website at
jamescalbraith.wordpress.com
for the latest news, book details, and other information

Copyright © James Calbraith, 2021

This book is a work of fiction. Names, characters, places and incidents either are products of the author's imagination or are used fictitiously. Any resemblance to actual events or locales or persons, living or dead, is entirely coincidental.

All rights reserved. Except as permitted under the U.S. Copyright Act of 1976, no part of this publication may be reproduced, distributed or transmitted in any form or by any means, or stored in a database or retrieval system, without the prior written permission of the publisher.
Fan fiction and fan art is encouraged.

THE LORDS OF BRITANNIA

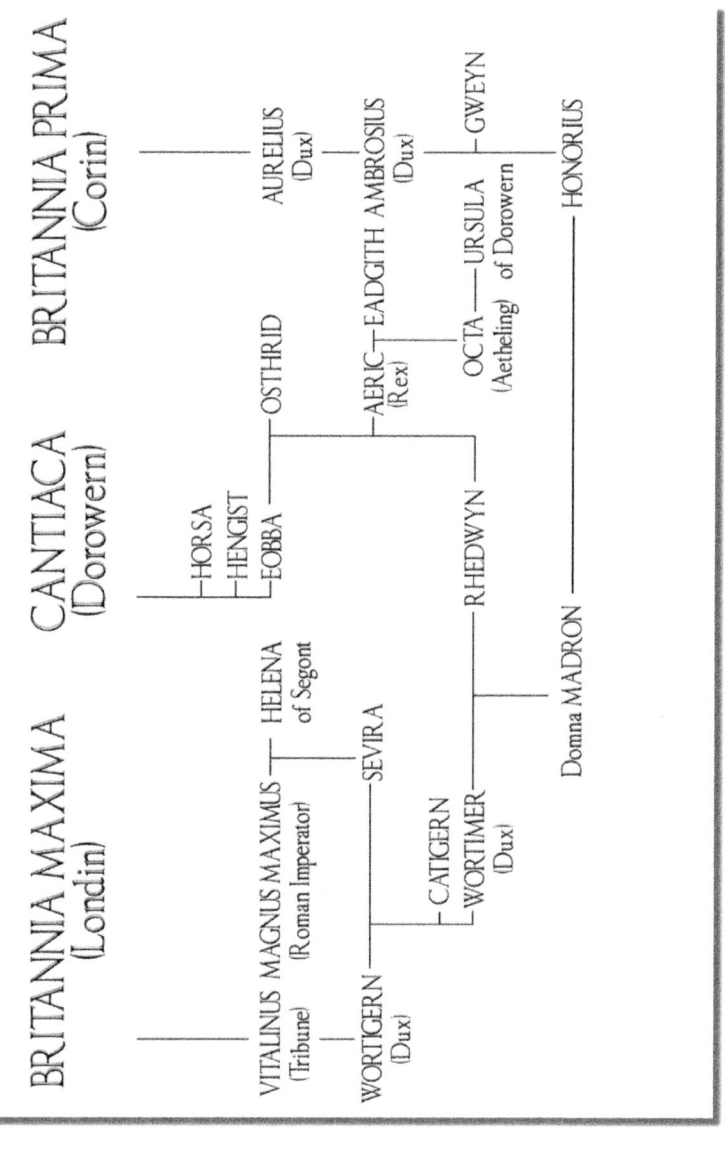

GAUL, c. 470 AD

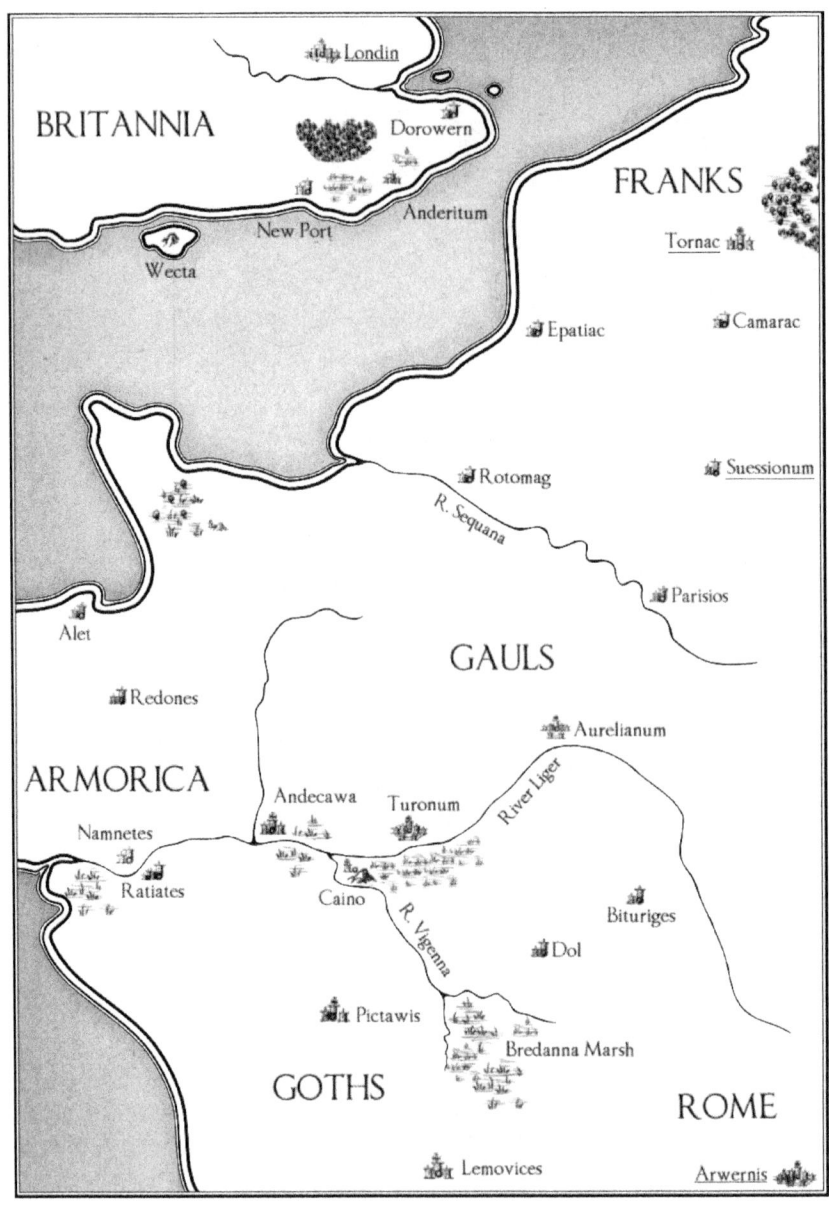

CAST OF CHARACTERS

Britannia

Aelle: *Rex* of the Southern Saxons
Albanus: *Comes* of Cadwallons, son of Elasio
Ambrosius: *Dux* of the western province of Britannia Prima
Bellicus: a veteran soldier guarding Londin's cathedral
Catuarion: a Regin noble, son of the last *Comes* of the Regins
Cissa: Aelle's son
Fastidius: Bishop of Londin, foster-brother of King Aeric
Haesta: Chieftain of the Iute clan of the Haestingas
Hilla: Aelle's wife, queen of the Southern Saxons
Illica: a warrior of Poor Town
Honorius: Ambrosius's son
Laurentius: Londin nobleman
Madron: also Myrtle, daughter of Wortimer, former *Dux* of Britannia Maxima, and Rhedwyn, princess of the Iutes
Mandubrac: *Comes* of the Trinowaunts
Riotham: Councillor of Londin, Ambrosius's representative
Wulf: Chieftain of the Poor Town district

Cantia

Aeric I: also Ash, Fraxinus: *Rex* of the Iutes, former Councillor of *Dux* Wortigern
Betula: also Birch; *Gesith*, commander of King Aeric's household guards
Octa: *aetheling* of Iutes, son of King Aeric
Pascent: son of Octa and Ursula

Seawine: chief of Octa's foot soldiers
Ursula: daughter of Cantian nobles, Octa's bride

Octa's riders:
    Audulf
    Croha
    Deora
    Eolh
    Ubba

Gaul

Ahes: *Comes* of Armorican Britons
Basina: queen of the Salian Franks
Drustan: *Decurion* of Armorican cavalry
Gelasius: Bishop of Pictawis in Gaul
Hlodoweg: Son of Hildrik and Basina
Marcus: Ahes's husband, commander of Armorican army
Budic: Armorican Briton patrician
Hildrik: king of the Salian Franks
Paulus: commander of armies of Northern Gaul
Syagrius: son of Aegidius, *Magister Militum* of Gaul
Victurius: vicar general of Andecawa

Riotham's army:

Abulius: a Londin nobleman
Atrect: an officer of Dorowern *vigiles*
Cait: Cantian tribal militiaman
Tammo: Peasant recruit

Goths and Saxons:

Adalfuns: a rebel warrior, former *gardinga* of King Thaurismod
Aiwarik: king of the Goths in Tolosa
Eishild: daughter of Thaurismod, rightful king of the Goths
Airmanarik: a rebel chieftain, loyal to King Thaurismod
Odowakr: Skir warlord
Sigegaut: chieftain of the Saxon pirates of Liger Mouth

GLOSSARY

Aetheling: member of the Iutish royal family
Amphora: large clay vessel for liquids
Angon: barbed throwing spear
Ballista: a missile-throwing siege weapon
Basilica: main public building of a Roman city
Bucellarii: private troops of a Roman nobleman
Centuria: troop of (about) hundred infantry
Centurion: officer in Roman infantry
Ceol: Saxon ship
Chrismon: a monogram symbol of Christ
Comes, pl. Comites: administrator of a *pagus*, subordinate to the *Dux*
Decurion: officer in Roman cavalry
Domus: the main structure of a *villa*
Domnus, Domna: Roman lord and lady
Dux: overall commander in war times; in peace time – administrator of a province
Equites: Roman cavalry
Francisca: throwing axe
Frauja, fraujo: Lord and Lady in Frankish
Fyrd: army made up of all warriors of the tribe
Gardingi: household guard of the Gothic king
Gesith: companion of the *Drihten*, chief of the *Hiréd*
Hiréd: band of elite warriors of *Drihten*'s household
Hlaford, Hlaefdige: Lord and Lady in Saxon tongue.
Mansio: staging post
Pagus, pl. Pagi: administrative unit, smaller than a province
Rex: king of a barbarian tribe

Seax: Saxon short sword
Sicera: Armorican drink of fermented apples
Spatha: Roman long sword
Villa: Roman agricultural property
Vigiles: town guards and firemen
Wealh, pl. *wealas*: "the others", Britons in Saxon tongue. *Walh* in Frankish
Witan: a gathering of elders

PLACE NAMES

Alet: Saint Malo, Brittany
Andecava: Angers, France
Anderitum: Pevensey Castle, Sussex
Andreda: Weald Forest
Ariminum, Wealingatun: Wallington, Surrey
Arvernis: Clermont-Ferrand, France
Armorica: Brittany
Aurelianum: Orleans, France
Bredanna: Brenne Marshes, France
Bituriges: Bourges, France
Caino: Chinon, France
Camarac: Cambrai, France
Cantia, Cantiaca: Kent
Dol: Deols, near Chateauroux, France
Dorowern: Dorovernum, Canterbury, Kent
Dubris: Dover, Kent
Gesocribate: Douarnenez, Brittany
Liger: River Loire
Lugdunum: Lyons, France
Mealla's Farm: Malling, Kent
Mutuanton: Lewes, Sussex
Namnetes: Nantes, Brittany
New Port: Novus Portus, Portslade, Sussex
Pictawis: Poitiers, France
Ratiates: Rezé, France
Rhenum: River Rhine
Robriwis: Dorobrivis, Rochester, Kent
Rotomag: Rotomagus, Rouen, France
Rutubi: Rutupiae, Richborough, Kent
Segora: Bressuire, France

Turonum: Tours, France
Vigenna: River Vienne
Werlam: St. Albans, Hertfordshire

PART 1: LONDIN, 468 AD

CHAPTER I
THE LAY OF UBBA

A squat merchant galley appears out of the dunes and limps fitfully towards the narrow channel between the Isle of Tanet and the mainland. She's mortally wounded. Her one striped sail is in tatters; half her oars are shattered. She's brimming with a heavy load, so that her deck almost touches the water, and her hull grinds against the seabed, dangerously shallow this close to shore. Still, if she can reach the safety of the River Stur, both the crew and the load will be spared; the Saxon pirates, however bold they may be, do not, yet, dare to enter the mouth of the channel – for that would mean sailing past Rutubi.

The ancient Roman fortress – what little of it remains after decades of locals quarrying its walls – once again guards the shore from the Saxons against whom it was once raised. My father did what he could to strengthen its crumbling ramparts. He had stones and timber from the nearby amphitheatre hauled to reinforce the embankments; he ordered building of a siege machine, devised according to the Roman war manuals I brought many years ago from my adventures in Gaul, and set it up atop a corner tower, from where it overlooks the entire width of the channel. When he's staying with his court in the mead hall, built to lean against the fortress's northern wall, his *Hiréd* guard mans the ramparts and patrols the coast, discouraging the sea raiders with their mere presence; but the king is not home today – he's moved to Robriwis for the summer, leaving only me and my men to protect the shore. Still, we should be enough to thwart any attacker foolish enough to challenge us in our own home…

And yet, here they come, and in greater numbers than ever before. Three *ceols* sail into the channel, slowly, carefully, hidden in the reeds, like wolves stalking prey through the tall grass. They hug the northern shore by the Isle of Tanet, as far away from Rutubi's walls as possible. Archers and javelin-men stare at the dunes, their

The Crown of the Iutes

weapons aimed at an unseen enemy, though I imagine they are more frightened of the wraiths of the Iutes buried on the island. This tiny speck of land was once a crowded, filthy home to the entire tribe of refugees, back when we had to beg the Britons to let us stay. Now, it's only a haunted graveyard, and a sacred ground where the priests perform the rites in memory of our fallen. Even I hesitate to visit it these days, though in my youth I would often cross the channel in search of quiet and solitude.

The Saxons are right to be wary. We have used merchant ships as bait before, though never this close to one of our coastal fortresses; but the galley is too great a prize to simply ignore. She sailed from Gaul, bearing the mark of Saint Peter on her sail, announcing that the haul and the passengers she carries belong to the Church; and that can only mean one thing: plenty of silver, maybe even some gold. Worth losing a few men or a couple of ships if the survivors can get away with their plunder – and the glory of victory over the hated *wealas*.

After passing the entrance to the channel, the Saxons pick up speed. These are not Aelle's men – they'd know better than to risk our wrath for such an uncertain gain. These new Saxons have come from across the Narrow Sea, to harass the walled towns and trade routes of the *wealas*, from Clausent in the west to Dubris in the east, and beyond, all the way to Coln in Trinowaunt land. There is little of worth for these sea pirates to find in the fishing villages and farmsteads of the Iutes besides some slaves and provisions, so we would have been safe to ignore all but the most daring of their incursions into Cantia – if not for the treaties the Iutes once signed with the Britons, which oblige us to defend Cantia's shores from all invaders, by land or by sea.

This new enemy first arrived at our shore four years ago, not, as we soon found out, from the Old Country where the Saxons lived of old, but from some mysterious new harbours they set up in Gaul, in the empty, unruly lands between the domains of the Goths, the

Armoricans and the few provinces still ruled by the remnants of Roman administration. And they've been growing bolder with every raid, reaching ever deeper, taking ever more, forcing the Britons back beyond their stone walls. Still, they don't know these waters as well as we do. If they did, they'd know where to check for ambush before venturing into the confined and treacherous currents of the Tanet Channel.

I blow the warhorn; the sorrowful sound booms across the sea, reaching from shore to shore. The mighty instrument is made out of an aurochs's horn, bound in bronze and silver: a gift from our ally, and my friend, *Rex* Hildrik of the Salian Franks, presented to me after his victory at Aurelianum, six years ago. The horn belonged to the Gothic general, Fridrik, slain by Hildrik himself at Aurelianum's gates. I took no part in that battle, but my men and I did help with the victory in a small way, defeating a force of Goths threatening Hildrik's western flank in Armorica, for which the Franks and the Gauls rewarded us richly.

At the horn's signal, three of our boats sail out of the thick reeds on the southern shore, while two more launch from a hidden cove on Tanet. The Saxons soon spot us, but they pay us little attention; we are a few small, hide-bound fishing boats, and it would be foolish of us to assault three large *ceols* full of seasoned warriors – if that was all we were.

As the galley slowly turns towards the mouth of the River Stur, and the Saxons launch into attack speed, I blow the horn once again. Three more boats join us from the opposite end of the channel, each with an archer standing on the bow, nocking a flaming arrow. This, at last, makes the raiders anxious – but they're too close to the galley to retreat now. They catch up to the cumbersome vessel, one on each side, with the third, the largest, in reserve. The warriors leap from deck to deck, launching with their *seaxes* drawn at what should be a terrified crew. Except this time, the crew fights back.

The Crown of the Iutes

They're all Iutes, too, twenty eager youths hoping to join the ranks of my warriors, led by Audulf, my finest officer. I had them sail to Bononia a few weeks ago, in preparation for this mission. I was sure the Saxons had their spies in the harbour, informing them which ships were worth pursuing, and I knew they would soon find out about a troop of Iutish warriors joining the merchant's team as guards; so as not to raise any suspicions, I had my men mingle among the ship's crew as regular sailors and work the ropes and oars on several journeys.

The ruse worked. The surprise is complete. Within moments, in a flash of steel and blood, a third of the pirates lie dead on the galley's deck, or float in bloodied waters around it. But the Saxons are too strong and experienced fighters to be so easily defeated by a mere pack of youths. After the initial shock, they push again, forcing Audulf towards the stern. Even as the battle rages on, other warriors grab the chests and *amphorae* from under the deck and haul them over to the waiting *ceols*.

Before the two *ceols* can depart, our boats reach the third one, drifting at the rear. Like the Scots pirates, whose ingenious tactics I imitate, we surround the drifting *ceol* from all sides before throwing grappling hooks to attach our boats to its hull. The archers and the javelin-men release their missiles; the flaming arrows strike the sail and the coiled ropes, soaked in tar, igniting them in an instant.

The Saxons expect us to board the *ceol* now, and engage in a deathly brawl on deck, in which they have a good chance of victory. But I'm not giving them the satisfaction; instead, I have half of my men draw hatchets, picks and great auger drills I brought from Dubris shipyards. While the remaining warriors cover them with shields from missiles thrown from the *ceol*'s deck, they strike at the hull, carving and cutting great holes in the timber, just below the waterline.

The other two *ceols*, noticing our efforts, break away from the galley; the Saxon warriors abandon the battle and leap back to their vessels in haste. But the *ceols* are now encumbered with plunder, and slow to turn in the narrow, shallow confines of the Stur's mouth. The Iutes on the galley drop their swords and pick up bows instead; they launch volley after volley at the fleeing *ceols*, reaping a bloody harvest.

At last, the Saxon *ceols* reach us and try to ram through to free their trapped comrades. I signal the boats to disperse. One of them is too slow; the *ceol* slices through it like a knife. I watch ten good men disappear under its bow, never to emerge again. But the others escape to the safety of the reed beds, where no ship can follow. It's now time for the last part of the plan.

The Saxons pass us by, slowed down by plunder and damage, the largest *ceol* listing to starboard and drifting dangerously close to the southern shore. We launch after them again; even the merchant galley joins the pursuit, rid now of the heavy load. I lead our little flotilla around the stern of the enemy, and close in from their port side, though for now we keep a safe distance, in case the Saxons decide to try their aim with arrows and javelins.

But their hearts are no longer in this fight. By now, they must have realised they were cheated. The chests, *amphorae* and sacks that they carried with such effort from the galley are filled with rocks and water; already, I see the men on one of the *ceols* throw the worthless haul overboard. There will be no glory or silver to gain today. All they can hope to get away with are their lives.

I wave at my men to row closer to the Saxons. The archers on the galley shoot again; the arrows fall harmlessly astern of the slowest *ceol*, but they add to the Saxon distress. On a sudden breeze, the front two *ceols* lurch forward, leaving the last one drifting behind; they must hope we'll halt to capture the easy prey, and let them get away. I leave one of the boats to shadow the wounded ship and press on with the chase. The Saxons swerve to the south-east, hoping to avoid our pursuit and reach the open sea quicker that way; exactly where I want them to go.

The faster of the two *ceols* is the first to fall into our trap. It hits the hidden shallows with such force that its bow launches a few feet into the air before coming crashing down. The second *ceol*'s helmsman desperately tries to avoid the unseen sand bank, but the breeze that was to be his salvation proves to be his doom, as it throws the *ceol* sideways into the reeds.

The captain of the third *ceol*, seeing the trouble befalling the other crews, deliberately points his vessel away from the open sea and straight towards the shallows. I nod to myself, approvingly. Whoever commands this expedition decided to stay with his men and fight to the last, rather than abandon them and flee for safety.

The Saxons must still think they stand a chance of surviving the battle. If they can fend off our assault, they could then repair the slight damage to their vessels and cobble together at least one that's again seaworthy. The warriors all leap from the decks into knee-deep water, and wade to the broad shingle beach to their south, hoping to reach it before we do. At their chief's command, they start to form a shield wall, two rows deep, facing the sea.

I gesture at the boats to scatter again, and we hit the beach in four different places. I tumble out, sword drawn, and gather two crews around me; the other two launch into a feigned attack at the shield wall's flank. The Saxon chief is too shrewd to fall for it, and beats the charge with ease, without breaking the line. I'm not giving him time to gather his men, and his wits, again. I put the aurochs horn to my lips and blow three short tones.

For a moment, nothing happens. I can see consternation in the Saxon eyes, as my men don't move from our landing place. Then they hear it – or rather, feel it, at first: hooves of a dozen war ponies, beating the shingle in a mad dash. The Saxon chief orders the shield wall to turn around to face the new enemy, but they're too late; a wedge of bearskin-wearing riders, led by Ubba, charges from beyond the dunes. The Saxons recognise the famous fur cloaks and shout out the name in panic: "The bear-shirts! The bear-shirts!"

It is from the Saxon hordes that we met in Gaul that I took the idea of cladding my warriors in bear-skin cloaks. In their armies, these marked the terrifying elite foot warriors, turned mad by a mixture of herbs and mushrooms. My bear-shirts are the finest of the Iute riders, mounting the best of moor ponies, hand-picked and trained by myself and my officers into a force that strikes fear into the hearts of all those who have heard of the ferocious bear-shirts. And they manage to achieve it even without the use of the secret henbane wine that my father's *Hiréd* drink before battle to make themselves fearless and immune to pain.

The cavalry wedge smashes into the Saxons like an armoured fist. Any semblance of order disappears in that instant; the chieftain falls first, his heart pierced by Ubba's lance. Only now I order the rest of my men into battle, to make sure no Saxons escape our trap. I needn't have worried. Seeing their commander dead, and their shield wall scattered, most of the warriors drop their weapons and kneel down with their heads low and hands high. A few make a feeble stand on the water line, preferring death in battle to the ignominy of surrender. We gladly grant them the glory of Wodan's Hall; the Saxons believe in the same gods as the Iutes, and we all know how important it is for a warrior to die with a sword in his hand.

But the rest prefer to choose another day for joining the ranks of Wodan's guests. Ubba's riders surround the largest group on a spit of sand, separated from the beach by a tidal channel. Ubba dismounts and waits for me to wade across to accept the Saxon surrender. We greet with an embrace. The bear fur on his back stinks of sweat and salt.

"A victory worthy of legend, *aetheling*!" he exclaims. "Three *ceols* captured with barely a man lost – your father will be proud!"

"I'm not doing this to make my father proud," I remind him. "But to defend our home."

"I'm certain after today they will think twice before coming here again."

"I wish I could share your good cheer, Ubba," I say. "I feel we only made them angry." I look around. "Where is Seawine?"

"*Rex* Aeric called him to Mealla's Farm just before we marched out of Rutubi."

I frown. "Seawine is not his to command, unless there's a war brewing. What does my father want with him at the Saxon border?"

"I wouldn't know, *Hlaford*."

I glance at the Saxons, and at their three vessels stuck in the shallows. "I guess this was the last great raid this season," I say. "See if you can salvage anything from these *ceols* for the Frankish boatwrights at Dubris. I trust I can leave you and Audulf to deal with whatever marauders may still come before winter?"

"We will manage. What about you, *Hlaford*?"

"I'm going back to my wife and son – I haven't seen them in weeks. But first, I think I'll see what so rattled my father."

The sound of dozens of spades, mattocks and pickaxes rings out all along the earthworks. The great dyke is slowly taking shape, growing out of the chalk slope of the Downs, with a ditch on the western side: the fastness of Mealla's Farm, one of several such rings of earthen banks and ditches that my father ordered built along the contested border with Aelle's Saxon kingdom. Here, the Medu River, traditionally the western border of Cantia, bends several miles eastwards, leaving swathes of fertile land on the other side; since Aelle's defeat at Robriwis ten years ago, these fields have belonged to the Iutes – but the scattered Iutish farms, and the important Roman road from Robriwis to the south coast that passes through here, are difficult to defend from the incursions of the insolent forest bands that still dwell in Andreda, beyond anyone's command.

When I arrive at Mealla's Farm, I expect the trouble to come from one such band – though I would think that the *Hiréd*, led by the dreaded one-armed shieldmaiden Betula, would be enough to deal with mere forest bandits on its own. A quick look at the gathered force – and lack of any damage from a supposed bandit raid – tells me that something else is the cause of my father's alarm.

I find Betula and Seawine standing on top of a finished stretch of the dyke, staring towards the wooded plain below. The forest looms menacingly, dark even in the middle of a sunny day, oozing cold, sinister tendrils towards the farms and villages. It takes a brave man to live in Andreda's shadow. The bandits are the least of our worries – at least they're flesh and blood. Many here – even the Britons – believe the wood to be a living being in its own right, a god or a demon, sending armies of wraiths and other dark spirits under cover of the night to frighten children, steal crops and harass the livestock.

The Crown of the Iutes

Between the dyke and the forest, the muddy, trampled plain is strewn with remnants of a recent battle – discarded weapons, torn clothes, crows gnawing on hacked-off chunks of flesh. The bodies are all gone, but I can tell the fighting was fierce at the dyke, if short.

"*Aetheling,*" the two greet me with bows and salutes.

"Can either of you explain what happened here?" I ask. "Were the *Hiréd* and my men really necessary to deal with some forest bandits?"

"They weren't bandits," says Betula. "They were warriors. Two bands of Saxon raiders, coming from the High Rocks fort, one here, the other at Beaddingatun."

"Aelle's own?"

"We think so. They didn't last long," adds Seawine. "Didn't seem to have their hearts in the fight, once they saw how firm our shield wall stood."

"But – why now? After so many years? And when the campaign season's nearly over?"

She shrugs. "Who's to say? But if they decide to strike again before winter, and with more keenness, I'm not sure how long we can defend these poor farmers. The dyke is nowhere near ready yet."

I slap away a midge biting at my nose. The marshy land near the Medu is still buzzing with annoying insects, even this late into the autumn.

"High Rocks? Are you sure?"

She nods. "We tracked them down as they retreated."

"I'm not much keen on assaulting a fortress on top of a sheer cliff," I say. "Not at the end of such a long year of fighting."

"Then what do you propose?" asks Seawine.

"I will go check it out myself," I say. "And if it's really Aelle, I'll simply ask him what's going on."

Betula raises her eyebrow. "Is that wise, *aetheling*?"

"I hope so. Just in case, post some men to that clearing," I say, pointing to a breach in the line of the trees to the south-west. "Have them set up a camp. Could be useful if it *does* turn out to be just a roaming forest band."

I know this place only from my father's stories – a range of tall bluffs of sheer grey rock, with remnants of an old hillfort on top, and ruins of several wooden buildings scattered throughout; once one of the main camps of Aelle's forest army, now supposedly used only by passing bandits and woodsmen for shelter.

Betula was right – there's an entire warband here, of well-armed and trained warriors, and one greater than any we've seen in recent years. But rather than gathering for a renewed assault, as we feared, it is already dispersing. As the guard leads me up a ladder to where I am to meet their warchief, I see small groups of warriors pack up and wander off into the woods. Still, there remain enough of the camp's renewed fortifications and a few newly raised permanent buildings to indicate that the Saxons are planning to return here before long.

The Crown of the Iutes

"*Rex* Aelle," I greet the Saxon king when we reach the top of the bluff. We meet within the walls of what once was a small mead hall, now roofless and with weeds growing over its rotting walls. Judging by the damage, this place hasn't been used in some twenty years. We sit on piles of furs, on either side of a smouldering hearth, covered from the elements by a deer hide spread out on four poles.

I can't remember the last time I saw King Aelle, but every time I do, I'm startled at how similar he looks to my father. The similarity is not so much a physical one – only that they're both pale-skinned fair-hairs, of almost the same age – but in how their parallel lives reflect in their gazes, their gestures, the way they speak and listen. They both came to rule their people in an inhospitable foreign land at roughly the same time, although Aelle was raised to be a chieftain by his father, while Aeric had to reach his position from that of a mere slave. Their relationship was as complex as only a relationship between two neighbouring rulers surrounded by common enemy could be: at times allies, more often rivals, ever wary of each other – but also, admiring one another's tenacity and ingenuity in surviving against the odds.

"You sound surprised," Aelle replies to my greeting. "Did your trackers not tell you what to expect here?"

"I knew there would be a Saxon warband – I didn't expect a king to lead it himself. You wouldn't find my father commanding a small expedition like this. Do you not have a trusted warchief who would do it for you?"

He grins. "My Cissa is still too young – and I like to do these things myself. Keeps me entertained. Unlike Ash, I find no pleasure in the daily goings-on of a peaceful kingdom."

"My father does it out of sense of duty, not for pleasure."

He chuckles. "I'm sure he does."

He runs his hand along the weapon lying at his side, as if he was stroking a cat. I know it well – the ancient, deadly *arcuballista*, a bolt-thrower of blackened wood, which featured in so many songs telling of Aelle's deeds.

"Why are you here, Octa?" he asks.

"Why are *you* here?"

"This is my land. I have every right to be here."

"Certainly – but that last attack was not an action of a determined warchief as skilled as yourself. It was only a probe, wasn't it? Are you planning to launch a full invasion after winter?"

Aelle's broad grin turns into a cold smile.

"What if I do?"

"You'd be mad to. We may only have a hundred shieldsmen on Mealla's fastness today, but by spring thaws my father will summon the *fyrd* to deal with the threat. Why would you risk your warriors to capture these few muddy farms?"

He locks his fingers under his chin – another gesture that I often see my father do; I know what it means – he's about to tell me something he finds difficult to say.

"I may have no choice."

"What do you mean? Who could possibly be forcing your hand?"

He leans back. "My people are not blind. They see their pirate kin plundering Cantia, and haul away great spoils."

The Crown of the Iutes

"And they want some of it for themselves," I guess. Now I understand why Aelle had to come to Andreda himself; there is unrest brewing in the Saxon kingdom. The clan chieftains must be losing their patience with the *rex* who hasn't led a successful raid in years. The Saxons have been plundering the Regin land for so long, there must be little left for the insatiable clan chieftains to plunder. If Aelle wants to keep his *rex*'s circlet, he must strike beyond his borders.

"Can't they join the pirate crews themselves?" I ask.

"Many do. That's my problem. I'm losing some of my best warriors to those *ceols*. I can't offer them what the pirates give them – glory and gold – without going to war myself."

I shake my head. "I will not let the Iutes lose their lives and livelihoods so that you can satisfy your warriors' urges."

"Would you rather I struck at the Meon Valley again? At Wecta? The farms are not as wealthy there, but would make for an easier target."

I wince. I don't need a reminder of what can happen when the Saxons strike at our distant western colonies. The last time Aelle tried to provoke a conflict there, his warriors slew my mother and slaughtered dozens of defenceless farmers and shepherds. As he says, there is little there now that would make a war worthwhile, except the pony breeding grounds in Meon's moors – even the pirates rarely pass by Wecta on the way to Cantia's shores. Still, if the Saxons did decide to launch another attack there, we would have no way of defending our people.

In my head, I run through all the possible solutions to Aelle's dilemma. It's clear to me that simply letting him launch an invasion would be a disaster for both of our peoples. Any war is a gamble; even if I were confident in the skill of my warriors, and the strength of our fortifications, there could never be a guarantee of victory against a warchief as skilled and cunning as Aelle. And the Iutes can ill afford losing good warriors when we still have the pirate menace to deal with next summer. Aelle knows it – he would never have agreed to launch this campaign if he didn't know how costly it would be for us, even if we did prevail in the end.

We could do what the Romans did in these circumstances – pay Aelle off, hoping a few sacks of silver might placate his clan chiefs without any blood spilt. But paying tribute, which in the short term might seem the easiest way, was a trap; the Saxons would only demand more next year, and then more again, until my father's chests were as empty as if they'd plundered them themselves…

I give Aelle a puzzled look. "Do you… do you want to bargain?"

"You came here for a reason, didn't you?"

"I came here to tell you to plead for peace and go home, before things go too far for both of us."

"If I do that, I might as well lay down my circlet and let the *witan* elect a new *rex*." He sighs. "I hoped showing them how well defended even these few muddy farms were, would calm their heads. But it only whetted their appetites. I'm afraid my hands are tied – you must tell your father to prepare for war and pray to Wodan, or whatever gods he believes in, that it is a swift one."

"I will speak to him as soon as he returns from Londin," I say. I did not find my father in Robriwis when I passed through the town on the way to the border – once again, he was away, doing whatever it was that he did on the mysterious, and increasingly frequent, missions to the great city. "Maybe we'll be able to come up with a better solution before spring time."

The Crown of the Iutes

"A warrior shouldn't think too hard about ways to avoid fighting," Aelle reminds me. "Or he'd risk Wodan's wrath."

"A warrior, maybe," I agree. "But a king must think of his people's well-being before his own glory."

"Is that what Ash has been teaching you?" Aelle chuckles. "I always knew all that time he spent among the *wealas* would addle his mind."

CHAPTER II
THE LAY OF PASCENT

The banner of the white horse, carried by Audulf in front of our column, flutters in the cool early winter breeze. The sailing season is over, and so is the threat of the sea raiders, at least until spring thaws. Now is the time to celebrate our victories, hail those who survived, mourn those who fell, and figure out what to do with those we captured in the recent battles.

The Rutubi Gate, washed, painted white and strewn with garlands of flowers and ribbons of painted cloth, is as good an imitation of a triumphal arch as was possible for the few remaining Briton citizens of Dorowern to arrange for our arrival. They prepared it more for their own sake than mine and my troops; for a day, it lets them feel Roman again, as if my "triumph" is supposed to bring back the memory of ancient glory, even if all that's left of it in the city is the looming marble ruin of the theatre, lonely walls and pillars of the *basilica* and the Forum, and the cracked domes of the baths. Time, fires, floods and sea raiders conspired to reduce the once-great capital of the *pagus* of Cantiaca to little more than a sea of waste and rubble. There are more barbarians living within the walls now, than there are Britons in their small huts sunk into the dug-up foundations, amid thatched wooden houses built with complete disregard to the network of stone streets. Some of the wealthy Dorowernians, like the family of my Cantian wife, Ursula, moved to the rural *villas* in the Downs, from which they descend once every few weeks to take part in a Mass at the city church, do some paltry trade in the ruins of the Forum, or attend the meeting of the increasingly ineffective tribal Council; those wealthier still fled with their families and servants abroad: west, to *Dux* Ambrosius's still Briton-ruled province, or to Armorica, now

The Crown of the Iutes

flourishing under the rule of *Comes* Marcus and his wife, One-Eyed Ahes.

But there still remain enough of the *wealas* in the province to line the sides of the city's main avenue and watch as a hundred Iute warriors march in a loud, bawdy, triumphant procession, followed by a long train of chained Saxon and Friesian captives, and carts filled with the spoils of war, towards the Forum, where the grateful citizens prepared a feast worthy of our victories. That the triumph is led by a heathen *rex*'s son doesn't seem to bother them – after all, Rome herself accepted triumphs from barbarian warlords in the past, if the old stories are to be believed. The Britons have no army to speak of – other than handfuls of *vigiles* watching over what's left of the walled towns, a scattered remnant of tribal militia and the nobles' *villa* guards – so they must hope to share in our glory instead.

The mud at our feet is hardened with cold, and I wince as I watch the townsfolk pick it up and pelt our captives. The warriors don't deserve the humiliation – they fought well, and their surrender meant fewer deaths on our side; but I can't deny this small act of vengeance to the people who had been threatened by the raids all through the year, frightened away from their fields and their usual trade routes, bullied almost into starvation. For too many, this year, despite all our efforts, was one of the most tragic they remembered since the Pictish raids of ten years ago. It was the poorest of Britons who suffered the most when the pirates managed to get through our defences and avoid our patrols. The raids only added to their misery. Abandoned by their Council, denied protection of Londin's soldiers, they lost what little precious items they still possessed – those that hadn't already been sold for food or buried deep in the ground for future, hopefully safer, generations: the ancient silver plate, the golden brooch, the jewel-studded earring, the goblet of Hispanic glass… Once the pirates attacked a farmstead or a village, they would take everything but the straw from the beddings, including those men and women who could fetch a good price at the Epatiac market. Little wonder, then, that those of the victims who survived the ordeal wish disgrace and cruel death on our captives.

Their wishes, however, will not be granted. The lives and freedoms of the Saxons belong to me and my father. Some – those most valuable – will be exchanged next year for the Iutes captured this year; others will be given to the Iutish families as slaves, to replace those they killed or took away. And a chosen few, whom my father will deem worthy of his favour, may perhaps be even allowed to join our kingdom, and given land to settle as a reward.

As we enter the Forum, I glance over my shoulder and wonder which, if any, of this autumn's captives will be granted this honour. The Saxon raiders proved surprisingly loyal to my father in seasons past; there are now enough of them to populate several large farmsteads on the desolate land between Medu and Crei, where they live freely among the Iute settlers and Briton serfs; far enough from the coast for them not to be tempted to return to their brethren – and far enough from Andreda to prevent them switching their allegiance to *Rex* Aelle's neighbouring kingdom.

Observing the feast spread before us on the stones of the Forum, I feel nothing but pity for the people of Dorowern. The nobles have set up a few tables for themselves and my officers within a makeshift enclosure in the shadow of the *basilica*'s tallest remaining wall, and those are heaving with an impressive variety of meats and cheeses. But the rest of the fare is so meagre, it's almost insulting to my warriors. My men eat better meals every day than these pots of thin potage, black loafs of bread and barrels of muddy ale that are presented to us – and yet, I'm certain that this is the best that the poor Briton townsfolk have to offer.

I nod at Seawine, my right-hand man and commander of my foot warriors. He reaches into the sack and throws several handfuls of bronze coins into the crowd of the gathered *wealas*. They rush to

The Crown of the Iutes

his feet to gather the pieces from the mud. I sense the annoyed stares of the Cantian nobles on me. With this gesture, once reserved to Imperators, I have come close to crossing the line. But I couldn't care less for the acceptance of the nobles. They have no power over me, even in their own city, not while I'm surrounded by a hundred of my best warriors, all dressed in shining mail coats and fur-trimmed cloaks.

There's only one noble in Dorowern whose opinion I care about. As I dismount, she puts down the three-year-old boy she's until now been holding in her arms, and rushes to me with outstretched hands.

I embrace and kiss Ursula, then stoop to pick up my son. I raise him high over my head as if he was the most precious of trophies, and shout out loud enough for everyone in the city to hear:

"Io triumphe!"

"Your family could not come?" I ask.

Ursula tightens her cloak before answering. Her parents are powerful Dorowern Councillors – even more so now that their daughter is wedded to the Iute *aetheling* – and should be present in the front rank at the feast. Despite the windbreaks spread around the tables and the thick cloth canopy over our heads, the winter breeze howls through the enclosure, turning all food cold the moment it's served from the cauldrons. I'd much rather celebrate our triumph within the twilight warmth of one of my father's mead halls, and so, I'm sure, would my warriors. But there will be enough feasting throughout the winter – there's little else to do in the cold, dark season between Yule and the first thaws for an *aetheling* and his guard than hunt, train and make merry. Today is the day when we acclaim our friendship with our hosts and allies, and if we have to suffer a little cold and wind for it, so be it.

"My mother caught some illness," she replies. "And at her age… We decided it's better for her and father to stay in the *villa*."

"An illness?" asks Audulf, leaning over the table. "Hope it's nothing serious. There was talk of a plague in Gaul before we left."

Ursula frowns and crosses herself. "Lord preserve us. No, it's… It's nothing serious. Just a bit of fever."

"In any case, it's best that we go straight to Robriwis from here, without stopping to see your parents," I say. "Can't risk little Pascent's health this close to winter."

I rustle my son's golden hair and smile at him. He giggles back and takes a bite of the honey cake.

"What about your father?" Ursula asks. "Shouldn't he be here, celebrating your triumph?"

"Today is my day," I reply. "His presence would only draw attention away from my achievements. He wants the people of Cantia to see I'm a worthy heir."

"What does he care about what the Britons think?"

I chuckle, softly. "One day, I'm sure, he'll deem it worthy of his time to share all his plans with me. Until then, I can only guess. All I know is that he's recently been spending more time in the cold chambers of Londin than in his mead halls."

The Crown of the Iutes

"You don't think –" She lowers her voice so that the nobles around us don't hear her. "You don't think he wants to become a *Dux*, after all those years?"

I force an incredulous laugh; but the truth is, I have been pondering exactly the same. Ever since I brought *Dux* Wortigern's diadem back from the West, nearly ten years ago, I have wondered what my father was planning to do about it, and about the legacy of ancient power that it symbolised. For seven of those years, he did nothing – at least, nothing that I would have been aware of. Only after Ursula gave birth to our son, whom we decided to name after Pascent, my father's master and adopted guardian from the years when he lived as a slave in a Briton *villa*, did he begin to show renewed interest in the politics of Londin and the surrounding provinces, what little of it was still happening; it was as if seeing my heir reminded him that his own life was not yet over – and that his name still meant enough for him to take part in the machinations of the greats and nobles of the ancient capital.

"I'll ask him all about it when we get to Robriwis. I hope this time I can finally persuade him to explain himself," I say and stretch my arms. "Or he can go fight the pirates himself next year."

At the end of every year of my father's reign, he would add a new precious ornament to the walls of the great mead hall at Robriwis, to mark the peace and prosperity of our tribe, and win the favour of the gods. Sometimes, it was a gift from the grateful people; other times, it came from the spoils that our warriors brought back from Gaul; a couple of silver shields hanging over my father's seat were given to us by Hildrik in gratitude for our continuing alliance. In the years of bad harvest or other misfortune, my father would reach into his dwindling family treasure stored in the grounds of his Ariminum *villa* and melt a handful of gold coins into some trinket. The resulting assembly of items, hung in rows between the door and the king's seat, presented a history of the Iutish kingdom as good as any chronicle, if one knew how to read it.

This year was no different, thanks to our victories over the Saxon pirates and the forest bandits. I reach into the sack and take out a silver goblet and an offering plate. Bowing low, I present them to my father, sitting at the far end of the long oaken table. He looks at the treasure with a raised eyebrow.

"This looks like church silver," he says.

"Perhaps," I say with a grin and playful shrug. "Who's to say whence the Saxons took their plunder?"

He gestures for me to slide the plate over to him. He raises it to the candle light. "It bears northern markings," he says.

"Do you want me to send it back to Lindocoln?"

He chuckles. "If the bishop ever comes down here, I will gladly give it back to him. Until then, it will be a worthy addition to my collection." He waves at a slave to take the items away and prepare them for hanging on the soot-blackened wall.

"How was Dorowern?" he asks.

"A cold, windswept ruin," I reply. "As always. Though I suppose you remember when it looked differently."

"It was already a ruin when I first saw it," the king replies. "It was too close to the capital for its own good. Londin wrapped its tendrils around places like Dorowern like ivy around an oak tree and sucked all their juices from them. The first thing that I saw when I came here, thirty years ago, were barges filled with plundered building material, destined for Londin's *villas*."

The Crown of the Iutes

"If you hate Londin so much, why do you spend so much time there?"

He smiles wryly. "You defend our kingdom with your sword and shield – let me fight for it with my words and mind," he says, tapping his brow.

"I didn't know we needed defending from Londin as well. Didn't you always say the *wealas* were a spent force?"

"Ten years ago this may have been true, son – but nothing lasts forever. And even a dying boar can strike one last time once roused."

"And what would have roused this particular boar now, of all times, Father?"

"Many things. The recent events in Gaul… The pirate attacks… Trouble in Aelle's kingdom… And, of course, *Domna* Madron's upcoming nuptials."

Madron – of course! How could I have forgotten?

Ten years ago, *Dux* Ambrosius arrived from the West to bind his son, *Domnus* Honorius, with *Domna* Madron, once known as Myrtle, daughter of Londin's last *Dux*, Wortimer, and the Iutish princess, Rhedwyn. Both children were too young to be wedded at that time – and so it was agreed that Ambrosius would return with his son after a suitable amount of time had passed. It was never supposed to have taken this long; but the *Dux* was too busy dealing with the many threats to his rule, both external and internal, to pay attention to the matter of his son's marital arrangements. And so it came to pass that Madron reached her sixteenth birthday, well into suitable wedding age, and still there was no news of the *Dux* and his son returning to finish what they started a decade earlier.

"She was promised to Ambrosius's son," I say. "What else is there to discuss?"

My father waves his hand. "Ambrosius is weakened, and far away. There are other nobles in Londin with sons of marrying age who think Wortimer's daughter should stay in her father's city… And know how much power they could gain through her."

"And what does Madron think about it all?"

"I wouldn't know. Fastidius keeps her locked away even from me. And he's wise to do so – though I worry she'll turn into a nun at this rate." He chuckles. "This is why I need *you* to go to Londin for me."

"Me? I haven't been to Londin in years."

"All the more reason for you to go," he replies. "You'll be less conspicuous than me. The nobles won't remember you. I'd like you to move there for the winter. At least for a couple of months. It's not like you're busy with anything else here."

"I have a wife and a young child, with whom I was hoping to spend some time, now that the fighting's over," I say. "Not that you would know what it's like."

"You'll have years to spend with them. This is important."

"My family's important!" I rise from the seat.

He scowls. "You can visit each other. It's only a few days' journey. It's not like I ask you to move to Gaul."

I sit back down. "What's so important about Madron's wedding, anyway?"

The Crown of the Iutes

"Everything."

He stands up and steps to the iron-bound chest in the corner. He unlocks it with an iron key hanging at his neck, rummages inside for a while and takes out Wortigern's diadem. The gold and the jewels gleam in the candle light.

"I knew it," I say. "You're still thinking about it."

"I'm not the only one," he says.

"Who else would know about us having the diadem?"

"No one for certain, as far as I'm aware." He sits down and puts the crown on the table. It shines with the reflected flames like a tiny sun. "That doesn't stop them from speculating. Ambrosius must've told someone he saw it in your hands... But it was so long ago, most will have forgotten about it – or dismissed it as mere rumour by now."

"So this is why you've been waiting so long."

He nods. "I knew sooner or later they would talk of having a *Dux* again. As far as I can tell, an odd alliance is forming in the Council, between those too young to know any better and those too old to consider how times have changed. A longing for the past –" he taps the crown with his index finger "– is a powerful force. Even if most of that past is invented. Or maybe *because* of it?"

"What does it have to do with Madron? And with us?"

"Think, boy, think! Whoever marries her into his family, will be able to call himself an heir to Wortimer – to Wortigern – to Imperator Maximus!" He grabs the diadem in both hands. "They will have no need for this trinket if they can get their hands on the girl." He throws it to the floor and leans back. A servant picks it up gingerly and packs it back into the treasure chest.

"I worry for our future," my father says, holding his hands behind his head. "Yours, your family's – and our tribe's. We are a small people, compared to the likes of the Goths or Franks – even the Saxons. There aren't any more Iutes sailing to join us from across the whale road. And there is nowhere for us to expand or invade – we are trapped between Aelle, the sea – and Londin."

"What about Meon and Wecta?" I remind him, but he dismisses me with a wave.

"A stretch of a damp moor and an island you can ride across in a day. Too distant to be of any use, too remote to defend. If it wasn't for your poor mother's memory, I'd have given it away a long time ago." He scoffs. "Diplomacy is our only strength, and I've been doing all I can to keep us balanced between the great powers of this world, with your help. We were fortunate Aelle didn't strike at us with full force this summer. I don't know what we'll do about him in spring, especially if he allies himself with the pirates, as I always fear he might. We can't afford to fight the Saxons from land and sea – and soon we won't be able to afford to fight anyone any more."

"How come?" I ask, surprised. "I train new warriors every month. We have enough spears and enough shields to arm them. It's true, we lack good steel for swords and mail for my bear-shirts, but surely that's only a temporary –"

"Our *fyrd* is not an *exercitus* – a standing army, like the Legions. We don't pay them salary; we don't provide them with armaments and grain paid for by taxes. An army like ours, just like Aelle's, lives off of what it plunders. And we're fighting a defensive war. I have the exact same problem as Aelle. It's not enough to take a few chests of spoils from the pirates, once in a while – most of it is stolen

The Crown of the Iutes

from our own land, anyway. When Aelle attacks, or the Britons finally gather their forces under a new *Dux*, we will need steel, we will need meat, we will need leather… All of this, we have to buy."

"What about your treasure in Ariminum?"

"How much of it do you think there was?" He laughs bitterly. "Ursula's dowry helped, but I ran out of gold two years ago, when I had to build that siege machine for Rutubi. I've been borrowing from Fastidius and a few friendly nobles since then, to keep up the pretence… But even their patience is running out."

I sit in silence. Needless to say, I had no idea the situation was so dire. The land that the Iutes settled on is lush and fertile and our sheep and pigs grow fat, so it is easy to believe we are a prosperous people. But of course, my father is right; one can't fight a war with grain sacks and mutton chops. The iron marshes of Cantia have long been depleted – the nearest ore fields belong to Aelle, as does most of Andreda, where the best wood for shields and spear shafts comes from. Everything we need to wage war, we have to buy in the markets of Dubris and Epatiac – with what little coin we can get from the Britons to whom we sell our produce, or with barter. The *wealas* merchants in Dubris and Leman are the only ones who can trade our wool and leather further on – and they refuse to share their profits with us.

I look around the mead hall again, and realise that despite the collection of precious ornaments gathered over the years, it is merely a shadow of Hildrik's opulent palace in his capital of Tornac or even the Council chambers in the still-Roman towns of Gaul.

So much about my idea of paying off Aelle.

"So, what *are* we going to do?" I ask. "What is it that you think you can get from the Britons?"

"I don't want from the Britons anything more than Rome gave to its allies in Gaul or Hispania. I want what should've been ours from the start, but that we were too weak to ask for – and too well-mannered, perhaps. We spoke of friendship, but the ties of friendship only go so far when money runs out. We need more than just a share of Briton land – we need a share of their coin. Their trade taxes and customs duties. If the *wealas* want us to defend them, they will have to pay for it."

"I thought the whole point of splitting from Rome was for the nobles to not pay their taxes. Wasn't this the problem even for Wortigern? Wasn't that why the Iutes were paid with land instead of gold, back in Hengist's days?"

"You've seen how the nobles live. There's still enough coin in their palaces to last us a generation, or more. The problem, as always, is how to get our hands on those hidden riches."

"And for this, you need a strong, friendly *Dux*. Another Wortigern."

"Or failing that, a weak one, far away."

"You'd prefer Ambrosius to be the *Dux* in the East? For the *wealas* to unite? Didn't we once fight a war to stop that happening?"

"With Ambrosius as their ruler, they would be anything *but* united," Father replies. "There are many who will think they deserve the seat better than him – Riotham, Albanus, maybe even Mandubrac…" He lists the names as if they were old friends, but I'm only vaguely aware of who each of these men is. "Divided, they would be easier to manipulate – and more fearful of someone like Aelle."

"As long as they're not *too* divided," I note. "We don't want the South to turn into the North."

The Crown of the Iutes

We know little of what goes on beyond the northern borders of the old Wortigern province, Britannia Maxima – less even than we know about the events in Gaul – but what rumours do get through, brought by terrified refugees, tell us a dire story of chaos and deadly strife: *wealh* tribes fighting each other using barbarian mercenaries as spear fodder; Saxon and Frisian pirates devastating the undefended coasts; heathen warlords taking over the villages and enslaving the locals in ways even Aelle wouldn't dare. And in all this, famines and plagues stride the land, decimating what's left of the tormented population.

"There was always trouble in the North, even in Roman days," my father says, dismissively, though I know how concerned he's always been about Britannia Maxima sharing the fate of its northern neighbours should our good fortunes reverse. "Trust me, we would have nothing to fear from a weak and distant *Dux* – it's a strong and capable one, with local support, but hostile to us, that would be a reason for worry."

"And if I do agree to go to Londin for you – what would you want me to do about it all?"

"Only observe, for now, nothing more. Winter is nigh, a time when the Britons gather in their warm homes to talk and drink. Gather gossip, make friends, find out who can be our ally, discover who is our enemy. I know this is what you're good at – perhaps even better than I ever was. I don't expect anything to happen this year, or next year – the mills of Londin grind slowly. But whatever happens, I want us to be prepared."

I rub my chin. "I'll have to talk to Ursula about this."

"Certainly. Our deal stands, as always, son – no orders, only advice."

"Thank you, Father." I stand up. "I'll bring Pascent later, when he's awake. I'm sure you can't wait to see your grandson."

"Please do. And, by the way –"

"Yes, Father?"

"If you do decide to go to Londin, I would have to ensure your stay there is made worthy of a king's son," he says with a mischievous smile.

"I thought you said you didn't have any money left."

"I can always find a little something for the family."

"Of course – *you* get to go to Londin, while I'm stuck here taking care of Pascent and my ailing parents."

This isn't what I imagined Ursula to protest about. I thought she'd try to stop me leaving her and the child for the winter – and I'd have a hard time persuading her to let me go if she did, for I myself wasn't yet sure if I wanted to obey my father's request. But all she complained about when I told her of what the king asked of me was that *she* couldn't join me in my exile.

"Londin is not Gaul," I repeat my father's argument. "You can visit me whenever you want."

She looks to Pascent, playing in a cold, muddy puddle with a little wooden *ceol*, and shakes her head. "It's not easy to travel with one as young as him – even to Londin," she says, and sighs. "It's been three years… four, counting when I carried him inside me. Four years since I went anywhere outside Cantia."

The Crown of the Iutes

I reach out and take her in my arms.

"I know this isn't the future I once promised you," I say. "I still remember the vision you had on Mona, how terrified you were of being stuck in one place forever. But this *isn't* forever," I assure her.

"Easy for you to say," she says bitterly. "At least you've been to Frankia for Hlodoweg's birth feast."

"It's only one more year. Next summer, I'm certain we'll be able to leave Pascent with a nurse and leave the island. See Hildrik and his boy, or visit Marcus and Ahes in Armorica."

"Marcus and Ahes…" Ursula repeats wistfully. "I do miss them."

Seven long years have passed since we fought the Goths in Armorica, alongside Marcus, then a *Decurion* in the Dumnonian cavalry, and Ahes, a daughter of *Comes* Graelon. After our victory, the *Comes*, disgraced by his alliance with the Goths, stepped down to make way for his daughter – and her new husband, Marcus. In the years between the war and Pascent's birth, we paid a couple more visits to their court at Worgium; but the journey across the Narrow Sea is long and dangerous, and we can't risk taking our son – the prospective king of the Iutes – with us onto a wobbly *ceol*. For as long as he's too young to be left alone, we – and especially Ursula – are bound by Britannia's shores.

"And they miss you," I say. "We'll sail come spring. I promise."

"What if there's a war with Aelle?"

"All the more reason to take little Pascent away from here."

The boy raises his head, hearing his name, and coughs. A blue stone, with the '*Pear-wood*' rune inlaid in gold, dangles on his neck.

It is a sign of protection that the gods of the Iutes give to those of Wodan's blood — my father wore such a stone as a child, and his father before him. Though we wish to raise our son as a Christian, he is not baptised yet — and we agreed to indulge the tribe's elders and priests who insisted that the boy wears the harmless trinket. My father, ever disinterested in the matters of faith, couldn't have cared less.

Ursula picks Pascent up from the puddle.

"Enough play," she scolds him. "You're going to catch cold."

"You look like you're about to be sick yourself," I note. Her face is pale, except the dark bags under her eyes, and her hair has lost its usual lustre.

"It's nothing," she says with a wave of her hand. "I'm just tired."

"Go back to the house, my love," I tell her. "Get warm. There's an ill wind about. I wouldn't be surprised if it snowed soon."

The Crown of the Iutes

CHAPTER III
THE LAY OF EISHILD

"How are you settling in, young man?"

I hide a wince behind an uneasy smile. At least the bishop doesn't call me a "boy", but I wonder how long he and my father are going to treat me as a mere youth? I'm twenty-eight this summer. A manly age. At this age, my father had already won the Battle of Eobbasfleot, and become Hengist's *Gesith* – and his foster-brother, Fastidius, was already the new, divisive Bishop of Londin, the youngest to ever hold the title. I even started to grow a beard and hair long, in the manner of Frankish and Gothic warriors, to show my father I was a grown man, but it seems to have no effect on the bishop.

"Everything here is so dear!" I laugh. "Last night I went to the shops by the Forum to buy some bread and sausages, it cost me half a silver piece! I don't know if my father's coins will last me until spring."

Fastidius chuckles. "Yes, well, that's Londin for you. If you need any help, remember you can always come here. The Church owes Ash greatly for protecting our ships from the pirates."

The bishop is one of the handful of people in Britannia who still call my father by his old slave name. All of them, like Aelle or *Gesith* Betula, knew him long before he became *Rex* Aeric – but the bishop has known him longer than any man alive. He was there at Ariminum when the Iute foundling was brought to the *villa* from the slave market, still crying and shivering; he was there when my father met my mother, before she was banished to a Iutish village; and he was here, in Londin, when my father was baptised as Fraxinus, the name under which he later served *Dux* Wortigern as his right hand and Councillor – until Wortimer's disastrous rebellion…

He has been a witness to everything that happened in Britannia since the Iutes landed on Tanet, forty years ago; he is wise with the age and experience of these stormy decades. And though I've known him since I was a child, though he's my father's foster-brother, sitting here in the bishop's private room at the back of the great Saint Paul's Cathedral and talking to him is almost as intimidating as was sitting in front of *Dux* Wortigern, ten years ago in Wened.

"Where are you staying?" he asks.

"At the Bull's Head."

Fastidius laughs. "Of course, where else! Ash is oddly fond of this place. Though it is nowhere near as opulent and popular as it was in our youth. But then, nowhere in Londin is…" he adds, and we both sadly nod, reflecting on the city's demise, though he would remember it as far more splendid than I could ever imagine.

Once the greatest city north of the Alps, Londin is now less than a shadow of its former self: it is a bad memory. West of the Cardo Street, the main north-south avenue, where once spread the civic buildings and temples, there is nothing left but a sea of ruin and cinders. Gone is the *Praetor*'s palace, gone is the *basilica* and the *porticoes*, and of the old Forum, only a stone square remains where a little local trade is still being done. Some of this destruction was an old wound even in Fastidius's youth, a remnant of the punishment inflicted on the city for a rebellion against one Imperator or other. But the rest is my father's doing, when he led his people to burn it all down at the climax of Wortimer's War.

People still try to eke out a life among these ruins, as simple farmers – there's enough space within the Wall for several villages; but the marshy soil, tainted with rubble and poisonous ash, bears little grain, and so entire swathes of the city remain inhabited only by wraiths and wild dogs. The city's life, such as it is, shifted eastwards, towards the cathedral, a sole beacon of civilisation and civic pride. The Bull's Head remains the only tavern still open on the Cardo; all the other inns have closed down or moved to the foot of the cathedral hill, to serve the pilgrims. The nobles of the northern district moved their palaces closer to the church or extended their grounds – swallowing the *villas* abandoned by their neighbours fleeing the city – so that at least the gates of their properties are bathed in the holy light. Altogether, in a city that once housed fifty thousand people, there now lives maybe a tenth of that number – and all of them clustered within the sound of the cathedral's bells.

Someone knocks on the door. The bishop invites one of the acolytes to enter, and he brings in plates of thinly sliced veal with spices, and sea fish in milk sauce.

"They don't serve things like this at the Bull's Head," I say, salivating.

"They used to, in Wortigern's days," Fastidius remarks. "Nowadays only the nobles can afford such delicacies, and they don't meet at taverns. I imagine it's all stews and potages these days. Cheap and filling." He sighs. "Lord knows I try not to abuse the Church's wealth, and spread it as far and wide as possible, but when the season for *vitulinum* is at an end, even I succumb to the sin of gluttony…"

He picks up the veal slice and swallows it whole, like a gull eating a fish, then wipes his lips with a piece of embroidered cloth.

The Crown of the Iutes

"You did not come all this way just to have a meal and a friendly conversation," he says, once we finish eating. "Nobody does that, not even your father."

I smile. "I suppose not. Though if I had known I would be eating *vitulinum* with black pepper, I would have come regardless of any other reason." I wipe my hands on my tunic. "I'm guessing my father told you why he sent me to Londin."

Fastidius nods. "It looks like you are to be our young spy."

"Our?"

"I, too, would like to know what the nobles and the Councillors are plotting – and they don't trust me as much as they should their shepherd. If it was up to them, they'd have replaced me with someone more to their liking a long time ago."

"Who is it up to, then?"

"Who, indeed!" He chuckles. "Not the Council, that's certain. Not while they can't agree among each other. A sufficiently powerful *Dux* might well force me out of the cathedral – and, more crucially, get his hands on its treasures."

"Ah. I see why you might be interested in the Council's doings."

"I care only for the well-being of my flock, my son," Fastidius says, his voice momentarily taking on the timbre of a preacher at a sermon. "I did not become the bishop for titles and power…"

"Not even for the *vitulinum*?"

He laughs again and shakes his head. "I know why you're really here," he says, his eyes suddenly sharp. He stands up and walks to a small window, secured with iron bars.

"Come here, Octa."

The window overlooks the inner courtyard of the cathedral hill. The entire enclosure is greater than any urban *villa* in the city – itself the size of a small town. I spot a large kitchen, a bath house, a smithy, several hermits' cells, a guesthouse and half a dozen other huts, where I guess the acolytes and servants dwell. On the far slope of the cathedral hill, in the shadow of the Londin Wall, several men till a vegetable garden.

There are two women down in the courtyard, fighting a mock duel with dull metal blades. They're both golden-haired, athletic and slim, and evenly matched – or, rather, both are equally poor. Judging by how they hold their weapons, how they try and fail to block and parry, they had no teacher to show them the proper way of fighting a short sword, but I can't deny their eagerness. Each clang of weapons is punctuated by a loud grunt.

"Wait –" I say. "Is that…?"

"Madron." Fastidius nods.

"Who's that she's fighting?"

"Don't you recognise her?"

I rub my eyes to see better. "Eishild?"

"The princess of the Goths herself," Fastidius nods.

The Crown of the Iutes

It was when we travelled to *Decurion* Marcus's wedding with Princess Ahes, six years ago, that I first met Eishild, daughter of Thaurismod, the rightful heir to the throne in Tolosa. Some time later, when the alliance of Gauls and Franks defeated the Goths in the Battle of Aurelianum, Eishild was among those captured, and – on her own request – brought to Londin with other prisoners.

"I had no idea this was where she was kept," I say.

"Neither does anyone else, I hope," says the bishop. "I had to use a lot of my wealth and influence to make sure she was moved here safely after we received news of Theodrik's death."

Eishild's father had many brothers; we met – and killed - one of them in Armorica; the other was slain at Aurelianum. Eventually, however, three years ago, Hildrik – always the best informed about what went on in Gaul – sent word that one brother prevailed over all others: the youngest, Aiwarik.

"Eishild is now the only threat left to Aiwarik's claim," Fastidius explains. "And not just because of who her father was, as I'm sure you understand."

In one of those odd conflicts about some obscure tenet of their faith that only the Christians were capable of understanding, the Goths have long been split between two manners of worship: the older, Gothic creed, and the updated one, as preached by Rome. Eishild and her father were among those raised in the new creed, while her other brothers still followed the old way.

"Surely she's safe in Britannia," I say. "Even the Gothic king's hand can't possibly reach that far."

The bishop rubs his chin. "There are some Goths living in Londin. Other captives, refugees fleeing from persecution, a few traders in the harbour… It wouldn't be difficult for Aiwarik to hide an assassin or two among that lot."

I look to the courtyard again. The girls have paused fighting for a moment, and are now sitting in the cathedral's shadow, drinking cold ale.

"Why – why are they fighting?"

"That, I believe, would be your wife's fault," Fastidius replies.

"Ursula? How come?"

"When you brought Madron here, she knew nothing of the world," he proceeds to explain. "And nothing of her mother's people. She lived in fortresses, among soldiers. When she saw Ursula and Croha, shieldmaidens fighting alongside men as equals, she imagined that this was what a Iutish woman, like herself, should do."

"I suppose it didn't help that Ursula came to visit so often, before Pascent's birth."

Fastidius nods. "Your wife would always bring new stories of war and glory – the Goths, the Saxons… Though it wasn't until Eishild arrived, another princess of a barbarian tribe, that the girl finally found herself a willing sparring partner."

"They need someone to train them," I say. "That's no way to hold a short sword. She's going to hurt herself."

"I cannot allow that. My duty is to keep everyone in my care safe, and teach them how to be good Christians, not to turn them into heathen warriors."

The Crown of the Iutes

"Yes, I can imagine how irritated Ambrosius would be if he learned you were training his daughter-in-law in war craft. He could barely stand the idea of you teaching her to read the Scriptures."

As I watch Madron and Eishild pick up their weapons again, I realise the shrewdness of Fastidius's plans. Of course, a man who became bishop before the age of thirty, while managing to shake off accusations of heresy, would know how to play the Briton nobles better than anyone.

According to the deal we've agreed to with Ambrosius, Fastidius was supposed to be nothing more than an impartial caretaker and tutor. By keeping any outside men away from the girl, be it my father, Councillor Riotham — Ambrosius's representative in Londin — or any other of the squabbling nobles, he created for her a world where the only role models were himself — and the women who were allowed to visit. And for a *Dux's* daughter, raised on a war-torn frontier, Ursula would be a far more attractive example than the meek nuns or handmaidens Riotham provided.

"Of course, we wouldn't want the princesses to hurt themselves…" Fastidius remarks.

"You'd let me down there? What if Riotham finds out?"

"Nobody in the city remembers who you are. Isn't that why your father sent you here?" He smiles to himself at some idea he just came up with. "Come back here in a few days. And make sure you're not seen."

They pause the duel and eye me suspiciously as I approach. I can tell they're exhausted with the fighting. The blades may be blunt, but they're still chunks of steel, and the result of the mock duel is a layer of bruises and cuts all over their hands.

Madron wears a short-sleeved, knee-length tunic, revealing supple, muscle-bound arms, and slim calves. She's wearing emerald green, the same colour her mother used to wear in my father's stories, even though it's impossible for the girl to remember this, since Rhedwyn died on the day of her birth. My father was right when he predicted she'd grow into a beauty; her face is smooth, glowing, as if chiselled from the finest marble, and wonderfully proportioned. The dark eyes, a mark of her descent from Wortigern's noble line, shine like two inlaid onyxes. Sweat makes the tunic cloth cling tightly to her body.

Looking at her, I have to remind myself of the secret that only I, *Rex* Aeric and Bishop Fastidius know: Madron and I are closely related: she is my half-sister. Her mother, Rhedwyn, was my father's sister, though neither of them knew about their close kinship when they were lovers. I promised myself that one day I would share this revelation with the girl – but for this, I will need to wait until my father's death.

Even after I throw down the acolyte's cowl, Madron is still giving me a wary look, until Eishild leaps towards me with a cheerful cry.

"Octa!" She throws her arms around me. "I almost didn't recognise you! How long has it been?"

"Seven years, I believe. Have I changed so much?" I reply with a laugh.

"Not at all – it's just the robes – and the beard…"

"I think it rather suits me." I run my fingers through the beard and turn to the other girl.

"*Domna* Madron." I bow.

The Crown of the Iutes

"*Aetheling...*" She bows back, still uncertain. She hasn't seen me in ten years – not since I brought her into the bishop's care. I was a youth then – and she was merely a child. If it wasn't for her meetings with Ursula, I'm not certain she would've even remembered who I was.

Eishild glances anxiously around. "Madron's not really supposed to –"

"It's fine. The bishop knows. I only came down here to show you how not to hurt yourselves while fighting."

I pick up the short sword – it's a good quality *seax*, worn and battered even before it was blunted. The weathered runic inscription on the blade claims it once belonged to some Saxon named Holm – and judging by the invocation to the sea gods on the other side, Holm must have been a pirate.

I put the *seax* in Madron's hand and wrap her fingers around the hilt. Her hand is soft and warm, except the calluses on the underside, ready to burst.

"This way you won't be getting those blisters, and your blows will have more power," I say. "Hold it straight, so the enemy's blade doesn't slide and slice your fingers off. Now, try."

"I hear His Grace worries about your uncle sending men to kill you," I say to Eishild as I parry Madron's swift but weak thrusts. The girl is keen, and with some training she might make a fine addition to the *fyrd*. Alas, it is not her destiny: as soon as she weds Honorius, she will be spirited away to Ambrosius's capital at Corin, where her only duty will be bearing and raising heirs for the *Dux*.

"The bishop should save his worries for Madron," Eishild replies, observing my fight with Madron intently. "I know all the Goths in the city, and there are no heretics among them. Indeed, the light of the True Faith seems to grow brighter every year. Drustan says —"

"Drustan visits you? I haven't seen him in a long time, either."

"Not often. He is a busy man, commanding the Armorican cavalry for Marcus and hunting Graelon's loyalists."

"I thought Graelon had died some time ago."

"He did — but there are still some who believe Marcus and Ahes are the wrong choice for Armorica. I hear Patrician Budic leads the nobles' resistance."

I shake my head. "Everywhere I look, people are fighting for one throne or the other. What's so great about being a ruler?"

"Easy for you to say — you're already destined to succeed your father."

"Believe me, if it wasn't for my sense of duty, I would give my title away in a blink of an eye."

"Every man thinks he's driven by some duty," says Eishild between strikes. "My uncles spoke of duty, too, when they murdered my father. In truth, it's the *ambition* that drives them — to madness. I'm glad my Drustan is satisfied with just commanding his riders."

"That's not the only thing that satisfies him," Madron says between strikes. She casts a bawdy glance at Eishild. "Don't look at me like that. Walls are thin in the bishop's guesthouse, and I have nowhere else to go at night."

"So that's why he was too busy to teach you two how to hold a sword," I say with a chuckle. Eishild's face turns bright red. "Why

The Crown of the Iutes

do you think His Grace should be concerned about *Domna* Madron?" I ask swiftly, saving her the embarrassment.

"I've been hearing rumours all over the city..." Eishild replies. "It would seem some of the Councillors are not content with giving Madron away to the *Dux* in far away Corin. But I'm sure the bishop will know more than I do. Now, let me have a go at that sword."

"Of course – here." I hand her the other weapon. It's a twin set; it was no mere pirate who owned these swords. Must have been a ship's captain. Was it someone I met, I wonder? The one I killed off Dubris just before Midsummer – or the one pinned to the mast of his own boat by Seawine's spear the week after Easter?

"I better go back to the bishop," I say. "We still have much to discuss."

"You will see us again, won't you?" asks Madron.

"I will try. I am supposed to spend the entire winter here. Remember the grip. Too tight, and you'll tear your skin. Too loose, and you'll get it struck out of your hand."

"Yes, *aetheling*," Madron replies, pressing the sword to her chest in a mock salute.

I bid my farewell to Fastidius just as the sun touches the rim of the Londin Wall outside the window. The days have grown short, and I don't want to go back to the Bull's Head in the dark.

Back in my father's days, this would never have been a concern. Londin was a city that rarely slept. All through the night there would be open taverns, whorehouses, baths, gambling dens, especially on the road from the harbour to the Forum. It was a loud, dirty, violent place, but at least it was alive. Now, the streets fall asleep shortly after nightfall, just as soon as the oil in the lamps in the ruined tenements and huts built on top of old foundations runs out. Even the *vigiles* don't dare to come out at night, unless there's a fire — and even then only when it threatens one of the noblemen's *villas*.

Even though it's still bright enough, I decide to take a northerly route back, away from the fishing wharves and the ruined districts to the west and south of the cathedral hill. As usual, one of the acolytes takes me to a small gate in the stone wall surrounding the cathedral enclosure. Like him, I'm wearing the dark robe and the hood marked with a small badge of swords and cross, though I doubt there's a single soul out in the back streets this close to dusk that would recognise me even without the disguise. I look to the courtyard, hoping to catch a glimpse of Madron's green tunic, but her training with Eishild is over and there isn't anyone there except a servant swiping dried leaves into the gutter.

The first time the acolyte showed me this exit, he seemed apprehensive.

"This path will lead you straight to the Augustan Highway, *Domnus*," he told me. "But… are you sure you don't want someone to accompany you?"

"I am a Iute warrior, brother," I told him. "As long as I have this by my side, I doubt I have anything to fear from the city roughs," I added, patting my *spatha*.

A few long weeks have passed since I came to Londin, and I still had little to report to the bishop about the inner goings-on of the Council. I met a few trusted nobles, friends of my father, and the word of my arrival began to spread among the wealthy and powerful, though they paid little attention to the news. They were more concerned with the Saxon king's growing ambition, and the worrying prospect of renewed pirate attacks come spring. If they were at all busy with finding themselves a new *Dux*, nobody was telling *me* about it. I was beginning to suspect sending me here at this time of year was a futile endeavour all along. Like bears and squirrels, the nobles grew fat and lazy in anticipation of the winter – all of them except, it seemed, Councillor Riotham, whose name I kept hearing mentioned everywhere and by everyone, often in connection with another name, not of a Councillor, but of Albanus, the *Comes* of the Cadwallons in the north; though what it was that they were both up to, I could not yet tell.

Passing through the gate, I spot movement to my left. A shadow leaps from the wall and runs off into the night: a man in a short, brown soldier's cloak.

This is new. *An assassin?* Or a spy for one? Have the Goths sent someone for Eishild after all? Whoever he is, I can't let him escape – it might be my only chance of stopping the attack. But following the cloaked man into the narrow alleyways means stepping off of the familiar path to the Augustan Highway. I don't know this part of the city well – and I don't know these back streets at all. It would be all too easy to get lost in here, or worse…

I test the draw on my sword and rush quietly after the shadow. He's in a hurry, but he doesn't yet suspect anyone following him, so I'm able to keep up with him for now. We leave the looming vastness of the cathedral hill behind us, cross the muddy stream that runs at the foot of the slope, and enter the burnt-out ruin of a once-grand district of tight streets and tall tenements. I wonder if the destruction is another result of my father's war with Wortimer, or some other disaster in the city's long and turbulent history. The tenements stare at me with the dark eyes of charred, empty windows. There is nothing behind them – not even a memory of the life that once bustled beyond those facades. The few people that still dwell here live more like serfs than city folk, tilling their small vegetable patches and taking care of a few goats or sheep in huts built of rubble, flotsam and whatever they could forage from the ruins.

My mysterious target finally spots me. I may be good in tracking prey through a forest or in the dunes, but this is not as familiar territory for me as it is for him. The first time I lose him, I manage to find him again after a few twists and turns of what must be a new dirt path carved through the old, regular grid of streets. The second time, I'm left alone in the middle of a small square space which, from the remains of pillars around it, I identify as an *atrium* of some long-lost *villa*.

With the darkness quickly descending onto the city, I'm loath to venture deeper into the narrow streets – but now, I'm not even sure if I know how to get back to the main road. I pause to get my bearings. I can't see the cathedral any more, hidden from view by the charred facades. The line of bright dots to my left marks the edge of the Wall – this, at least, tells me I'm still headed in the right direction.

A few turns past the *atrium* I reach a blocked alleyway. I can tell this is a man-made barricade, rather than just a randomly fallen wall; I've built a few like it myself back in the day. I turn to circumvent it, when a voice calls after me from behind the rubble.

"Are you lost, brother?" a man calls and laughs. I remember I'm still wearing the acolyte's brown robes. "Need to find a way back to the cathedral?"

I ignore him, and continue looking for a way out. I reach another blockade. The barricades seem to be linked together by ruins and rubble, into a wall of sorts; if they continue like this either way, they must be encompassing an entire district bound by Londin's two main avenues.

The Crown of the Iutes

I know now where I am: the Poor Town.

I'm surprised this place still exists. This city within a city, this den of bandits, beggars, whores, refugees and anyone else looking to stay away from the *vigiles* while still hoping to enjoy what Londin has to offer, was once home to my father's army of rebels, fighting to overthrow the tyrant *Dux* Wortimer. It was already a sea of ruin filled with tents and poor huts even then. I was certain it had burned down to the ground in the final battle of the conflict – but whatever has happened since then, it looks like the Poor Town has grown back to almost its original size in the intervening years.

Two men appear before me, holding long knives. The third one sneaks up behind me. They're all wearing drab, grey, crumpled tunics, the colour of the weathered stone around us, making them almost invisible in the twilight.

"We asked you a question, brother," one of the men says. He's a fair-hair, his mud-straw locks falling in long, thin, dirty clumps on his shoulders, though judging by his manner of speech he was raised in Londin. "It's only polite to answer."

"I want no trouble," I mumble, pulling the cowl deeper onto my brow.

Another rough appears on a low ridge made from piled-up rubble and refuse, juggling a small throwing axe. The fair-hair comes up to me and looks under my hood.

"Come now, brother. We know you church folk only pretend. Nobody could really be this poor and miserable."

He reaches under my robe, searching for some precious trinkets he imagines I'm carrying underneath – but instead, he finds the hilt of my sword.

"Hey!" He leaps away. "He's armed! Boso, get him!"

In the corner of my eye I glance the axeman grasp his weapon and throw it at me. I reach out, grab the fair-hair and pull him in. The axe strikes his back. I throw him aside, draw the *spatha* and turn around to face the one behind me.

"Go get the others, Boso," he shouts. "He's not one of the bishop's men."

The axeman disappears behind the ridge of rubble. I strike at the bandit before me, cutting him on the wrist; he drops the knife with a squeal. I kick him down and spin to face the last of the attackers just as he lunges at me. He almost gets me – the acolyte's robe gets in my way, and I can't dodge fast enough; the knife blade slices through my tunic and scratches my side. Still, he's no match for the *aetheling* of the Iutes. I slash through his right arm, then draw a shallow, painful line across his chest. He trips and falls on his back.

I don't want to kill them. It's not their fault they mistook me for easy prey. I just want to get moving after my quarry. I press my sword point to the bandit's neck.

"A man just passed through here, in a soldier's cloak – have you seen him?" I ask.

"Fuck you," the bandit spits.

I hear a flutter of an arrow, and duck, instinctively. The missile flies over my head, lands in the rubble. I look up: two archers stand on the ridge. Three more bandits run at me from the sides, with clubs and axes. It's as if I've stepped into a nest of angry ants – suddenly they're all over me. I pick up the bandit and use him as a shield. The second archer shoots before noticing what I do, and his arrow hits the bandit on the shoulder.

The Crown of the Iutes

"Get back!" I cry. "I don't want any more of you to get hurt. I have nothing worth stealing – just let me through!"

The commanding boom of my voice makes them step back in hesitant confusion; I'm now used to leading entire warbands into battle – a few city roughs don't frighten me. But they're too many even for me, and they know it. They start approaching me again from all directions. I push the one I'm holding forward and, hiding behind him, I run at the nearest of the archers. He's not used to shooting at a target coming straight for him; the arrow flies high above my head. Before he can nock another, I cut through his bow, barge at him and throw him down, then keep on running, climbing up the ridge. Behind it, I see more bandits. There must be a dozen of them now altogether, and those new ones look like trained warriors. Certainly the man leading them is a greater threat than any of the ones I have fought until now: tall, bearded, wielding a great staff. The earth trembles under his strides. I grasp the *spatha* in both hands and swirl it over my head before bringing it down upon him. He takes it on the staff, and tries to hit me in the head; I dodge in a split second. The staff grazes my brow. I strike again, under his block. He's faster than I'd expect of a man his size, and swerves aside, but my blade cuts his flank – a graze for a graze.

One on one, I'd beat him, eventually; but the others reach us now, and grab at my arms and legs. I slash to my sides and feel the blade squelch into a body; I don't care about their lives any more, only about getting out of here alive. I tear my arm out from somebody's grip, punch back with an elbow: a snap of a broken nose. I kick with full force: a cracked shin. I untangle myself from the robe and roll down the rubble heap, the shards of brick and pottery tear painfully at my skin.

"Hold him!" the bearded man commands. "Don't kill him." More arms on me, and bodies, throwing themselves at me. I punch, and kick, and bite, but my sword is torn from me, and my legs buckle under me. With one last burst of strength, I roar, grab two bandits hanging each on my shoulder, thud their heads together and throw them to the sides. I find the bearded man standing right in front of me, staff raised to a strike.

His weapon flying towards my face is the last thing I see before everything goes dark. The last thing I hear is the bearded bandit's order: "Take him to Wulf."

The Crown of the Iutes

James Calbraith

CHAPTER IV
THE LAY OF ILLICA

A man's voice breaks through the black mist. He sounds like my father, only hoarser, whistling through a few missing teeth. He's asking someone a question, but I can't quite make out his words.

"...a deal with the bishop..." I hear. "...why send this warrior?"

"I wasn't sent by anyone..." I force an answer. There's a pause in the man's questioning, followed by a bucket of water splashing painfully at my face. This, at last, allows me to open my eyes and take a look around.

I'm inside a large, half-ruined stone building – not a *villa* or a bath house, but a public chamber of some sort, maybe a local *curia*. It once had an upper floor – I spot a staircase leading nowhere in the corner, and remains of a wooden floor still protruding from the wall halfway up – and was topped with a dome, of which nothing is now left but one segment, sticking out like a cracked, crooked tooth. Instead of a roof, the interior is shielded from the elements only by what looks like an old, tattered sail, spread from wall to wall.

The man before me is a Iute; of that, I have no doubt. And he is, roughly, my father's age, though his face is more ravaged by scars of time and war. The left half of his face is marked with deep burns; his left eye is white with blindness; his nose is broken in so many ways that he has to breathe through his mouth. He sits on a sort of barbaric throne, built from the base of a pillar, padded with sheepskin. We're surrounded by a ring of armed guards and, behind them, a small crowd of onlookers – men, women, even a

[69]

The Crown of the Iutes

few children, fair-hairs, *wealas*, and a few other, more exotic faces; most of them in rags, wrapped in blankets, huddled around meagre campfires on this cold night.

By law and treaties, there shouldn't be any Iutes dwelling permanently in the city; and I can't think of a reason why they would *want* to be here, when there's empty land aplenty in Cantia for them to till, plenty of fish in the sea to catch. When my father lived in this place, the Poor Town folk were trapped within Londin's walls by the war raging outside. But the war is no more. Could it be that these people prefer this life of thievery and poverty to the simple drudgery of a serf's existence?

"I wasn't sent by His Grace," I repeat. I switch to Iutish. "I was chasing after someone, and they fled into the Poor Town – I think. I was hoping you'd help me."

"Why would I help you catch one of our own? Who are you? I can see that you're a seasoned warrior – you took out five of my men in that brawl. And I trained some of them myself."

"I didn't mean to hurt anyone," I say.

He scowls and waves his hand. "They'll live. I don't like to repeat myself, but – who are you, and what are you doing here?"

I look about me and hesitate. I don't know how the folk of Poor Town will react to mentioning my father's name. The last time anyone here saw him, he led most of them to a suicide charge on Wortimer's palace, in which half the city burned down, with many of the townsfolk perishing in the conflagration.

Like the Free Folk of Andreda, these are people without masters and laws. They wouldn't take kindly to no king's son, no *aetheling* trying to extend his father's control over them. If they find out who

I am, will I get a chance to explain to these poor wretches that I want nothing from them?

"I am Octa," I say. "Son of Eadgith and Ash."

A murmur spreads through the crowd around me, though not as agitated as I'd expected. It would seem my father's name is not remembered here as well as I thought.

The man on the throne stares at me, then chuckles.

"I should've guessed. You have her eyes. And her hair."

"So I've been told," I say. "You're from the original Poor Town, then? Before the fire? I wasn't sure if any of you survived."

"Not many – and most of those who did, moved to Cantiaca, when they heard your old man declared himself – what was it? A *Rex?*" He scoffs. "But there will always be enough suffering poor in Londin and the provinces to fill up a place like this in no time."

"And they took you for their leader? Who are you?"

He straightens himself and puts his hand to his chest.

"I am Wulf. Maybe you've heard of me."

"Wulf – as in Wulf, Birch and Raven?" I exclaim, and rise from my seat, only to be brought down by a guard's stiff hand on my shoulder. "My father's band of thieves! Of course I've heard of you!"

He steps down from the pillar base, and comes up to me so close I can smell the ointments applied to the old burns on his face. He must be in constant pain.

The Crown of the Iutes

"So, Ash sent you to spy on his old comrades-in-arms, did he?" he asks, baring his teeth. "What does he want from us? There's nothing here worth taking; he of all people should know it."

"How many times – I didn't come here on purpose! My father doesn't know I'm here. Nobody does. I'm chasing a man. Maybe you've seen him – he wore…"

"Yes, yes, I heard it the first time." He sits back down. "Do you really want me to believe Ash's son just happened to pass by my domain?"

"Is this what you call this place?" I laugh. "Your *domain*? Listen, I don't care what you want to believe. There's a room at the top floor of the Bull's Head that I would very much like to be in right now, instead of this arse-cold *curia*. I want nothing to do with you or your Poor Town – unless you can help me find the man in a brown soldier's cloak."

Wulf glances to one of his men. "You know what he's talking about?"

"Maybe he means Illica," the bandit replies. "The lads on the northern rampart have seen him disappear towards the cathedral most nights. We thought he was out robbing pilgrims."

"That's him!" I say. "I saw him at the cathedral."

"Why did you go after him?" Wulf asks.

"I was coming back from a visit to the bishop and saw a suspicious man wandering about the cathedral." I shrug. "I wanted to know what he was doing there."

"So you ran after him across half the city? I assure you, the bishop's guards don't need your help chasing away intruders."

I glance to my sides. "Fine, I admit it. I had a good reason for my pursuit – but I'm not going to share it here, with all those people around. If it was indeed one of your men, he may not be the only one in service of my enemies."

Wulf smiles bitterly. "Enemies, plots… Bad omens follow your family like stink after a dog. I *almost* missed that." He waves at the guards. "Take him to my hall, and make sure we can't be heard by anyone. And find me Illica. No matter what he was doing there, I don't need my men poking around the bishop's fortress."

"You've had problems with Fastidius before?" I ask.

In the corner of the *curia* that forms the centre of the Poor Town, Wulf has built himself an imitation mead hall, from the same amalgamation of rubble, flotsam and driftwood as the rest of the huts in the district. A fishing boat forms its roof; the walls are adorned with an assorted collection of various items stolen and found over the years, none of them particularly precious – except a candlestick of tarnished silver and a golden crucifix studded with jewels, hanging over Wulf's bedding next to his spear.

"He's a good man," Wulf replies. "One of few in the city. Helped us greatly after your father left us. But some ten years ago, something changed. He locked down the entire hill, put up more guards, stopped letting in beggars and pilgrims except on great holidays, as if he had brought in some great treasure…"

"Wait – you mean you didn't know? All this time?"

"Know about what?"

The Crown of the Iutes

"About Madron. Myrtle, Princess Rhedwyn's daughter."

He furrows his brow. "Rhedwyn. There's a dark name from a bleak past. It was in Rhedwyn's name that we followed Ash into oblivion." He shakes his head. "I didn't even know she had a daughter. You're saying she's being kept in the cathedral?"

"Only until *Dux* Ambrosius comes to take her back West, where she is to wed his son. They were betrothed seven years ago – surely you remember the great ceremony on the hill."

"Is that what it was?" His eyes open wide. "We grew rich on all the merchant caravans and countryside nobles that came to the city that time. But no, I never had any interest in finding out *why* the rich and the powerful do what they do. Nothing good ever comes from asking too many questions." He scratches his burnt cheek. "*Rhedwyn's* daughter… That's why you've been visiting the bishop?"

"She's one of the reasons."

"And you think whoever hired Illica to spy on the cathedral wants her harmed?"

"I can't be sure if Madron was his target. There are other guests seeking sanctuary at Fastidius's house from spies and assassins, and I would loath for any of them to get hurt."

He rubs his temples. "This is just like talking to your father all over again. Hired killers, politics, diplomacy… It's all poison. I don't want my people involved in any of that."

"But they're already involved. What do you think the bishop would say if he found out your men are spying on his guests?"

"Illica is not one of my men. Not quite. He only joined us a year ago. He came with two others, claiming they were deserters, from Gaul. He proved his skill in a few bouts with the *vigiles*, so we let him and his two friends join the watch. But I never fully trusted him. We don't get many foreigners around here – the furthest my people tend to come from is the forests of Andreda or the misty hills of the Cadwallons…"

"You have Free Folk from Andreda coming here? Why?"

He shrugs. "Who am I to question why people do what they do? Maybe they get bored of eating pinecones and lichen in winter. Or don't want to stand in the way of Aelle's raiders when they march on the Iute farmsteads. Is there anything else you wanted to know about Illica?"

"Gaul, did you say?" I ask. "He wouldn't say which part, exactly?"

"Even if he did, I wouldn't remember. You can ask him yourself when my men bring him. Does it matter?"

"Perhaps. It would help explain why he was lurking around the cathedral."

Wulf gives me a suspicious look, but says nothing. Instead, he leans back against the wall, and pours me a cup of murky, rotten-smelling ale.

"How's Birch doing?" he asks, watching with a wry smile as I try to stomach the drink.

"She goes by Betula now," I reply. "She's the king's *Gesith*. The finest warrior in the kingdom."

Wulf nods. "Still no man, though?"

"No man. But a daughter, of sorts – a girl from Wecta that she took in and raised into almost as fine a warrior as herself."

He sighs. "Tell her I'm still thinking of her when next time you meet."

"I'm surprised neither she nor my father tried to contact you after all this time."

"I suppose they don't want to revisit bad memories. Besides, my people are better off without Ash's meddling. I'm sorry if this sounds harsh to you –"

"Not at all," I reply. "I understand what you mean. And I'm sure you're right. My father has often visited Londin in recent years, he has had plenty of chances to find you. He couldn't have been this busy with the Council to –"

Wulf raises his hand and shakes his head. "I don't want to know anything about what your father does in Londin. Keep your politics to yourself. It's the best for us all."

"As you wish."

One of Wulf's warriors enters the hall. The chieftain claps his knee.

"Have you got him?"

"No, *Hlaford*," the warrior replies with an uneasy bow. "We – we couldn't find him anywhere. Illica's disappeared from Poor Town."

The next morning, the landlord at the Bull's Head tells me some men are waiting for me outside. By the look of disgust on his face, I guess they must have been sent by Wulf.

There are three of them – and they're holding the fourth one, a Gaul, wearing a short soldier's cloak.

"His name is Claudius," they tell me. "One of the three. We found the other one dead. Illica must have killed him. Do with this one whatever you want, just don't involve us any further. *Hlaford* Wulf doesn't want any trouble with the bishop or the nobles."

"Tell him I'll do what I can to keep the Poor Town safe."

I take Claudius behind the inn, into the dark, secluded space that was once a part of the stables. Facing my wrath and my sword, Claudius drops to his knees, pleading his innocence and ignorance of his companion's plans and whereabouts.

"Why are you protecting him?" I ask, drawing blood from his cheek in a slow motion. "Are you afraid he'll kill you like the other one? I assure you, it's nothing compared to what I'll do to you if you anger me."

I cut his other cheek, hoping he doesn't notice how loathsome I find the torture, even as slight as this one. Even when I tried to gain information from the pirate captives regarding their next lethal raid, I could never bring myself to cause them true harm, leaving this instead to the more brutal among my men.

"Or is it that you're working with him?"

But the Saxon pirates were tough barbarians; when they departed for their raids, they expected to die or be maimed. Claudius is a deserter, fleeing, according to his own words, from a Gaulish

The Crown of the Iutes

Legion and the dangers of the Gothic frontier. He breaks down under my questioning like a scorned child.

"There was a man," he tells me. "A noble. He offered us all silver, but only Illica took it."

"A Gothic noble?"

"Goth? No amount of silver would make us work for the Goths."

"A Briton, then? Someone from the city?"

"From the northern district."

"You know where he lives?"

"I followed Illica once – but it's a dangerous place for someone like me. Full of guards…"

"You'll be safe with me."

"Me? I'm not going anywhere!"

I press the blade to his neck. "You can either take me to that nobleman's house, or stay here – forever."

"Are you sure this is the place?"

The Gaul nods eagerly. From our hiding place on the top floor of a tall, burnt-out tenement, I observe the grounds of an enormous *villa* in the northern district. There aren't many such palaces left in this part of the city, and whoever owns this one made good use of the abandoned properties, swallowing his immediate neighbours on either side of the old fence. The enlarged grounds now span both sides of the Mithras Brook, the muddy stream that flows through the centre of Londin. The owner clearly cares more for the size of his land than for its maintenance. Only the main path linking the gate with the *domus* is cleared from weeds and lined with a few headless and armless stone statues as it runs past an imposing, but long broken-down, fountain; its bowl, sculpted into leaping dolphins and sea nymphs, is filled with murky rain water. The rest of the gardens is overgrown with a wild tangle of scrub, as thick in places as the undergrowth in Andreda; except the plants that were allowed to take over this territory are, as much as I can tell from their winter-black shapes, of a more exotic sort than ones that grow in the old forest. A sprawling fig tree grows in one corner, a gnarled chestnut in the other. A few rosemary bushes as tall as a man explode in heady, evergreen clouds of fragrance, crossing the *villa*'s boundary and encroaching onto the street before it. All of this variety is being choked by ivy, burdock and thistle, entire mounds of dry, dead weeds rising over the remains of the *villa*'s outbuildings.

Claudius was right – there are too many guards, both *vigiles* and privately hired soldiers, roaming the streets for us to get any closer to the *villa*. Its owner is clearly concerned for his own safety – or at least, wants everyone else to think so. The amount of protection afforded to this weed-overgrown patch of empty land is almost ostentatious. Whoever lives here must be one of the richest and most powerful of the nobles still left in Londin. A member of the Council, no doubt. And unless the Gothic king started bribing Briton nobles to do his bidding, this means Eishild was right: the real threat from the hired swords is to Madron, not to her.

I don't know enough about the Council to even start guessing who the *villa* might belong to. From what my father and the bishop explained, there are a few factions that might benefit from standing against Ambrosius's plans; but whether the nobles who hired Illica wanted simply to stop Madron's union with Honorius, or force

The Crown of the Iutes

another husband onto her, that they were sending spies to the cathedral proved they weren't planning on achieving their aims in a peaceful, lawful manner.

With nothing else to do, I can only stay in our hiding place and observe the entrance to the palace, hoping to gain some insight from watching whoever might be coming to visit the mysterious nobleman.

"I'm hungry," Claudius complains. I reach into my satchel and throw him a bread roll filled with sheep's cheese. He devours half of it and keeps the rest for later.

"Were you really a soldier in Gaul?" I ask him. He's younger than me, but not by a lot. If he fought Goths for Aegidius, it's possible we took part in the same campaigns.

"I was. A spearman."

"Were you at Aurelianum, seven years ago?"

"I guarded the camp. Didn't see much of the battle itself."

"Why did you run away?"

He scowls. "A soldier's life was easy under Aegidius. After Aurelianum, there was peace on the border. The Goths didn't bother us; we didn't bother them. The Bacauds were subdued. I got lodging and three meals a day just for leaning on my spear from dawn to dusk, staring at the flowing Liger…"

"What changed?"

"When Aegidius died, his son was yet too young to rule. *Comes* Paulus and *Rex* Hildrik took over the command of the defences, and they were more warlike than Aegidius or his boy. Paulus believed attack was the best defence, and had us march out on raids deep into the heathen lands – but we were neither trained nor equipped for this kind of war. One time, less than half of us returned alive from a raid. That's when Illica, Armin and I decided to run away."

"Why here? Why Londin?"

He shrugs. "We boarded the first ship out of Andecawa that agreed to take us out of Gaul. Londin seemed like a place where it's easy to disappear."

I sense he's not telling me everything, but I have no time to ask him any more questions. Two carriages arrive at the palace's gates and drive up to the porch of the *domus*. They bear strange markings, of wild boar and a leaping horse. A man steps out of the first vehicle, accompanied by armed guards – he's a redhead, like me, with bushy beard and a mane of unruly hair. Gold rings glint on his arms and neck.

"Do you know who that is?" I whisper.

"I've never seen this man before," Claudius replies.

Just as the redhead steps up to the gate, the door of the *domus* is flung open. Two burly guards emerge, dragging a man with them to the street.

"That's Illica!" says Claudius.

The guards throw Illica out into the gutter, to the redhead's amusement, then throw a small coin bag after him. Some silver coins rattle out onto the pavement. The Gaul rummages after them ravenously, bows to the guards and shuffles away.

The Crown of the Iutes

"Stay here," I say to Claudius, threatening him with the sword. "Don't move."

He retreats into the corner and nods, clutching onto his bread roll.

"I showed you Illica. What more do you need me for?"

"I don't want you running away to warn any other friends you may have here. Now stay down. I won't be long."

At first, it seems Illica is going back to the Poor Town. But soon he reaches the Augustan Highway and crosses it into the north-eastern district of the city. If I remember my father's stories correctly, this was once the territory of the Angles, Ikens and members of other tribes who infiltrated the city's Wall from the north. It doesn't appear that anyone lives here anymore. Even the sunken huts built into the foundations of the tenements have rotted away. The marshland that binds the city from the north and east penetrated here, slowly swallowing the abandoned ruins into an oozing mire.

Illica reaches the outline of a crossroad, stops and looks over his shoulder; I hide in a shadow behind a fragment of a stone wall. He whistles three times. After a moment, three other men appear on the crossroad from some unseen hiding place. Fair-hairs, all. Two of them wield *seaxes*, the third one carries an *angon* spear on his back, and the manner of the clothes and hair they wear is unlike that of any Iutes or Saxons I know. When they open their mouths, their coarse, rising accents confirm my suspicion: these are Angles, the mighty tribe that settled far beyond Coln, just outside Wortigern's domain, and managed to subdue the native Britons long before the Iutes and Aelle's Saxons even considered rebelling against their masters.

Illica hands each of them a few coins from the purse.

"You know what to do?" he asks them. They grunt back affirmatively.

"Is it just the four of us?" one of the Angles asks. "I hear the bishop has strengthened the guard recently."

"Two more are waiting by the Coln Gate with a cart, once you get the package. But this is a mission of stealth, not strength. My employer doesn't want to start a war with the Church – if he can help it."

Three armed men. Even if they're trained warriors, I feel like I'll have no trouble taking them all on, especially since, unlike in the fight with Wulf's bandits, I will not care about killing them. But should I do it now, or should I wait for them to reach the cathedral, to make sure I know what their plans really are?

A piece of weathered foundation crumbling under my foot makes the decision for me. The Angles turn in my direction, but before they can spot me and realise what's going on, I charge at them from behind the wall. I reach the spearman first. He reaches for the *angon*; he's too slow to draw it before I thrust my *spatha* in his chest.

I spin to avoid a falling *seax*, grab the swordsman's tunic and draw him in; the impetus of his blow propels him forward, head-first into a mound of waste. The third Angle steps back, raises his sword over his head in a battle stance, and rolls his cloak around his arm as a shield.

I accept his challenge and raise the *spatha* to my ear. Judging by his confident stance, he must be an experienced fighter. I grab the sword in two hands and whirl it into a powerful slash. The Angle raises his shield-arm to accept the blow – but it's a feint; at the last moment I switch from cut to thrust, reaching under his guard and carving deep into his right armpit; and just like that, the duel is over – though the Angle doesn't know it yet.

The Crown of the Iutes

Blood erupts from the gash like a waterfall. The Angle, overcoming what must be a terrible pain, tries to strike at me, but his short *seax* doesn't have the reach. I stab again; another red flower blooms on his chest. He stumbles and falls to his knees. With a slash to the neck, I end his suffering. I turn around, remembering the third Angle is still alive – but seeing me unharmed while two of his companions lie bleeding out in the dirt, he turns tail and disappears into the marsh.

Illica tries to run away, too, but fear buckles his legs under him. I grab him, pin him to the crumbling wall and press the sword to his stomach.

"If you don't want to see your guts spilt all over this mud, you better tell me who you're working for. Who's paying you?"

He stares at me in fear and surprise.

"I don't know," he says. "I swear. He never told me his name."

"But you saw him?"

"All I know is that he owns the *villa* I was in today."

I let him go. He collapses to the ground. It shouldn't be difficult to discover the owner of the vast palace.

"Come with me," I say. "You'll tell the bishop everything you know."

CHAPTER V
THE LAY OF WEROC

"The great *villa* by Mithras Brook?" the bishop's eyes widen in shock. "Are you sure?"

"I saw Illica get thrown out of there with my own eyes."

"He could've been there for any other reason."

"Illica has no motive to lie to me," I reply. "He's not from Londin; he doesn't know any other nobles. Why is this so hard to believe? Whose palace is it?"

"Councillor Riotham's," Fastidius replies. He flicks his thumb against his chin in thought. "It just doesn't make sense. I can see why Albanus would want to meddle in the city's matters – his father always believed *he* should've been the *Dux* after Eobbasfleot, and his son is no different." From my description of the redhead and his carriage, the bishop soon deduced that the noble visitor at the northern *villa* was none other than Albanus, young *Comes* of the Cadwallons, so named after the saint whose sacred bones stored at Werlam were said to cure him from disease in childhood.

"But Riotham is Ambrosius's right hand in Londin," the bishop continues. "Why would he want to harm the girl and ruin his master's plans?"

"You don't think he's capable of rebelling against his *Dux*?"

"Do you think he decided to change masters? To join Albanus? But how would abducting Madron help either of them in any way?

The Crown of the Iutes

They don't need ransom – Riotham's already the richest man in Londin. A hostage? But for what purpose? Surely he can't imagine Ambrosius would let him get away with anything for the girl's sake."

"Maybe he *is* doing Ambrosius's bidding. Maybe they're planning something against my father. Madron is like a daughter to him, and…"

"Riotham's never shown any interest in the Iutes or your father before." Fastidius shakes his head. "It must be something else –"

"It's Weroc."

We both turn to see Madron standing in the door. She's wearing the same brown acolyte's cloak as I do when sneaking in and out of the cathedral – it hangs loose on her slender body.

"*Domna* Madron!" the bishop protests. "What are you doing here? What if somebody sees you?"

"I think it's too late to worry about that."

"How much have you heard?" I ask.

"Enough."

"And who's 'Weroc'?"

"Riotham's son," the bishop replies instead of Madron. "How do *you* know about him?"

The girl enters, uninvited, and sits down on Fastidius's bed. She throws off the robe and shakes off the dust of the courtyard. A fresh bruise on her forearm tells me she's been practising the sword again — and that Eishild got the better of her, for once.

"He's all Antonia ever talks about," she replies with a shrug. "The handmaiden Riotham sent me. She thinks she's being subtle about it, but I have long suspected there's something odd about how she praises him. Apollo merged with Hercules, with the mind of Constantine." She scoffs. "As if she wanted me to fall in love with him just from the description."

"How old is this Weroc?" I ask.

"I don't know for certain, but he can't be more than a couple of years older than me," Madron replies.

"About the same age as Honorius, then," says Fastidius. He clenches his hands together. "He couldn't possibly be thinking…"

"Does it matter what he is thinking?" Madron asks. "You said you stopped his men. What more do we have to worry about?"

"If I know Riotham — and I know him better than perhaps anyone in Londin," the bishop says, "this will only be a minor setback for him, and his new patron. He's spent the last ten years building a position of great wealth and influence in the city. I heard he's been getting silver and men from Aegidius in Gaul, but it might just be rumours. What isn't a rumour, however, is that he's raised an entire private army, the *bucellarii* — I'm sure you've seen some of them around his *villa*. They're almost as numerous as Wortimer's old army, back in the day. I thought he was doing it to pave way for Ambrosius's takeover — but now it's clear he wants the power for himself."

"Albanus won't be the only one who would support his bid for power," I say. "Some of the nobles in the West have been looking for someone to replace Ambrosius after the disaster in Wened, that

The Crown of the Iutes

much I know. If Riotham manages to arrange a marriage between Madron and his son, instead of her marrying Honorius, as planned, it would all but ensure his success."

"I would never agree to wed Weroc," Madron protests. "He sounds awful, even in Antonia's claims."

"I'm afraid Riotham wouldn't care much for your approval," says Fastidius. "Our deal was with Ambrosius, not with him. If he couldn't convince you to marry his son, he'd force you to it."

He stands up. "We have to move you somewhere more secure," he says to Madron.

"Where can be safer than the cathedral?" I ask.

"If Albanus is involved, the cathedral is no longer a safe place. He hates that I'm a bishop, and never hid that he'd want to move the bishopric to Werlam, where the saint's relics lie. He will not care for the sanctity of this house if it stands in the way of his goals. What about Cantia? Can we move Madron there?"

I shake my head. "My father won't want to risk a fight with someone as powerful as Riotham. Besides, this is not what was agreed with Ambrosius. *You* were supposed to be the girl's only guardian."

"And it's exactly what I'm doing. Guarding her. Keeping her from harm."

"Shouldn't we let the *Dux* know about this?" asks Madron.

"Of course," says the bishop. "I will send out messengers at once. But it's the middle of winter. It will take months for Ambrosius to be able to respond in any way – and even he might not be strong enough to take on the combined might of Riotham and Albanus. Especially if all we have for proof of the Councillor's scheme are the words of some Gaul deserter."

"We will have proof if we provoke him."

"What do you mean?"

"Madron must stay here," I say firmly. "But we will make it known that she's leaving for Cantia. This will spur Riotham to a brazen assault on the cathedral, before all his machinations come to fruition. When we defeat him, we will strike a dire blow not just to his army, but to his reputation. Forget about becoming the new *Dux* – he'll have a hard time staying on as the Councillor."

"And if we don't defeat him?" Fastidius says. "I cannot risk the well-being of my guests and servants. It's not just Madron. A battle like this would put everyone in danger."

"This place is a fortress," I insist. "It would take siege machines to break through its walls. And you're the finest strategic mind on this island. My father always said you taught him everything he knows about the art of war." I notice the compliment raises a faint smile. "With you and God on our side, we can beat any army."

"I will not have Madron be used as bait," he says, still unconvinced.

"I don't mind," the girl replies. "Octa is right. Right now Riotham's strategy is in disarray. We caught his spies; we killed his kidnappers. If we give him too much time, he'll only use it to come up with a better plan, and to strengthen himself further. We can't beat him with wealth or influence – but we can beat him in plain battle."

I look at Madron and smile appreciatively. The girl is young, but she's bright – and already sly as a fox. It's no wonder: she's had the best education in Britannia; but that's not everything. Both her

The Crown of the Iutes

father and her grandfather were *duces* in Londin, both won the title for themselves by force and cunning, rather than have it handed to them by the Council, even if one of them turned out to be a bloodthirsty monster. Their shrewd blood burns in Madron's veins, mixed with the courage of the Iute warriors that was her mother's — and my — inheritance.

"I need to think about it," says the bishop. "And pray for guidance. Leave me for now, both of you. Octa, I will send for you as soon as I make my decision."

"Of course, Your Grace."

"And — take care of yourself. I don't suppose Riotham yet knows who thwarted his ploy, but if he does find out, I won't be able to protect you outside these walls."

"I'll be fine, whatever Fate may throw at me."

I lay my hand on the sword's hilt, seeking the usual assurance, but somehow, this time, I find none.

The door to my room is unlocked and slightly ajar. I reach for the sword and draw it halfway before pushing the door open.

A young woman is sitting on my bed. I've never seen her before, but I know her kind well. She wears a tight dress of garish cloth, slit open over her chest and thighs, with no undergarment. Her hair is bound up and dyed red. A fur-lined cape lies thrown on the floor; it's a cold night, and her skin — plenty of which can be seen through the openings in the dress — has a bluish tinge, poorly concealed by a layer of lime paint.

"I think you got the wrong room," I say.

"You are Octa, son of Aeric?"

"I don't remember ordering anyone."

There's always one or two of her kind sitting in the inn's main hall, waiting for patrons; they never have to wait long —their services are as much part of the inn's trade as food and drink. I hired one of the girls before, when my loneliness grew too strong; but though she skilfully satisfied my flesh, my spirit remained empty, yearning only for Ursula's soft, if often reluctant, touch, and I haven't tried that sort of thing again.

"I am a gift," she says. "Already paid for."

"A *gift?*" I frown. "Who from?"

She lies down on the bed, slowly unlacing the front of her dress. "Councillor Riotham, they said."

Riotham. Everything becomes clear. She's not a gift – she's a warning, and a challenge. The Councillor is letting me know he knows all about me and my plans.

"Get out of here," I say.

With a wounded grimace, she sits back up. "I'm paid for the whole night," she says. "I have nowhere else to go."

"Tell the landlord you need a room. I'll pay for it."

"Sounds like a waste of silver," she says, fluttering her eyelashes and pouting her lips seductively.

"I'm in no mood today for – wait." I might use the woman after all, though not in the way she intended. "Who ordered you to come here?"

"I told you – Councillor Riotham."

"But it wasn't the Councillor who spoke with you, or gave you the money."

She scoffs. "No, of course not. I'm an army whore, not a nobleman's courtesan." That explains why I haven't seen her at the inn before. "It was just some officers."

"Officers – from Riotham's army?"

"The troops that train north of the Wall," she says. "They're some of my best customers."

That Riotham sent me this pox-ridden soldiers' whore adds an insult to the threat. I could easily afford a courtesan fit for a noble if I needed this sort of entertainment.

I sit down beside her. "What's your name?"

"Lucia."

"How many of those soldiers are there, Lucia?"

"I'm a whore, not a clerk," she replies, picking at her yellowed teeth. "But I'd reckon there's a good few hundred there at a time."

"At a time?"

"They come and go. I can always count on new customers," she grins.

"Any horses?"

"Only for the officers and messengers." She shrugs. "This is boring. I was paid to hump, not talk of soldiers and horses."

I walk up to the small scroll-reading desk by the window and pour her some of the wine – the good one that I asked the innkeeper to bring me from the Forum, rather than the swill he serves his regulars. Lucia sniffs the mug suspiciously, then downs it in one and belches.

"This is what the officers drink," she says. She looks around. "And this is the most expensive room I've ever been in. Are you a Councillor yourself?"

"No, but my father was." I sit back. "I am a Iute, from Cantiaca."

"Oh, like Wulf."

"You know Wulf?"

"Of course. I was born and raised in Poor Town. I thought all Iutes were bandits or peasants."

I chuckle. "Not all. I'm an *aetheling*. A king's son."

She laughs and sprawls herself on her bed. "I am at your command, *aetheling*!"

"Maybe later. Tell me more about those *bucellarii*. How often do you meet with the officers?"

She scowls. "There are other girls, more popular than me – younger, wilder. Barbarians. But I am still a favourite of one or two, who prefer more… old-fashioned ways."

The Crown of the Iutes

"Then I will need you to do me a favour."

"A favour."

"I will pay, of course. Whatever you got for coming here. All you have to do is meet with one of the officers who sent you here and tell him what I'll tell you."

She ponders my proposal for a moment, with a finger to her lips. As I look at her bare flesh through the unlaced dress, a bout of melancholy washes over me. I wish Ursula was with me here. I wish she could join me in the battle against Riotham. She would have loved taking a stand against a corrupt Councillor, and fighting alongside Bishop Fastidius. This is exactly the sort of thing we used to do in our youth, before my duties as *aetheling* stopped me from going on adventures, and before having to take care of Pascent stopped her.

I reach out and touch Lucia's breast. She smiles and raises herself on one elbow, letting the breast fall out of her dress.

"Fine," she says. "I'll relay your message. And I'll do it for free, because you're Wulf's kin, and a king's son. Just – don't make me spend this night alone. I *am* a professional, after all."

"Alright, if you insist." I untie my breeches, already bulging. Ursula still hasn't come to visit me in Londin, and there's only so much I can do with my own hands. "But use only your mouth," I add, wary of how many soldiers from all over Britannia and beyond must have passed through the girl's fleshy gates.

"A man of taste," she chuckles as she lowers her head.

"Are you certain they'll come?" the bishop asks, looking with doubt down from the battlement onto the street below. A carriage, marked with Paul's and Peter's insignia, is being prepared for departure, accompanied by a small retinue of mounted guards. A short while ago an identical carriage left from the cathedral hill in the direction of the Londin Bridge. This one is supposed to head for the Coln Gate. Neither of them carries Madron – both are just decoys, to lure Riotham's men into thinking today is the day when we're finally moving the girl into shelter, beyond the city walls, beyond the Councillor's grasp.

"I'm certain Lucia will tell them what she's meant to say. I can't guarantee what Riotham is going to do with this information."

"I don't know if I feel comfortable with putting so much faith in a… woman of sin."

"'Seest thou this woman?'" I recite. "'I entered into thine house, thou gavest me no water for my feet: but she hath washed my feet with tears, and wiped them with the hairs of her head'."

He laughs. "Well said. I am schooled by my own pupil. I see you have not forgotten your education."

The battlement from which we observe the preparations is a short stretch of the cathedral enclosure's defensive perimeter, facing north-west, the only one built entirely out of stone: a large piece of retaining wall salvaged by the bishop in its entirety from some dismantled basilica or a bath house. Soon after Wortimer's War, when the cathedral hill avoided destruction only through good fortune and my father's warnings, Fastidius began strengthening his defences; at first, he merely surrounded the grounds with a taller fence and added more guards, but his intuition was proven right time and again. Without a *Dux*, surrounded by enemies, and impoverished by its isolation, the whole city had become as unruly as the Poor Town, and especially violent here, in the outskirts.

The Crown of the Iutes

There had been several attempts at an open rebellion against the Council, and plenty more smaller skirmishes, brawls, bandit attacks; after each such incident, the bishop demanded more land and resources from the Council to expand his ramparts. The church territory grew in the process, the sides of the cathedral mushroomed with attached smithies, storehouses and barns, until the fortress into which the cathedral grounds turned reached the Londin Wall itself.

Beyond the Wall, the boundary is a combination of earthen walls, palisades and makeshift barricades – enough to keep out the bandits or an occasional hunger riot. But will it be enough to halt an outright assault by Riotham's *bucellarii*? And will the Councillor indeed be bold enough to try striking the sacred ground of a church?

"Won't he be afraid of you excommunicating him?" I ask the bishop. "Like Germanus did with Wortigern?"

"That's why he's working with Albanus," Fastidius replies. "Once he becomes the *Dux*, the two of them will have little trouble convincing the other bishops to denounce me as a heretic and annul any of my decrees. My position here has always been tenuous – you've heard what they say about me in the West. I only lasted this long because the Council's too weak and too self-centred to worry about me – and I made sure not to remind them of my presence too often. To be honest, this entire business with Madron is the most I've been involved in the city's affairs in years."

"Then – why *did* you get yourself involved in this? If Riotham is taking a risk, then you do tenfold. You could die. We could all die. Why not just give the girl to him?"

He smiles bitterly. "Do I really need to answer this, Octa, son of Aeric? We both know who she is. Your father would protect her with his life – I will do no less."

"I'm not sure if my father wouldn't prefer to hand her over to Riotham, rather than Ambrosius."

"Oh, but I am. Riotham as *Dux* would be the worst thing to happen to the Iutes since Wortimer. And it wouldn't be that good for Londin, either." He rubs his eyes. "I prayed long and hard on this, Octa, and I have made my peace with God. I have lived a long life. If it ends tonight, so be it."

"You sound like a Iute warrior." I chuckle.

"I suppose I've learned something about war from your father, too." He leans down to the courtyard. "I think you're just about ready, aren't you?"

A female servant, disguised as Madron, looks out of the carriage. "We're ready, Your Grace."

The carriage rolls off down the slope, then turns towards the Augustan Highway. For a long while, nothing more happens. At length, the lookouts return from the north.

"Alpinus?" the bishop calls to the rider in front. "Still nothing?"

The rider shakes his head. "It's like Sunday afternoon after the Mass out there, Your Grace," he replies. "Not a soul to be seen, except the guards at the gates."

Fastidius turns back to me. "I think we've waited long enough, Octa. I'm afraid your night acquaintance did not sound convincing enough for Riotham's —"

A whistle sounds in the distance. Moments later, a messenger comes running up the western avenue.

The Crown of the Iutes

"They're coming," he announces, breathless. "From the old fort by the amphitheatre."

"How many?"

"I don't know - a hundred, two hundred... A whole army!"

The herald, wearing a woollen headband and carrying a branch of peace, climbs up the dirt avenue to the accompaniment of brass horns. The rest of the enemy force remains at the foot of the cathedral hill. From my vantage point I count maybe a hundred and fifty men, all armed with swords and spears, some, though few, clad in mail and helmets. I notice the two carriages we sent out as decoys, captured, at the far back of the formation. I hope Riotham's men didn't harm any of the innocent servants riding in the carriages. The Councillor himself is nowhere to be seen, just as the bishop predicted – he wouldn't want to be present at the battle this early.

We meet the herald at the new gate to the enclosure, punched through the chunk of stone wall set up halfway across the hillside. The wall and a palisade on its either side separate the slope into two parts, which not only adds to the site's defences, but makes it easier to manage the crowds gathering in front of the cathedral on holy days.

Devised by Fastidius's strategic genius, the two wings of the palisade form a wedge, which would funnel any incoming assault and focus it on the gate and the stone wall. In the far corners of the wedge stand two wooden towers, from which the bishop's soldiers can pelt an attacking force with arrows and darts. It must be a daunting view for the troops gathered at the bottom of the hill, made worse by the great banners Fastidius hung from the palisade, painted with the *chrismons* and the swords of Saint Paul, to let everyone know that if they strike at this wall, they're striking at God himself.

The herald glances at the gate and the rampart above. He notices me – and the *spatha* in my hand – and winces before turning back to the bishop.

"By the order of the Magistrates of the City of Londin and the Council of the Province of Britannia Maxima," he announces, in a loud, clear voice which echoes from the palisades, resounds throughout the courtyard, and flows downhill on the breeze, "you are hereby commanded to release *Domna* Madron, daughter of Wortimer, into our custody."

He presents the bishop with a sealed missive. Fastidius cracks the seal and peruses the document, before tearing it in half.

"The Council has no power here," he replies. "I respond only before God and His Church."

The herald looks over his shoulder, to the army gathered below, then back to the bishop. "Are you sure this is how you want to end this, Your Grace? Over some half-heathen wench?"

"She is my guest. As is everyone else behind this wall. I swore to protect her until her betrothed returns. I will give her away only to *Dux* Ambrosius or his son, Honorius." He speaks calmly, but his voice booms louder than the herald's, fortified by decades of experience preaching to great crowds. "Are *you* sure you want to sacrifice your mortal soul for the sake of your master, son?"

The herald steps back, as if slapped. The soldier behind him makes the sign of the cross.

"Your Grace, I implore you –"

The Crown of the Iutes

"God sees you, my son, and judges all your deeds, good and bad."

Fastidius crosses himself, too, and extends his hand in a blessing over the herald and the soldier. Instinctively, they bow before the gesture. "Go to your master. Tell him whatever happens here today is on his conscience."

"Y-yes, Your Grace," the herald stutters. Gone is his haughty demeanour. This is the man who a few weeks ago would've stood inside the incense-filled cathedral hall, praying, listening to the bishop reciting the word of God, trembling before the majesty of the Heavens. How could he now proclaim edicts against the very same holy man who held sway over the souls of everyone in the city? Even if the rumours of the bishop's heretic inclinations are true, it isn't up to the Council to resolve religious disputes – and certainly not by force…

The herald turns and sulks back to his men. The bishop climbs back onto the rampart as the gate shuts behind him.

"You're in good cheer, Octa," he remarks.

"With just a few words, you've inflicted more damage to the Councillor's army than a barrage of arrows," I say. "If even a third of them now feels the way the herald looks, I suddenly don't feel so bad about the chances of our survival."

Fastidius shakes his head. "This is why Riotham only sent these few today," he says.

"A *few*? You were expecting more? Several days ago, we were fearing an attack by a handful of hired swords, now we're facing an entire army – and you call them a *few*?"

"The time for ploys and subterfuge is over. Riotham must win this battle, now that he's got the entire Council involved in his plans.

He won't stop until either all our men or his are slain. This is only a fraction of his army – he knows those in the first wave of attack will be filled with the most doubt. We will have a lot more trouble with whoever comes next."

The sound of trumpets and whistles announces the beginning of the charge. To my surprise, the bishop remains at the gate, even as the head of the enemy column comes ever nearer.

"Shouldn't you find some shelter, Your Grace?" I ask.

"I'm not just a general today," he replies. "I am a shepherd, and my place is with my flock. Besides," he adds with a wry smile, "I command better from the front line. Brace yourselves!" he shouts to the guards behind the wall. "Load your bows! Here comes the battering ram!"

The Crown of the Iutes

CHAPTER VI
THE LAY OF BELLICUS

The ram is made out of a ship's mast, a thirty-feet-long beam of fir-wood bound with iron clamps, to which are attached the carrying ropes. Eighteen muscle-bound men wield it up to the gate – some of them fair-hairs – clad only in woollen breeches and army boots. It's a primitive weapon – but then, the cathedral gate was built to lock out crowds of rioters, not to withstand sieges.

Each of the eighteen holds a small round shield over his head, guarding him from missiles thrown from the rampart and the wooden towers. The rest of Riotham's army have no such protection, as they rush to scramble over the earthen banks and the palisades. On each tower stand two of the bishop's men: an archer, and a missile thrower, with a basket of *plumbata* darts and a bundle of javelins. They rarely miss. With each shot, with each throw, one of Riotham's men crumbles and disappears from sight, trampled by his compatriots.

They may be wearing the drab robes of acolytes now, but these men were soldiers once, as were many others fighting for the bishop: not just Wall guards or former *vigiles*, but members of Wortimer's old army, veterans of Eobbasfleot and the fighting in Londin. They took up service in the cathedral as penance for the atrocities their side committed in the war with the Iutes, and now they finally see a chance to repay for all their sins at once, by protecting the cathedral and the innocents within.

There are fewer than a hundred of us capable of bearing arms with some skill. Fifty, at most, are veterans. A few dozen more – servants, slaves, cooks, young acolytes – volunteered to help in any way possible, whether by carrying supplies, taking care of the wounded, or building the defences. Everyone else hid inside the cathedral building, a nigh-impenetrable fortress of black and white stone, where they assist our fighting in the way that, to many, seems the most important: through prayer.

The bishop counts the strikes of the ram against the gate. The oaken beams shudder and creak, the inch-thick iron bar thrown over the leaves groans and bends under the blows. At the tenth strike, he calls a retreat.

"Spears and shields, to the second line!" he cries. "Archers, cover us."

I throw one last dart from my stock; it hits one of the ram-carriers on the shoulder, but he shrugs the pain off. I climb down the wooden steps and join the bishop in his retreat.

The second line of defence is a crescent-shaped barricade thrown across the outer courtyard, stretching from the stables to the north to a row of stalls to the south, where traders sell keepsakes and victuals to pilgrims on holy days. We built it over the past few days from whatever rubble we could find around the foot of the hill, and the great bricks and stones of the Londin Wall; a large section of which, near the wharf gate, succumbed to the Tamesa's raging tides a few years ago. Nobody bothered to clear or repair the breach, since the pile of rubble was still high enough to deter most sea raiders brave and fortunate to reach this far up the river. The Council's negligence proved our blessing, providing us with enough material to set up or reinforce barriers and barricades throughout the enclosure, and split it into a number of easy to defend sections.

It's not as imposing as the stone wall and the gate, but the low barrier is more suitable to the kind of fighting we expect here today: gruelling hand-to-hand combat, bashing shields, thrusting spears, hacking and slashing with axes and long knives. For this, we need to be on the same level as the attackers; the arrows and *plumbatas* can only last us so long.

At the twentieth strike of the ram, with the crack of a splitting thunder, the gate finally gives way. At the same time, the southern palisade comes crashing down, and with it, one of the archer towers. Riotham's men pour through the two gaps, only to face the new barrier. Dismay and fear paint the faces of the first soldiers who reach the outer courtyard. They can now see the entire front line of the enclosure: the network of barricades and embankments, the imposing edifice of the cathedral itself – and beyond it, at the far back, the most threatening of all: a *ballista* on top of one of the Wall's towers, aimed at anyone who would dare to breach the final line of fortifications.

Nobody told them they would be capturing a fortress. Breaching the outer wall was challenge enough, and they paid dearly for it – and it seemed the real battle has only just begun. A bristling hedgehog of spears and shields, as many as we could find in the bishop's stores, once again surrounds and traps the attackers in a crescent of wood and steel.

Riotham's commanding officer is not without skill. I spot him, in a plumed helmet, as he passes the broken gate and rallies his men around him. I can't hear him over the din of battle, but I can imagine what he's shouting: that the barricade is just a pile of rubble, not an impenetrable wall; that we are outnumbered, and few of us truly know how to fight; that beyond this one last, thin line, lies victory – and that they should not fear God's wrath, for the bishop is a heretic of the worst kind: a Pelagianist. That his sort had been all but vanquished in this island by the efforts of the great Germanus, and the light emanating from the sacred bones at

The Crown of the Iutes

Werlam; but unbeknownst to anyone, the Adversary had woven his final nest in the very heart of the capital.

Whether this is what his speech is about, or something else altogether, it works. The soldiers regroup at the gate and push forth in one concerted charge, at the centre of the barricade's crescent. This is the weakest point in our line – if they break through here, nothing will stand between them and the cathedral door. This is why the bishop entrusted its defence to the most experienced commander at his disposal: me.

I have twenty soldiers with me, all of them Wortimer's veterans. It is the oddest of feelings, to lead into battle all these old men who, sixteen years ago, fought on the side of my people's mortal enemies. Did one of them take part in the slaughter of my mother's village? Did they fight my father at the Augustan Gate? I don't ask them any questions. Fastidius assures me that they left that part of their lives far behind, that they have truly repented for their sins and repaid for them with years of faithful service.

They certainly don't seem to bear me any ill will; they heed my orders as if I was a Briton officer. I don't need to rouse them into battle. It's enough that they're fighting again, led by someone who knows what he's doing. It helps that I have studied the Roman ways of war, the same they are now recovering from the depths of their memories. I would have preferred to have my bear-shirts with me – and most of all, I wish Ursula was here at my side; but in their absence, and despite their advanced age, the twenty Britons appear a decent enough force with which to stop Riotham's advance.

I don't have much to do at first. The veterans know their job well; this is exactly the kind of battle they were trained for: holding a firm line of tall shields, against which the attackers crash like waves against a harbour wall. I stand in the centre of the line, the keystone in the arch, shield forward, sword over my head, not only because I'm the commander but because I'm the youngest and expected to last the longest against the enemy onslaught. This does not inspire my confidence; the oldest of my subordinates, Bellicus, is coming on seventy years, and was already a seasoned veteran when he stood against King Drust and his Picts at the Iken beach. His arms are wiry, sinewy, and his bones brittle; his face is a dried raisin, darkened with age. I fear, like quite a few of my men, he will die today, not from the blows of Riotham's swords, but from sheer exhaustion.

But for the time being, we hold. This is, by now, an all too familiar exercise. I stab over shield, I slash under, I duck and block, I dodge the spears, I reel from stones hitting my helmet; I find openings through which to thrust when the enemies try to wrestle shields from the men standing next to me. Before long, a pile of bodies grows at the foot of the barricade. The attackers' feet slip in the blood of their fallen comrades. My shield-arm grows numb, my sword blade is chipped into dullness on the bones of the enemy warriors. I lose track of passing time. How long can this last? There were a hundred and fifty of them when the battle started. A dozen at least fell fighting at the gate. I myself must've slain five or six already. There can't possibly be many more of them left, unless Riotham threw in some reserves I haven't seen before.

The Crown of the Iutes

And then, the line breaks.

Not my veterans; I can't think of anything Riotham could launch at us that would break through our wall of shields, short of a heavy cavalry charge. After more than an hour of fighting, none of my men is so much as scratched. No, the line breaks on our left flank, where Riotham's light troops finally find their way through the labyrinth of overturned stalls, crates and sand-filled barrels, and pierce through our weakest formation – a group of young acolytes, armed with clubs, rakes and kitchen knives, guarding the approach to the cluster of dormitory huts appended to the cathedral's southern wall. These huts are the only home they know, and they fight bravely to defend them, but they're overrun within moments of the enemy reaching their line.

"Bellicus!" I call to the old man. "Take eight men and come with me. Rest of you, fill in the gaps."

"We're too few!" Bellicus replies.

"We'll be too *dead* if we let them take our rear. Lose those shields and grab your swords!"

I should wait until we're in formation, but there's no time. We strike at the enemy piecemeal, one by one, as quickly as we can. I cut down one foe and leap aside to dodge a spear of another. Bellicus comes from the side, whirls his *spatha* and slams it into the spearman's shoulder, hacking it clean off. I'm surprised at the strength hiding in his bone-thin arms. I hit again, and again. Another enemy falls, but two more rush past me. One of the veterans drops to the ground, his head cracked by some blunt weapon. I pick up his short sword and use it to block a falling axe. A spear blade scratches my side. I thrust with the *spatha*, hitting the arm that holds it, step forward, cut again with the short sword, but the enemy pulls back and my blade cuts through the air.

"There's too many," says Bellicus.

"I know," I reply.

Riotham's commander poured all his reserves into the gap on the southern flank. With our backs to the cathedral wall, we're split from the fighting at the barricade. I see the line of shields rolled up as my soldiers fall one after another. Some of the men from our northern flank rush to their aid, only to find themselves cut off from the rest by another wave of enemies.

I gather the surviving veterans – there's only seven of us left – and form a wedge, with which I charge at the side of Riotham's reserve. It is a futile strike. We down a few more men in the initial chaos, but lose three of our own, and are pushed again back to the cathedral wall, where we can only defend ourselves and watch as the rest of the barricade falls to the enemy onslaught.

Just then, the great door of the cathedral swings open. I can't believe my ears at first: the air fills with the sound of an angelic choir. I turn to look, astonished: a procession of young men and women in white ceremonial robes descends the stairs. They hold candles and crosses and sing a solemn psalm. Bishop Fastidius marches in front, wielding his crooked staff. The swiftly setting winter sun gleams off the silver and jewels on its top.

The Crown of the Iutes

The effect on the battlefield is immediate. Both my and Riotham's men pause the fighting. Some kneel – but they're swiftly admonished by their officers, who remind them of Fastidius's heresy. We all wait to see what the bishop's plan is. Can he really hope to win the battle with just song and prayer? Germanus claimed to have done this once, in the West, when he fought the rebel *Comes* of the Cornows… I like to think of Fastidius as a friend – or at least, a friend of the family – but even I can't tell whether he truly believes prayer alone can turn the tide of battle, or is it all just another ruse?

Whatever the bishop himself may believe, the transformation that his intervention brings is clear. In the sudden lull, the enemy's momentum is lost. The rush of impending victory recedes from the eyes and faces of Riotham's men, while our soldiers momentarily regain their strength and conviction. It is a brilliant, if risky, stratagem. I glance to Bellicus. He nods and strengthens the slippery grip on his sword, ready to throw himself back into the brawl.

Fastidius stops, and the entire procession halts behind him, a mere few feet from the nearest enemy. The soldier looks to his officer in fright, but before either can react, the bishop raises the staff high – and strikes the man over the head, cracking his skull in an instant. Blood spurts from the wound onto the bishop's snow-white vestment. The youths of the procession drop the candles and crosses and draw long knives from under their robes.

"Now!" I cry.

In the shocked stillness, my call resounds throughout the courtyard, and we attack from all three sides at once at the wedge Riotham's force carved into our southern flank. I lose sight of the bishop and his youths as I immerse myself into the bloody clash at the foot of the stairs. It feels as if the wind has changed direction and is now blowing dust in the eyes of the enemy. They're no longer fighting to win – now it's their time to fight for survival. I kill another young soldier – he can't be more than sixteen, and he dies quickly from a cut to the neck; but when I search for another man to fight, I can't find one.

The trumpets call retreat. Riotham's surviving soldiers turn around and trample each other on the way out, scrambling over the barricade and the market stalls. We let them flee, too weary for pursuit. The sword drops out of my hand and clangs on the marble of the cathedral stairs. Knees buckle under me. Someone rushes to support me from falling – it's one of the young acolytes, his white robe now soaked red in the blood of the enemy.

By some miracle, I escape the first day of the battle with only a few scratches and bumps, none of them serious enough to prevent me from falling into a dead man's sleep, lasting until dawn.

The vast hall of the cathedral was turned overnight into a field hospital. The blades of light coming from the windows under the vaulted ceiling carve the vision of carnage out of the darkness. The marble floor is slippery with blood. Nuns and acolytes rush from one wounded to another, carrying wrappings and buckets of water taken from the baptistery well.

The Crown of the Iutes

I find Madron and Eishild among those helping the injured. Neither has any experience in field surgery, but they're doing what they can to bring relief to the young acolytes, a dozen of them sitting under the southern wall, bound in blood-soaked wrappings torn from their own white robes.

A few years ago, Madron stood in this very same hall, waiting for her betrothed. A mere child then, unaware of her own importance, the importance which made all these young men willing to throw their lives away in her defence.

She spots me and rushes to greet me.

"Are you hurt, *aetheling*?"

"No, I'm all well, thank the Lord," I reply. It feels fitting to be grateful to the Roman God for my salvation; it is his house we're defending, after all. "You?"

"I was never in any danger – the bishop had us hide in the crypt, though I wanted to join the fight."

She looks shaken by all the death and pain around her; her face is pale; her eyes bloodshot; her hands tremble. Though she's a child of a burning frontier, I don't think she's ever been this close to battle before. I hold her hands.

"Everything will be alright," I assure her. "His Grace knows what he's doing. Where is he?" I ask, not seeing Fastidius anywhere in the hall.

"He's out the back," she says. "With – the dead."

There's no place to bury the fallen in the small graveyard behind the apse, so the bishop ordered that one of the frost-hardened vegetable patches in the shadow of the Londin Wall be dug up, to the sorrow of the hermits dwelling in the cells nearby, who use it to grow their simple tubers and roots. The burials are all but finished by the time I find him.

"How many?" I ask.

"Nearly half," the bishop replies.

"Riotham must have lost a lot more."

He nods. "But he's got a lot more to spare."

"I really hoped Wulf would send some of his men to help us," I say. I visited the Poor Town a couple of days before the assault, to warn Wulf of a possible battle near the borders of his "domain" – and to test where his loyalties lay. He threw me out before I could even tell him who was coming to attack the cathedral, and why. "Did you know he still keeps that crucifix Betula stole from you all those years ago?"

The bishop chuckles. "I lost count of how many times I bought it back from the thieves' market only to let them steal it again. We don't know what's happening in the Poor Town – they may be fighting their own battle right now. We'll just have to depend on our own strength."

"Should we surrender, then?"

"Not yet. We can withstand one more day like this, now that our… lines are shortened."

This isn't a pitched battle, and there are no set lines, but I understand what he means – with fewer men our supplies will last us longer, and within the impenetrable walls of the cathedral we

The Crown of the Iutes

can only hold out as long as we have enough food, arrows and wound ointments.

He crosses himself and blesses the gravediggers with his staff — the half of it that remains after the battle; it must have snapped on the bones of some unfortunate attacker.

"Look at it," he says, showing me the staff. "My pastoral is as broken as I am."

"What do you mean?"

"I have sinned, Octa. I brought death to the House of Lord. I splattered my vestments with the blood of the innocents."

"They weren't innocent. And you did what you had to do."

"All are innocent before they're judged by the Lord," he says.

"We only survived thanks to your arrival."

He chuckles. "Thank you, Octa, but I can deal with my own conscience myself, with the Lord's help. Let us focus on what's coming, instead. Come, I'll show you something."

He leads me to a narrow wooden staircase which takes us to a scaffold attached to the cathedral's southern roof, used to repair the tiles and to douse fires from lightning strikes. I can see far into the city from here — to the west, over Poor Town, all the way to the Bridge; to the north, into the empty marshes past the Augustan Highway, and the *villa* district to the west of it.

Riotham's soldiers have pulled back beyond the gate, leaving only a ring of guards on the courtyard. There's no camp — there's no need, when most of them could just return to their barracks in the north of the city, or even to their homes, only to get back to the battlefield when they're called to fight again. This is what makes our position so odd: it's as if we are fighting Londin itself.

The bishop points to something to the north. Out in the field of rubble between the hill and the Coln Gate, I see a slowly gathering crowd. They're not in formation, or in any sort of order; a chaotic mass of people, coming from all directions, in small groups or alone.

"Who are they?" I ask.

"Onlookers," the bishop explains. "It may be a fight for life to us, but to the people of Londin this is the best entertainment they've had in years."

"Whose side are they on?"

"Nobody's but their own. *This* is the city," he says, sweeping his arm over the gathering crowd. "These townsfolk, rich and poor. Not the Council, not the soldiers. If the cathedral is taken, they'll come to plunder it, of course, but not out of malice. For now, they're just watching things as they unfold. But as long as they're there, we can make use of them."

"How?"

"Gossip spreads easily in crowds like these," he replies. "I managed to send a few men out there, with rumours that the northern slope is not as well defended as the front gate."

I study the space between the crowd and the northern palisade. The postern is the only remaining entrance to the cathedral enclosure, now that the main gate has been captured. It's not as easy to reach as the gate – the winding path to it leads through a maze of ruins and up a slope that's steeper here than in the west.

The Crown of the Iutes

But there are no stone walls here, and no fortifications other than the palisade and a low earthen bank, reaching from the Londin Wall in the east to the stables in the south-west. No battering ram is needed to break through the postern – a few strong men should be enough to tear it down, and in this way gain easy access to the enclosure's entire northern flank.

"You think Riotham will buy the ruse?" I ask.

"I would be surprised if he's not thinking about it already. His men will be wary to attack the main gate again after yesterday – they'll be eager to try something different."

"It's a narrow path. With all these onlookers in the way, he won't be able to send his full force against us."

"I'm sure he's aware of that. But this is too good an opportunity for him to pass."

"And you really believe we can win this? After yesterday?"

He turns to me. "I was praying all night for guidance. The Lord told me to stand firm. Whether that means He wants me to die a martyr, or that he will save us all at the last moment, I don't know… But I'm not letting anyone just march into my cathedral, not after they drowned its stairs in blood."

"Then I'd better find Bellicus. We'll need that wall of shields again."

A whole day passes before Riotham manages to gather his men again – by the northern wall, just as the bishop predicted. There's fewer than a hundred of them this time, and most of them coming fresh from the *bucellarii* barracks.

The delay allows us all to rest and heal the worst of the injuries. Our remaining force is a meagre one – some thirty soldiers, not counting the veterans, but those who survived the first day are the toughest and fittest of the bishop's men; we may be fewer in numbers, but our strength and resolve has barely diminished.

This is to be our final stand, so I gather all thirty of us in one place, a line two-men deep just behind the palisade. Bellicus and his veterans line up in a crescent-shaped shield wall in front, leaving some fifty feet of open space between the postern and our ranks – just enough to, hopefully, trap the enemy again inside a deadly funnel. As Riotham's force starts to climb up the northern slope, we all take our Last Rites from the bishop. We all feel that there can be only two outcomes of today's battle: we either win – or we die.

It starts to snow.

We watch, helplessly, as the enemy loops ropes over the tops of the palisade poles and drags them down. The postern gate shatters under the axe blows. Riotham's soldiers pour through the gaps in an unruly cascade. Standing on top of the steep slope, we make the best possible use of the high ground. From behind the shield wall, we lob what little missiles we have left – darts, javelins, sling bullets, then rocks, chunks of marble carved from the cathedral walls, and blocks of granite lifted from the pavement. This seems to halt the enemy for a moment. They pull back to find cover, regroup, and return – this time with shields over their heads.

I put a horn to my lips and blow retreat. Other than the veterans, my men are not well trained, and I worry that the manoeuvre we devised with the bishop will fail through their lack of skill – but they prove remarkably disciplined for a random assembly of

The Crown of the Iutes

acolytes and former slaves, and the plan goes as smoothly as if they were a *centuria* of legionnaires.

We feign a flight, under the vaulted gateway of the northern guesthouse and into the cathedral's inner courtyard. Riotham's men break past Bellicus and his shields, and chase after us with howls of triumph. They fail to notice the trap until it's too late. As soon as they all pour into the courtyard, the first missile strikes the dense crowd of attackers. The bolt hacks off the arm of one and severs the leg of another before raising a plume of dust where it hits the ground.

Since it's the bishop's duty to maintain the stretch of the Wall around the cathedral, it's his own soldiers who man the massive *ballista*, one of the few still defending the city from pirate raids. We didn't use it on the first day of battle, deliberately, to make the enemy think that it wasn't functioning, that it was merely an expensive decoration – there was no need for it to waken from its slumber in years. But it was there all the time, looming like some sleeping monster, waiting, ready to bring death from above with its six-foot-long iron-tipped bolts, and nobody knew better what a devastating weapon this was than Fastidius, the hero of the Iken Beach.

The effect is immediate. The *ballista* brings terror to all foot warriors far greater than the damage it causes, especially when they have nowhere to run from its deadly missiles. As I rally my men to a renewed assault, panic spreads throughout Riotham's ranks. With a great twang of springs and ropes, another bolt flies through the air, shatters a shield and pins a tall, burly warrior to the ground through his chest, killing him in an instant. The sight is enough to spur his comrades to terrified flight. Trampling over each other, they rush back through the vaulted gateway, the same way they came, dropping their weapons in fright.

Bellicus's veterans turn around, their shield wall now preventing the enemy from fleeing instead of keeping them out. Riotham's soldiers fall onto their spears and swords as they blindly run out of the inner courtyard. There's no mercy this time; we're not letting anyone run away. We are still rested, battle rush still burning in our veins, and we know that the more enemy blood we spill onto the snow today, the fewer men Riotham will be able to send against us tomorrow.

If the people who came watching the battle from the safety of the marshes were expecting a long, gruelling spectacle like yesterday, they must be sorely disappointed. By noon, mere two hours after the start of the battle, I blow the aurochs horn, ordering my men to halt their pursuit and pull back towards the cathedral. The onlookers wait for a while yet, hoping for Riotham to throw in his reserves, of which he still must have plenty, but when nothing else happens, the crowds, by now frozen to the bone, grumpily disperse.

Despite the victory, our losses are grave. More than half of the veterans lie dead, the thin patch of snow around their bodies turned deep crimson. We have no more fortifications behind which we can withstand the next attack: no more palisades, no more barricades. Throughout the rest of the day and night we can only watch, helplessly, as Riotham's soldiers gather once again for an attack, on both slopes of the cathedral hill this time, knowing that this one will be our last stand – unless the bishop relents.

As I wait for the last of my men to enter the cathedral for the night, I spot a small, lonely figure in an acolyte's hooded robe, skulking across the main courtyard through the falling snow. I rush after it, sword drawn, thinking it might be a spy or a deserter. When I grab it by the robe and turn it around, I'm astonished to see Madron's face under the hood.

The Crown of the Iutes

"What are you doing here?" I whisper, pulling her aside into the shadow of the stables. "Have you gone mad?"

"I'm giving myself up," she says, tearing herself from my grip. "I don't want everyone to die for my sake."

"It's not just about you anymore," I tell her. "Do you think Riotham will just give up now, after he's lost so many men? The Council decreed that the bishop, and all who stand with him, are heretics. We are no longer protected by any law. The cathedral's treasure is for the taking; those of us who survive will be sold into slavery. You're just another prize to them."

"Then what are we going to do?" she asks, her voice trembling with terror as she suddenly realises the danger she's in. "We're all going to perish here."

"Trust in His Grace, and your Lord, Madron. We survived two nights already, and still we live. Riotham can't throw his men at us forever."

"What if he can? You don't know how many soldiers he's got left. But I've seen how many we have lost. All those poor boys, bleeding on the cathedral floor…"

I pull her to me and hug her. "We will win this, I promise. This can't last long. Riotham must be feeling the pressure already – how many more times can he lose? I know those Councillors – they can't wait for him to slip up, to show weakness. Three days of fighting in the middle of the city, and so close to Christmas – that can't be good for anyone, not for trade, not for the safety of the townsfolk… I'm sure it will all be over soon."

"It will be – one way or another."

"We will win," I repeat. "Now, let's go back before anyone spots us. I'd rather die from a sword than from a stray arrow of some anxious guard."

The Crown of the Iutes

James Calbraith

CHAPTER VII
THE LAY OF RIOTHAM

The ram's booming strikes echo throughout the crypt like a great bell. It's been going on for hours. The heavy bronze door, barricaded from inside, is nigh impervious to the sort of primitive siege methods available to Riotham. The cathedral was built as a mighty fortress, the last place of refuge for Londin's faithful in case the barbarians, heretics, pirates or whoever else threatened the city breached all of its defences – and the crypt is the last refuge within it, for the living as well as for the dead.

Nobody can get in here – and nobody can get out. We've been trapped here, among the stone coffins storing remains of the previous bishops and other church luminaries, for two days now, ever since Riotham's men managed to finally set fire to the cathedral's timber roof. It was their only way to get through the church's defences – and amounted to absolute blasphemy, proof that Fastidius was right: Riotham's ally Albanus, driven by pious zeal, thought nothing of the cathedral's sanctity, deeming it a mere den of heretics and heathens.

As the burning rafters fell on our heads, and the gate buckled from heat, Riotham brought his entire remaining army to finish us off, bearing clubs, axes and more torches. Our *ballista* silenced after launching its last bolt, our barricades breached, the outbuildings around the cathedral all set ablaze days earlier, we had no choice but to retreat further inside the great hall, pulling as many of the wounded with us as we could. When it was clear we couldn't even hold the line around the altar, the bishop ordered our remnant force to retreat behind the crypt's bronze door.

The Crown of the Iutes

"How are we for food?" I ask Eishild. We are not short of water – the crypt is built on top of a deep well, which also supplies the baptistery's pool; looking around the cave's ancient walls, much older than the hall above us, I'm guessing it was once used for some pagan mysteries before the hill was consecrated in Saint Paul's name. But most of our food stocks were kept in a storehouse at the back of the cathedral, which we were forced to abandon during that final assault.

"There's nothing left," she replies, wiping a smudge of blood mixed with dirt from her face. "I haven't eaten anything since yesterday – I shared my last bread with some poor dying boy." She hides her face in her hands. "Oh, when will this hellish banging stop!"

I struggle to remember why Riotham is so eager to break through the crypt door. We keep no treasures here. We have nowhere to go, buried alive like the corpses around us. They could hold us in until we starve; the bishop's fervent prayers, his voice rising over the din of the battering ram, is the only thing that keeps our faint hope alight – hope for what, I wonder? – but it will only take a couple more days before hunger and despair will start driving us all mad.

I look around, and in the dim light of the few remaining candles, my eyes fall on Madron's soft face. Somehow, in the chaos of battle, I forgot we were fighting for her. *She* is the treasure that Riotham wants, and he wants her alive – alive enough, at least, for his son to wed her in the eyes of Briton law. If I could think more clearly, I'm sure I could wonder about the layers of irony of our situation – it is Wortimer's blood in Madron's veins that is both the cause of our suffering, and may yet prove our salvation.

Just then, a deadly silence falls on the crypt.

"They – they stopped…" whispers Eishild.

"Maybe they're just resting. They've paused like this a few times before."

But this time it's different. We can't hear the usual rustling of men rushing around the cathedral seeking another hidden entrance to the crypt, or the striking of mattocks against the door frame. Something's changed.

All we can do is wait; we wait for hours, wary of a trap. As the last of the candles dies down, we are shrouded in darkness. I fall into deep, dreamless sleep; when I wake up, I see that even our watchmen succumbed to weariness. Had the enemy managed to find a way in at night, we'd all be dead by now. Still, there is nothing outside but silence.

All of us who can still move gather by the small altar at the far end of the crypt and join the bishop in a quiet, weary prayer. At long last, I decide we've waited enough. I send one of the altar boys to climb up the narrow stair and look out through the small spyhole in the bronze door.

"What do you see, son?" the bishop asks.

"Nothing," the boy replies.

"What do you mean, nothing? Is it still too dark?"

"No – it's already day, and there's plenty of light now that the roof is gone… But there's nobody there. The hall is empty. Only dead bodies and discarded weapons."

"It might still be a trap," says Bellicus hoarsely. Somehow, throughout all this, he still lives, though his wounds are severe, and the bishop has already given him his Last Rites.

The Crown of the Iutes

"No, wait –" the boy continues. "Somebody's coming."

"Riotham's men?"

"Can't say. There are only few. They're coming over here – slowly, carefully…" He pauses. "They're armed. The one in front is a fair-hair."

I hurry up to the door, push the boy aside and start wrestling with the heavy coffin lid that barricades it from inside.

"Octa!" the bishop protests. "Stop! What are you doing?"

"It's not Riotham," I reply. "Help me get that door open," I command the guards. "We're finally getting out of here."

I rub my eyes and blink as my sight adjusts to the brightness of the day outside. The battlefield presents to us a mystery. There are a few dead bodies in the hall and by the cathedral gate, and some weapons and shields thrown on the floor, amid the burnt debris and blackened stone; the battering ram lies discarded by the scorched crypt door. But I see nothing that would explain the sudden disappearance of the besieging force.

Wulf approaches the altar cautiously with five of his men.

"Octa. Your Grace." Wulf bows, but stays at some distance from us. "You're all well – and alive." He sounds genuinely surprised to see us.

"Not all of us," the bishop replies morosely. "We lost many good men in this battle."

"That's not what I –" Wulf looks up. "You mean, you don't know?"

"Don't know what?" I ask. "What happened here? Was it you who chased Riotham away?"

He shakes his head. "We only dispatched the remaining guards when everyone else left." He nods at the dead bodies.

"Left? Why?"

"You really don't know…" He sheathes the sword and scratches his face. "There's pox in the city."

We reel back. A murmur spreads throughout the survivors. Even Fastidius crosses himself in pious fear. *Pox*. The terrible disease hasn't struck Britannia in a generation, but everyone has heard the stories of its horrid, morbid touch, sweeping through the cities in Gaul and beyond; in the aftermath of Attila's invasion it was said to slay more people, and in more gruesome ways, than the Huns themselves. It is the worst of diseases, as it covers the body in black scabs, brings in fever, diarrhoea, bloody vomit, until within a week all that remains is a wretched, famished half-corpse, begging for swift, merciful death.

"When did it start?" the bishop asks, his lips turning pale.

"Five days ago. The first ones to die of black shits were the sailors and whores at the wharves," Wulf replies. "The nobles all packed up and ran away soon after. Everyone else started fleeing yesterday. You must be the only people left in this part of the city."

"We were cut off for two nights," I say. "Did Riotham flee, too?"

"I don't know about him, but all his soldiers are gone, or trying to leave."

"What about your men? What about the Poor Town?"

He shrugs. "We have nowhere to go. And now the city belongs to us. The pox doesn't kill everyone it touches – those who survive will be kings of these ruins."

I turn to the bishop. "If the pox is in Londin, it must be in Robriwis, too. I have to go to my family."

Fastidius nods. "Take Madron and Eishild with you," he tells me. "They'll be safer in the countryside."

"What about yourself?"

"My flock needs me. This isn't the first pestilence to strike the city, and not the last. I will open a hospice in the cathedral – what's left of it... Wulf, if any of your people need help, don't hesitate to bring them here."

"Thank you, Your Grace. But Octa will have a hard time getting out of the city. There are great crowds at the Bridge and in the harbour. All the ships are gone."

"Not all," says Fastidius. He leans to one of his acolytes and whispers something in his ear. The boy runs off back to the cathedral.

"I have a boat on the eastern quay," Fastidius says. "Fast one – used to belong to an oyster merchant I once knew... I'll give you a pass – but you'll have to get to it on your own."

"I'll send two of my men with you," says Wulf, struck by remorse for not sending his warriors to help us during the siege. "You'll need muscle to get through the mob in the harbour."

The unmissable – and unmistakable – stench of death welcomes us at Robriwis beach. The disease must've struck Cantia soon after I left for Londin. It couldn't have been ravaging the *pagus* for long, or my father would've sent me a message before the battle for the cathedral had begun – but the devastation it brought is staggering. Robriwis, always a small and struggling town, is now completely empty, its people, like those of Londin, seeking safety from the plague in the open country. With tight throat and pumping heart, I slog down the desolate path linking the beach with the fortress, my mind still dazed from the scenes in Londin harbour, where immeasurable crowds stormed the few remaining boats; more people would have drowned in the shallow waters, trampled by their fellow townsfolk, than would perish from the disease. If it weren't for Wulf's two brawlers accompanying us, I would've had to use my sword to cut a line through the throng. When we finally reached the eastern quay, the helmsman of the bishop's boat was all but ready to depart. Even with Fastidius's seal on my letter of passage, it took the point of my blade at his throat to finally convince him to let us on board.

All this chaos is now behind us. The fortress looms over the dead town in grim silence, a black cloud of crows circling above it. A few old men and women skulk about the walls, seeking solace in the ancient lore that this particular pestilence cuts a deeper swathe through young and the children than through the old: all the more reason for me to hurry to see my family.

The gate is shut and there's nobody manning the ramparts, but the fort is not empty: I can hear a distant wailing of mourners, the crackling of flames from the burning pyres, and the ringing of

The Crown of the Iutes

pickaxes digging graves in frozen dirt. The gods of the Iutes, like the God of the Britons, clearly haven't managed to protect their own from the disease.

I bang at the door with the pommel and call for the guard. There's no answer.

"What now?" asks Madron. She and Eishild are leaning on each other, both exhausted by the events of the past few days, and cold. We've barely eaten anything since leaving the cathedral; we haven't had a moment to rest. Even I'm light-headed from weariness and hunger.

"Don't worry," I say. "This is my home – I know how to get us inside."

Built over the steep riverbank, a section of the western walls of the Robriwis fortress long ago crumbled down into a tall pile of rubble; my father had since patched some of it, but what remains is still an easy enough climb – assuming one isn't close to collapsing from exhaustion.

My fingers slip on the wet, cold stone; my feet struggle to find purchase. I have to pause several times along the way. Even when I reach the summit, I'm forced to halt to rest. Black spots dance before my eyes. My stomach churns. My hands tremble.

I look down at the scene of gloomy devastation. I count at least ten fresh graves dug in the new burial ground by the eastern wall, some of them heartbreakingly small. I'm covered in sweat, despite the cold. One of those graves could be…

I leap down. Nobody pays much attention to me – in any other circumstances, an arrival of the *aetheling* would cause at least some clamour. Everyone is too busy dying, mourning or waiting for salvation behind closed doors. The only armed guards stand in front of my father's mead hall, but even they appear shocked into numbness by everything that's happening around them.

I fight the urge to immediately search for Ursula and the child, and remember why I climbed over the wall. I rush to the gate. There's only one guard left here, sitting on a stool, holding on to his spear. What happened to my father's warriors once the plague struck? They can't have all succumbed to the disease already; did my father send them out into the country to protect the refugees – or did they, also, flee the fortress as the world broke down around them? I can only hope Aelle's Saxons are in similar dire straits to us; otherwise it won't take much for them to overrun what's left of our defences.

"Didn't you hear me banging and shouting?" I cry at the guard, shaking him from his stupor.

"*Aetheling*! What are you doing here? We weren't told you were coming."

"Just help me open the gate. And then let the *Rex* know I've arrived. I assume he's in his mead hall?"

"He is – but, *aetheling*…"

His face takes on a morbid hue, and his eyes fill with sorrow at the news he's about to tell me – but though I suspect what it is, I don't want to hear it yet.

"Don't," I stop him as we pull on the gate. It grinds heavily, with ice crackling between the boards; it must've been shut for days. "Whatever it is, I'd rather hear it from my own family than from the first Iute I meet."

The Crown of the Iutes

"At least he didn't suffer long, with Lord's blessing."

Ursula stares at our son's pox-blackened body on the pyre. He looks smaller and lighter than he did when he still lived, as if the disease sucked the flesh from within. Pascent was to be buried in hallowed ground when his time came, but like all plague victims, Christian and heathen alike, he is destined for the flames.

Ursula's voice is cold, emotionless, her eyes glazed over, dull. Her skin is grey and sallow, though with no marks – somehow, the pox spared her. I feel the acute pain of loss piercing, tugging at my heart, pushing tears out of my eyes whenever I remember what happened, and Ursula's numbness surprises me; but, I remind myself, I've only just learned of little Pascent's death, while she had to endure his agony for days, herself struggling with the disease – and the grief of having just buried her own parents.

The plague struck the walled towns of the *wealas* first, and worst, like flash flood after a thunderstorm, Death cutting a dark swathe through the narrow streets, leaving no house untouched. Ursula's parents died one after another. Her aged, feeble father, succumbed fast, when nobody yet suspected a plague. Soon more people took ill in Dorowern, their skin covered with red marks; Ursula took Pascent and fled to her family's *villa* with her mother – but it was too late to save the child and the old woman.

"It was all my fault," she says.

I don't know how to react to the change in her spirit. It's as if she was replaced by a changeling when I was in Londin – the same person in body, but someone completely different inside. I have never seen anyone close to me in such deep mourning before; my father fell into a pit of melancholy after Eadgith's death, but even then he remained unmistakably himself. Every time Ursula speaks, I startle, and have to remind myself she's the same woman I fell in love with, who bore my child, and who spent the last ten years sharing the home and bed with me.

"Don't speak such foolishness," I say. "You did what you could to save him."

"He died because of me. Because of my blood in his veins. Because of the Briton curse."

"A curse?" I scoff bitterly.

"Look around you. The Britons perished in their hundreds, while the Iutes and the Saxons survived almost unscathed. It's because we are fading away. We bear few children, we die easily. Our time is gone. And Pascent suffered for it."

I remember this Ursula – though I haven't heard her in many years. Before Pascent's birth, before our marriage, she would often talk of her fear of her people disappearing, like the builders of the stone circles, replaced by the fair-hairs and other barbarian invaders. I know she's not the only one to believe so, though in the joy of rearing our firstborn, that particular worry seemed to have perished for good; my heart breaks at seeing it return.

I wrap my arm around her – but she remains cold to my touch.

"*You* survived. And many Iutes died, too."

"Only those who lived too close to us, in the walled towns. The curse got them, too. The others were protected by their gods."

"So was Pascent," I remind her. "The runestone…"

The Crown of the Iutes

"I took the runestone from him when the plague struck – and had him baptised at Dorowern. I thought my God would be stronger than the heathen ones. I was wrong."

"Grief speaks through you," I tell her, shocked by the confession. Neither of us ever treated the trinket seriously – we often jested about it; but she seems serious now. If even Ursula's faith wavered from sorrow, what hope is there for anyone else? "We will have another child. More children. My blood is strong enough for the two of us," I try to laugh.

She shakes her head and pulls away. "No," she says firmly. "I could not bear going through all of this again."

The way she says this, the way she flinches from my touch – I'm not certain if she means merely the risk of another child's death, or what needs to be done for such child to come into the world. Though she's grown fond of my warmth, and we learned to satisfy each other at night so that I wouldn't need to seek the solace of other women, we have only lain together a few times over the years – and even fewer after Pascent's birth. She took little pleasure from these trysts. Indeed, no man, not even I, has ever been able to bring her as much pleasure as the *drui* woman, Donwen. I knew she agreed to bear Pascent out of love for me, and out of respect for my duties as the *aetheling* – part of which was providing my father's dynasty with a future heir. But if she refused to do it again, how could I ever persuade her differently?

"You are deep in mourning," I say. "As am I. Today, we bid farewell to our child. It's no time to talk of the future. Come," I add, helping her up, "let us start the fire."

In the end, like everything else in life, the plague also passes.

[134]

As the refugees return from the woods and hills with the spring thaws, as everyone counts the dead and the living, we learn that the outbreak, outside the walled towns, was not as devastating as everyone at first feared. By Easter, we get the first good news back from Londin. Fastidius survived, as did most of his acolytes. The plague ravaged the city, especially the Poor Town, taking at least one in five of its inhabitants – but the bishop was full of hope the capital would convalesce in time. Most importantly to us, Riotham and his machinations no longer seemed as much of a problem as they did before the plague struck; busy with the recovery, the Council had no time or patience to deal with his ambitions, or his conflict with the bishop, who was now a hero of the city for the role his cathedral played in saving many of those touched by the disease from terrible agony. Even *Comes* Albanus's star shone darker now, as his namesake's sacred bones failed to stop the plague from cutting as bloody a streak through Werlam as it did in Londin.

As the winter storms abate, ships start to cautiously arrive from Gaul, bearing news from the continent. The plague disappeared from there as well, as swiftly and unexpectedly as it came; a few towns, harbours like Epatiac, suffered greatly. Others the disease bypassed altogether. What happened beyond the frontier, in the kingdom of the Goths, or in southern Gaul, we could only guess; but for now, it seemed, as everyone was reeling from the aftermath of the pestilence, there was to be peace on all borders again.

"It's time to send the girls back to Fastidius," my father says one calm day, after receiving another letter from Londin.

"Are you sure they'll be safe there?"

"Riotham and Albanus had their chance. Neither is going to try anything anytime soon. Meanwhile, Ambrosius is growing impatient," he says, tapping the letter, marked with the Imperial Eagle seal. "He's reminding me of our contract, and I have no more reason to keep Madron here now that her safety is assured." He looks up at me, and his gaze softens. "How are things at home?"

"Ursula buries herself in her new duties – she took over as a Councillor in Dorowern after her mother… But I can see how she suffers."

"And you?"

"I have wept enough."

He nods. "Have you given any thought to the future yet?"

"The future?"

"The kingdom needs an heir, Octa."

I scowl. "Father – we are still in mourning."

"I understand that, son. But I am not a young man. I must be sure that –"

"Maybe you should've given me a brother, then, instead of wallowing in your *own* grief for decades."

I immediately regret my outburst, seeing the change in my father's face. I'd prefer him to be angry with me; instead he falls back into that black melancholy that still sometimes takes him over, though I'm the only one who ever sees him like this.

He's only ever loved two women – Rhedwyn and Eadgith; both died in short succession some fifteen years ago, when he was still a hearty, fairly young man. He could've taken another woman and spawned a number of potential heirs if he so wished, easing my burden of continuing the dynasty.

"I had the best heir I could've ever wished for," he says with a sulk.

"But you took a risk by having *only* me," I say. "I might die any day. In battle, of plague, in an accident. What will happen to your precious dynasty then?"

He smiles weakly. "Then, I will give the kingdom to Haesta and his sons," he says, and I can't tell if he's jesting.

Before even Eishild and Madron can begin to pack for the journey back home, word comes of a grand procession coming Robriwis' way from Londin.

They arrive in three silver-plated carriages and twenty horses, with a long train of slaves, servants and carts carrying tents and provisions, in tow. The first carriage bears the Imperial Eagle mark of Ambrosius. The second one is from the cathedral, with the crook and crossed swords of Saint Paul's. And the third one carries a crest that I don't recognise: a sword and galloping horse.

"That's Mandubrac, son of Peredur. From Coln," my father explains as we watch the carriages roll into the fortress.

"What's the *Comes* of the Trinowaunts doing here?"

"I have no idea. I haven't seen him in years. Whatever's going on, this is bigger than just Londin."

"And you haven't had any messages about this?"

[137]

The Crown of the Iutes

"No – but Fastid is here, and he wouldn't ride out of the city with no good reason."

As the riders of the escort follow the carriages, I spot the familiar red cloaks and golden helmets of the Dumnonian *equites*. Eishild spots them too; she squeals in glee and runs to the first of the riders.

Drustan leaps from his horse and welcomes Eishild with a warm embrace. The other riders dismount as well and approach to greet us. I recognise most of them, though many years have passed since we fought together, in Wened first, then in Armorica against the Goths.

"I don't understand," I say. "Why are you here? Why did you come from Londin?"

"I'm not quite sure myself," Drustan replies. "We did not expect to arrive here in such great company. We came to Londin with news – and to take Eishild back to Gaul." He nods at the Gothic princess.

"Me? Back to Gaul? Why now?"

"All will be explained," says Fastidius as he emerges from the carriage. He puts his hand on my shoulder. "I'm so sorry for your loss, Octa." He looks around. "Where's Councillor Ursula?"

"In Dorowern, helping with the city's recovery."

He shakes his head. "We'll need to summon her here as well." He calls one of the riders from his escort. "You will go to Dorowern."

"I need a fresh horse, if I'm to reach it swiftly, Your Grace."

"I'm sure King Aeric can spare one of his ponies. Right, *aetheling*?"

"Ri-right," I stutter, momentarily distracted by the sight of Councillor Riotham himself disembarking from the third carriage, in the grey, drab sackcloth robe of a penitent.

"Before we talk of the urgent matter that brought us all here," Riotham begins, once we all sit down at the horseshoe-table at my father's mead hall, "I want to beg your forgiveness, *aetheling* Octa."

"My… forgiveness?"

"I brought needless suffering to you and to *Domna* Madron," he says. "I struck at the House of God, I struck at the servants of God – and for that, I brought punishment not only on myself, but on all of Londin – indeed, on all of Britannia."

"What brought this change, Councillor?" my father asks. I can sense amused suspicion in his voice.

"Isn't it obvious?" Riotham says. "The pox struck Cantiaca on the day I launched my assault on the cathedral. It reached Londin on the day I was about to breach the crypt door." He shakes his head. "If this is not a clear sign from the Lord, I don't know what is."

I look to Fastidius. The bishop nods. "I would urge you to accept the Councillor's remorse, Octa," he says. "I can vouch for its seriousness. He has confessed his sins to me and started on the long road to penance."

His voice leaves no place for doubt: whether he himself believes Riotham's conscience was truly shaken by the plague, is neither here nor there, but for matters at the table to progress any further, I must express my generosity.

The Crown of the Iutes

I stand up and bow. "Lord Councillor, I'm sure you believed what you were doing was the right thing to do at the time. We all make mistakes. I forgive you and accept your repentance."

We embrace briefly to the cheers of everyone gathered and return to our seats.

"This is only the beginning of my penance," Riotham says. "I have come here with a certain... proposition for you, *Rex* Aeric, that I hope will benefit us both."

"It is rare indeed that I hear any propositions coming from the Londin Council," my father replies. "And even rarer still that I deem them worth my attention."

"This is why I'm here, Ash," Bishop Fastidius says, using my father's old slave name to remind him of the youth they both spent in a Briton patrician's *villa*. "To make sure you at least listen this time."

My father winces, but nods.

"*Decurion* Drustan, I trust you the most of everyone gathered here, on account of your friendship with my son," he says. "Why don't you tell us what brought you back to Britannia?"

Drustan glances to his sides, where far more prominent men than himself sit, takes a sip of *mel*, and begins his brief tale.

The plague came to the kingdom of Goths before it reached Britannia's shores, and ravaged the land between Tolosa and Burdigala, though not as badly as further north. It was enough, however, to cause some disquiet and unease – especially when the Roman bishops in the cities recently occupied by the Gothic army started blaming what they perceived as heretics for the disease.

"You are aware of the religious issues tearing the Kingdom of Tolosa apart, *Rex*?" Drustan pauses to ask.

"My son explained some of it to me," my father replies with a bored nod. "Though they worship the same God, the Goth lords and their Roman subjects go about it somewhat differently – enough that it causes some strife between them. It's one of the reasons Princess Eishild dwells with Fastidius instead of with her own kin, I understand. That is as much as I care to know about it."

Drustan chuckles. "Yes, Octa also never bothered himself with the intricacies of the Gothic faith. Suffice it to say, there is quite a significant amount of unrest brewing in Tolosa – and both my master Marcus, *Comes* of Armorica and Paulus, who commands Gaul's armies in the name of Aegidius's young son, agree that this might be the best opportunity we've had in years to weaken the Goth hold on their land."

"You want me to return to my people," says Eishild excitedly. "Just like we've always planned. Lord's wounds, I didn't think this day would come!"

"What is this about?" my father asks.

"Since we brought the princess to Londin," Fastidius leans to explain, "we have always hoped that one day we would take her back to sit on the Tolosan throne, where she rightfully belongs."

"And bring the Goths into the fold of your Roman Church, no doubt," my father adds. "But what does any of that have to do with me and my Iutes? I have no quarrel with the Goths."

"But you *are* a trusted ally of *Rex* Hildrik of the Salian Franks, and of the *Magister* of Gaul, are you not?" asks Riotham. "Lord knows you boasted about it often enough."

The Crown of the Iutes

"I had to *remind you* about it often enough, when the Council bothered me and my people," my father replies. "What of it?"

"They're hoping to use the chaos in the Gothic kingdom to march against Aiwarik – and his allies, the Saxons of Liger," says Fastidius.

This, at last, catches my father's attention. And mine. A chance to defeat the Saxon pirates on land, for good – rather than merely respond to their raids, hoping that eventually they may run out of men and ships and leave us alone... The longer the Saxons of Liger menace our shores, the greater the risk grows of them allying with Aelle and the Saxons of Britannia, and together overwhelming our defences.

"It is a tempting prospect," I say. "And I'm sure *Rex* Hildrik will request our aid if he decides he needs it – and when he does, we will respond accordingly."

"*Comes* Paulus, who commands Gaul's armies, *did* request our aid," says Riotham. "And I have decided to sail to Gaul myself, leading my men and those of any allies I can gather, including *Comes* Mandubrac here."

The leader of the Trinowaunts bows. His is the last *pagus* of Wortigern's old domain that still acknowledges the nominal control of the Londin Council – though they were always too small and weak to be of much use to anyone. I wonder what "men" he can offer for the expedition – the Trinowaunt coasts have of old been defended by clans of Saxons who, like Audulf's family, have dwelled there long enough to think of themselves more as Britons than foreign barbarians. Unlike Aelle's people, these east Saxons have always been friends of the *wealas*, but are they friends enough to march to a distant land in their name?

"So, you are gathering an army to cross the Narrow Sea," my father muses. "Do you think yourself another Constantine? There are no Legions left for you to take."

"No – but with the help of Trinowaunts, Cadwallons and Cants, I may be able to gather some two thousand men. Half a Legion should be enough to destroy the pirates for good."

"The Cants?"

Ursula raises her eyes from the plate of cold meats before her, as if the name of her tribe is the first thing she's heard all evening.

"Should the Dorowern Council permit," says Riotham.

Ursula glances to me, then to my father. "You know very well we have no soldiers. There are barely even any *vigiles* left in Dorowern."

"We don't need warriors. We would recruit volunteers from among the townsfolk and serfs, if you allow us. They would get training in Londin and weapons in Gaul – and the Lord would provide victory," says Riotham, to Fastidius's barely noticeable wince.

"An ambitious man could do a lot in Britannia with half a Legion," my father remarks. "Wortimer started a war with less. And you're nothing if not ambitious, Councillor. Are you certain fighting Saxons is all you need these men for?"

"I understand your doubts," Riotham replies. "But I assure you, all I think about is penance for my sins. I want nothing more than to destroy the heathen pirates who so threatened the churches throughout our land – and I would hope you will join us in this mission."

The Crown of the Iutes

"I am prepared to spare some of the Church's treasure to fund this expedition," notes Fastidius, surprising almost everyone at the table. We were certain his support for Riotham would only be symbolic, considering how much money would be needed to rebuild the cathedral. "It is a noble enough goal."

"Two thousand men…" My father scratches his chin. "Whether you win or fail, this might well be the last time such a force of *wealas* warriors is seen in Britannia. Even if I don't add my men to this army, I admit I would very much like to witness it march before I pass from this world…" He reaches for the cup of ale and takes a long, thoughtful sip. "I will need to consider your proposition with much care and attention. *Decurion* Drustan, you must have fought those Liger Saxons before – they're just on Armorica's southern border – what can you tell us about them?"

CHAPTER VIII
THE LAY OF CATUARION

Late at night, when all the noble and less noble guests retire to the tents raised on the muddy plain of the Medu, the *Rex*, the bishop, Ursula and myself meet in my father's house, a two-chamber wooden building attached to the rear wall of the mead hall. It's tiny compared to Hildrik's palace in Tornac or the *villas* of the Cantian nobles, and its sparseness reflects my father's solemn and stark spirit. The hearth room is barely furnished, except the scroll cupboard lining the wall and a chest of valuables in the corner, next to the desk. In the room next door, a blazing furnace is heating water for the king's bath later. It's small, cramped and hot here with all four of us; there aren't even enough chairs and Ursula and I have to sit on the sheepskin on the floor – but it makes this meeting of old friends feel appropriately intimate.

"Does he really believe all that talk of sins and repentance?" my father asks.

The bishop shrugs. "Some of it, yes. Certainly not as much as he shows. But it doesn't matter what *he* believes. He failed in all his plans, and he needs to prove himself in some way if he wants anyone at the Council to take him seriously again. And there are many in Londin who *do* believe his ungodly behaviour brought the Lord's punishment down onto the city. I made certain of that myself," he adds with a wry smile. "Besides, with Ambrosius finding out what his representative busied himself with over the winter, Riotham will want to be away until things calm down."

The Crown of the Iutes

"But why go fight the Saxons in distant Gaul?" I ask. "Why not move against some easier target, like the Picts or the Brigands? No *Dux* has done anything like this since before Wortigern."

"You've just answered your own question." Fastidius smiles. "A victory on the continent would make him equal to the great *duces* of old. Some of it is your own doing, Octa. Yours and your father's. The Council in Londin has been watching you with growing concern and envy. They want what Cantia has under your rule: peaceful borders and links with the continent. They want to share in your friendship with the Franks and the Gauls, and in your trade. Albanus can't offer that, locked in his province with no access to the sea, and Mandubrac is too poor and weak. If Riotham can deliver on his promise, all his past transgressions will be forgiven – and the diadem will be his."

I glance to my father, then to the chest in the corner. Of course, the bishop doesn't mean the actual diadem of Wortigern, only the symbol of power. I don't know if my father ever told him what I brought from the West ten years ago.

"And you support him in this – why?" my father asks.

"To show the generosity and forgiveness of the Church, of course," the bishop replies with a soft laugh. "May I remind you, he *did* almost destroy my cathedral – something even you failed at, if I remember correctly. If, Lord willing, he returns from Gaul triumphant, I will need to be on his good side. As will you."

"Then you'd advise me to send my warriors with him?"

"Don't you want to destroy those raiders? You'd have better chance with Riotham than on your own."

"Assuming the *wealas* don't betray us in some way again."

"You won't be in Britannia anymore. Your son and his men are more at home in the lands across the Narrow Sea than anyone in Riotham's army, the Councillor included. They'd be surrounded by friends there – Marcus, Hildrik, Paulus… I doubt Riotham would dare to try anything in these circumstances."

"What makes you think I'd send Octa?"

"It's obvious I would have to go, Father," I say. "Nobody knows Gaul as well as I do. And I will need to take my bear-shirts with me."

"You have just lost a son," my father replies. He reaches out to put his hand on Ursula's shoulder. "You have to take care of your family – and your family duties."

Ursula and I glance at each other. We both know what he means; and we both know it's the last thing on either of our minds right now.

"Somebody will have to command the Cantian contingent," says Ursula quietly. She's gazing at her toes with the same blank stare she had when watching our son's body burn.

"You are the mother to my future grandson," my father says. "You should not –"

"I am a Dorowern Councillor now, *Rex*," she replies, her voice ice-cold. "Not one of your shieldmaidens. I will decide what is best for me and my people."

"Father," I interject hastily. I've never seen Ursula so incensed with her father-in-law before, and I fear another wrong word might cause a rift that will be too wide to ever span again. "Perhaps it will do us both good to leave Britannia for a while. You know yourself how bad memories can linger and burn in your soul. Remember how you felt about Londin after Rhedwyn?"

A shadow mars my father's face. He wipes his red eyes with a weary gesture and blinks. It's getting late, and we all drank a lot of ale tonight.

"Is this really what you want, Ursula?" he asks. "To go fighting the barbarians in Gaul, like in the old days? Feel young again?"

She shrugs. "It's not about feeling young. I can't stay here, where every corner reminds me of Pascent. I hear his laughter in the streets of Dorowern and Robriwis; I see his bright eyes in the flowers on the Downs." She hides her head in her knees for a moment, then looks up again. "And there will be many in Cantia who feel the same. I spoke to families in Dorowern. Fathers who lost their sons… Husbands who lost their wives… Riotham will have no trouble filling his cohorts here."

"If I am to agree to this – if I am to spare my warriors, I will need more than just assurances of Riotham's good will, Fastid," my father says, turning back to the bishop. "I will have my own trouble to deal with this year."

"You mean Aelle," I guess. "The plague may have slowed him down, but I doubt it will stop him, especially if he learns we have sent our best warriors abroad."

The bishop rubs his chin. "I'm not sure if Riotham can handle a war with Aelle *and* the pirates in the same season…"

"A war will not be necessary," my father says. "Aelle is no fool, and I don't hope we can subdue him for good, even with two thousand men. But we can ensure at least he's no threat while Riotham's army is away."

"How would we do that?" I ask.

Father waves his hand. "There's no point discussing it now, when Riotham can only command a handful of his own soldiers. When he comes back with this half-Legion of his, we will talk again."

He stands up – and so do we all. Even the bishop raises himself slowly and heavily from the bronze chair.

"You, Octa, can do as you please, as always," my father says with a sigh. "And I have no power over the Cantian militia. It will take a long time to prepare an expedition of this size," he adds. "Plenty of time for any of you to change your minds."

"What if Hildrik requests our assistance directly?" I ask.

"I will have Betula prepare the usual centuria of younglings."

"A hundred youths may not be enough this time." Over the years, this has been our standard response to the Frankish requests for assistance with whatever border skirmishes they were troubled with. It was a mutually beneficial agreement, as our youths – those who survived – gained valuable experience they wouldn't get otherwise in peaceful Cantia. "Not for a war with Goths, not when the Britons send twenty times as many. Rome might start thinking Riotham's a more reliable ally than us."

"I don't need to prove my worth as an ally to anyone." My father glowers. "And a hundred Iute warriors, even young ones, is worth a thousand *wealh* roughs whose only experience is chasing thieves and dousing fires." He stifles a yawn and waves at me and Ursula impatiently. "Leave us now, children. I want to talk to Fastid. We meet so rarely these days."

The Crown of the Iutes

"You know you are always welcome in my cathedral, brother," the bishop says with a polite smile. He reaches for the flask of mead on my father's table and pours himself a full cup.

My father scowls. "As you are here in my mead hall, brother."

"Come, Octa," Ursula says, pulling me outside. "Let's leave these old men to their bitterness."

To the surprise of everyone, himself included, just in time for the start of summer campaigning, Riotham manages to gather – and provide with rudimentary training – an astonishing four full cohorts.

The first of the cohorts Riotham formed mostly of his own men – four *centuriae* of the *bucellarii* remaining from the battle of the cathedral, and two more formed from an assortment of servants, freed slaves and camp followers, lightly armed and with no armour or helmets. The second cohort is made up of *vigiles*, bodyguards and other volunteers from Londin and surrounding *villas*, the owners of which have been reimbursed by the bishop for the lost labour – and a *centuria* of Cadwallon militiamen, whom *Comes* Albanus managed to spare from defending his contentious northern borders.

The assembly of the third and the fourth cohorts proved the truth of Ursula's words. The ranks of the tribal militias of the Cants and Trinowaunts – what little of them was left after years of depending on the heathen swords for defence – swelled when news of Riotham's expedition reached the towns and farmsteads of the Britons.

"It wasn't just the plague that brought them," Ursula told me. "It was pride, too. Some of these men have watched the Iutes and

Saxons fight in their name for a generation, while they did nothing but tend to their fields and concern themselves with petty disputes and trade. And while most simply revelled in the peace it brought them, others felt they could no longer rely only on the barbarian might. They know it might be the last chance to prove the worth of Briton swords."

Riotham made good on his promise to prepare his own men, and those of the Londin cohort, but few of the new tribal militiamen have ever held a real weapon. Even Madron is a better warrior than most of them, after what little I managed to teach her. Still, when I arrive in Londin to oversee the last few weeks of training of the Cantian contingent, I see that what the Cants and the Trinowaunts lack in combat ability, they make up for in ambition and perseverance.

"This will not help them against my uncle's army," notes Eishild, observing our training.

"No," I agree. "But it might be enough against the Saxons. Pirates don't fight as well on land as on water."

"Your bear-shirts are coming, too?" she asks.

"Of course. Fighting pirates is our job, whether here or in Gaul."

I have little time to turn the Cants into warriors, though I try my best. The summer campaign season grows ever near, and by Whitsun we must march out of Londin – south, across the Regin border, towards New Port, where a fleet of transport galleys, provided partly by the Church and partly by *Comes* Paulus, awaits our arrival. Aelle has enough sense to not try to stop our two-thousand-strong force from entering his domain. We know he has enough warriors in his *fyrd* to destroy us, if he so wished – but it would be a bloody war, one that would leave his kingdom

The Crown of the Iutes

vulnerable to other enemies. And he has no reason to fight us – as far as he's aware, we're merely passing through…

Aelle looks around the walls of the seaside *domus* with a scowl. Catuarion, who lent his *villa* to Riotham for the duration of our visit to the harbour town, is one of the few wealthy Regin nobles still remaining in Britannia – son of the last *Comes* and New Port's *Praetor*. Most of the remaining *villas* around the coast have been taken over by Aelle's courtiers and clan chieftains who, not sharing the Briton taste for stone walls and cultivated gardens, proceeded to dismantle them and build their wooden halls and barns on the ruined foundations.

The Saxon *Rex* arrived in a bronze-plated carriage, with a grand retinue of warriors and all the trappings of a powerful ruler, but none of this theatre can hide the fact that for him to be summoned to this place like a common supplicant *Comes* is a grave insult to his prestige. Aelle has had no need to heed anyone's demands since taking over the Saxon *witan* after his father's death. But now that he's allowed four cohorts of strangers to be stationed in and around the main city of his domain – with his family trapped inside – he has little choice but to answer Riotham's summons.

"What do you want, *wealh*?" he grunts at the Councillor. He notices me and Ursula at Riotham's right side and gives us a slightly friendlier nod, then glowers at Catuarion, sitting at Riotham's left. The magistrate retreats into his chair in fright, knowing he will be punished for his part in this once we're gone.

"Respect as befits the representative of the Great Council of Londin, heathen," Riotham replies with equal terseness. "And guarantees of peace while we're fighting in Gaul."

Aelle's eyes narrow. "You have no power here, Councillor," he replies. "Your own laws say so." He points to Catuarion, who sulks even further. "The Regins accepted me as their ruler. They care not for Londin's orders."

"They didn't seem to care much for you, either," I note.

Our arrival into New Port was an odd spectacle. The Briton townsfolk lined the Roman highway with flowers and triumphant cries, greeting us as if we had come to liberate them from under the heathen yoke. Riotham, though clearly glad with the welcome, was forced to painstakingly assure the Saxon king that our intentions were peaceful. It changed little in how the Regins treated us during our stay. Even as Aelle arrived at the seaside *villa*, he did so to the accompaniment of the noises of the great feast thrown to celebrate our troops.

I see how all these *wealas* rejoicing has unnerved Aelle. As far as I know, the Regins never gave him much trouble before. Beaten into submission by the mutinies of Saxon mercenaries in the dark years before Aelle's father forged his kingdom, all they could do was watch with dismay as their farms shrivelled, their cities shrank and their *villas* grew poorer – or move. With every visit, I saw more homes abandoned, inns closed, wharves emptied of goods and their roofless walls left to the elements. The harbour's timber piers have been dismantled, to build palisades for the feuding Saxon clan chiefs or new halls for Aelle and his warriors. Bronze and lead from the wharves and the breakwaters was robbed and melted into weapons and ornaments. Without protection from the tides, the harbour began to silt up; there was barely enough space remaining for the small fleet that was to take us to Gaul. The road to Londin had grown over with weeds, the bridges crumbled into the rivers. *Rex* Aelle – ever a warchief, never much of a magistrate – had little concern for maintaining the port and its trade links with the continent, and the Regin merchants, though at first glad of lower taxes and duties, at length grew disillusioned with the neglect which followed and shifted their business to Londin and Cantia's harbours. The nobles either sailed to Armorica, or walled themselves inside their *villas*, there to live their lives to the end, surrounded by memories of past glories and what little luxuries they hoarded. The serfs in the countryside simply shrugged off the change of masters, knowing the Saxons wouldn't heed their grumbles any more than the Briton lords did.

But now it seemed that the townsfolk of New Port – and there was only New Port left, other towns of the *pagus*, like Regentium and Mutuanton, having long ago turned into half-deserted clumps of ruin – knew how to keep a silent grudge. Half a generation may have passed since the Saxons took over running the *pagus* from the tribal council, but there still remained a dangerous memory – a memory of once belonging to something greater than just the small, forgotten harbour town: of being a Briton, a proud citizen of a mighty island and, before that, of an Empire whose trade routes spanned the entire known world. Riotham, with his demeanour of an Imperial aristocrat, with the half-Legion of Briton warriors at his command, and with a fleet of Roman galleys waiting for him in the harbour, represented this memory here just as much as he represented the vision of Rome to Londin's city folk and its Councillors. His arrival brought something the Regins hadn't felt in a generation: hope for the future.

Civil unrest in the town that provides him with the only link to the riches of Gaul and the world beyond is the last thing Aelle needs right now. Riotham must know it as well as I do; but he also must know to strike a careful balance. Push Aelle too far, and he will snap. There's only so much humiliation the Saxon king can accept in exchange for seeing us all promptly leave on the broad-decked galleys that crowd his harbour.

"I don't need a heathen lecturing me on the laws of my people," Riotham scoffs. "But you're right, it is not for me to tell the Regins what they should or shouldn't do in their own land. And it's not what we're here for."

At Riotham's nod, I slide a scroll across the table. Aelle unravels it with a frown, and scowls again. It's written in Imperial Latin – another deliberate slight, as Aelle didn't have my and the Councillor's education.

"And what's this supposed to be?" he snarls.

"A peace treaty," I say. "The Saxons never officially signed one after Eobbasfleot. It's time to put an end to hostilities between you and Londin."

"You want us to be the lapdogs of the *wealas*, like the Iutes?"

I swallow the affront with an innocent expression. "Read it yourself," I say. "It's only an acknowledgment of the existing situation. I'm sure your *Regin* subjects would rejoice at you agreeing to the treaty and settling matters between you and Londin after all those years."

Aelle grunts and proceeds to decipher the Imperial letters, with his tongue sticking out in the corner of his mouth.

He moves the scroll to Catuarion. "What's this about Anderitum and Port Adurn?" he asks, pointing at the few words he clearly understands.

"It's about the new garrisons for the forts…" the magistrate starts.

"The Saxon Shore forts are too crucial for the defence of all of Britannia to be left only in your care," Riotham interrupts him. "You've let the pirates sail past your shores too many times – clearly you can't handle them on your own."

The Crown of the Iutes

"We want the forts manned by a mixed crew of Iutes, Britons and Saxons," adds Ursula. "It's only fair, since we all depend on them for our safety."

"Absurd demand," Aelle replies and throws the scroll back. "You might as well ask for my *Rex*'s circlet."

"Come now, Aelle," I say. "You knew we'd have to ask *something* of you. What use are these empty stone walls for you, anyway? I know for a fact you don't even keep a garrison in Anderitum anymore – and you've always had trouble holding on to Adurn."

"It was my father's home for many years," replies Aelle. "My son was born there. As was an entire generation of Saxon warriors."

"But the Saxon warriors didn't build these walls," says Riotham. "Rome did. By law – the same law you just invoked – they still belong to us. You're only renting them from us in exchange for your swords, just like the Iutes… But at least the Iutes still perform their duties."

"All of that is ancient history," Aelle replies. "I will not just hand over my forts to a bunch of *wealas* and their Iute dogs."

"Then we'll have no choice but to stay here," says Riotham. "I can't risk leaving Londin without a peace treaty with its strongest neighbour." He glances to Catuarion. The magistrate swallows. I feel almost sorry for him. We would be, of course, staying in his *villa* until Aelle changes his mind, dining at his expense – and Councillor Riotham is used to a quality of life far beyond the means of even the wealthiest of Regin nobles…

The Saxon king bites his lower lip. Breathing heavily, he stares at me, not at Riotham, with a mixture of hate and scorn.

"You can't force me to do your bidding," he says, "I am a *Rex* of the Saxons."

But I can hear the resolve in his voice weaken. In his mind, he's calculating which course of action to take. I know he doesn't care about the forts as much as he's making it seem. He doesn't need them to wage war on the Iutes or the Briton tribes to his west – and he's not as bothered by the pirates as we are. The navy harbours that they once guarded have long silted up. The great curtain walls of Anderitum require more men to guard them than he can spare, and for little gain. A Iute and Briton garrison within his kingdom would be a threat to his rule, yes – but they could be easily rendered harmless by simply containing them inside the ramparts…

It is time for the last strike. I nod at Riotham – and he claps his hands. A slave brings in a small chest and puts it on the table before Aelle. The Saxon opens it carefully, as if expecting a snake to leap out.

His eyes open wide and gleam with the reflection of what's inside. The chest is filled with treasure – coins and jewels on top, but underneath, gold dust and bits of silver hacked from tableware. Aelle runs his hand through the chest and lets the dust run between his fingers like sand.

A warlord on the continent, like Hildrik or Aiwarik, would have laughed off such a meagre offering. It's only a fraction of Riotham's own treasure, topped off with a few precious pieces given by other nobles at Fastidius's urging. But I can see in Aelle's eyes it must be the most gold he's seen in a long time. He's bled his own kingdom dry – and this small chest must seem to him like a pitcher of water in the desert.

"And this… treaty," he asks with suddenly parched lips, "is that all you want from me?"

The Crown of the Iutes

"This, and to swear an *ath* that you will not break this peace," I say. "We would, of course, do the same."

"*We?*" Aelle scoffs. "I thought this was only peace with the *wealas*. What do they care about what goes on between us, fair-hairs?"

"*I* speak for Cantia," says Ursula. "The Iutes are our shield and spear. You attack them, you attack all of us."

Aelle smirks. "So, it's come to this – the mighty Iute warriors are hiding behind *wealh* skirts... This almost makes it all worth it." He picks up the scroll again. "I will have my elders go through this," he says, by which I'm sure he means he'll have some Regin magistrate – one more trustworthy than Catuarion – translate the difficult legal language of the treaty into Saxon. "I'll come back with my response tomorrow."

He reaches for the chest, but Riotham lays his hand on the lid, and smiles.

"And we will give these to you – tomorrow."

Ours is the last galley to set sail from New Port harbour. It carries the final detachment of the Iute contingent: my thirty bear-shirts, our ponies, and bundles of weapons and armour wrought by Iutish blacksmiths especially for the campaign.

Even when we learned that Riotham assembled the promised four cohorts, it wasn't easy to convince my father of sending more than the hundred younglings into Gaul. We may have been marching to defeat the pirates in their home ports, but that didn't mean there were no more threats to Cantia: the Picts and the Brigants would still raid from the North, and Frisians and Franks might still strike from across the Narrow Sea to our east, if Hildrik failed to subdue them this year. And there was still the matter of trusting Aelle at his word, even if sealed with an *ath* of blood before the Saxon gods.

"He doesn't believe the wrath of Wodan any more than I do," my father told me. "Having our men hold the shore forts is good precaution, but it's not enough – and certainly will not stop Aelle from sending his 'forest bandits' against our farms, claiming he doesn't control the Free Folk of Andreda."

In the end, I was only able to add another hundred of Seawine's spearmen to the *centuria* of youths. A meagre effort considering what we were up against in Gaul – and how little we could trust the Briton cohorts to bear the brunt of fighting if the Goths sent their warriors to aid their Saxon allies.

Over the years of defending Cantia's coast, I've discovered that the best way to swiftly deal with numerous threats was to divide my thirty finest bear-shirts into five "blades" – detachments of six riders, with a number of spearmen attached to them, each commanded by one of my old comrades-in-arms. Four of these are assigned to dedicated stretches of the long shoreline, from Rutubi to Leman. Audulf's is the strongest, made up of men he often took to Frankia and Gaul to fight alongside Hildrik; Ubba, Eolh and Deora command the other three. The fifth "blade" rides the lightest and swiftest ponies, and in Cantia their usual task is to take messages between the other commanders – but in Gaul, once we march into battle, I want them to be our forward patrol. The six young shieldmaidens that ride in this detachment follow Croha, the dark-eyed beauty from Meon, armed with twin throwing axes – the rare skill she learned from Betula.

It may be early summer, but the Narrow Sea is restless as always. The ship heaves and rolls in the waves. A few miles ahead I see two bobbing dots of the vessels sent before us. I doubt this stretch of the Narrow Sea, between New Port and Rotomag, has seen this

The Crown of the Iutes

much traffic since Constantine departed with his Legions sixty years ago.

I look to Ursula, standing next to me at the railing, tears roll down her face. The salty wind squeezes moisture out of my eyes as well, but I've known my wife long enough to tell her tears are not caused by the weather.

I wrap my arm around her, and say nothing. Over the years I've learned it's best to let her decide whether she wants to share her feelings with me or not.

"I've dreamt of seeing this coast again for so long," she says at last. "It was supposed to be a joyous occasion. One full of freedom and hope. We were going to show it to our son."

"There's always hope," I say. "We're alive. And for now, we are free. As much as one can be in a war."

"What do you think is waiting for us in Gaul?"

"Drustan and his *equites*, for a start," I say. "They're supposed to join us in Rotomag, and march with us to Aurelianum, to the border with the Goths."

"I fear there will be more politics there than fighting," she says. "Things are never straightforward in Gaul, and there are too many factions vying for power. The Franks, the Armoricans, the Goths, the Saxons – and above all this, Romans, as confused as they ever were… I've read letters my mother received from her friends in Armorica. There is no order or peace anywhere on the continent, except in Aegidius's old domain – what's left of it."

"This is nothing new. All we've been doing is keeping the floods of chaos away for a few more years. A generation at best. There was a time when this island could send entire Legions to help Gaul's defences, not four cohorts of barely trained men."

"Is this supposed to make me feel better?" Ursula scoffs.

"But it's not all bad," I say. "When my father was young, he feared the shrinking of the world. Wenta of the Ikens or Callew were the limits of his knowledge, travel to another *pagus* was an expedition. Now going to war in Gaul sounds as easy as crossing from one side of Cantia to another. Not all is lost yet. Britannia and the Britons still have a role to play on the world's stage. And – we've finally made peace with Aelle."

She shakes her head and wipes her tears away. "I do not share your hope. Your father was right – the world *is* shrinking. At least for the Britons. The Councillors of Dorowern can barely see beyond the Medu. The nobles spend all their energy fighting for the right to rule over Londin – but what is Londin now but a pile of ruins inhabited by wraiths? This campaign is the last gasp of my people. And it's a foolish waste. Imagine what we could achieve if we put all these men to some peaceful work, rather than send them to die in Gaul. How much we could rebuild."

"There would be no glory for Riotham in civil work," I say. "He wants to be seen as a great warrior, not a skilled magistrate. And it's easier to destroy than to rebuild. But who knows, maybe once we've dealt with the pirates and return home with plunder…"

"I wonder how many of us will return," she muses. She brushes her hair back – she cut it short before our departure, though not as short as she used to wear it when she was a shieldmaiden, fighting in Gaul at my side. Being made a Councillor in Dorowern transformed her into a Briton noblewoman – though she still prefers to wear breeches and short tunics wherever possible, and certainly didn't forget how to carry a sword and a shield.

The Crown of the Iutes

"We'll find out soon enough," I say. I look to the sky – a dark cloud looms on the eastern horizon, beyond the grey cliffs of Bononia. "I hope we reach a safe harbour before the storm breaks."

PART 2: GAUL, 469 AD

CHAPTER IX
THE LAY OF BASINA

There is a certain routine now to these travels around Gaul, one that I'm slowly settling myself back into. The excitement of the journey is subdued by the familiarity of surroundings, and soon I feel as if I've never left this land of gently rolling hills and slow rivers, winding lazily through shallow, marsh-bottomed, green valleys. Not much has changed since we last travelled down these old stone roads – except it all seems a little busier and livelier than back then. The years of peace under *Dux* Aegidius allowed the people to return to their towns, repopulate their farms, replant their crops, though with the plague's devastation some of that progress has been reversed again. The disease struck hard here, even in the countryside. Black crosses dot the roadside on the approaches to towns, spilling out of the old graveyards. Once in a while we pass a tragic sight of an abandoned farm, with all the hopes of an unfortunate family dashed by the cruel sickle of the pox.

As we come nearer to Aurelianum – through a land none of us has seen before – I notice some of the newly built farmsteads along the stone road look different to those inhabited by Gauls or their Frankish allies. The houses are square, their thatched roofs upturned in the corners in imitation of tent cloth. The walls, of thin wattle daubed with lime, are painted in colourful, geometric patterns around doors and windows. There are horses everywhere – small, sturdy, fast-looking ponies, dozens of them out on the pastures. The people appear different, too. They wear long tunics of dark green or brown cloth, lined with ribbons in the same patterns as their houses, and long, pointy woollen caps. The older women have their heads squashed long in the Hunnic manner, reminding me of Queen Basina, but the younger of them seem to have abandoned the custom. Some are dark-haired, most are fair-haired or red, some men wear moustaches, others not, but all have distinct noses, broad, flared and hooked, and dark, piercing eyes.

The Crown of the Iutes

"Alans," explains Drustan, noticing the interest with which I observe these people. "Fine horsemen and good allies. Saved the day at Maurica, and countless times after that. They practically own Aurelianum these days, and we're all the safer for it."

"Where did they come from?"

"They came with the Goths, from the eastern plains, like so many of these horse tribes," says Eishild. "But before that, they rode with the Huns, from whatever sun-scorched wastes birthed them."

"What wonders they must have seen on the edge of the world," I say, shaking my head with amazement. My knowledge of the continent beyond Gaul is faint, despite years of studies under Bishop Fastidius's tutelage; to the east of Italia I know only of the New Rome and the islands of the Greeks, where Ulysses travelled, though I can scarcely tell which ones are real and which are just places from legend.

There is a world outside the Empire's *limes* of which no ancient author could write anything certain, a world of deep, dark forests and vast seas of grass, where Sarmatians once ruled, where Eishild's Gothic ancestors fought great cavalry battles with the Huns, where Gepids fought Thuringians, where Burgundians waged epic struggles with the Vandals, all of it remembered only in the songs of their *scops*, if at all. My own people come from this darkness beyond all written knowledge, though from the North rather than the East; our arrival in civilised, Roman Britannia was a shock that transformed the politics and life of the entire island. I can't even begin to imagine what the arrival of all those hordes of horse archers and other nameless tribes did to idyllic Gaulish countryside.

If I hadn't met the Gaulish country folk before, I wouldn't be able to tell anything here was out of place. The Alans may have come from the edge of the world, but they seem to have settled in this land as if it was their own. The young ones, those of the generation born in Gaul, greet us in fluent Vulgar and wear tunics and cloaks of local design, something I haven't seen any of the young Iutes do – quite the opposite, in fact, as some of the Cantian youths, even in the army that marches with us, have taken to wearing Iutish garb and interspersing Iutish and Saxon words in their speech.

Ursula's mood lifts somewhat as we ride southwards. I still long to see her smile at least once – but the darkness fades from her eyes, replaced by a faint glint; the warm summer sun paints our exposed arms and faces the shade of ripe apples. Wheat greens in the fields, whitebeam trees are in full bloom and blackbirds trill in the branches.

It's hard to believe we're riding for war.

Aurelianum itself is a small, heavily fortified square of a town, on the northern shore of the River Liger. Protected by the Alan contingents, it appears to have been spared the ravages of past conflicts. Its walls and gates are intact, the streets are clean, the tenements still stand tall. Positioned on the main highway from the north of Gaul to its centre, with a great ancient bridge thrown over the Liger marshes still serving trade passing through, it is as prosperous a place as any I've seen in this part of the world.

Chimneys of the many forges belch black smoke into the blue sky all around the city, and leather mills and tanneries line the riverside. It's only a remnant of the great armament factories of Gaul, which once supplied weapons, armour and siege machines to the Legions throughout the Empire – but the production is still going on at an immense scale, unlike anything still remaining in Britannia. We will have no trouble arming our four cohorts with the finest steel.

The Liger itself is a broad, slow, sprawling river – not as great as the Rhenum, but wider than the Tamesa in Londin. Split into many shallow branches by wooded islands and patches of weedy

The Crown of the Iutes

marshland, it forms a formidable barrier, and I can easily imagine countless hordes of invaders drown in its waters when faced with the city's powerful garrison.

Beyond the bridge, on the other side of the river, a small fortified checkpoint marks the beginning of the Gothic territory. We expect to find the bulk of the Gaulish army here, but other than the Alans manning the walls and training horse muster in the field outside in their exotic armours of shiny steel scales and peaked helmets, there are only a few legionnaires wandering the streets, looking as if they're on leave – and a wing of Frankish cavalry, their mounts tied in front of the town's largest inn, one of them a familiar Thuringian war mare.

Basina, Queen of the Franks, looks even more striking than when I last saw her. Her face has gained a sharp, mature beauty. Her hair has lost some of its lustre, but it still falls in magnificent dark locks down her shoulders and back. She's gained the round hips and the full breasts of a woman who's given her husband many children, and is ready to give him many more.

"I'm so sorry for your loss," she says, giving us both a warm, thoughtful embrace. "I always hoped our little Hlodoweg would one day have a play companion in your son."

"Thank you. How is your boy?" asks Ursula.

"Tengri protected us," Basina replies. "We were out hunting in the Charcoal Forest with Hlodoweg and his sisters accompanying us when news came of the plague at Tornac. We waited most of it out in a camp in the woods."

"Thank the Lord." Ursula raises her eyes to the sky.

"Have the Franks suffered greatly?" I ask.

"Not as much as the Gauls – only in the South, around Camarac. But we have been weakened, and our warriors are not yet ready for the war. This is what I came here to warn Paulus about – but he's already gone, leaving the town to Aegidius's youth, Patrician Syagrius."

"Gone – where?"

"That's what I'm about to find out. Come with me to the *Praetorium* when you're ready."

On the way out of the inn, Basina gives another of her warm hugs to Audulf. This isn't the first time they have seen each other since I left both of them wounded at Icorig, ten years ago –Audulf has visited Frankia numerous times since then with his "blade" of riders. I can tell by how they greet each other that Audulf and Basina have become good friends over these years and feel an odd pang of envy.

"Who are these men that you brought?" Basina asks as we march towards the *Praetorium*. "The ones camping outside the northern wall. They're not Iutes."

"A Briton army," I reply. She raises her eyebrow. "Four cohorts, from Londin and the surrounding *pagi*."

"Do you trust them?"

"Not at all. Half of them barely even know how to fight, and the other half tried to kill me a few months ago, including their commander."

"I don't think I've ever seen a Briton 'army' before."

The Crown of the Iutes

"There hasn't been one in Gaul in a generation – and there likely won't be another in our lifetime. But if you've seen Marcus's Armoricans, you've seen how the Britons fight."

"I only saw his *equites*. Fine riders."

"Some of the *equites* are here, too, with *Decurion* Drustan."

"And what are *they* doing here? Never mind – you'll tell me later. We're here."

We reach the heavy oaken door of the *Praetorium*, a small, handsome building by the Forum, with a domed roof raised on pillars over a sculpted frieze – it must've been a temple to the heathen gods once. Only a few of the bronze rivets in the door are missing, the others are green with patina. This little detail reminds me once again that the town was spared conquest – any plundering army would have taken all the precious metal with them and burned the wood for fuel.

The man waiting for us inside is similar enough to his father that I have no trouble recognising him as the son of Aegidius, the previous *Magister Militum* of Gaul – and a man I counted among my friends. When Basina called his son a "youth" I expected someone in his early twenties – but he looks older than me, and I'm surprised to have never met him before in my travels.

"*Domna* Basina." He stands up and salutes her, with visible deference to her status as the Queen of the Salian Franks. He then studies me and Ursula, trying to guess who we are and why we are bothering him. Once we introduce ourselves, his eyes light up in recognition, and he invites us to sit with him in the building's atrium. There's a working fountain here – a small round basin with a statuette of some river deity pouring water from a pitcher: an astonishing extravagance, when compared with the overgrown ruins of Londin's palaces.

"I was expecting to find Councillor Riotham here," I say. "Or at least someone from his retinue. They only sailed out a few days ahead of us."

"You just missed them. They left as soon as I told them Paulus wasn't here."

"And where *is* Paulus?" asks Basina.

"In Andecawa – or on the way there, with the better half of a Legion," Syagrius replies with a grimace of annoyance. He doesn't seem to take kindly to everyone disregarding him as commander, despite him being the son of the great *Magister*, a feeling with which I can certainly relate.

I look to Basina for an explanation. "It's the closest garrison city to the mouth of the Liger," she says, and turns back to the Patrician. "That means he's decided to deal with the Saxons on his own?"

"I imagine so. Not like he thought it necessary to share his plans with me."

"Aren't you a *Magister* here?" I ask. "A *Dux*, as your father?"

He winces again. "I wish. I'm barely a *Praetor* in Suessionum, my own home town. Yes, my father prepared me to be the next *Dux*. But then he came into conflict with the new Imperator, and Rome never confirmed my title, so I'm stuck with no real power and no real army to command except my *bucellarii*: a simple chief magistrate dealing with the boring civil matters of the province, while Paulus and Arbogast do all the fighting."

"What sort of conflict?" asks Ursula.

The Crown of the Iutes

"Politics." Syagrius scowls. "My father never accepted any of the eastern usurpers who came to the throne after Maiorianus — and they, in turn, refused to acknowledge his command. There's probably some poor man in Arelate calling himself *Dux* in my place, but I wouldn't know — we've been cut off from the South ever since one of the usurpers graciously decided to give Septimania back to the Goths."

"The Empire is friendly with the Goths again?" asks Ursula.

He shrugs. "I can't keep up with the dealings between Rome and Tolosa. Myself, I strive to stay on friendly terms with the Goths — they're just across the river, after all, and they are better neighbours than they are enemies. This is why I'm in Aurelianum now, to assure Aiwarik of our peaceful intentions. Tolosa buys our iron and leather, and pays in silver for it. Rome is faraway, and fickle. They fight the Goths one year, and give them land the next. I'd rather not have anything to do with it. Unless you know otherwise?"

"We were told to expect a new war with the Goths," I say, not certain how much Syagrius should know about the plans of Eishild's rebellion. "Riotham and we were supposed to fight the Saxons on the western flank, while Paulus and *Rex* Hildrik —"

"I told you, the Franks are not ready yet," says Basina. "And neither, by the looks of it, is Paulus, if he decided to march against the Saxons himself."

"I know of no new war, except the usual trouble with the bandits," the Patrician says. "And I'll thank you for not starting one. Paulus wasted too many good men trying to recapture the lands the Goths took after my father's death. I told him I don't care about those empty marshes. Two years now we've had peace, and I'd like to keep things that way."

I glance to Ursula. "Then Drustan and Eishild…"

"They're expecting the Franks and the Gauls to help them with the unrest," Ursula whispers.

"Did you say 'unrest'?" asks Syagrius, frowning. "Do you mean the Martinians?"

"The Martinians?"

"The *Praetor* of Pictawis asked my help to deal with some Bacauds bothering the border," says Syagrius. "Though oddly enough, I haven't heard a word from his bishop about it." He scratches his stubbly chin, then shrugs. "I was sure my father had dealt with the menace for good, yet here they are, raising their ugly heads again. It would have been a better use of my soldiers than chasing the Saxon ghosts all over the Liger, but Paulus thought otherwise." He looks into his cup and winces when he sees it empty. "Is there anything else you want from me?"

"I think we're good for now," I say. "Thank you for your help, *Dux*."

He welcomes my flattery with a grimace, but I can tell he likes being addressed by his father's old title. "You know where to find me," he says. "I'm not moving from here anytime soon."

The stench of the riverside tanneries, working late until dusk, permeates inside the inn, making all the food and drink smell of boiled leather and urine, whether it be morsels of Gallic fowl in a creamy stew, or goblet-fuls of heady red wine mixed with herbs and honey, or any other Gaulish delicacy served at the city's largest and wealthiest tavern, where Basina – as befits a Queen of the Franks – asked us all to meet and discuss the latest news.

The Crown of the Iutes

"I've heard nothing certain of these Martinians," says Eishild, who spent the day seeking out the few Goths dwelling in Aurelianum whose word she could trust. "But I fear the uprising has already started without us, at least near the border. News of our arrival travelled fast."

"We have to warn them," I say. "Without outside help Aiwarik's army will slaughter them like they did the Bacauds in Armorica."

"If they haven't already," says Ursula.

"You heard Patrician Syagrius – if the *Praetor* of Pictawis asked the Gauls for help, that means the Gothic army hasn't arrived yet in force. There was peace for the past two years; the city and the *pagus* are likely defended just by the local militia while Aiwarik's armies are busy elsewhere."

"Where is this Pictawis," asks Seawine, "and what people live there?"

"Across the river, south of Turonum," replies Basina, the most familiar of us with this part of Gaul. "It is a proud and ancient city, from what I heard, and it's guarded by the Taifals – another barbarian tribe of horsemen settled there by Rome, much like the Alans here. They have no love for Goths. I'm not surprised they took this chance to rise against their new masters –"

When she first heard of Eishild and Drustan's plan to rouse the Gothic faithful to a rebellion against their *Rex*, Basina was far from impressed. The scheme struck her as poorly thought through, and with little chance of success. She seemed glad and relieved when the Gothic princess announced her new plan after her meetings in Aurelianum: to try to convince the rebels to lay down their arms and hide, now that the expected assistance from Gaul and Frankia was not forthcoming.

"Is it far?" I ask.

"You should be able to reach it in a week, if you travel in a small enough company and avoid the main roads," says Basina. "But I thought you were in a hurry to join Paulus in Andecawa?"

"I will send Seawine and the main Iute force with Riotham," I say. "And we will travel light to Pictawis to help Eishild: only my bear-shirts and Drustan's *equites*."

"I'm not sure Riotham is going to Andecawa," says Seawine. "From what I overheard, he was boasting about marching at the Goths without waiting for Paulus or the Franks."

"On his own? With just four cohorts?" Drustan scoffs. "Has he gone mad?"

"Maybe he knows something we don't know," muses Ursula. "He did seem oddly unperturbed with the news."

"I'll talk to him in the morning," I say. "Maybe it's just a misunderstanding, though I wouldn't put anything past Riotham…"

Basina grins. "I sense there's no great friendship between you and those Britons."

"Most of the men in the cohorts are just common city folk, fighting for their bread and salt," I say. "But you won't see me mourn Riotham and his fellow nobles if they happen to suffer some misfortune along the way."

"Four cohorts will simply melt away in the sea of Gothic warriors," says Drustan. "But they would help Paulus greatly in his offensive against the Saxons."

The Crown of the Iutes

"This *Comes* Paulus everyone's talking about," I ask. I've heard the name many times before, but I simply assumed he was one of Aegidius's officers, before being struck by a sudden thought. "He can't be the Paulus of Ake, who fought with us at Trever?"

"The same," nods Basina.

"He's come far," I note. "What is he the *Comes* of?"

"Andecawa and Cenomans."

"To think, when I first met him he was only a small town *Praetor*, about to throw away his life in pursuit of a band of Saxons."

"And he's still chasing Saxons to this day," says Basina. "Only now, he does it as the commander of a great army. He could've been the *Dux* and *Magister* after Aegidius's death, but he refused to accept the titles. All he wants is to fight the barbarians."

"And what about Arbogast of Trever?"

"He's practically a ruler of his own country now," she replies. "Though still an ally when we march against Alemanns or Burgundians."

"Then he's gained the independence Odowakr promised him, after all."

"Rome's grasp has been ever weakening. Aegidius only kept his ties to the Empire out of sentiment, and friendship with the previous Imperators. Anyone who wants to rule as a sovereign, can do so without asking the Imperator's permission."

"Even Hildrik?" I ask with a grin. She grins back, but doesn't answer, wary of the spies in the dining hall who must be listening to our every word.

The wine flask runs dry at last, and Drustan and Eishild bid us good night, to prepare for the mission to Pictawis. Not long after, Seawine departs to his dwelling in the Iutish camp outside the city walls, leaving only me and Basina by the tavern's flickering, smouldering hearth.

The Queen of Franks calls for more ale, then sits between the two of us, wraps her arms around our shoulders and pulls us close.

"This is good," she murmurs contentedly. "Friends, together again."

"I'm surprised you remember us so fondly," says Ursula. "It's been so long since we fought together."

"Too long," says Basina. "And I'm not talking only about fighting." She grins and pinches my rear. "What's this I hear about you two discovering some *drui* magic?"

I glance to Ursula, my cheeks burning. "You told her?"

Ursula shrugs. "I didn't think there was any need for secrets between you two."

Basina downs a mugful of ale. "The night is still young. Why won't you show me what you've learned since we last lay?"

I choke on the ale. "I have a wife now," I say.

"And I a husband. But I've given Hildrik so many children, he doesn't care what I do in my bedroom and with whom. I'm sure

The Crown of the Iutes

Ursula won't begrudge me this one last time, for old time's sake, will you, love?"

To my surprise, Ursula shrugs with a wistful smile. "I don't know why you'd want him, but I'd rather he quenched his urges with you than some local wench."

Her candour renders me speechless, until Basina stands up and pulls me to her. "Come, *aetheling*. The beddings here are soft but sturdy. Don't think I haven't noticed you staring at my tits all day – you'll have more than enough of them before morning!"

Sprawled on the skins and furs, thrown by our passion all over the wooden floor, Basina's regal, brazen nakedness oozes sweat and moist heat, like a furnace in a bath house. Her black hair, tall and long in the Hunnish manner, flows like a dark, meandering river. And though we've been riding each other all through the night until we both grew sore, as soon as I reach out to feel one of her heaving, life-giving, milk-tasting breasts under my hand, I grow painfully stiff again.

"Hildrik is a fortunate king to have such riches," I say.

"He has nothing that he hasn't won for himself in battle."

"With such plunder in his treasury, no wonder he feels like he doesn't need to prove himself as warlord anymore."

She raises herself on an elbow.

"You put your cock in a man's wife once, and already you think to question his valour?" she asks with an amused smile.

"It was a lot more than once," I reply with a grin. "I'm just saying, if I had what he's got, I wouldn't want to risk losing it all, either."

"Are you calling my husband a coward? Greater men than you paid with their manhoods for such words. No matter how skilled they were."

"A coward? By Donar's hammer, never!" I protest. "I saw him fight. The man knows no fear. Although… Maybe he's grown a little lazy on Gaulish gold? After all, with all those Roman taxes coming into his chests, what need is there for campaigning – even if an ally is in need?"

"I told you – the plague ravaged Frankia in winter. If not for it…"

"We, too, had the pox," I remind her. "It took my son and many others. And yet here I am, with two hundred Iute warriors. Even the *wealas* gathered an army the size of which hadn't been seen in Britannia in a generation. Are the Frankish warriors not eager to drown the pain of their loved ones' deaths in the blood of the enemies?"

She grows serious, then laughs out loud. "May Tengri's bolts shoot you! You want me to goad Hildrik into helping you against the Saxons!"

"I wouldn't need his help if I could rely on Riotham's soldiers," I say. "But if they're marching on the Goths, my centuries alone will mean little in the coming fight. This might be our last chance to defeat the pirates before they decide to join sides with Aelle and conquer Britannia. And after several seasons of plundering the coasts, their chests must be overflowing with silver."

She raises her hands in surrender, still laughing. "Enough! I preferred you when your mouth was full of my cunt. Do you always talk so much after humping?"

The Crown of the Iutes

"I don't often get to hump a queen."

"Then shut up and make me scream again."

She takes my hand and puts it between her thighs. Just as she starts to grind it, the door slams open.

"Ursula!" I jerk my hand back in shame. "What are you –?"

Ursula takes in the scene before her and grows red-faced, though I can't tell if it's from anger, shame or excitement, before composing herself.

"Put on your breeches, Octa," she commands. "It's already morning."

"What's going on?"

"You were right about Riotham. Something's happening. My Cants just got orders to march out – and so did Seawine's Iutes."

I leap up and stumble for my clothes, rolled into a sweaty bundle in the corner.

"The Iutes take no orders other than from Seawine or myself!"

"Seawine will wait to hear from you before doing anything, I'm sure," says Ursula. "But the Britons are under the Councillor's command. You said you would talk to him. His men wouldn't even let me see him."

"I'll see what I can do," I say as I slide into the breeches and throw the tunic over my shoulders. "Though I doubt I can stop Riotham from whatever new foolhardy scheme he's come up with."

I reach for the door. Ursula turns to join me, but stops when Basina calls her name.

"Let the men deal with each other, *walh*," the Queen says, as she spreads herself invitingly on the furs. "And let us women take care of ourselves. I can see the flame in your eyes burn even brighter than your husband's."

Ursula looks at me hesitantly, then back at Basina's dark cave. Now I have no doubt what urge paints her cheeks the burning crimson.

"I think I can manage Riotham on my own," I tell her and nod at the Queen of the Franks. "I'm just not sure if you can manage… *her*."

I find the Briton camp all but empty, save for a couple of guards, a few stragglers, and a handful of wretches who caught some sickness along the way to Aurelianum. The Iutes are all dressed, packed and ready to march, but at Seawine's orders they're waiting for my confirmation to join the *wealas* cohorts.

"Riotham will be on the bridge by now," Seawine tells me. "He tried to convince us you've agreed to everything, but I had to wait to hear it from yourself."

"And you were wise to do so. Did he tell you where he wanted to take you?"

"Only that we were to cross the river, and then head south."

"Tell the men to go back to their tents, but stay wary. I trust neither these Britons nor Syagrius. This may not be over yet."

The Crown of the Iutes

As I gallop back across the city, I notice the Alan guards gather in the streets in numbers far greater than before; they're riding in from outside the walls, in detachments eight-ten men strong, as if readying for battle. But I have no time to worry about this new development. At last, I catch up to Riotham just as he crosses the Liger Bridge. All four cohorts are already on the other side of the river, watched cautiously by the guards at the Gothic checkpoint – far too few to stop the marching army. I hold the Councillor's horse by the reins and make him stop and turn about to face me.

"Where are you taking them?" I demand.

"To march against the Goths."

"We're supposed to fight the pirates. *Comes* Paulus awaits us at Andecawa."

He scoffs. "A greater destiny awaits me in Gaul. The Imperator marches on Tolosa, to bring down the heretic kings. We are to meet his army at Arwernis, and help on the northern flank. Between our pincers, the Goths will perish forever!"

"That's the first I have heard about any of this."

He laughs, mockingly. "And who are *you* to know the secret deals between the noble Christian lords, heathen?"

"Then this was never about penance," I realise. "You never planned to fight the pirates. Do you even feel any remorse for your attack on Saint Paul's?"

"I only needed the bishop's blessing to fill my ranks with enough men, and his gold, for the weapons and ships. The Imperator promised me more than I could ever gain in Britannia, more than I could win from the Saxon filth. When I return triumphant, Londin will bow to the will of Riothamus Gothicus – and so will all you meagre heathen tribes!" he boasts.

"You will perish along the way, like so many before you," I say. "You have no idea of the true might of the Goths."

"The Lord marches with us." He shakes his sword. "He will smite the heathens and lead us into victory, regardless of their greater numbers."

"Boastful words for someone who stormed a House of the Lord and had to flee before His wrath," I remind him.

"Your jibes matter not. The Goths are in disarray, distracted. The plague, and now the rebels in their North. There will never be a better time to strike. And when we're done with the Goths, yes, we'll come back to deal with your Saxon pirates. You can join me if you wish, and share in the glory and the rewards that Rome will lavish upon us – or waste time hunting other heathens in the marshes."

"Neither of you is going anywhere!"

We both turn to see Syagrius, on horseback, surrounded by a retinue of grim Alan riders, all wearing coats of scale armour and brandishing heavy spears or curved bows with steel-tipped arrows.

More Alan riders ford the river on either side of the bridge, to cut Riotham and me off from the southern shore, where the Briton cohorts await.

"My father worked hard to ensure peace with the Goths, to turn them into good neighbours instead of mortal enemies," Syagrius says. "I won't let you ruin his efforts with some ill-fated expedition."

The Crown of the Iutes

"You'd defy the will of the Imperator?" asks Riotham.

"The will of some Greek upstart, sent from New Rome to ensure the East's hegemony over the West?" the Patrician scoffs. He seems to assume Riotham and I are aware of what he's referring to, but I can see the Councillor is as much in the dark regarding Rome's politics as I am. "Yes, I dare say I do. My relations with Tolosa are more important to me than whoever sits on the throne in distant Italia. And as for you –" He points his *spatha* at me. "I already ordered your friends thrown in jail. Yes, I've learned all about your little scheme! The last thing I need is more Martinians at my doorstep."

"You took Eishild and Drustan?" I reach for my sword. The Alans lower their spears and raise their bows. "You'll pay for this. They have powerful friends."

"Doubt it." He chuckles. "Nobody will miss an exiled Gothic princess, and I have little reason to fear the wrath of the Armoricans." He spews the last word out with noticeable disgust. "If you don't wish to join them, you'd both better pack your tents and go help Paulus – or better yet, go back to Britannia. Lord knows I didn't ask either of you to come here."

Behind him, behind the line of armoured riders, at the bridge gate, erupts a noisy commotion. A brief clash of arms later, new riders appear on the bridge: the Franks, their swords red with Alan blood, their mounts foaming at the mouths. Basina – half-naked, wearing only her leather breeches and a breast band – storms her way past the dumbfounded Alan spearmen to Syagrius's side and presses the tip of her lance to his chest.

Through a gap in the Alan line pours a wing of Armorican *equites*, with Drustan and Eishild, wearing drab prison tatters, in front – followed by my own riders, led by Ursula and Croha.

"Go, Octa!" cries Basina. "There are more of them coming – I don't want to fight a pitched battle inside a city!"

"What about you?"

"I'll be fine – he won't dare harm the Queen of Franks. Will you, small prick?" she goads Syagrius in a way that makes me think I wasn't the only one she shared a bed with during her visit in Aurelianum.

"You barbarian filth – " the Patrician seethes, but the point of Basina's lance piercing his tunic makes him shut up.

At my orders, the *equites* and the Iutes proceed to disarm the Alans barring our passage into the land of Goths. As soon as a gap opens in the Alan blockade, Riotham grunts, spurs his horse around and gallops towards his troops without a word. The Gothic watchmen step aside and hide even deeper into their checkpoint, wary of drawing attention of either of the sides – though I imagine they're already preparing a report to send to their king in Tolosa, giving him a detailed description of the strange happenings on the Aurelianum Bridge.

"I will take your Iutes to Andecawa, as promised," Basina assures me. "We'll be waiting for you there."

"And what about Hildrik?"

She grins. "I'll see what I can do. But I'm sure you'll be able to manage without our help. Now, go – even I can't hold them for long!"

The Crown of the Iutes

CHAPTER X
THE LAY OF ADALFUNS

There are birds in these woods that I have never heard before. They come out at dusk, when we finish setting up our camp, and sing their strange songs until dawn, telling of long, bright summers and sweet, abundant fruit of the distant lands of the burning sun.

I've never been this far south. The nights are warm and bright here, and we only light the campfires more out of habit than for heat. We're keeping to the main Roman highway, following the trail of Riotham's cohorts, at a safe distance in case the Briton army draws too much enemy attention to itself. And in case the Goths do come searching for us, we shun village inns and roadside *mansios*, choosing to camp in the wild instead. Not that there are many inns here that can accommodate fifty riders, for that's how many we are when joined by Drustan and his *equites*.

I return from an evening piss. I can't see Ursula anywhere in the camp. Croha notices my confusion and nods towards a nearby brook. It takes me a while to find her: in a sunken nook where the brook spills deep enough for her to bathe. Watching her glistening with cold water in the golden light of the setting sun, I feel suddenly overwhelmed by a torrent of emotions: lust, love – and shame.

"Why did you let me do it?" I ask when she emerges back onto the muddy shore. She sprawls on the grass beside me, letting the warm night air dry her out. I know every inch of this body – I've known it for years – and yet it's as if I was seeing her for the first time. I reach out to touch her belly, remembering how it swelled four years ago, when she carried Pascent. She stirs, but does not flinch.

The Crown of the Iutes

"Did you not enjoy it?" she replies.

"At the time, yes. But the bile of remorse I now feel in my throat wasn't worth it."

"I didn't send you to Basina to shame you. There was no subterfuge. I know what men need. I know what *you* need. And what your father demands of you."

I laugh, incredulously. "I'm not going to spawn an heir with Basina!"

"Not with her, no. But I was hoping once you did it with her, you'd be able to do it with anyone."

"Anyone?"

"There are plenty of suitable girls who'd take your seed. One of Croha's shieldmaidens, maybe. Or even Croha herself."

"Croha?" I blurt, surprised. "I couldn't – she's like a sister to me."

"But she's *not* your sister. She's a fine warrior, and a beautiful woman. You do her dishonour to not even consider her as your mate." She lifts herself on an elbow. "We have to be mature about this. It's not the end of the world for a king's son to take a concubine. What if I was barren?"

"But you're not."

She sighs. "I might as well be." She puts her fingers to her lips in a dreamy gesture. "You know, I could taste you inside her…" she says enigmatically.

"I don't care about heirs, or who you choose to lie with," I protest. "I care about *us*. Being together. And nothing's going to change that."

She runs her hand down my cheek.

"My sweet Octa. My foolish Octa…"

I don't understand what her words mean, but when she leans down to kiss me I sense the warmth of her love passing from her lips to mine, and it calms me down.

She's still mourning Pascent, I tell myself. It will pass. I've waited for her before – this is nothing to worry about.

"Six riders," reports Croha. "They're heading this way purposefully – doesn't seem like a random patrol."

I raise my hand and make a fist. The order ripples down the ranks, as thirty Iutes dismount and lead their horses down a field path to a nearby copse, to hide from the approaching Goths. Only Croha, Audulf and I remain on the road, waiting.

Upon reaching the crossroad at a town called Bituriges, whose small Gothic garrison fled seeing Riotham's arrival, Drustan and I decided to abandon the cover of Briton troops and turn west, in search of the Bacaud rebels. The Pictawis highway was well marked with milestones and *mansios*, but on either side spread a wild frontier, a stark contrast to Liger's civilised northern shore: a great, dark wood, interspersed with scattered farmsteads, most of them ruined, and abandoned fields overgrown with scrub. To our south, the land rises in sharp, dark spurs and to our north, it sprawls into midge-infested swamps and marshes. If we had enough time to prepare this journey, we could've got a guide from Aurelianum, but

The Crown of the Iutes

the hasty manner of our departure meant we were left to our own devices to find our way across the Gothic kingdom.

We decided that my Iutes and I would keep to the stone highway; I didn't fancy getting lost in the marshes or tangled in the woods. But fifty riders would have been too conspicuous – especially if twenty of them bore the red cloaks of Roman cavalry – and so Drustan and his *equites*, more familiar with this territory, took to the wooded hills to try to find an alternative route.

Keeping to the highway meant inevitably stumbling upon the Goth checkpoints and armed patrols; by now, no doubt, news of the Briton army at Bituriges would have reached the garrison at Pictawis, and made them wary of any riders approaching from that direction. We are in no way a threat to a walled city – we couldn't even assail a fortified watchtower – but the soldiers on the frontier are always anxious, especially with rumours of the Imperator marching for Tolosa from the South, and they might well take us for a vanguard of an invading force.

Before long, the six riders appear over a hump of the road. Croha was right – they are trotting hastily onwards, wary, watchful and focused; it's not an accident that they're here.

"Shall we kill them now?" asks Audulf, caressing the pommel of his long *seax*.

I gesture to him to calm down. "Not yet."

The Goths spot us and slow down. I raise my hand in salutation.

"Hael."

They respond with their own word of greeting, then halt and study us and our mounts. All three of us wear mail, and are well armed, but we are too few to seem a threat on this vast, empty plain.

"Where are you going?" asks the patrol's commander. Long, straw-coloured hair flows from under his helmet, and his cloak and shield thrown over his back are painted red and green into dragon and crow shapes.

"To Pictawis," I reply.

"What business do you have in Pictawis?"

"We heard in Aurelianum there's work for hired swords there," I say. "We're Saxons, from beyond Rhenum."

"Saxons?" The Goth eyes me suspiciously. "Why aren't you with your kin, at the Mouth of Liger?"

"They're not our kin," says Audulf, and spits in disgust. He, at least, really is a Saxon, and his northern accent and manner are the most convincing. "Not all Saxons are the same. We're decent lowland folk, not some sodden pirates – I'd sooner fight with Franks than those fish-eaters."

The Goths chuckle. "Suit yourselves. You're right about the mercenary work – there are Bacauds abroad not far from here that will need dealing with."

"Is that who you're after?" I ask.

"How do you know we're after anyone?" The commander grows tense, and his hand shifts towards the throwing axe at his side.

"I have eyes, don't I?" I say. "You were clearly looking for someone before you spotted us."

The Crown of the Iutes

The Goth smooths his moustache. "If you've come from Aurelianum, you must have heard of the great Gaulish warband marching south," he says.

"They barred our way at Bituriges," I nod. "But they didn't seem to be heading this way."

"It's not them we're worried about," the Goth replies with a grin. "Our king will deal with them in his own time. But there's talk of another troop about in these parts – a wing of Roman cavalry. Nobody knows why they're here, and what they want – but with the Bacauds roaming in the North, and the Gauls over in Bituriges, we can't afford to dismiss any rumours."

I look to Croha and Audulf, then back to the Goth. "We came down the only highway from the West, and haven't seen anyone but merchants and farmers."

"I told you they wouldn't stay on the main road, Ibbas," one of the Goths complains. "They must have gone down one of the marsh routes."

"Indeed. Looks like we're wasting our time here. Thank you, Saxon – you've saved us some pointless wandering in this blasted heat."

He salutes me farewell. The Goths ride past us, then stop again, on the crossroad with an old droveway. The commander looks around, exchanges a few words with his men and points towards the nearby copse – the same one where I hid my warriors. He sends three of his riders down the droveway to investigate.

I curse, and nod at Croha and Audulf. Silently, we draw our swords and turn our mounts around. "Be quick about it," I say. "We can't risk any of them getting away."

We cut short across the field, towards the three Goths on their way to the copse. They are too late to notice my charge. I cut one down before he can draw his weapon. The other two try to flee, but in the field their horses are slower than our ponies. Audulf and Croha reach the second one in a few pony strides: Audulf cuts low and is blocked; Croha cuts high and her blade digs deep into the Goth's neck.

Some of the hiding riders, seeing our fight, emerge from the copse to help us, but I can tell they'll be too late to catch up to the commander, who turns and spurs his horse to a gallop. I leave the other Goths to my men, and launch into pursuit. I must get to him before he reaches the cobbles of the highway, where his warhorse will easily overtake my moor pony. He looks over his shoulder, draws the flying axe and throws it. I duck – the axe, deftly thrown, bounces off my helmet and dazes me for a moment. I sheathe the sword and draw the lance. The longer shaft lets me reach the back of the Goth's horse. Approaching at an angle, I strike from the side and cut a deep gash in the horse's flank. The poor beast neighs desperately and launches into an even more feverish gallop – but in doing so, it ignores its rider, and runs straight across the highway, into the muddy field on the other side.

The Goth struggles with the reins; this lets me ride up to him. He draws a long sword, with a jewel-studded pommel – I can tell by his stance he's a veteran, and wonder briefly what sins he committed in the Gothic king's service that destined him to patrol this miserable, distant frontier; was he a loyalist of the previous *Rex*, perhaps?

I will never learn the truth. Our swords clash. He's a fine fighter, but the large round shield at his back hampers his movements; he's more used to fighting on foot than on horseback. He's got an advantage of height – his mount is taller, and so is he. I can cut swiftly with my slim *spatha* under his skilful blocks and parries, but though my blade reaches far enough to give him a few nasty cuts, I can't break through his defences to deliver the deadly blow.

I rear my pony high, and as I fall, I smash against his parry, holding my sword with both hands. Unable to balance, the force of the blow throws me from the saddle – but not before my blade cracks through his and crashes into his clavicle. We both hit the mud at the same time. I roll back up. The Goth tries to crawl; blood spurts from his shoulder with each move. His horse, panicked, bolts and gallops away, further into the field. He reaches for the sword, lying in the dirt. I step on his hand, and shove my blade into his neck, severing his spine.

Croha and Audulf ride up. Audulf's left arm is bloodied, but the injury is slight. One of the Goths lies sprawled in the high grass only a few feet away, with Croha's axe in his back; if not for her skill with the blade, he would've caught up to me while I was still on the ground. His horse stands over his body with its head low, as if waiting for its master to awake. I search for the other warhorses in the fields and nod, satisfied, when I count all six of them, riderless.

"Are you alright, *aetheling*?" Croha asks.

"I'm fine. What about you?" I point to her chest. Her tunic is torn and her leather chest wrap is slashed through by some stray blow, revealing a shallow wound – and giving me a good view of her finely shaped breasts. I sense the battle rush recede from my limbs – and flow to my nethers, instead. I spot Ursula approaching us from the copse, and I remember her urging me to find a mate among the Iute shieldmaidens…

Croha looks down and covers herself up, reddening. "It's only a scratch."

"Get rid of those horses," I order the riders as they emerge from their hideout. "Can't leave any trace of this fight behind. And be quick about it – we need to get to Pictawis before they send out any more patrols our way."

Drustan and Eishild arrive at the gates of Pictawis a day after we reach the city's suburb, sprawling east of the river that binds it on three sides. I notice two of the *equites* are missing, and a few others bear light injuries. Drustan himself is wounded – he barely sits in the saddle, his left thigh tightly wrapped in blood-soaked cloth.

"Goths?" I ask.

Drustan shakes his head. "Bacauds. We disturbed a band of them yesterday. There are great numbers of them hiding in those marshes, roaming like swarms of angry wasps."

"Aren't they the ones we're supposed to talk to?" asks Ursula.

"Not these ones," Eishild replies. She's visibly shaken by the encounter, and I know her enough to tell it's not just because of the violence. "These ones didn't want to talk. But somebody is leading them – gathering them all in the marsh. That's the person we need to find."

"How do we go about it?" I ask.

Eishild nods at the city walls. "We'll find out in there. I know someone in Pictawis who can tell us more of what's going on."

We leave the men to set up camp in a fallow field on the eastern bank of the river. With Ursula, Drustan and Eishild, I march to the bridge gate and introduce us as commanders of the reinforcements

The Crown of the Iutes

sent by Patrician Syagrius at the local *Praetor*'s request. The guard looks at our camp doubtfully.

"I hope there's more of you coming," he says.

"Is it that bad?" asks Drustan. "We thought it was just some bandits."

"We'd handle them ourselves if they were just some bandits," the guard scoffs and nods the way towards the city. "The *Praetor* will brief you on everything."

As we march down the *Decumanus*, between rows of thick stone columns of the many *porticoes*, I'm on the lookout for the mysterious Taifals; but if they're here, I'm unable to tell them apart from other fair-hairs living in this crowded place. Pictawis is a sizable settlement – greater than Aurelianum, and similarly untouched by most of the recent wars. The southern side of the street is lined with merchant warehouses, though most are empty and boarded up, a memory of the greater prosperity that the city must have enjoyed in the Empire's glory days; the northern side is piled high with rubbish and rubble, from which grow the tall tenements of the poor townsfolk.

Instead of reaching the *Praetorium*, Eishild leads us to a cathedral complex, rising upon a mound in the south-east, with its back to the city wall, in an arrangement much reminding me of that in Londin. The church itself is modest, but what draws the eye is a magnificent baptistery, all bright brick and gleaming marble, with lofty columns reused from some pagan temple.

Eishild tells us to wait, and knocks at the door of a small, but well-built, whitewashed *domus*, standing between the church and the baptistery. A servant appears at the porch and they exchange a few quiet words, after which the servant hurriedly vanishes inside. Before long, a short, portly man wearing a tunic embroidered with

Saint Peter's keys and lined with gold ribbon runs out of the *villa*, struggling to tie up his belt.

"Princess!" he exclaims. He glances around, then repeats in a whisper. "*Princess!* What if someone recognises you? Come inside, quickly."

"Your Grace, my friends –" Eishild points to us.

"*The bishop?*" I whisper. "Your contact is the bishop?"

"Yes, yes, of course, all of you, come in," the bishop says, wringing his hands. "Octavius, call Maryam, this man needs medical attention. And then run to the *taberna*, fetch us some roast lamb. Apologies, I have nothing prepared –"

"It's quite alright, Your Grace. We haven't come here to feast. We have matters of great importance to discuss."

"Naturally." The bishop looks to Drustan and me again. "And I think I can guess what these matters are."

The road, straight and level until now, begins to descend in lazy curves down a sharply falling slope. This isn't a Roman stone highway, but a path of ancient ages, stamped by uncounted feet through the wooded hills, leading almost exactly due north from Pictawis, to the old ford on the River Vigenna. It is on the river shore overlooking the ford that the Martinian band is supposed to have set up its chief settlement, according to Gelasius, the bishop of Pictawis.

The sharpness of the road's descent tells us we must be coming into the Vigenna valley, which, from what Gelasius told us, is

The Crown of the Iutes

deeper and steeper than that of the sprawling Liger. The woods part, revealing a grid of narrow fields, separated by low drystone walls and overgrown hedges. A few farms appear still to be inhabited — not everyone fled before the Bacauds, it seems.

I slow down, letting Eishild's horse catch up to us. She's been in a foul mood ever since we departed from the city, leaving her beloved Drustan and other wounded in the bishop's care. There are only a dozen of us riding down the narrow road — six Iutes and six *equites*; we don't want to frighten the Bacauds into thinking they're being invaded. The rest of the men are to wait for my signal in Pictawis — or ride to our help if we're not heard from in a week.

"What's wrong?" I ask the princess. She lifts her head slowly; her eyes are filled with sadness and worry. "I thought you'd be glad. You're riding to meet your kin."

"Yes — but to tell them to lay down their arms, not to rouse them into battle," she replies.

In truth, we don't exactly know who, or what, we're going to find at the rebel camp — or what we will tell them when we get there. The bishop's tale was as confused and uncertain as the Bacaud army itself.

"There is an old nest of dissenters on Vigenna's shores, in a place called Caino," he told us. "*True* Martinians, not like those rebellious serfs that later took the saint's name to justify their crimes. Followers of Maximus, who was one of Martinus's first disciples in Turonum. But for many years, they kept to themselves, and we didn't bother them. Most of them are decent, god-fearing people. They would sometimes visit the city for trade, or to see their families. We had no trouble from them — until a few months ago."

"What happened?" I asked.

"She did," the bishop replied, nodding at Eishild. "Just as we planned. Rumour of Thaurismod's daughter returning to Gaul was enough to spark a flame of rebellion throughout the North. There are many Goths loyal to the Roman Creed around Pictawis – and not just the Goths. The Taifals never took to the old heresy, either. But only the heretics are allowed to serve in Aiwarik's garrisons – and so the followers of the Roman Creed were soon forced to flee into the marshes, where they joined with Martinians and other rebels. Now, it's as if a new nation was being born on Vigenna's shores. All who find their lives unbearable flock to Caino – runaway slaves, deserters from Aiwarik's warbands, Bacauds from all over Gaul… An entire army, waiting for your orders, Princess."

"I have no orders for them," Eishild said. "Other than to go home. The allies I promised will not come this year – the Gauls fight the Saxons in Andecawa, and the Franks are not coming at all. All we could count on are four cohorts of Britons, but now they are marching south, to Arwernis, and from there onto Tolosa, and will be of little help to us here in the North."

Blood ran from the bishop's face. He raised his hands in despair. "Then all is lost. I spoke to the *Praetor* yesterday. All that was stopping Aiwarik from dealing with the rebels once and for all was fear of Gauls and Franks striking at his flanks. A great warband is waiting at Vesunna for his orders, only a few days' march away. And of course, we all know what the Goths did at Vesunna four years ago…"

I didn't ask about the events in Vesunna, but judging by how both Eishild and Drustan lowered their suddenly ashen faces in prayer, Aiwarik's warriors must have committed some terrible atrocities in that place against the followers of the Roman Creed – enough to terrify all the faithful in Gaul at the mere mention of the name.

Eishild's horse stumbles on a hole in the road. I grab the reins to stop her from falling. She thanks me softly.

"All those years in Londin," she says when she settles back in the saddle, "I was preparing myself to one day lead my people in righteous revolt against my heretic uncles. And now that they've finally risen... I'm supposed to tell them, what – that it was all a mistake?"

"They just have to wait a little more," I tell her. "This is only a temporary setback. The Imperator is marching against the Goths. Who knows, maybe with Riotham's help he'll be victorious after all – or at least weaken Aiwarik enough for your rebellion to succeed later in the year."

"And what if it's too late? You've heard the bishop. A warband from Vesunna is coming our way... Where will all those people go?"

"They're bandits. If there's one thing they know it's how to hide."

"And what if they won't believe me? What if they won't listen to me? They don't know me. I haven't been here for years. Most of them aren't even Goths. What authority will I have to order them to disband?"

Ursula, hearing our talk, rides up to Eishild's other side.

"You worry too much, Princess," she says. "Let's see what's going on in Caino first, before we try to figure out how to deal with it. Put your trust in the Lord – He wouldn't have brought us all here if He didn't have a plan."

Eishild nods. She's not sensitive enough to Ursula's voice to know her superficially pious words carry little hope, but they're enough to lift the princess's mood. "Thank you, Councillor. You're right." She raises her eyes to the sky. "The Lord will not fail me."

The road bends, and enters into a ravine, its sides topped with low-grown but dense, dark wood. I raise an open hand – a signal to my men to be watchful. This is an obvious place for an ambush. I nod at Eishild to ride forward, with one of the *equites* before her, carrying the great banner of Saint Peter, golden keys on white, gifted to us by the bishop as proof of our honest, and godly, intentions.

"We're being followed," reports Croha. "They're hiding, but not very well."

"Then they'll be waiting for us at the mouth of this ravine," I say. "Sheathe your weapons. Make sure they know we mean peace."

Just as I guessed, the Martinians have set up a barricade of logs and thorny bushes, with just enough of a gap in it to let through a single horse. This must be one of the borders of their makeshift kingdom. There aren't many guards at this checkpoint – that I can see, at least – and should we wish, we could charge through or around it with little trouble, but I can feel dozens of pairs of eyes staring at us from the dark wood above, and I'm sure each of those eyes looks down the shaft of a nocked arrow.

The Martinian guards approach us with brandished spears. I notice one of them is a Goth, or at least wears his hair and tunic like one.

"Lord bless you, good men," I say, raising my hands in prayer. "Are you the disciples of the holy man, Maximus?"

The guards' expressions soften, but they remain cautious. "What if we are?"

"We are here to join you in reverence of Martinus," I say. "And in your fight against the heathens and heretics."

The Crown of the Iutes

He looks at me and my men suspiciously. "Are you not heathens yourselves?"

"They are coming with me," says Eishild. "I vouch for their faith."

"And you are?"

"She is Eishild the White, the rightful princess of the Goths," says the Goth guard. He comes up, pushes away the first Bacaud's spear and kneels before the princess. "I wasn't sure if I recognised you until you spoke, *fraujo*."

"You know me?"

"I was in your father's *Gardingi, fraujo*. I was banished after your bastard brothers killed him. My name is Adalfuns."

"I remember you." Eishild dismounts and lays her hand on his head. "Though I was only a child – how could you know me?"

"Your beauty shone even then, Princess. You have the light of your mother's wisdom in your eyes – and of her faith."

"Is she the one whose arrival was prophesied?" asks the spearman. I glance around – the other bandits emerge from the woods on either side of the ravine. As I suspected, most of them carry bows, javelins or shepherd's slings.

"This is she."

"Prophesied?" I ask.

"We were told you'd be coming, Princess," Adalfuns says. "Please, come. All of you."

As the Goth leads us towards the river, Eishild leans over to me and Ursula. "For the last couple of years my loyal followers, like bishop Gelasius, were sending out agents to the Faithful, to prepare them for my arrival," she explains quietly. "I didn't know they'd disguise it as a *prophecy*."

"It might work in our favour," I say. "Should make it easier to convince them on what we have to say."

We reach a small, grey beach; a flat-bottomed boat has been dragged onto the sand. Before us flows the Vigenna. At first, the river seems shallow and narrow enough to be crossed on horseback. Looking closer, I realise that what I took for the opposite shore is only a flat, grassy island in the middle of the current. The real northern shore rises beyond it, in a line of imposing sharp, grey cliffs. I spot the ruined ramparts of an old Roman fortress, once defending this crossing point, peeking over the tree tops, and a few scattered huts at the bottom of the cliff. This must be the place called Caino.

"Leave your ponies here," says Adalfuns, pointing to an enclosure by the beach, crowded with the mounts of the Bacauds. I spot a few warhorses, but most are just dray mules and ponies. "They'll be kept safe, I promise. There's no place for them on the other side."

"You keep no horses on the mountain?"

"There are too many of us in the caves as it is," Adalfuns replies. "Besides, there are few riders among the pilgrims, apart from us Goths and some of the Taifals."

"Caves?" asks Ursula.

Adalfuns smiles. "You'll see."

The Crown of the Iutes

Like the *Labyrinthus* in the ancient legends, the myriad caves cut into the soft, light-grey rock of the Caino hills form an impenetrable maze of great and small grottoes, roughly hewn columns, tunnels branching into the darkness, hidden entrances and unexpected exits. The caverns are long but shallow, cut just below the cliff's surface, and spreading along its walls – once in a while, a crack or a gap in the rock serves to brighten the tunnels with the light coming from outside. I cannot even begin to guess how many people live in these underground dwellings, but there must be hundreds of them, judging by the amounts of provisions we pass gathered in the storage caves at the main entrance to the complex.

We reach a large, domed hollow, deep inside the maze. Its walls are carved with Christian symbols – crosses, *Chrismons*, fish, loaves of bread. At the far end, illuminated by the beam of light shooting from a hole in the vaulted ceiling, stands a stone altar, with a figure of a majestic Christ painted over it in charcoal, ochre and chalk, staring intently at those gathered before him. Water drips from the ceiling and gathers in pools along the walls.

"This is a church," I exclaim, astonished. Eishild and Ursula cross themselves, as do the *equites* – I give my men a slight nod, to signal that they should do the same.

"One of two in Caino," Adalfuns declares proudly. "The new one we had to raise on the surface, for all the new recruits. It's where your men will have to worship – but of course, there will always be a place for the princess and her friends in Maximus's great hall."

He leads Eishild, Ursula and myself to the altar. We all kneel down before the large, flat stone, brightened with dozens of candles.

"This cave is where everything started," says Adalfuns. "After Martinus died, Maximus, as many of the great man's disciples, sought a place where he could dwell as a hermit, and illuminate the land with the light of True Faith. The Lord led him here, when it was only a small, natural hollow. Before long, people started coming here from all over Gaul, drawn by Maximus's piousness and virtue. For nearly a hundred years, his disciples carved these tunnels, building this underground monastery in imitation of their master. And now, he is buried here, under this altar, sanctified by his holy bones."

"We are humbled to be in the presence of his remains," says Eishild. "And I hope Maximus's light will shine brightly on our plans." She looks around. "And where is your priest?"

"We have no need for priests here, Princess."

A man stating this, in a rough, gravelly voice, enters the cave from some hidden entrance behind the altar. He's another Goth – older than Adalfuns, and taller. His long beard, golden with patches of grey, cascades in curls almost to his waist. He wears a patch over his right eye, and his face is carved with deep scars. Over a black leather tunic he dons an armour of steel scales; a long sword with jewel-incrusted pommels hangs at his belt.

"We live like the first Faithful," he explains. "We have no hierarchy, no bishops. Whoever is the most senior, in age or experience, at the Mass, celebrates the Eucharist. Of course, that's how we do things here, underground." He nods upwards. "Out there, in the new church, we still keep up the pretence."

"Are you another of Thaurismod's guards?" I ask, stepping in front of Eishild.

He smirks. "I was a nobleman at his court, and a servant of his father before him, but I wasn't of the *Gardingi*. My name is Airmanarik." He salutes us.

The Crown of the Iutes

"You're the chieftain here, I'm guessing," I say, eyeing his armour and sword.

"You have a good eye, Briton." He nods. "Though only in matters of war – we have no magistrates here, either. What plans were you talking about, Princess?"

"I would like to discuss them with you in private, after we've eaten and rested."

"Of course." He bows. "Adalfuns will take you to your temporary quarters, while we prepare something more suitable."

CHAPTER XI
THE LAY OF AIRMANARIK

"You have gathered quite an army here, Airmanarik," I note as we sit down to a simple supper. The Bacauds are not quite starving – not yet, at any rate – but their fare is that of a poor peasant: dark bread, porridge of lentils and barley, with no salt or spices, and a little wild honey as the only luxury. Looking around I see that the leaders and elders of the community share the same meal as everyone else, including us.

"We're close to a thousand armed men now," the Goth boasts. "And still more come every day. They're not all here, of course – scattered throughout the marshes and woods, spreading the word of our rising to the towns and farms from here to Tolosa, making themselves ready."

"Ready for what?" asks Ursula.

"For the day we strike at that filth Aiwarik, and all his heretic kin," Adalfuns says, slamming his fist on the table. "And send them to Hell where they belong."

"You would need ten times as many men to attack my father's capital," says Eishild, giving me a wary glance. "And more still to keep it."

"Not when Aiwarik is busy fighting off the Gauls, Franks and Romans. With him and his army out of Tolosa, we will march into the city, its gates open by the Faithful inside, and slaughter all who stand in our way until only those of the True Creed remain."

The Crown of the Iutes

I chew the dark, hard bread in grim silence. We are surrounded by marks of the Christian faith on every wall – faith of peace, faith of love, but the bloodlust in the Goth's words is more akin to that of a heathen warrior, vowing to vanquish his enemies. This isn't surprising from someone who was chosen to lead an army of the Bacaud rebels – I fought enough of them to know their vision of Christ's kingdom on Earth is baptised in the blood of the pagans and heretics – but I can see Eishild is still disturbed by Airmanarik's passion for cruelty.

"You will do no such thing," she says, at last.

"I'm sorry?" Airmanarik furrows his brow.

"I did not come here to lead you on Tolosa."

"There is no help coming from Gaul or Frankia," I explain hastily. "No armies coming to distract Aiwarik and lure him out of Tolosa, except a small warband of Britons – likely marching into a trap as we speak. Instead, it's the Goths that are coming *here*, from Vesunna. To destroy you."

"And how do *you* know this?" Airmanarik grows even more suspicious. I notice the mention of Vesunna has the similar gloomy impact on the men at the table as it did in bishop Gelasius's room.

What happened in that town?

"We are Britons ourselves," says Ursula. "The princess was hiding out in Londin these past few years. We came as her escort and retinue. I myself am of a noble Briton family."

Airmanarik grunts. "From what I heard of Britannia, it's as much a seed of heresy and heathenry as Gaul, if not more."

"Why do you think we came here?" I say with a wry smile. "But while we sailed with that warband of Britons, we learned all about the Roman plans for this year's campaigning. Hildrik is not coming south of the Liger this summer, and neither is Paulus. Worse still, the Imperator himself marches on Arelate and Tolosa, which means Aiwarik will likely hunker down in his capital, waiting. You're on your own, and your plan is destined to fail."

"You must stay your hand, Commander," Eishild pleads. "Tell your men to lay down their weapons and wait in hiding for a better time – or come with us to fight the Saxons."

"No!" The Goth rises and bangs the table, letting the wooden plates and clay mugs fly. "We cannot wait anymore! And we won't abandon the holy caves. Let the Goths come! Let's see them try to repeat what they did in Vesunna! We will fight them here, and here we will defeat them!" He sits back down and points at Eishild. "Is this why you came? To destroy everything we've been building all this time?"

Adalfuns leans over the table. "*Frauja* Airmanarik, the arrival of the princess was prophesied – we were told to do whatever she orders…"

Airmanarik scoffs and throws a mug at Adalfuns. The younger Goth barely dodges the clay missile; it smashes into bits on the cave wall behind him.

"You know what I think about these prophecies. Did Maximus himself foretell this? Did Martinus? No, it was only a rumour spread by strange men arriving from Lord knows where. Men who, for all we know, were in league with this princess and her Briton accomplices."

It is now time for Adalfuns to rise in indignation. "Hold your tongue, Airmanarik. You may be a chieftain here, but you were merely a cup bearer at Thaurismod's court. This is Princess Eishild you're talking about, and I trust her word more than anyone in these caves. If she says we should lay down our weapons, lay down our weapons we will."

I expect another outburst from Airmanarik, but instead he leans back with his hands behind his head and a mysterious smile on his lips. "Very well. I'm willing to discuss this further tomorrow – but for now, our guests must still be weary after the long journey."

"Indeed we are," I say, sensing there's nothing to be gained from pressing the point further tonight.

He waves at a guard, bids him to lean over and whispers something in his ear. The guard frowns for a moment, looks at us, then nods.

"Your quarters are ready," says Airmanarik. "Lupinus will take you there. These may not be the palaces that the Briton nobles are used to," he chuckles, "but I trust you will be pleased."

"We are content with merely being here, Commander, in the presence of so many godly men and sacred relics," I say with a nod. "Until tomorrow, then?"

"Yes – perhaps," he replies enigmatically.

At a crossing of tunnels, I bid farewell to my men, who are led towards their surface dwellings. Following Lupinus and a few other guards, we descend further into the maze. The corridors grow darker, narrower and more damp, until we can only walk two abreast, each one of us accompanied by a guard.

"Is this really where you keep your most honoured guests?" I ask, increasingly annoyed as freezing water drops at my neck.

"Patience, Briton."

We reach a small cave which looks like a vestibule leading to another network of tunnels. There are two more guards here, spearmen.

"Your weapons," says Lupinus, extending his arms.

I grab hold of my sword. "What's the meaning of this?"

Lupinus smiles. "We'll take care of them here," he says, nodding to a rack of knives, maces and axes on the wall. "You have no need for weapons in your bed chambers. It is our duty to guard your peaceful sleep."

I glance at Ursula – she shrugs and unbuckles her sword belt. I do the same, and Eishild hands over her slim Gothic dagger. At Lupinus's prompting, we enter the darkest and the narrowest corridor yet, brightened only by a couple of oil lamps hanging under the wet ceiling. Before long, we reach a row of entrance holes, disappearing into the shadows, each locked by a wooden door. Lupinus opens the nearest.

"I don't like this," says Ursula.

"Neither do –" I start to say, before the guard behind me kicks me in the back and throws me into the chamber behind the door. Ursula and Eishild join me moments later, cast unceremoniously to the cold, stone floor. Ursula scrambles up and rushes to the door – but Lupinus shuts it in her face. She bangs her fists on the wood and screams – only once, in helpless fury.

[211]

The Crown of the Iutes

"I knew it," she says, sliding to the floor, despondent. "It always ends like this."

"It must be some misunderstanding," whispers Eishild.

"No misunderstanding," I say. "It's clear Airmanarik will do everything to stop you from disturbing his plans of revenge and conquest. I'm surprised he hasn't simply killed us off."

A voice speaks out in the darkness. "Airmanarik doesn't kill his guests. This whole place is a holy ground – he wouldn't defile it with your blood. He just keeps us here until we join his side – or rot."

"Who's *we*?" I ask. Ursula and I shield Eishild with our bodies as I try to pierce the darkness with my gaze. "Who are you?"

The light of the oil lamps outside penetrates faintly through a hole in the door, just enough for me to make out a silhouette of a man, sitting by the far wall.

"My name's Megethius of Arwernis," he introduces himself. By the movement of his shadow I guess he's bowing. "I am – or, was – a courier in the employ of Seronatus, *Praefect* of Gaul. Before the Bacauds captured me on my way up the Liger."

Arwernis. Where have I heard of this place before?

"A messenger – to whom?" asks Ursula.

A chuckle. "To Odowakr, the warchief of the Saxons."

"Odowakr?" I cry out. "Odowakr leads the Saxon pirates?"

"You know him?"

[212]

"I —" I hesitate. "I've met him once. What messages did he exchange with this… Seronatus?"

Megethius retreats under the wall. "I'm sorry, these are confidential matters between my master and the Saxon warchief."

I scoff. "Look around you. We're set to rot in this prison for Lord knows how long. What point is there in secrets?"

"I may not ever leave this place, but something tells me you will," says Megethius. "Besides, I don't know much myself. I only carried sealed letters."

"Did Airmanarik see those letters?" asks Eishild.

The courier sighs. "He took all my saddlebags, but whether he cared to read them – I couldn't tell you."

I look to the shadow by the door, where Ursula sits. "I wonder if he read something in them that gave him confidence his plans will succeed?"

"What does it matter?" I hear her shrug. "Right now we have to worry about getting out of here. We don't know how long they're going to keep us here – or what they're going to do to our men out there."

"We'll think of something," I assure her. "For now, we should try to rest. Things always look brighter in the morning."

"How will we even know when it's morning?" Ursula asks gloomily.

The Crown of the Iutes

A guilty looking Adalfuns, accompanied by two armed guards, who remain watchful in the door, visits us the next day.

"Are you harmed?" he asks.

"We are fine – for now," replies Eishild coolly.

"My apologies, Princess. I had no idea Airmanarik would do this. I don't know what he wants from you – but I know he won't dare hurt Thaurismod's daughter."

"It's pretty clear what he wants," I say. "He wants Eishild to give her blessing to his march on Tolosa. Which is clearly never going to happen."

"I wouldn't be so sure," says Eishild. "I may be left with no choice – what if he threatens you or Ursula?"

"We'll be fine," says Ursula. "Don't worry about us. This isn't the first time we've been captured."

"If there's anything I can do to ease your time here…" says Adalfuns. "I was told I'm allowed to treat you as guests, rather than prisoners."

He nods at the guards. One of them presents a tray of food – the same bowls of porridge and chunks of dark bread as yesterday. I give my portion to Megethius, who devours it eagerly.

"We need beddings," I say. "And light. And clean water."

"Of course. I'll get right on it."

"There is something else I need you to do," says Eishild.

"Anything in my power, Princess."

She steps closer to him. The guards grunt, nervously, and lower their spears at us.

"There are some letters in Airmanarik's possession," she whispers. "Sent by Odowakr, warchief of the Saxons. This man was carrying them," she adds, nodding towards Megethius. "Can you get them for us?"

Adalfuns clears his throat nervously. "I – I will do what I can, *fraujo*."

She lays a hand on his shoulder. "You were one of my father's *Gardingi*. His bravest warriors. I know there is valour in your heart greater than in Airmanarik's. I know I can count on you."

"Yes, *fraujo*."

"What good will those letters do us?" asks Ursula when Adalfuns and the guards leave.

"I'm not sure. But I have a feeling you're right – whatever is in those letters made Airmanarik believe he could take on Aiwarik in Tolosa. When we get out of here, I need to know what we're dealing with."

"*When* we get out of here?" I ask. "You have a plan?"

"I may have." She smiles. "But I will need your help, *aetheling*. Remember how you tried to teach me fencing, back at the cathedral…?"

The Crown of the Iutes

"Trial by combat? What do you mean?" I ask.

I weigh the stick in my hand. Adalfuns brought us two of them – axe shafts, by the look of it – on Eishild's request, for us to train with as much as we can in the tight confines of the cell.

He did not, as yet, manage to provide us with the letters; Airmanarik, he tells us, keeps the courier's belongings in his own chest, as if it was some precious war plunder – thus confirming their importance.

"You Northerners wouldn't know it," Eishild explains, "but it's still common among the likes of Burgundians and Longbeards. The Goths used it too, back in the days of heathenry. Still, if Airmanarik truly believes himself a Gothic nobleman, he would not dare to decline a challenge."

"And *you* would fight him?" asks Ursula. There's a little too much mocking disbelief in her tone for Eishild's liking. The princess scoffs and lunges at me with a surprising strike, which I barely manage to parry. She slashes under my block and hits me on the knuckles. I drop the stick and rub my bruised hand.

"Madron and I have been training all spring since the siege," she says. "We've practised everything you showed us back at the cathedral."

"Airmanarik is a large man," I say. "And, I'm sure, a veteran of many duels. Even I would be wary to stand against him."

"He will never expect me to have any skill with the sword," Eishild says. "And I may be small, but I'm fast and nimble. You just have to teach me a few more tricks."

Ursula looks at me and raises her eyebrow. "The girl's almost as good at making mad plans as you once were."

"Hey!" I laugh. "I can still come up with a plan or two if need be." I pick up the stick. "How do you even know he will accept?"

"I must count on his honour as a nobleman."

I shake my head. "This will not do. I don't know many Goths, but I know noblemen – and most will only obey their honour if they have no choice." I rub my chin. "We have to force his hand."

"How would we do this?"

I grin. "That's what I'm here for."

I come up to the door and call the guard.

"What is it now," he asks wearily.

"What day is it today?"

"Sabbath – why?"

"We have been without the Eucharist for a long time," I say. "Surely you cannot deny us a Mass?"

The long silence is promising – the guard, like all the residents of the caves, is fiercely devout, and missing a Mass must, to him, be equal to the worst of tortures. I hear him walk away from the cell, no doubt to discuss my request with his superiors.

"I conveyed your plea," the guard says upon his return and then, after a pause, he adds: "I will pray that it is accepted."

"Lord bless you, good man," says Eishild, in her sweetest and most alluring voice. I can almost hear the young guard blush.

The Crown of the Iutes

It is just as Airmanarik explained when we first met him; there is no priest at this strange Mass, and the rite sounds ancient and unfamiliar to my ears, used to Fastidius's lofty prayers. It is the Goth captain himself who is the celebrant today – he reads from the Scripture, and calls us all to rise and pray, while the acolytes portion a loaf of the same dark bread we ate for our suppers, and pour wine into a dusty silver goblet.

"'Be strong and of good courage,'" Airmanarik reads from the Book of Josue. "'Be not afraid, neither be you dismayed: for the Lord your God is with you wherever you go.'"

Airmanarik looks at the congregation from under his bushy eyebrows, waiting for the meaning of the words to penetrate even into the dimmest of minds. The gathered no doubt appreciate the unusual importance of today's Mass. I don't know how many of them are familiar with the "prophecies" – but every once in a while, one of the Bacauds casts an intrigued glance back towards Eishild, standing with us at the far end of the sacred hall behind a wall of armed guards. Our legs are tied, but our arms are free so that we can raise them to the Heavens in supplication at the right time.

"'Then Josue commanded the officers of the people,'" Airmanarik continues, "'saying: Pass through the camp, and command the people. Tell them to prepare their provisions. For within three days you shall pass over Jordan, to go in to possess the land, which the Lord your God gives you to possess.'"

It doesn't take a scholar of the Scriptures to discern the meaning of Airmanarik's chosen passage. This is a call to war; he is Josue, and the River Vigenna is the Jordan, behind which lie the lands of heathens and godless heretics, ready for the taking.

The Goth is not finished yet. "'And they answered: All that you command us we will do, and wherever you send us we will go,'" he booms, then raises an accusing finger and points it to Eishild: "'And whoever rebels against your command and does not heed your words, in all that you command him, shall be put to death!'"

A confused murmur spreads throughout the congregation. They see the princess in chains and under guard, but do not yet understand the reason – nor do they grasp the source of Airmanarik's wrath. Was Eishild not foretold to lead them against the heretics? Wasn't *she* the prophesied Josue – or at least, his Rahab, sent by the Lord to assist in the conquest of her own homeland? But now, she seems to be facing an accusation of treachery and rebellion against the Lord's command …

Eishild does not stand for the accusation. She pushes herself between the warriors – one of them is the young prison guard from yesterday, and he lets her move forward so that she can speak freely.

"For her princes are like the wolves tearing the prey, to shed blood, to destroy the people, and to get dishonest gain!" she cries, quoting another verse from the Scripture. "Her prophets plastered them with whitewash, seeing false visions, and divining lies for them, saying, 'Thus says the Lord God,' when the Lord had not spoken!"

"Silence her!" Airmanarik commands. "The Snake speaks through her!"

"Commander," the young guard opposes, "she merely recites the Lord's words."

"Seize him, too!" Airmanarik orders the other guards, but they all hesitate, waiting for Eishild to finish her outburst.

The Crown of the Iutes

"I am no snake," says the princess. "It is you who lies to your people and conceals from them the truth. Why didn't you show your men the letters from the Saxon warchief? Why didn't you share with them what I told you about the plans of Gauls and Romans?"

"More lies," Airmanarik seethes.

"There is a simple way to prove which one of us is lying and which one is telling the truth."

The Goth scoffs. "And what would that be?"

"Fight me. In the old way. The Lord will decide."

Airmanarik laughs. "I would crush you like an insect, little one."

"As Goliath said to David," I say to a ripple of laughter. Airmanarik turns red at the mockery. The plan is working; most of the Bacauds may not be aware of the Gothic customs, but there are some fair-hairs among them who know what Eishild's challenge means. And there are enough Goths in Airmanarik's retinue to witness the stain on their commander's honour if he refuses her.

He grunts. "Very well," he says. "You *are* a Balthing, a scion of the kings. I cannot deny you a hero's death, if that is what you wish. We will speak of this later. For now, let us finish this Mass in peace." He waits for Eishild and me to return tamely behind the line of the guards, before nodding at the acolytes to bring out the bread and the wine.

"You can still change your mind," I whisper.

"Never." The princess's eyes gleam. "The Lord will send me victory, just like he sent us one at the cathedral."

It was the thickness of the cathedral's walls and Fastidius's skill in war craft that saved us in Londin, not the Lord's grace, I think at first – but then I remember the sudden onset of the plague which brought an end to the siege, and so I just nod and smile.

There's only one place suitable for a duel to the death in Caino. It can't be anywhere near the caves – the ground around Maximus's tomb is too sacred for this sort of pagan ritual, so all the participants and observers of the contest board the flat-bottomed boat, which takes us to the green island in the middle of the Vigenna.

There are just over twenty of us gathered on the muddy meadow: Adalfuns and Airmanarik with their retinues, two Bacaud elders chosen to ensure justice and honour of the entire congregation, which hinges on their chief commander remaining honest and truthful, is preserved – and six more armed guards, two of each assigned to Eishild, Ursula and myself.

Greater crowd has gathered on the northern shore of the river, at the foot and on top of the grey cliff, watching us as if we were gladiators in an amphitheatre. Unlike an audience in an amphitheatre, however, they remain mostly silent and uneasy; nobody dares to cheer for the princess while Airmanarik remains the captain of the rebel warband – and, it would seem, few are keen to support him against the daughter of Thaurismod, whose arrival they've all been awaiting so eagerly.

After the two combatants stand in a circle of rope laid out on the grass, Airmanarik removes his tunic. He's oiled and glistening underneath, the muscles dancing on his chest. The sight is clearly supposed to intimidate the frail princess. As is the choice of arms. He unbuckles his sword belt and instead reaches for a great, two-handed axe. It is a slow, heavy weapon, and one that exposes him to swift jabs from Eishild's blade – but wielding it shows he's not afraid of any harm the girl might bring him.

"He could cleave you in two with one blow of that axe," I say, giving the princess my own sword – the light, narrow cavalry *spatha*.

"He'll have to find me first."

"Be careful," says Ursula, eyeing Airmanarik's thick, rippling muscles. "You'll need to cut him more than once to fell him."

"Once should be enough," I say, "if you hit the right spot."

"Once *will* be enough," Eishild agrees, weighing the sword in her hand and throwing it from side to side. She ties her hair with a headband, and rolls up her breeches over her knees, before stepping into the rope.

"Do you not wish to yield, girl?" Airmanarik asks, dragging the axe blade in the mud. "It is a shame to waste a life so young."

"Do *you*?" Eishild asks back, and leaps forth, with the same speed and agility she showed in training. The ferocity of the attack surprises Airmanarik and he lets the *spatha*'s blade cut his left arm. He swings the axe; it cleaves the air inches from Eishild's chest. She leaps back, throws the sword to her left hand and lunges again, with an upwards slash. She almost cuts him again, but this time Airmanarik reacts swiftly enough and leans away just in time.

They exchange a few more blows, each too weak and slow to cause any harm, and then both pull back and stride along the arena's edge, measuring each other's mettle. Eishild dances, skipping from left foot to right. Airmanarik huffs, catching his breath. I can tell now that his muscles are more for show than for fighting. He is a big man, but he's in bad shape. Still, all he needs is one fortunate blow…

He lifts the axe and whirls it over his head, then, with a roar, brings it down on Eishild, weaving it up and down in a figure of eight, drawing a deep scar in the mud each time the weapon lands in the dirt. Eishild leaps back, and to the sides, dodging, ducking and skipping. She makes no effort to counter-attack – it's too dangerous, with the great blade swinging so close. She waits for Airmanarik to grow weary of this exercise – or make a mistake.

The Goth commander slashes the air one last time. The princess skips back, and feigns a stumble, supporting herself on her left hand. I'm the only one who spots her picking up a handful of gravel. Airmanarik steps away and goads the princess to make her move, with a beckoning gesture and some Gothic slurs I don't understand. Eishild glances to me. I nod.

"Now," I whisper, wordlessly.

The princess raises the *spatha* overhead for a great blow. Airmanarik grins, knowing where the sword will fall from how Eishild turns her body and leans onto her left leg for support. He raises his axe with deliberate slowness. Eishild slashes downwards – but before her weapon strikes the shaft of Airmanarik's axe, she moves up her right leg, throws the gravel in Airmanarik's face, shifts the sword to her, now empty, left hand, and shoots forward and down, right under the Goth's blind parry, the thrust of her sword digging deep into Airmanarik's thigh.

She jumps back to avoid the falling axe. Airmanarik, still propelled by momentum, steps forward and lands on his injured leg. With a cry, he collapses; the shaft of his axe stops him from falling face-first into the mud. Eishild kicks the axe away from him and puts the blade of her sword to his neck.

"Do you yield *now*, Airmanarik?" she asks, breathless from exhaustion.

The Crown of the Iutes

He grunts, pushes the sword away and staggers up. The wound on his thigh spouts blood in great spurts. He grows pale and points to his guards – not at Eishild, but at me.

"A heathen ploy!" he roars. "They're not Christian at all – they're all heathens from the North. Or will you deny it? Your men told me all!"

"If you brought harm to any of my warriors, I swear –" I step forward, but Airmanarik's guards grasp my arms and pull back. They do the same to Ursula; others stand in front of Adalfuns and the Elders, spears drawn. As the two bands of guards face off, Eishild raises her sword – not for a blow, but in prayer.

"It's no ploy," she says. "I beat you fair. The Lord led my arm, like he did David's in the Valley of Elah. You're bleeding out. If you don't take care of that wound, you'll be dead before you reach the shore."

"The Lord will give me strength," Airmanarik replies with effort. "And he will smite you like he smote the Amalekites." He struggles to raise the axe again.

Just then, I hear a thunderous splash on the southern shore of Vigenna. I twist my neck to see them: twenty warhorses and thirty moor ponies storming over the shallow water, crimson cloaks and bear-skins fluttering in the spray, and leading them all in the charge, with a lance raised forward in his left hand, his helmet gleaming in the sun – Drustan.

"The *equites* are coming!" I cry.

"Octa – catch!" Eishild throws the sword back to me as the guards are distracted by the sudden assault. I catch it and in one neat move slice through the back of the guard holding Ursula. She tears herself from his grasp, draws a knife from the guard's sheath and thrusts it in his chest.

A thrown lance pierces another of Airmanarik's men. I swirl and cut down the third one. Adalfuns rushes to Airmanarik, while his warriors rush at the enemy. The two Goths grapple. Adalfuns overcomes the wounded commander and throws him to the ground.

Drustan's mount climbs the muddy shore and reaches us in a couple of leaps. Airmanarik's men drop their weapons and run for the river.

"Look out," I shout to Drustan, seeing his *equites* launching into pursuit after the Goths. "The river is deeper on the other side!"

The Dumnonian halts his men, dismounts and rushes to Eishild's embrace.

"My love – are you alright?"

"I'm fine," the princess replies. "You came just in time."

"As always," I say, approaching them. "I've lost count of how many times our lives were saved by the Dumnonian cavalry."

Drustan looks around at the defeated guards, at the two confused, frightened elders, and at the two Goths, still tussling in the mud, and scratches his head under the helmet.

"What, on Lord's Sacred Wounds, is going on here?"

The Crown of the Iutes

CHAPTER XII
THE LAY OF ODOWAKR

"You're now the leader of the Bacauds, Eishild," I note, amused. "A Queen in the Marshes. What are you going to do with all that power?"

She stays serious despite my jests. "Those who wish to continue in peaceful worship can stay in the caves. I'm sure not even Aiwarik will dare to defile this holy ground with the blood of the innocent faithful. Others will have to disperse and go into hiding until another time."

"They're bandits," says Drustan with scorn that makes our host, Adalfuns, wince. "Rudderless, they will only return to their bloody ways, plundering the farmsteads and threatening travellers on the highways. Sooner or later, they will bring Aiwarik's wrath on this place."

"You do them injustice, Drustan," I say. "These are not the same ruthless rebels you and I fought in Armorica. They are disciplined, and trained by Gothic and Taifal officers."

Eishild throws up her hands. "Then what would you have me do with them?"

"That depends on what's in those letters," I say, reaching for the bundle of scrolls taken from Airmanarik's war chest.

The Goth survived the duel – his constitution proved stronger than anyone expected, and he shrugged off the injury within a day, Eishild's cut leaving him only with a slight limp. The Bacauds were always famous – or infamous, to their enemies – for the way they

The Crown of the Iutes

fought fiercely until they could no longer stand, despite wounds and weariness. Perhaps their faith really did grant them the power to heal themselves faster – or at least, ignore the pain, the way henbane did for the Iute warriors.

Humiliated by his loss, Airmanarik retreated to his cave dwelling, where we put him under guard of the *equites*. We're under no illusions that this is the end of his power over the Bacauds; a man of his stature and influence must still have many followers among the bandits, who will flock back to him as soon as he calls on them.

Ursula and I unroll the scrolls one by one, to check which ones were brought by Megethius. With the Caino camp set up so close to the main trade routes of northern Gaul, and his men roaming freely in the wilderness from Turonum to Pictawis, Airmanarik found himself in possession of many such missives. But most of them were trifle matters: secret messages from noblemen to their mistresses; urgent dispatches from wealthy merchants to their creditors; tedious stories of everyday life exchanged between what few Roman men of letters remained in Gaulish cities. The really valuable information – spy reports, orders, military assignments – was sent by armed couriers, who knew how to avoid bandit ambushes. Capturing Megethius, with his precious load, was a singular stroke of fortune.

"It's here," says Ursula. She holds two densely written scrolls in her hand. I've never seen Odowakr's writing before – didn't even know he *could* write. The letters are rough, broad and hasty, but skilled, with only a few errors in the Imperial Latin.

"I never took Odowakr for a man of learning," I say.

"Maybe he dictated it to someone," says Ursula.

"The writing's too uneven for a secretary." I stretch out the scroll. "Let's see what was so important about this letter."

The missive is addressed directly to Seronatus, whom Odowakr titles not just as *Praefect* of Gaul, but as its *Magister Militum*, with his seat in Arwernis. I remember now where I have heard this name before: it was when Riotham was taking his cohorts to meet with the Imperial Army – or so he believed…

"…the trap is all but set," Odowakr writes confidently. "Paulus is stuck in Andecawa, waiting for enough reinforcements to strike at my harbours. I pray you ensured they will not arrive. I am poised to launch my ships when he least expects it. We passed Namnetes already. All I need is the promised provisions and weapons from the Arwernian forges – you will find the list of requirements on the separate sheet."

I glance at the second scroll – it is a long and detailed inventory of anything an invading army might need; I hand it over to Drustan.

"Can you tell how large a force this could supply?"

"I'll try – but I don't know about Saxon ways of war…"

"If he runs his army the way he writes his letters, it will be more a Legion than a barbarian warband," I say, and return to Odowakr's letter.

"…as agreed, I'm waiting for you to confirm that you and Aiwarik have caught Riotham in your snares. But I will not wait forever. I have, as you know, made the same mistake with your predecessor, and my patience grows short. If I do not hear back from you before Ides of August, I march on Andecawa and take it for myself, our deal with Aiwarik be damned. Time is precious. My spies report that Hildrik's not ready to campaign this year. Syagrius is a weakling, too reliant on his allies, who I'm certain will betray him as soon as they smell blood – and as you inform me, there's no love between him and Paulus, so they're unlikely to join forces. Black crows are already circling his domain. You can either be there for

The Crown of the Iutes

the feast, or watch from a safe distance as we tear into the dying corpse, knowing that you will be next. The choice is yours, Roman."

I look up sharply from the note.

"Bad news?" asks Ursula.

"Just as I feared, Riotham is marching straight into Aiwarik's trap."

"It's too late to warn him."

"It's not Riotham I'm worried about. Whatever happens to him, he brought on himself. What day is it today? By Roman reckoning."

"Seventh of August," replies Drustan. "Why?"

"See for yourself." I give him the letter and rub my eyes, weary from deciphering Odowakr's letters. "I sent Seawine's Iutes to Andecawa, thinking they'd be safer there, and now... We don't have much time."

"Namnetes is on the Armorican side," Drustan says, turning pale. "I must ride back to Marcus. If the border cities are in danger, he will need all his *equites*."

"I'm coming with you!" says Eishild, reading Odowakr's letter over Drustan's shoulder.

"I'd rather you didn't," I say.

"What do you mean?"

"You have here what amounts to more than a cohort of good warriors, Goth and Taifal riders among them. They all now believe you came to lead them against the heathens and heretics. And what are Saxons if not a heathen scourge?"

I look to Adalfuns and he nods in agreement. "Many of us fled from the pirate menace. They would gladly take revenge, if they had a chance."

"If we strike fast, we will have surprise on our side," I add. "Odowakr doesn't expect anyone except Paulus to stand against him."

"How far is it to Andecawa?" asks Ursula, who by now has also familiarised herself with the content of Odowakr's message.

"Depends on the route," says Drustan. "The quickest would be through Turonum, but…"

"But the Gauls would not just let a warband of Bacauds march through their city," I say, nodding. "Even if they all claim to be followers of Martinus. By the time we had explained ourselves, it would be too late."

"There is another way," says Adalfuns. "Across the marshes on Liger's southern bank. It's how the Roman courier got here. If the roads are still good, it would only take three days at a soldier's pace."

"It's better to assume they aren't," I say. "We should march out as soon as possible, even if it means we can't gather all the Bacauds in time."

"If time is of such essence, we may need to get Airmanarik out of his cave and convince him to work with us," says Ursula. "Eishild may be the one the Bacauds want to follow, but he's the one who knows how to organise them into an army."

The Crown of the Iutes

I nod. "I fear so, too. But it may be easier to convince him than you think. After all, he'll get to lead his men into the just war he so prayed for."

"We should reach the village of the ferrymen today, if our directions are accurate," I say. Our ponies wade wearily across another flooded marshland. Once there was a road here, judging by the tops of milestones peeking above muddy water, but in the devastation of the ages past, the dykes, canals and other waterworks that once hemmed the mighty Liger in its valley had all but perished, and now the river spews as far and wide as the flat plain allows, swallowing new swathes of land with each spring thaw and summer rain.

The flooding meant that we had to pass some of the earlier crossings over the Liger – the fords swelled, and the ruined bridges crumbled under the pressure of current. We are now heading towards the last of the points marked by Megethius on my crudely drawn map. We are already near Andecawa – indeed, we seem to have passed it by some time ago; the city itself lies beyond the confluence of Liger and another, smaller, river to the north-east of where we are now. According to the notes the courier left us, a handful of fishermen dwells at the southern end of the confluence, supplementing their meagre income by ferrying occasional travellers on their flat-bottomed boats across both rivers.

We are alone again now, just me, Ursula, and my bear-shirts. Drustan and his *equites* galloped at great speed back to Armorica, by the short way of Turonum. Eishild remained at Caino, to prepare the Bacaud warband which she – or rather, Airmanarik, under her orders – would lead to Paulus's help. While all that happened, it was up to us to patrol the road ahead and, if possible, try to reach Andecawa before the pirates, to warn Paulus; though first, we have to discover the exact manner of Odowakr's trap…

I could not believe that we would be facing the dreaded warchief again. Ten years have passed since I last saw him, after helping defeat his siege of Trever. He did warn us back then that one day he would return – but I never expected the once-great general to return as a mere pirate captain!

"Something's strange about it all," I murmur to myself.

"What is it?" asks Ursula.

"How can a band of pirates even consider capturing an entire walled city, manned by Paulus's legionnaires? We fought them back so many times in Cantia. The Picts were more of a threat than those Saxons."

"The ones who sailed to Britannia must have been only raiding parties. Foragers for the greater force. Didn't Odowakr claim in his letter he already passed one fortress along the river?"

"Namnetes." I nod. "But we don't know if he took it, or just sailed past. Andecawa is supposed to be a strong fortress – wait. Do you see that?"

I raise my hand and the riders behind me stop. A pillar of thick, black smoke rises over the tree line on the horizon, some three miles ahead.

"That's where the ferry is supposed to be!" I exclaim. "To arms, Iutes! If we hurry, there may still be some villagers left to save!"

I spot a watchman on top of the wooded dune, and cut him down before he can cry for help. Moments later, we charge out onto a broad strip of sand and mud, with the remains of a few smouldering huts to our left and right, and bodies of the fishermen scattered between them. In the middle of this destruction, dragged out onto the beach, lie four ships: medium-sized Saxon *ceols*. I know this type well – I helped sink many of them over the past few summers. Some distance beyond them, in the current, I spot the hacked and charred remains of the ferry, slowly sinking in the calm waves.

The Saxons are here, too; we catch them setting up camp amid the ruined huts. Stacks of sharpened stakes pile around the perimeter, waiting to be turned into a palisade, but there are no fortifications around the tents yet. The surprise is complete.

"Bear-shirts!" some of the pirates cry in shock, recognising us from their raids on Cantia. "Why are the bear-shirts *here*?"

At first we storm through the camp with little resistance, our lances flying left and right, stabbing and slashing, slaying anyone unfortunate enough to get in our way. But four *ceols* carry many warriors – twenty or thirty men each – and as more pirates pour out of their ships, I bid my men turn around and regroup on the mud plain south of the village.

"Audulf!" I cry. "Take Ubba and Deora around them, ride a shield! I'll punch from this side."

Audulf nods. The three "blades" under his command ride out in a long column, turn in a sweeping crescent to the north of the ruined huts, and back towards the ships. As the Saxon warriors turn to face the threat, I form my riders into a sharp, thin sword blade, with Croha and Eolh to our sides. We skirt the edge of the water, the hooves splashing in the wet mud, and slip between the camp and the ships, splitting the warriors already on land from those still leaping off the decks.

James Calbraith

As I watch my men perform these complex manoeuvres, I feel a swelling pride. I know there are few cavalry formations left in Gaul who know how to ride like this – and none, perhaps, in Britannia, now that Marcus's *equites* have moved with him to Armorica. Years of training these men using old Roman manuals, followed by years of sending them off to fight Alemannic hordes or Saxon warbands in Frankia to gain valuable experience, helped forge my bear-shirts into a small but exceptionally cohesive armoured fist, able to break through all but the finest enemy defences.

"Shield wall!" cries Croha, pointing to my left. Somehow, in the chaos, a dozen Saxons managed to line up in a semi-circle, their backs to the river, with their shields raised and spears thrusting outward; but they're too few, and they can't catch their footing in the slippery sand.

"Not yet," I reply. We swerve towards them. I take Croha and Ursula – our ponies are the tallest – and we wade around the rear of the Saxon line, in chest-deep water, while the rest of my wedge strikes from the flank. It's not a comfortable place to fight; as I thrust at the first Saxon, the wet shaft of my lance slips from my hand and splashes into the river. I draw the sword and slash another enemy on the shoulder. The Saxons in the wall fight well, but they are too few and their feet have no purchase in the soft mud; the line breaks and they're scattered into the waves.

More pockets of resistance form on the flood plain. The battle now enters the final phase, and one that I'm always the least fond of: the long, gruelling single combat, charging and breaking off, riders chasing after fleeing footmen, spearmen seeking ponies' flanks, *spathas* crashing against shields. And although our victory is all but certain – more than half the pirates painted the mud grey with their blood – this is when the fight is at its most dangerous; in the desperate chaos, a stray spear thrust or an axe glance can bring a swift and unexpected death. I tug the reins just as my pony is about to smash into a suddenly emerging spearman. Croha rides past us and thrusts her lance in her back. I nod at her with a grateful smile, and then glance around the battlefield to assess the situation.

I notice that the surviving Saxons are all slowly moving towards one of the four *ceols*, a ship with a black sail rolled up on its single mast. Those who are already there have formed themselves into a crescent, defending the vessel from the riders, while its crew pushes it off the beach back into the current. In their hurry, they forgot to throw off the gangway – the plank drags a deep line in the mud.

I reach for the horn and blow an alert.

"Audulf! Ursula!" I call over the din of battle, and point to the black-sailed ship.

"I see it!" Audulf cries back. Ursula only nods. Together, we gather as many Iutes as can break away from the fight. We form a new wedge, broad and shallow this time, with Audulf and Croha's detachments on its point, and turn towards the ship and its defenders.

"Careful," I tell Croha. "This mud is treacherous."

She nods, before feinting a charge straight at the side of the crescent of spearmen. A few Saxons turn their weapons towards her shieldmaidens in a reflex – revealing their flank to me and Audulf. Croha swerves aside, while I smash into the first of the pirates. The impact throws me from the saddle and I land head-first in the water; Audulf and his pony slip and fall next to me – but it's enough to make a gap in the Saxon line between which the rest of the riders push through.

Ursula is the first to storm up the plank, the hooves of her pony sliding dangerously on the wet board. Three more riders join her – Deora is one of them; I can't see the other two through the spray in my eyes. There's no space on deck for more ponies, and there's no need for more. The Saxon crewmen leap into the river, fearful of the rampaging beasts. For a moment, I must focus on my own survival, as several pirates surround Audulf and me in the knee-deep current, and I lose sight of what's happening on the black-sailed ship. It takes all my strength and attention merely to block, parry and dodge oncoming blows – there are too many of them for me to think of countering. Audulf at my side is more fortunate; he manages to grasp an axe falling on his head with his left hand, twist it out of the enemy's hand and strike him back on the forearm. I spin and stab the wounded Saxon in the gut, but I pay dearly for the momentary distraction. Another warrior's powerful kick in the stomach tosses me into the water. I emerge gasping and spluttering, and see an iron-studded club heading straight for my face. I duck at the last moment; the club grazes my brow. Lightning flashes in my right eye – and a sound of horns blasts in my ear. I slash my sword, blindly, and hit only air. The sound of horns repeats.

I rub water from my eyes and look around. The horns blow for the third time, and this time, I'm certain – the sound is real, and coming from the deck of the black-sail ship. All around me, the surviving Saxons drop their weapons in surrender. I shove my way through them to see what's going on. There are only three ponies left on the deck – the fourth lies dead in the water, crushing its rider with its body; but Deora, Ursula and the third Iute – one of Croha's shieldmaidens – are still alive; Ursula stands dismounted, surrounded by the Saxon crew, who all hold their hands in the air, their weapons at their feet. I leap on deck and push the pirates out of my way to see the cause of the sudden capitulation.

Kneeling before Ursula, hands behind his head and the blade of her sword at his neck, is a dark-haired, dark-eyed man, staring defiantly at his captors. I recognise him in an instant as Odowakr the Skir, son of Edeko.

The Crown of the Iutes

Whenever I pass Odowakr, he bursts out laughing and shakes his head in disbelief. It's no different this time – but this time, I'm here to talk to him at last, having finally dealt with our casualties and the Saxon prisoners.

I sit next to him on one of the palisade logs. He licks his parched lips. I hand him a water flask.

"What is so amusing?"

He didn't recognise me at first – we've only met once in the flesh, and I gave him a different name then – but he knew who I was after I introduced myself; though the force I brought into the siege of Trever was insignificant compared to the great armies that clashed there, my Iutes and I have made enough of an impression for him to remember us even a decade after his defeat.

"Why haven't you tied me up?" he replies with a question.

I shrug. "What's the point? Your only way out of here is across the river – and this place is the last good crossing for days. Or would you care to brave the marshes, full of Bacaud marauders?"

"And what about my men?"

"Those who suffered light or no injuries, I put into the hold of your ship. I haven't yet figured out what to do with them next. Others, I had to take out of their misery. I only have enough herbs and ointments for my own men."

"I understand." He nods. "You've done more than I would have in your place. Have you found Christ since we last fought, Iute?"

"I'm neither a Christian nor a heathen, Saxon…" I say, waiting for him to finish drinking. "Or should I call you a Skir?"

"You remembered. I'm touched." He chuckles, and then shrugs. "Who knows *what* I am… My father is a Skir, as is my brother – but my mother was a Hunnish wench… I've spent all my life wandering from one tribe to another, in whatever army asked for my services. I was called a Saxon, an Alamann, a Herul, a Thuringian…"

"A Roman?"

He looks up. "How do you know?"

"I saw your handwriting. You've had Roman education."

He raises an eyebrow. "My handwriting? Ah, you must have intercepted one of the couriers…" He chuckles again and leans back, putting his hands behind his head. "I was a hostage as a youth. In the East, where my homeland is. I know how to write Greek, too." He stares at me for a moment. "I see it now. This is why we are so alike. You, too, were raised among the Romans. Is this why we keep stumbling upon each other like this, friend?"

"This is only the second time I have met you." I scowl.

"Ah, but you're a Iute from a distant, misty island, and I'm a Skir from the grass seas of Pannonia, far beyond Rhenum. We shouldn't have even met *once*. And yet, here you are, meddling in my plans once again. I don't know what gods you *do* believe in, fair-hair, but you must appreciate the intricate game they're playing with our lives."

"Is this what makes you laugh? The thought of us being mere playthings of Fate?"

"How could it not? Clearly, whoever holds the threads of the universe together intended for us to meet here. Why else would

The Crown of the Iutes

you have come to *this* place, *today*? What are you even doing here, Iute?"

"Don't act so surprised. I know you're aware of the Briton army which landed in Gaul a few weeks ago."

He nods. "Of course. And my spies even told me they saw you with them. But I expected you to march with Riotham to Arwernis."

"Right into your trap."

"Not mine. It's all been settled between Aiwarik and the Arwernians. They want to divide Gaul between themselves and their allies. I only found out about the plan after I was sent here, and decided to tear myself a slice of the honey cake they're baking."

"*Sent* here? By whom?"

He laughs. "You haven't searched the chests on my ship, yet, then."

"I was busy burying my men. And yours."

"I understand. But why don't you go see what's in them, first? Then everything will become clearer."

"You could just tell me."

"Ah, but where's the fun in that?" He scoffs. "Are you in a hurry somewhere?"

"You know I am. I have to warn Andecawa about your coming."

"Paulus is not a fool. He already knows we're here. And it's too late to stop us, anyway. My fleet will be here tomorrow."

"Without their warchief."

"My officers know how to follow the orders without me nursing them."

I stand up, noticing Ursula on the deck of Odowakr's ship, calling me and waving something in her hand.

"Do your officers not know how to build a palisade?" I ask, wiping my arse from dust. "Why did *you* come here yourself, to this insignificant village? Why risk everything like this?"

"We heard of an army of Bacauds marching this way. I know how fiercely they fight – I needed this crossing secure." He scratches his cheek. "Turns out, it was just a band of Iutes. My spies are not always completely accurate."

"Your spies were right," I tell him. "The Bacauds *are* coming. We are merely their vanguard."

His eyes widen, and he laughs again. "You are full of surprises today, Iute!"

On my way to the ship I pass a makeshift table heaped with food laid out for my hungry men – from our own provisions and from what we found in the camp – and pick up a damp bread roll and a dried Saxon sausage before leaping onto the deck of Odowakr's black-sail vessel.

The Crown of the Iutes

"You'll want to see these," says Ursula, waving a couple of sheets of parchment in her hand. "We found them –"

"– in Odowakr's chests," I say. I bite the sausage and smack a midge on my neck. "More letters from his co-conspirators in Arwernis?"

"Something more interesting than that," she says and hands me the first parchment. I examine the broken seal. It shows a bust of a man in profile, wearing a pearly diadem and armour, with the legend *THEODOSIVS PF AVG* around it.

"*Avgvstvs,*" I decipher. "This is an Imperial Seal!"

"I thought so, too."

I read on. The missive is not a recent one – the parchment is yellowing on the edges. It is a letter of praise for valour, addressed to a certain Odowakr, son of Edeko – a centurion on the Moesian border.

"He was in Rome in his youth." I nod. "He told me about this."

"Not just in his youth," she says, presenting me with the second parchment. This one bears the name of Anthemius on the seal: the current Imperator.

"So that's it…" I murmur. "He said someone *sent* him here, to command the pirates. He meant the Imperator himself!"

I take another bite of the sausage and wipe the fat dripping from my mouth. "Come with me," I say. "Odowakr will have a fascinating story to tell us."

She holds my hand. "Shouldn't we hurry on to Andecawa? We've wasted enough time here."

"The main Saxon fleet will be here by tomorrow," I say. "If we go to Andecawa now, we'll just be trapped within its walls with everyone else."

"Then you'd just abandon Paulus and his soldiers to these barbarians?"

"Not at all." I shake my head. "But we can achieve more from outside. Just like in Trever. Just like in Armorica. I'll think of some way to stop the pirates – but first, I want Odowakr to explain these to me," I say. I shake the parchments, then roll up them up and shove into my sword belt.

"Yes, I act on the Imperator's orders," Odowakr admits when we confront him with the letters. "Strictly speaking, it is you and your allies who are the traitors to the Empire, not us."

"How?" Ursula asks, astonished. "And… why?"

He stands up and asks us to follow him into the river. He removes the torn tunic, revealing a back of scars and bruises, then splashes the cold water all over his face and chest, at last washing off the dried blood of the battle.

"The world is more complex than you imagine, Iute," he says, rubbing water out of his eyes and blinking. "And it changes faster than any of us can keep up. Romans, barbarians, Imperators, chieftains… These are just words. None of it means anything anymore."

The Crown of the Iutes

"Your words don't mean anything, either," I say. "Speak clearly, or don't speak at all."

He chuckles. "Very well. Let me tell you a story of how Rome has been dealing with her enemies ever since she's grown too weak to simply beat them into submission."

He puts the tunic back on, and we return to the camp. I ask Deora to bring us something to drink from Odowakr's ship. "See if you can find some wine. His tastes would've grown more refined in Rome's service."

"So I'm guessing after Trever you decided to march for Rome," I say when we sit down. "*Dux* Arbogast thought you might."

"Not at first," says Odowakr. "My star darkened after that battle, and it took me years to repair my reputation as a warchief. My younger brother took over the command of my father's armies, and I was all but banished from my homeland while they fought the Goths... I will not bore you with the stories of how I prevailed, suffice it to say, after many tribulations, I gathered a great band of Skirs and Heruls, and crossed into Italia. At that time there was no Imperator to stand against us, and the Vandals were ravaging the country as they pleased."

"I heard about this – it was three or four years ago," says Ursula. "But I haven't heard about you."

Odowakr nods, and sighs. "I was a hasty fool. I thought Italia was like Gaul or Germania, a ruined country of tired slaves and idle landowners, only with more plunder... But it is like another world, even in its diminished state." His eyes turn misty at the memory, as if he was describing a former lover. "We were like flies on an ox's back. A barely noticed annoyance. When the Romans finally came to deal with us, they wiped us out in a single battle."

He falls silent and grim, remembering what must have been to him a terrible disaster. How many men did he lose that day? Thousands, if his army matched what he brought to Trever…

Deora returns with a flask, stamped with the mark of the Augustodunum vineyards. Odowakr raises his head. "I was keeping this one for the victory feast," he says.

"This *is* a victory feast," I say, pouring the wine into cups. "Just not yours. What happened after the battle with the Romans?"

I raise the cup to my nose. The wine smells of wild cherries and a sweaty saddle.

"We fled beyond the River Sontius when the night fell," Odowakr continues. He sips the wine and closes his eyes, savouring the aroma for a while. "I thought these were my last moments. We had nowhere else to go – another cohort landed at our rear… But Fortune blessed me one more time. Instead of an army, a messenger arrived at our camp with a chest of silver, offering to hire me and what remained of my men into a Roman Legion. Someone noticed how well I commanded the troops in battle, even in the midst of the defeat."

"The Imperator?" I ask.

"Someone much more powerful," replies Odowakr. "His name is Ricimer, the *Magister Militum* of all the West – like Aetius before him. He is the true power in Rome. He ruled in the Imperator's place when there wasn't one, and now he rules in the Imperator's name."

"Then it was he who sent you here," I guess. "But why?"

"To bring a rebellious province to the fold!" Odowakr says, laughing. "Unlike Aiwarik, always a loyal servant of Rome, at least

The Crown of the Iutes

on paper, Aegidius resisted Ricimer's rise to power, and plotted with the Vandals against him – and now his son refuses to even acknowledge the new Imperator. I was tasked with weakening Syagrius's western flank and taking a bite out of his armies, before Ricimer launches the campaign against the mutinous *Magister*." He looks at me with a wry smile. "As you can see, Iute, you've chosen the wrong side in this war."

"I chose the side of my friends and my father's allies," I tell him. "It's the Franks and the Armoricans that I'm here to support, not Patrician Syagrius – and I couldn't care less for Imperial politics."

Odowakr nods. "That's clever. I don't know much about Armoricans, other than how well they defend their coast, but Hildrik is shrewd – he may yet come out victorious from all of this, if he throws his lot right. You'll notice he hasn't come to Paulus's help."

"His people are still recovering from the plague," says Ursula.

"Is that what he told you?" the warchief asks mockingly.

"I still don't understand," I say. "If you were sent here as a Roman commander – then why do you lead a fleet of pirates? Why did you send your men in *ceols* to raid Britannia and Armorica – shouldn't you have a cohort of legionnaires at your command?"

Odowakr shakes his head. "It wouldn't be much of a secret mission if I marched a thousand warriors across Gaul, right under the noses of the Goths and Burgundians. When Ricimer sent me North, all I had with me was my Skir house guard and a cartful of Roman silver with which to buy the first band of Saxon mercenaries. I only plundered your coasts to gain more gold and more men – and to disguise my true purpose."

This, at least, explains why the pirates never bothered to ally with Aelle against my father. For any other pirate warlord, conquering Cantia would have been a prize worth all the blood and glory – for Odowakr, it was little more than a ruse in his ever growing plans…

"And what about the Arwernian plot?" I ask. "You said you didn't know about it until arriving here."

"I told you the truth. This is something the Arwernian magistrates concocted on their own with the Goths. They tried the same thing last year, but the plot was found out, and their magistrates were tried for treason."

"And now they're trying again – with your help," notes Ursula. "This alliance with the Goths… If it succeeds, it would be a greater blow to the Empire than Syagrius's mutiny." She rubs her forehead. "You're right, this is all too confusing. Which side are you on, really?"

Odowakr smirks. "I don't plan to be Ricimer's hound forever. I have my own future to think about."

"You're surprisingly cheerful for someone who's just been taken prisoner," I note. "I could end your future with one stroke of a sword."

"True." He nods. "And yet, here I am, still alive and well, drinking the finest wine this side of Falernus." He smiles. "You see, I can sense when death is near, Iute. It's a gift I've gained by challenging Fate a few times too many."

"And what is your gift telling you now?" asks Ursula mockingly.

He sips the last of the wine. "It's telling me I'm safer here with you than I ever was with those Saxon mercenaries."

The Crown of the Iutes

CHAPTER XIII
THE LAY OF SIGEGAUT

As the last of the *ceols* departs from the muddy beach, the captives we left on the eastern shore give us a quick lesson in Saxon curses and rude gestures.

"You'd think they'd be grateful for us sparing their lives," notes Audulf. He calls back to his kin, repeating some of their insults and adding more of his own.

"They'd rather die in battle than be freed," I say. "As would any of us."

"They will soon get a chance when the Bacauds get here."

"If they have any sense, they will disperse into the marshes long before then."

I turn away and watch the opposite shore approach swiftly. The oars of the *ceol* are in part manned by some of the pirate crewmen, who chose to join us rather than face the wrath of the Bacauds. They are mercenaries, after all, and their loyalty lies with whoever promises them greater plunder and glory – and right now, it appears Odowakr is in no shape to promise them anything anymore.

There's a village on this side, too, larger than the one on the eastern shore and intact, but empty, the fishermen having fled before Odowakr's ships. The landing beach is long and broad, more suitable to large vessels, but I order the *ceols* be anchored down in the current, in waist-deep water, rather than beached; I want them to be ready to set sail at a moment's notice.

The Crown of the Iutes

"How will the Bacauds reach us?" asks Ursula.

"They'll have to figure it out on their own," I say. "Those four boats wouldn't be enough for Eishild's entire army, anyway." I turn to Audulf. "Take your men down river as soon as they're ready. The main fleet should only be a couple of hours away. Once you're done, I want you to ride to Andecawa yourself – tell Paulus what we've learned, and tell him to be watchful. We still don't know what deceit Odowakr has prepared."

He nods and leaves to give orders to his riders. I look at the river, trying to imagine what an entire pirate fleet sailing up it might look like. The Saxon captives told us we should expect a hundred ships, but that is clearly an exaggeration; I don't expect anyone but Odowakr and his officers to know how many vessels there really are in the fleet, scattered throughout the marshy islands of the Liger Mouth, and though Odowakr was more than eager to share with us his life story and reasons for coming to Gaul, he remained tight-lipped about the details of the force sailing to take Andecawa.

"Why are we keeping him?" asks Croha, watching in disgust as Odowakr wades out onto the beach, flanked by two Iute guards. She was only a child ten years ago – she doesn't remember or care about the siege of Trever, and of Odowakr's wars in Gaul. To her, he is just the Saxon chieftain, the captain of the pirates who have been menacing Cantia's coast and who cost the lives of so many of her comrades-in-arms. "Why not just kill him?"

"He's an enemy commander," I tell her. "It is a custom. We might use him as hostage later, or exchange for ransom. I would hope he'd do the same if I were to fall into his hands."

She scoffs. "So it's one rule for soldiers, another for chieftains."

"It is how it's always been, and always will be," I reply.

Mere thirty ships. That's how many Croha reports from her patrol. Carrying maybe a thousand men altogether. A great enough number for a devastating raid — and if a warband this size ever reached Cantia, they would've overran our defences with ease — but nowhere near enough to capture a Roman fortress with Paulus's half a Legion inside, unless…

"You have another army coming by land," I guess, confronting Odowakr on the river shore. He sits cross-legged in the sand, chewing on a reed, and watching my men load up his four *ceols* with bales of hay and bundles of firewood.

"Now, what makes you say that?" he replies with a grin.

"Nobody expects a bunch of pirates to be able to take a walled port."

"And they're right. It would be foolish to try."

"You've kept them hidden all this time. Who are they? Burgundians? Alemanns?"

His grin grows wider. "How would I keep an army of Burgundians hidden for two years?"

I wipe my nose in thought. *How indeed?* Yet another mystery that will solve itself in a day or two…

I notice Ursula approach, dragging with her what looks to be one of the villagers. The poor wretch bends in a deep bow and raises his hands up in supplication.

The Crown of the Iutes

"Found a few of them hiding in the dunes," says Ursula. "We may be fortunate. He claims there's a village of pitch burners in the nearby forest. It's where the rest of the fishermen are hiding."

"Pitch?" Odowakr overhears us and rises his eyebrow. "So that's what you're doing!"

"Get as many men as you can and go find that village," I tell Ursula, ignoring the warchief. "We don't have much time. If you're not back before the Saxon fleet passes that island –" I point to a wooded spur of land some one and a half miles downstream from the beach, with ruins of some ancient temple gleaming white among the trees " – we'll have to start without you."

"Don't you dare."

"My poor ships…" muses Odowakr after Ursula departs with half a dozen riders towards the dark forest looming in the west. "Must it really end this way?"

"I lost count of how many of your *ceols* I sank at Cantia's coast," I say. "Four more won't make a difference."

He chuckles, then grows serious. For the first time, the faint smile vanishes from his lips. His eyes narrow, and his gaze grows steely. I feel a shudder run down my spine, and suddenly I understand how this unassuming warrior from the distant lands was able, time and again, to gather such great armies under his command, despite the many failed campaigns.

"You've been a thorn in my side a few times too many for my liking, Iute," he says coolly. "I know how to hold a grudge."

"Am I supposed to be afraid of *you?*"

I draw my *spatha* and put it to his neck. His stare remains cold and calm.

"Do it," he says.

"What makes you so sure I won't?"

The wry smile returns. "You and I both know you'll need me when your side loses this war. I'm your only guarantee of safe return home."

"We're not going to lose."

"If you really believe this, you'll have no problem killing me right now."

I bite my lip and press the sword to his skin, drawing a rivulet of dark blood, then mumble a curse and put the weapon back in its sheath. I summon Croha.

"Get him out of my sight," I tell her. "Make sure he doesn't talk to anyone. Not even our men. If he gives you any trouble, you have my permission to do whatever it takes to keep him silent. We may need him alive – but we don't need him unharmed."

"Yes, *aetheling*." She licks her lips. "It will be my pleasure."

The island splits the river into two streams of unequal width. The broader one is further from our shore, and it's there that the first sails of Odowakr's fleet appear. The vessels are of many types – large and small, some long and sleek, *ceols* built by the pirates themselves for use in their raids, others short and squat, galleys taken from merchants to carry troops into battle. They all struggle

The Crown of the Iutes

to row upstream – the Liger flows in a powerful current this close to the sea, and they have to be wary of the reed beds and shallows threatening their course from either side.

I can tell they're expecting trouble by how carefully they sail, in a broad column, with the sleek *ceols* in front, archers and javelin-throwers on their bows. They haven't heard from their warchief and those who came with him in days; they must suspect he's fallen into some ambush set by Andecawa's defenders. But even with Odowakr missing, the plan is too far gone to be abandoned now, and I'm sure there are enough ambitious men in the Saxon army to rejoice at the prospect of not having to share the plunder with their Skir master.

I can't see their faces, but I can imagine the relief that must show on them when the forward crews spot the four ships heading towards them at full speed, the black sails on Odowakr's vessel filled with auspicious northerly wind. I hear their hails as we approach, and whoops of joy. The warchief is safe – and all will be well. In two or three hours they will reach Andecawa, take her harbour, scale her walls and plunder, burn and ravish the city and its people for days until there is nothing left to plunder and burn, and no one left to ravish.

But the hails turn to shouts of concern and confusion as the four ships press on without any sign of slowing. At my signal, the rowers drop their oars and, one by one, leap into the river, where they wait to be picked up by the fishing boats that follow close behind us. They did what they had to do – now the Liger's current is enough to propel the *ceols* into the middle of the Saxon fleet.

"Now!" I cry and blow the aurochs horn. On each ship, the remaining Iutes put torches to the pitch-soaked bundles of hay and firewood. The flames spread in an instant, leaping from the hold to the deck, and from the deck to the sides.

"We should go," urges Ursula as the fires rage before us. I can barely see the enemy anymore through the high, bright flames, but I can hear their terrified cries as they try to turn their ships back or get them out of the way of the *ceol* missiles. In panic, they steer into the shallows, entangle them in the reeds, crash them onto the beaches. My face itches from the heat, my hands, holding the steering oar, grow sweaty.

"Not yet," I say. "I have to make sure. We only have these four…"

As the bundles burn through, they explode, sending sizzling sparks in all directions. The black sail catches ablaze and turns the mast into a giant torch, beaming dark, wet smoke high into the sky, like a blacksmith's chimney. I stare in morbid fascination at the fiery spectacle, until Ursula pulls me with her from the deck.

I hit the water just when the first of the fire ships strikes the side of the leading Saxon *ceol*, in the apocalypse of blaze, smoke and deafening noise.

I sneeze, wipe my nose and take one last glance at the river. At least a third of the Saxon ships either lies aground in the shallows and reed beds, or drifts downstream as burning, dead hulks. I don't wait to find out the full extent of the destruction wrought by our attack. In the end there's only so much damage that four ships can do to a fleet more than six times greater. As the captains scramble to salvage as many of their vessels as they can, and bring a semblance of order to their continuing plod up the Liger, I order the Iutes to mount up. Before we ride out, I tie Odowakr to the saddle behind me.

"Just put me on one of your ponies," he pleads. "I see you have some spare ones. I swear I won't be any trouble."

The Crown of the Iutes

"With your army so close?" I shake my head. "I don't think so. Just hold tight, we'll be in Andecawa in no time."

I'm worried about Audulf and the men who rode with him. It's only an hour or two on horseback to Andecawa, and even if it took them a while to reach the *Comes* and relay to him the news, they should've returned a long time ago. I trust Audulf to not have fallen into a pirate ambush – something else must've stopped him…

The reason becomes clear as soon as we reach the outskirts of the city. Andecawa itself lies across the narrow channel of the Liger's subsidiary, the name of which escapes me – spanned by a stone bridge thrown over some muddy islands, next to which lies a small harbour, cleared now of all merchant ships in expectation of the coming Saxon fleet. On the shore opposite the city, beyond a small suburb, sprawls a vast *villa*, one of the largest I've ever seen; its immense grounds are nearly the size of half the city itself. From a tall ridge marking the *villa*'s southern border we can see not only the entire riverside suburb, but also over the ramparts, and into the city below. As far as I can tell, there's no damage to the walls or the gates. A stretch of a sodden flood plain, near the bridge, is taken up by a camp of an enemy force – far too small to besiege the fortress, but large enough to stop us from breaking through.

"They can't be more than a couple of cohorts," says Ursula. "And a thousand Saxons coming on those ships, at most." She turns to Odowakr. "How do you hope to capture the city with so few men?"

The warchief scoffs but says nothing. I notice a small group of warriors on the far end of the bridge, trying to push to the city gates through a detachment of guards, but other than that, I don't see any fighting going on anywhere else around the city. Not that there's much that the enemy could achieve here. Andecawa is bound by a mighty wall, in the shape of a rough oval, with more than a dozen tall turrets, a few of them still carrying the *ballistae*, though I can't tell from this distance if they're working. It is a small city, but a magnificent fortress, an impassable barrier for anyone who'd wish to cross into Gaul this way. I see no siege machines in the camp, not even an attempt to build a battering ram of the sort I saw in Trever. A hundred soldiers could hold Andecawa's walls against this handful of men. Even if the entire pirate fleet sailed up the river now, I can't see how they could do anything to the city other than burn down its harbour, trample its fields and raze the suburbs.

"I can't see any markings or banners from here," I say. "Who *are* they?"

"Whoever they are, they're preparing for battle," notes Croha. To the sounds of trumpets and officers shouting, the warriors in the camp gather at the foot of the bridge, forming into neat squares, lining the mudded river bank in an orderly queue.

"This isn't a barbarian warband," I say. "These men were trained in Roman ways."

"Why have they marched forth now? Do you think they spotted us?"

"No," I reply. I point to the river behind us. "They spotted *that*."

Somehow, the first of the Saxon ships managed to make up for the time lost recovering from the inferno. There's no trace of a formation; instead of one mighty forest of masts, the surviving *ceols* move towards the city in piecemeal manner, in groups of two or three, the fast ones leaving the slow ones far behind. Seeing the prize so near, the captains throw all caution to the wind, as if they were afraid that the infantry will steal it from them if they don't hurry. The broad, sluggish troop carriers at the back appear the most damaged – they wouldn't have gotten out of the way of the fire ships as swiftly as the sleek warships; many must have been left behind, others limp at the back of the column, still smouldering and taking on water.

The *ballistae* on the walls turn slowly towards the approaching fleet, but even this is not enough to put fear into the pirate hearts. I can hear the twang of the powerful strings from where I'm standing; the bolts tear through sail and board alike, as if through parchment. One of the stricken *ceols* sways to port and drifts into the shore. Another halts, turns in place and starts to sink. But the others press on unperturbed. The *ballista* crews notice the slow merchant galleys at the back and shift to these easy targets. One by one, the bolts shatter the decks of the already wounded vessels. It doesn't take long before the first of the ships is sent to the bottom of the river, with water around it turning pink with the blood of the fallen pirates. The fastest of the *ceols* now come into bow range – to their doom, as Paulus's archers shower their decks with well-aimed flaming arrows.

"It's going to be a massacre," says Ursula. Again, she addresses Odowakr angrily. "What were you thinking, bringing these men here?"

"I'm surprised you care for my warriors so much," Odowakr replies. "But as much as I appreciate it, your concern is misplaced. *Vide!* Just watch."

The Saxon ships swerve and smash into the shore wherever they can; the pirates stream from their decks and hurry across the fields towards the city walls, approaching from the south and east in a haphazard manner, even as the defenders continue to pelt them with arrows, *ballista* bolts and sling shot. I still can't see a way for them to take the walls. They carry no ladders or ropes; they don't stop to shoot back at the soldiers on the ramparts.

It is only when they reach the southern gate – and the forces on the bridge finally make their way across from the west – that Odowakr's terrible plan is fully revealed. In the end, nothing we did mattered. There was no way we could've saved the city – the Skir had prepared for every eventuality, even his capture – even the loss of a fourth of his fleet did not slow down his plans.

At the blast of trumpets, both gates fly wide open – from inside. I watch with helpless despair as, with great roars, the Saxons and the mysterious army on the bridge rush into the city in unstoppable streams, like a swelling river through a broken dyke, sweeping aside what little opposition awaited them behind the walls. The treachery is as surprising as it is complete. The soldiers on the ramparts are still throwing missiles at the warriors below, even as the enemy pours down the city's streets behind their backs. The pirates immediately turn to plunder, and their advance falters as soon as they reach the houses of the wealthy near the Forum. But the foot soldiers remain disciplined, and they move in a tight column towards the *Praetorium*, where Paulus is desperately trying to mount lines of defence from the few *centuriae* he's got available inside the city.

Paulus's soldiers, realising now what has happened, make spirited attempts to break through from the ramparts back to the city centre; even with the treachery, even with the shock, the battle hangs in the balance: Paulus's men are fine warriors, and they are still equal in number to the invading force, and though they're cut off from their commanders and forced to make their way through the winding streets in small groups, they do not fall easily to Odowakr's warriors – but this only serves to prolong the city's suffering.

"We have to do something!" cries Croha.

I look to my men – their faces are grey and grim as they stare at the slaughter below.

The Crown of the Iutes

"They are too many," whispers Ursula.

"When did that ever stop us?" I reply.

I grab Odowakr and throw him off my pony. "Tie him up," I order, "make sure he stays in the mud until we return."

I draw my sword and raise it high. The Iutes welcome the sight with a proud war cry.

"Octa," Ursula says simply. There's a warning in her voice.

"Don't worry. I know what I'm doing."

"If you say so."

She spurs her pony and gallops down the slope before I can give the order. I kick my mount's sides and storm after her. I know I don't need to shout the command now, I don't even need to look over my shoulder to make sure – I know that behind me, twenty warriors, clad in gleaming mail and cloaks of bear-skin, the finest riders in Britannia, join the thunderous charge.

We smash into, and through, the enemy camp. It's emptied of all soldiers: only the guards and camp followers attempt a feeble stand, but we brush them aside like stalks of grain. I slow down only to make note of the markings on the tents, banners and discarded shields.

"Armoricans!" I call to Ursula. "They're Armoricans!"

"Impossible!" she cries back. "Marcus would never betray us."

"Not Marcus – Patrician Budic, and other old Briton nobles. Graelon's supporters. Odowakr must have promised them help in overthrowing Marcus and Ahes."

"Those bastards! They're like night bugs – what will it take to get rid of them?"

"I don't know – but we'll try to get rid of as many as we can today."

We reach the bridge. Most of the Armorican army is already inside the city, but there are still some queuing up before the gate: stragglers and marauders, cowards waiting for the fortress to fall before they get their turn at the plunder. They stand no chance against us. I order our wedge to unravel along the breadth of the Roman road – ten abreast, in three rows, with me, Ursula and Croha up front. We sweep down the bridge, our lances whirling and glinting in the sun; each enemy soldier we face stands before a blink-of-an-eye choice: to stand against the oncoming, relentless storm of mail and blade, or to leap into the river below, where there is at least a hope of survival. Most choose the latter. Those who don't, perish under our hooves.

We shatter the Armorican rear, and carve a gash through the enemy line all along the road from the bridge to Andecawa's western gate; none of my men is so much as glanced, and we must have slain at least thirty of the Armoricans in the charge – but that is as much as I dare to risk. I halt just before the gate. In a cloud of dust, the Iutes halt around me, puzzled.

"Why did we stop?" Croha asks, breathless. The right sleeve of her tunic is soaked in blood, none of it hers. "We were doing so well!"

"Out in the open field, against a bunch of cowardly stragglers. In the narrow streets, we will all perish. Trust me, a city is not the place for cavalry."

The Crown of the Iutes

"What now, then?"

I look around. Behind us, the bridge drips with the blood and guts of the fallen Armoricans. Before us, the city burns, ravaged by the combined forces of Budic's legionnaires and the Saxon pirates. But the enemy have noticed our arrival; already, the Saxons who remain in the harbour gather against us – and some of Armorican officers in the city are calling on their men to prepare the defences at their rear.

"Now, we retreat," I say.

The Iutes groan and shake their bloodied lances.

"A month ago, none of you even knew this city and its people existed," I tell them. "Now you wish to die in their defence? This isn't the last battle in this campaign. Eishild and the Bacauds are marching from the east – Marcus and Drustan ride from the west. We will beat the Saxons yet."

"What about Audulf?" asks Deora. "And Seawine and his Iutes?"

With a wince, I look back across the bridge, to the slowly approaching Saxons. They see our bear-skin cloaks, and are as puzzled by our presence as their fellow pirates were at the ferry village.

"Ursula, come with me. The rest of you, go back to the ridge and bring me Odowakr. I will get our people back," I assure them. "You have my word."

If they're still alive.

I ride slowly down the bridge, its stones still rust-red with the dried blood of those we slew in the charge. Odowakr shuffles wearily behind me, tied to the saddle of my pony; I no longer treat him with the respect I once believed he deserved. Seeing the treachery and slaughter of Andecawa hardened my heart and those of my men.

Waiting for me on the other side is the commander of the Saxon fleet, the man as responsible for the victory as Odowakr himself: Sigegaut. He alone came to meet me; Budic and his Armorican soldiers do not care for the Skir's fate, and are still busy plundering the city of all its riches, as if they themselves were the barbarians they claim to hate so much.

Behind Sigegaut and his guard, Andecawa burns. Thick pillars of black, wet smoke rise into the Heavens as if it was an offering on a heathen altar. From the city gate to the ships in the harbour, the Saxons carry off what spoils they took for themselves, carts heaped with precious goods – and, surprisingly, a couple of the *ballistae*, taken from the city walls, each riding on top of a special platform made from two flat-bed drays tied together, dragged by mules. The surviving townsfolk are being led in a long, wretched column, tied up in ropes and chains, destined for whatever distant slave markets will accept Gauls as commodity. I study the faces of the captives – marked with both the physical and emotional scars of the battle – to see if I can recognise any of them, but it seems the Saxon commander has delivered on his promise. All the surviving Iutes from Seawine's force are here, gathered in a mud field at the far end of the bridge, bound together in a small crowd; judging by how many of them bear fresh wounds, none of them shirked from the fight. Seawine is there, too, a deep, dark scar running across the left side of his face, as is Audulf, with fresh burn marks on his arm and side. Only two of his men are still with him.

I hear Odowakr chuckle. I turn back. "Shut up," I snap.

The Crown of the Iutes

"Is this what I'm worth?" he says. "Two hundred of your best warriors?"

"I don't know yet. It depends on your man over there. Sigegaut!" I call. "Come forward!"

The Saxon captain walks towards me with his right hand up to show he holds no hidden blade. I dismount and approach from the other side, and we meet in the middle of the bridge. He takes off his helmet, marked with a wild boar figurine. He's older than both me and Odowakr. A drooping moustache binds his lips, scarred from some old blow that also took out a couple of his front teeth.

"Do you understand the terms, Saxon?" I ask him.

"You hand over my warchief – I give you back your men, and we all part ways," he says, whistling through the teeth gap.

"And we are free to go about as we please."

"As long as you stay away."

"Do you give your word?"

He produces a dagger and cuts across his right hand. I extend my right hand for the cut. Our bloods mix.

"I swear on Wodan the Allfather and Donar the Thunder-wielder, I swear before Tiw the Just and Frige the Merciful," Sigegaut declares. I repeat the *ath* after him, as our mixed blood drips on the stones of the Roman bridge.

He looks over his shoulder and waves at his men to start releasing the Iutes, one by one.

"Do you know what happened to *Comes* Paulus?" I ask.

"What's it to you, Iute?"

"He was my friend."

He gives me a surprised look. "I can see about getting his body from the *wealas*, if you want to give him a good funeral."

"I would be grateful."

He summons a young warrior and whispers something in his ear. The messenger runs off towards the city.

"Your men fought well," Sigegaut says as the first of the Iutes pass us by. "But they gave up too soon. They brought you dishonour with their surrender."

"Don't talk to me about dishonour," I scoff. "You only took the city through treachery. There was no valour in dying in that fiery trap. They did what I trained them to do. There will be other battles for them, other chances to gain glory."

"Wodan sees all," says the Saxon with a grimace. "There's no place in the Mead Hall for those who fear death."

"No warrior of mine is a coward. But they all fight for something more than just a place at Wodan's Mead Hall. They fight for their king."

Sigegaut shakes his head, then nods at Odowakr. "This one talks like you."

"I know," says Odowakr. "I noticed that myself."

The Crown of the Iutes

The last two Iutes – Seawine and Audulf – shuffle past me; we nod at each other in stern silence. Odowakr raises his bound hands.

"We've kept our part of the bargain," he reminds me.

"So you did." I cut his binds with a single slash of the dagger. "Go away."

"Wait." He gestures for Sigegaut to step back. "Give us a moment," he tells the Saxon captain. "I wish to speak with Octa one last time."

"What more is there to speak about?" I ask when we're left alone.

Odowakr rubs his wrists, burning red from the rope marks.

"What will you do now?"

I look to the East, beyond Andecawa. "Now, I will wait for reinforcements and crush your little army before it can do any more damage to Gaul."

He laughs.

"Why are you doing this, Iute? Why do you care about this land and its people, when they couldn't care less about you? Go back home. Prepare for war with *Rex* Aelle. Your father needs you more than Patrician Syagrius."

I stare at him in amazement. The two of us have never spoken about Aelle before.

"Yes, I know all about what goes on in Britannia. Did you think I only sent raiders to your country? I sent spies, too. For a while, I considered joining forces with *Rex* Aelle. Cantia would have made a suitable addition to my domain, even if I could only hold some of it, and briefly."

"Why didn't you?" I ask, feeling a sudden chill, realising how close we were to being conquered, without ever knowing it.

He winces. "Aelle didn't impress me. He lacks spirit. He is a small, petty ruler, like those cousins and uncles Hildrik has to deal with in his own kingdom. All he thinks about is how to capture a few more ruined towns, how to expand his borders to the next river, how to reach the next coast… His greatest ambition is to control a slightly greater swathe of Britannia than his father did."

"And what is *your* greatest ambition?"

"Isn't it obvious?" He grins. "This is the time of great change. The world shifts around us. The Romans are retreating everywhere. The king of the Western Goths rules half of Gaul and most of Hispania. In the East, other Goths took Illyria. The Vandals remain unbeaten in Africa. The Franks hold the North. The Burgundians rule Lugdunum. Everything that was once Rome's is free for the taking."

"And you would like a slice of that honey cake yourself." I nod. "I know. You told me before."

"Not just the slice." Odowakr says. "*All* of it."

"You'd want to rule the Empire?" It is my turn to laugh mockingly.

"And why not? Right now, Ricimer, scion of the Goths and Suebians, controls Rome and decides who wears the Imperator's diadem – but he's old and will not live forever. Somebody will have to take his place."

The Crown of the Iutes

"*You?*"

"Anyone. Even you, Octa, son of Aeric."

"And all of this…" I wave towards the smouldering city. "Is just means to that end?"

"All just steps on the road to Rome… But, I'm sure you understand this."

"Me?"

He lays a hand on my chest. "That Aelle of yours… He would never have come to fight me at Trever. He would never ally with Aegidius, or become Hildrik's friend. It takes a special kind of man – a special kind of warrior. There is a fire inside you that makes you wander and seek greatness." He puts the other hand on his chest. "The same fire burns within me. If you would join me…"

"I will not."

"Perhaps not yet. You have your honour. Your oaths. Your father, the king. But you will grow weary of these bonds, and of your misty little island, one day. I will be waiting for you."

"If there is indeed the same fire within us, I doubt you'll stay in Gaul that long."

He chuckles. "Ah, then you do understand. Well, then…" He nods, sadly, and steps away. He glances to the city, then back to me, his eyes narrow. "Reinforcements, you say?"

"You'll see soon for yourself."

"Andecawa's walls still stand strong," he says with a menacing undertone in his voice. "And there are no more traitors left inside to open the gates for you. I know all about the Bacauds and of the Armoricans... Unless you can summon another miracle from the thin air, I would strongly advise you to rethink your alliances before it's too late."

"You will not frighten me."

He raises his hands. "I'm only trying to help!" He turns back to the Saxon captain. "We must prepare our defences. Octa here thinks he can defeat me – and he's already done it twice!" He chuckles.

Sigegaut gives me a wary glance. "Stay away from our walls, Iute, until it is time to do battle," he warns me. "I swore an *ath* and my men will keep to it – but I can't vouch for Budic and his *wealas*. I heard them howl for your blood when they learned of your presence here."

"This doesn't surprise me." I give him a slight bow. "Thank you for the warning."

"I just want the privilege of killing you to myself." Sigegaut smiles. "It will please Wodan more if it's a Saxon that slays a Iute, instead of some Christian coward."

"I will make sure to seek out your sword when it's my time to die."

The Crown of the Iutes

CHAPTER XIV
THE LAY OF VICTURIUS

*C**mes* Paulus's funeral pyre still smoulders on top of our ridge when a great cloud of dust rising in the rust-red barley fields to the east announces the overdue arrival of Eishild and her band of Bacauds. They march up the Turonum highway, the rebel warband too sprawling and too unruly to keep to the road. With the Saxon boats patrolling both shores of the river, our forces are completely cut off from each other, and once again I can only watch as a troop of Budic's legionnaires sallies from Andecawa to surprise Eishild's vanguard in the open field, before they can prepare any sort of defence. The skirmish is brief – the Armoricans are grossly outnumbered by what appears to be a full cohort of the rebels, and they're smart enough not to risk the enemy's greater numbers overcoming them; but as they retreat, in orderly squares, back to the city, they leave behind a smattering of corpses – men and horses – in the young barley. I can only hope Eishild wasn't anywhere near that brief bout.

With Andecawa's mighty gates shut before them, the Bacauds start setting up their camp in the fields by hanging two banners on tall poles. One is the emblem of Martinus – a red torn soldier's cloak on a pole; the other one I don't recognise – a blue dragon circling a blue pearl.

"Are they planning a siege?" asks Seawine, scratching the scar on his face. "They'll have an even harder time of it than Odowakr's men."

His was a harrowing tale. When the Iutes reached Andecawa with Queen Basina, Paulus at first assigned them to service duties: as provision porters, arrow fletchers, construction workers helping

The Crown of the Iutes

with digging ditches and piling up earthen banks around the city. It was only after Seawine led a detachment of his men into victory against a Saxon patrol boat that the *Comes* agreed for the Iute warriors to join his garrison on the ramparts.

The Armorican contingent arrived soon after, and overran Andecawa's makeshift defences in the grounds of the suburban *villa* with ease which, Seawine admitted, should've raised suspicion from the start. The Iutes took no part in that battle – their task was to patrol the eastern shore and assist with keeping the peace in the besieged city's streets. Paulus, trusting in the might of his walls and siege machines, made no attempt to retake the *villa*; he knew the main thrust of Odowakr's assault would come from the river, and paid little attention to Budic's feeble attempts at breaking through the fortified bridge.

"Not all of the Armoricans were trained legionnaires, at first," Seawine said. "There was a core of trained soldiers, but the rest resembled more the roughs we had to fight in Britannia, bandits and small town brutes, seeking easy fortune. We destroyed them all in a few initial skirmishes, until only the legionnaires remained. This gave us false hope. No enemy ever took Andecawa's walls by force, Paulus told us – and it didn't seem as if it would happen now."

"It wasn't the enemy force that he should've feared," I remarked to Seawine's dejected nod.

By sheer accident, he happened to witness the moment when the traitors let the enemy inside. He stood in the middle of the *Decumanus*, after dispatching another detachment of Iutes to the harbour wall, from which they would shower the Saxons with javelins and darts: "just like at Cair Wortigern," he added with a wry scoff, when he saw what looked like two detachments of city guards fight each other at the western gate. One squad quickly overwhelmed the other, and they opened the gate before Seawine could intervene.

"I only had a few men with me at that moment," he said. "Everyone else was either on the ramparts, in the infirmary, or somewhere in between. When the enemy poured in, we barely managed to save ourselves. We took shelter in a nearby inn, and barricaded ourselves inside. I sent out messengers over the roofs of the tenements, to try and gather as many Iutes as possible around me. I hoped for little else than a chance to make a last stand."

They were fortunate. The Armorican soldiers took them for their Saxon allies, while the Saxons themselves were too busy plundering and chasing after Paulus's legionnaires, easily recognisable in their army cloaks and steel helmets. Once Seawine decided he could no longer wait for any more stray Iutes to join him, he formed them into a battle column and started fighting his way through towards the nearest gate, hoping to break out of the burning city.

"I saw you through the flames and blood," he continued. "Mowing down the enemy on the bridge. I knew then you'd find a way to save us – we only had to survive long enough. Just then, the Saxons must have stormed the *Praetorium* and killed Paulus. The mournful horns announced the garrison's surrender – and as soon as I heard, I ordered the men to lay down their weapons."

"A wise decision."

Thirty out of the initial two hundred Iutes lay dead in the streets of Andecawa – but thanks to Seawine's leadership, it was a small loss compared to the slaughter inflicted on Paulus's soldiers, few of whom lived to see the next day. Now, the remaining warriors are resting and healing their wounds in the camp on the ridge, while we wait for the arrival of one last force to strengthen our mixed gathering of warriors – too scattered and disparate to be called an army.

The Crown of the Iutes

They appear, at last, in the evening, storming down the northern highway, from Redones. An entire wing of the crimson-cloaked Dumnonian cavalry, led not by Drustan this time – but by *Comes* Marcus himself. Riding next to him in a chariot, with a patch over her missing eye and her long hair flowing in the wind, looking like a heathen queen of ancient legend, is his wife and the true ruler of Armorican Britons: Ahes the Fair.

We rush down the ridge to greet them and lead them to our camp, before they can get too close to the city and find themselves in the same sort of trouble as the Bacaud vanguard had the day before.

"What happened?" Marcus asks, dumbfounded, seeing Andecawa burnt down and us hiding in the forest above it. "Are we too late?"

"Yes – and no," I reply. "I will explain everything, but first you need to get out of the range of those *ballistae*."

"Where are the Martinians?" asks Drustan, searching desperately for his beloved among my men. "Where's Eishild?"

"On the other side." I nod towards the opposite shore, where the campfires of the Bacauds start to glimmer in the quickly falling twilight. "At least, I hope she's there."

Under cover of the night, a single small boat crosses the river, bringing Airmanarik, Eishild and a third man I don't recognise to our camp on top of the ridge. Below us, in the city, the fires still burn. All through the day, the Saxon *ceols* plied back and forth, ferrying the spoils and the enslaved townsfolk over to some intermediary anchorage downstream. Despite this, the Saxons are still, somehow, finding new ways to plunder and destroy what little remains of Andecawa's glory. Only the church remains untouched in the middle of the city, defended by Budic's men against would-be robbers – though the bishop's house next to it succumbed to the ruin.

We are brought this last bit of news from the city by Victurius, a vicar general secretly sent out by Andecawa's bishop with a few acolyte refugees, to seek out any allies who could help with retaking the city. Victurius also provided us, at last, with the answer to the riddle of who betrayed Paulus and opened the city gates.

"A few days after the siege started, we welcomed two *centuriae* of volunteers sent by the *Praefect* of Arwernis to help us with the Saxon menace," he told us. "We rejoiced – the Arwernians were once our allies against the Goths and the Huns. There weren't enough of them to make a difference in any upcoming battle – but Paulus, to his doom, posted them as guards at the main gates, out of respect for their valour. I don't know what they were promised for their betrayal…"

"I think I can explain," I told him. "Come to the war council in my tent later tonight."

It is a lofty name for a gathering of a few captains, each of whom commands a mere handful of men. The mood, both in the tent, and in the camp outside, is as dark as the night around us; it worsens when the wind brings the cries of woe and despair from the smouldering city below.

"We have the numbers," says Marcus, after Eishild and I report on the state of our forces. "And skill."

The Martinians brought some six *centuriae* from Caino – less some fifty dead in the skirmish on the first day. They are warriors of varied quality, but all itching to face the heathens who threaten their homeland; they grew even more eager once they found out that the army that took Andecawa was made up of Budic's and Graelon's old soldiers. There are still many among the Bacauds

The Crown of the Iutes

who remember the Britons' bloody conquest of Armorica, who had their homes stolen, and lives destroyed, by Graelon's brutes, and who burn with renewed desire for revenge.

"But we have no way to wage a siege, and not enough foot soldiers," I reply.

Marcus and Drustan arrived at the head of a full wing of what was once a Dumnonian, and now an Armorican, cavalry, fifty men strong. Many of Eishild's best warriors are heavy riders, too – Taifals of Pictawis, represented by the third man who came on the night boat, their chieftain Saphrax. Together with my bear-shirts we would make an unstoppable force in an open field, but one next to useless when trying to take a walled city.

"We have him trapped," says Ahes. "He can't last long in a city he only just took over. We will destroy his foragers. We'll starve him out."

"I fear it might be you who will starve," says Victurius. "*Comes* Paulus was preparing for a long siege himself. He gathered provisions from the entire *pagus* in the city. You won't find fresh food or fuel anywhere for miles. And now Odowakr has it all."

"And his ships will bring him more, when needed," adds Ursula. "We have no way to stop them."

"Odowakr didn't come here to stay in one city forever," I say, and tell the others what I've learned from the Skir about his true plans. Neither Eishild nor Airmanarik are particularly surprised; as Goths, they are familiar with the way Rome uses her enemies against each other, just as she now uses Odowakr's Saxons against Syagrius. But Marcus is struck by the revelation implied by my story: that in the intricate web of alliances, counter-alliances and shifting loyalties, it is he and his men who are now enemies of the Empire, while Patrician Budic's supporters are fighting on Rome's side.

"I wouldn't worry about it too much," says Victurius. Hearing about the part the Arwernians played in the plot seems to have hardened his heart. "Imperators come and go. There were three of them in the last ten years! And each one had to rewrite his alliances from scratch. It is to Patrician Syagrius that we owe our most immediate allegiance – and to the people of Gaul, not to some politician in Italia."

Victurius is a young man – younger than me and Ursula, and younger still than Marcus, and I can see the impression his bold statement makes on the Armorican *Comes*. Like me, he must wonder what the boy's words could mean for the future of Gaul and the Empire itself. Are the Gauls – at least here, in the north – now on their way to split from Rome for good, just like the Britons did two generations ago? There may be no Narrow Sea to separate them from the rest of the Empire – but there remains only the thin corridor of Lugdunum linking the North with the South and Italia, and even this route may one day disappear, swallowed by the ever-expanding barbarian kingdoms. What, then, of Syagrius? What of his allies, the Franks and the Iutes?

But those are questions for another time. If Odowakr and his fellow conspirators are successful in their plot, there may be no Gaul left to speak of. With Paulus and his army gone, we may well be the only force standing between Odowakr and the western part of Syagrius's domain. The Saxons are too few to conquer it all – but they are now free to raid and plunder, maybe even all the way to Aurelianum. And once they reach that city, how will its Alan defenders react? After all, Odowakr marches in the name of the Imperator. When the Gaulish auxiliaries are forced to choose their loyalties, their answer may not be as straightforward as young Victurius would wish.

"Odowakr is not here to be the new *Praetor* of Andecawa," I continue. "He is the Imperator's dog, and wants as large a slice of

The Crown of the Iutes

Gaul for himself as he can swallow. He will march on another city sooner or later – sooner, if I know him."

"Turonum is the closest," says Drustan. "And it only had a small garrison when we passed through it."

"We'll be able to catch him on the way there," I say. "Out in the open, our horses will make all the difference."

"Not if he boards the ships again and *sails* to Turonum," says Saphrax, the Taifal. "Unless the Lord grants us the power to ride on water, those Saxons are out of our reach."

"Then we'll have to make sure he doesn't have any ships left to board."

"There they go again," whispers Ursula. Another Saxon boat splashes into the river. The warriors on board all carry covered lanterns to help them light the way and illuminate the shore, as the boat navigates the shallows and reed beds in the pouring rain.

This isn't the first such patrol of the night – and this isn't the first night of increased patrols along the river. The Saxons have grown anxious, and in their anxiety, they managed to cut us all but completely off from the other side; we have had no contact from Eishild and her Bacauds in days.

"They must have spotted her boat when she was coming back," I say.

"Or they're simply worried about all the troops gathering around the city," replies Ursula.

I tighten my cloak, thankful for the fine workmanship of the Armorican tailors: for this one night, I'm wearing the uniform of an *eques*, exchanged with Drustan for my bear-skin. Ever since I spoke to Odowakr on the bridge, I have tried to keep the continuing presence of myself and the Iutes in the vicinity of Andecawa a secret, hoping to confuse the defenders into thinking some new force arrived to battle alongside Marcus and his Dumnonians; when I needed them to ride out to forage or patrol, I had them wear the *equites'* red cloaks and silver helmets, and mount their warhorses instead of the ponies. Not that there was much for them to do in these disguises. Victurius was right: there was barely any food left to find in the farms and villages around the city. The barley was still too green in the fields, and the fruit in the trees was small and sour. We had to act fast if we didn't want to go into battle with groaning stomachs.

With the river now an impassable barrier, coordinating any assault between us and the Bacauds was bordering on impossible. Fortunately, the operation we agreed on at the "war council" didn't need much further planning. All we had to do was wait for an opportune time – and hope that the other side would spot that opportune time as well.

Tonight is just such a moment. It's the day of the first of the late summer storms, and it's been pouring and howling since early morning. Thunder rolls in from the north in earth-shaking rumbles. The river's swollen, though not yet breaking out of its banks. When Donar's angry, there can be no sailing – apart from an occasional rowing patrol – and so the Saxons have beached all their ships, waiting for a change in weather. Andecawa's harbour, fit to only take in an occasional merchant's galley or two, is too small to accommodate all the vessels of Odowakr's fleet; the *ceols* are strewn all along both shores. The ships are gathered in groups of three or four, crews huddling together for safety and warmth, like seals on a sand bank in pupping season. The campfires sizzle out in the rain, and so the only way to keep warm is for the Saxons to drown their

The Crown of the Iutes

misery in ale and mead. Mournful songs ring out throughout the camps, songs of loves lost and of distant homelands abandoned for the sake of adventure. These Saxons are even further away from home than we are, having come here from the mist-shrouded, dark-wooded shores far beyond the Rhenum; on a miserable night like this, many must wonder if sailing here was worth their meagre share of plunder.

"Do you think the Bacauds will be here?" asks Audulf.

"We can only hope," I reply. "But we don't need them to be. The Saxons are as cut off from each other as we are. Focus on our part of the battle, and don't worry about the Bacauds."

We mount up in silence. We're coming towards the boats from the north, having drawn a wide arc around the suburban *villa*, to further the enemy's confusion. The bridge looms in the distance, marked out more by the noise of rain hitting its polished cobbles than by the gloomy line of shadow rising over the churning waters. I check the weight of the lance in my hand. The blade has dulled and chipped in the battles in the fishing village and on Andecawa's bridge, and there was no chance to re-forge it. Some of my men got new weapons from the spares Marcus and his men brought with them, but there wasn't enough for all, and I preferred to hand them to the younger riders, who need all the help in the coming battle they can get.

We ride out into the wet darkness, guided by the sounds: the singing, the shouting, and the screams of tortured captives; drinking and gambling are not the only ways in which the pirates entertain themselves tonight. As we approach the first huddle of boats, I taste blood and realise I've been biting my lower lip all through the ride.

"Can you make out the bridge?" I ask my men before the charge, pointing with the tip of the lance. They murmur in confirmation.

"Remember where it is. Once we're done here, we're going across the river, to join with the Bacauds. Seawine's men will keep it open on our side, but they won't be able to hold it for long. Understand?"

"Won't the Saxons try to stop our crossing?" asks Deora.

"They will *try*," I say. "But we are Iute riders of the Cantian plains, and they are mud-dwelling pirates. We are the bears of Wodan and the wild boars of Donar, while they are like fish and frogs, and we will trample them into dirt if they stand against us."

They raise a subdued cheer. Lightning crackles somewhere on the other side of the river; the thunder rumbles under the hooves of our ponies.

"Draw your weapons," I command. "May your lance blades flash like lightning, and may your swords blast the enemy skulls like Donar's thunder!"

The night is too dark, and our approach path too narrow and muddy for us to try any sort of formation. An attack at night is difficult enough; a coordinated charge is an impossibility. My men simply ride close behind me, in a loose line, following the sound of each mount's hooves. The best we can hope for is not to lose anyone along the way, and reach the first pirate camp together. Not that we expect our foe to be anything but a drunken mass of sailors and half-asleep guards. Our targets are the ships' crews – and the ships themselves, if we can get to them, though how much damage we can really do to them tonight is anyone's guess. The storm that trapped the vessels on shore, enabling us to attack them, also renders them impervious to fire, so it will be down to our swords and axes to rip holes in the boards, shatter the oars and slash through ropes and sails.

The Crown of the Iutes

I don't imagine the Dumnonians to fare any better than ourselves. They're riding from the south, sweeping up the tall riverbank, where the ground is supposed to be firmer – our moor ponies may fare well enough in the sodden mire into which the rains turned the shore by the bridge, but the warhorses of the *equites* would only break their legs if they tried to charge here. Should it still prove too difficult to ride, they may have to dismount to fight, losing their main advantage – but Marcus and Ahes assured me their men can fight just as well on foot as on horseback.

"We've been fighting these pirates just as long as you have," Ahes told me with a confident glint in her only eye, "and we had to defend our borders from Goth marauders, Bacauds, and uncounted other foe. We know what we're doing."

The conditions are so miserable that we almost pass by the first of the enemy unnoticed. My pony's flank brushes against a Saxon spearman, standing, or rather, dozing on his spear, in a dip between two dunes, guarding the only approach to the strand from the north. I cut his throat mid-shout for help. It is a sloppy cut, a blind slash in the dark, and he falls to the ground, gurgling and writhing, before Croha thrusts her lance in his back, ending his agony.

The encounter makes me feel uneasy, but there's no time for worry as we emerge onto the strand, shifting from trot to a messy charge; there's neither place, nor ground, for us to gallop. Ankle-deep mud splashes under the hooves of ponies, announcing our arrival louder than any war cry. Careful not to get tangled in any tent cloth or ropes, I wade and weave through the camp, stabbing my lance into anything that may look like a sleeping body. Those of the Saxons who are still awake, rush towards us with unseen weapons. I aim at their cries: only when they're in sword range can I make enough of their silhouettes to know where to strike.

It is harrowing work; we fight almost blind, guessing that we hit the enemy only when their shout is cut short, or when the blade digs into something soft; sometimes, a splash of warm blood on my hand is the only thing telling me I struck somebody. It's a miracle we don't hit each other, and that only because we're all mounted, aiming our blows deliberately low. The noise of clashing arms, cries of agony, and ponies neighing in distress fills the night air with a disorientating clamour. Moving randomly from one foe to another, I suddenly find myself by one of the *ceols*. There is some light here – a storm-proof lantern of Roman design hangs on the bow, a single bright point at which I can, at last, focus my attention.

"To me, Iutes!" I call through the storm. I repeat the summons until most of my men make their way to the ships. Judging by how silent the night has become again, it seems we've already slaughtered most of the men guarding the beach.

"Destroy what you can," I order. "Be quick about it – we have to move on to the next anchorage before they notice what's happened here."

I climb on board the first *ceol* and pause to peer into the darkness. I'm trying to make out the noise of battle from the opposite shore, where the Bacauds should already be storming the Saxon landing sites, but the dense curtain of rain is impenetrable to sight and sound alike.

Just then, another lightning strike nearby turns the darkest night into a bright day for the blink of an eye. In that one blinding moment, the entire deck of the *ceol* is revealed before me – and I see that it is filled with warriors, waiting in silence with their swords drawn.

Odowakr outwitted me once again.

I stumble back and leap off the deck as the horde rushes towards me.

The Crown of the Iutes

"It's a trap!" I yell through the rain. "Mount up! Retreat!"

The campfires of the Saxons glimmer in a scattered line along the river shore. I hear their songs of glory born on the cool breeze. There are no songs in our camp – only prayers of the Martinians, mourning their fallen, and grumbles of the Iutes, angry with me at failing to deliver them another victory.

"One more such loss, and the young ones will start wondering if they shouldn't join Odowakr," I say.

On any other day, losing four of the bear-shirts would have been a disaster. I feel their loss acutely; I trained each of these men myself, I fought with them in every battle on Cantia's beaches. But it was a miracle that any of us survived at all in the chaotic flight from the strand. Odowakr not only had his warriors wait for us in the bowels of his ships, but he also sent a detachment of Armorican shieldsmen to cut off our retreat, rightly guessing that we would try to break across the river. They clashed with Seawine's younglings in a bloody brawl on the western end of the bridge, both sides surprised to stumble upon each other in the darkness.

As soon as our ponies reached the higher ground, the night turned into our ally. Even Odowakr's strategic wits couldn't account for the training of my bear-shirts. Given enough open space for manoeuvres, my Iutes knew how to form up with their eyes closed. On the slippery stones of the bridge, the shieldsmen could find no purchase, and in the chaos of the fight with Seawine, they couldn't see us coming in time to strengthen their grips on the shields. Our tight wedge punched through their line like a spear blade thrusting through a boar's fat flank. Moments later, we were on the other side – but not safe yet.

I split my force in two, sending Audulf south, into the narrow space between the harbour and the city walls. With the other half, I returned to the bridge, to save as many of Seawine's men as I could. I managed to gather some fifty youths around us and rush them across, just as Andecawa's gates opened wide to spew forth a *centuria* of Budic's legionnaires.

We barely avoided a rout. Audulf charged before us, scattering one hastily formed line of Saxon defence after another, clearing our way towards safety, as the Armoricans pursued us in grim silence. I only knew we had broken free when I heard the rustle of barley stalks under the pony's hooves and saw a wing of Taifal riders coming towards us, lighting their way with torches. Budic had no intention of fighting heavy cavalry in the darkness and pulled back behind the walls before the Taifal charge turned his sally into a costly defeat. With remarkable discipline, his men turned about, the vanguard turning into a rearguard, bristling with spears to protect the garrison's orderly retreat.

The Bacauds, we soon learned, had an even worse night. It was against them that Odowakr sent the main force of Budic's legionnaires, joined by a large number of Saxon axemen. In the bloody mire, in the dark confusion, they fought a slogging retreat from the pirate anchorages, ending only once they reached the fortified borders of their camp. They still haven't finished counting their dead. Airmanarik himself fell in the rearguard of the fleeing warband, pierced, as those who witnessed his death claimed, by half a dozen spears. Adalfuns barely made it back, cut in the left arm and across the back. Eishild, at least, escaped unscathed, protected by her Taifal bodyguard. Saphrax's riders were busy everywhere on the battlefield, their valour and skill preventing the night from becoming a complete disaster. After a brief rest in the Bacaud camp, we even joined them in one last brief charge, to mop up any enemy left in the barley fields, and salvage at least some victory out of the night of defeats; but trampling Saxon marauders

The Crown of the Iutes

and finishing off wounded Armoricans was poor consolation after the earlier slaughter.

The worst of all is the uncertainty about the fate of Marcus and his cavalry. We heard nothing from them, or the Iutes who remained with Seawine on the western shore. In the morning, we saw pillars of smoke coming from the ridge: the Saxons discovered and destroyed our camp in the woods. But the *equites* were fine warriors and well led, and it was hard to believe that they couldn't escape the ambush on their mighty warhorses. Most likely, they were hiding somewhere in the woods and marshes to the west, waiting. At least, that's what we chose to believe…

Ursula finishes sharpening her knife on the belt, sheathes it, and checks the wrappings on her shoulder where a Saxon arrow struck her.

"Maybe it's time to face the truth," she says.

"What truth?"

"That we can't do anything more to help anyone here. That we should pack up and go back home, while we still can – while the Saxons haven't yet cut us off from all harbours."

"We've never given up before."

She scoffs. "We were never failed by so many allies before." She starts counting off on her fingers. "We came here to fight alongside the Britons – and Riotham took them off to be slaughtered somewhere in the South. We came to honour our alliance with the Franks – and Hildrik is nowhere to be seen. We came to help the Gauls – but Syagrius just sits in his fortress, waiting for us to do his fighting for him, while Paulus let himself get killed. Eishild's rebellion was quashed before it even started. Everything that could have gone wrong, did. What other reason is there for us to stay here?"

"We came here to defeat the pirates — and they're still here."

"Because we thought they would join Aelle and threaten our shores. But now we know it was only to help Odowakr conquer Gaul…" She shrugs. "And would it be that much worse to have him as a neighbour than Syagrius or Hildrik?"

"I don't know," I admit. "It's possible we might even be better off. For all his trickery, he seems a decent man, guided by a pure ambition. Educated in Rome… I sense my father would be fond of him, if they ever met."

"Then leave Gaul to him, and give your men an order to march home. There's nothing to be gained from us staying here even a day longer."

"What about our friends and allies?"

"Marcus and Drustan will return safely to Armorica, and take Eishild with them — I doubt Odowakr will bother chasing after them. As for the Franks…" She shrugs. "They will fend for themselves, like they always do. I'm sure Hildrik will know how to stay on Odowakr's good side."

"Do you not even wish to wait and learn what happened to the Briton cohorts? To your kin?"

"They are all dead or enslaved by now," she replies with bitter certainty. "All Riotham's scheme amounted to was hastening the demise of my people. If we could —"

The Crown of the Iutes

She stops and stares at something behind me. I follow her gaze, but at first, I can't see what she's looking at.

"What is it?"

"There's someone there."

In the dark vastness between our camp and Andecawa's walls, I spot silhouettes of five horsemen, in hooded cloaks, trotting slowly, away from the city – and towards us.

I call Audulf and order him to ride out with a few Iutes to intercept the strangers. The shadowy travellers make no attempt to fight or run away. Before long, the five men arrive peacefully at our camp.

"Odowakr!" I exclaim when their leader removes his hood.

He puts a finger to his lips. "A little discretion, if you please. I wouldn't want to announce my little escapade to my men."

"You're running away?" Ursula guesses.

"Indeed I am, *Domna*. Congratulations, you have bested me once again."

"But why? Our attack couldn't have possibly damaged your forces this badly."

Odowakr smiles. "You're right. This isn't Trever, and however bravely you and your warriors have fought, you alone would have made little dent in my army – or impact on my plans... But your actions did cause me some troublesome delay. I would have to wait for more boats and men to arrive from Frisia, to continue my conquest – and, I'm afraid, I can no longer afford to wait."

"Have your men finally grown weary of your duplicity?" I ask curtly.

"Nothing of the sort – quite the opposite." He chuckles. "But, I'm sure you will find out the reason for yourself – tomorrow."

"Tomorrow? Why not tell us now?"

"And spoil the surprise?"

I give Ursula an annoyed look. I could hold Odowakr here and force him to divulge the cause of his flight – but I am strangely intrigued by the mystery, and willing to wait until dawn for the reveal.

"And where are you going?" I ask.

"Back to Italia. To get my just reward."

"Reward? For what?"

He raises his arms and waves vaguely around. "I have achieved all that Ricimer asked of me! I killed Paulus, destroyed his army and weakened Syagrius's flank, and all with just a cartful of Roman silver. Not bad for a barbarian chieftain, eh?" He winks. "It is now up to the Imperator to come and pick up the pieces – if he dares."

"What about Gaul? What about the Arwernian conspiracy? Don't you want your slice of the honey cake anymore?"

"Eh." He shrugs. "This one was always a gamble. As you will find out tomorrow, Fate conspired against me once again. Or perhaps…" He looks at me curiously. "Perhaps it wasn't *just* Fate… Was this your doing, too, I wonder?" He asks, enigmatically, and shakes his head. "No matter. I must hasten back to Italia. My fortune awaits me there."

"What makes you so certain we'll let you go?" asks Ursula.

"A twisted web of alliances may have made us enemies when we first met, *Domna*," replies Odowakr, with a gentle, pleading smile. "But there's no reason why we shouldn't part as friends. I have no quarrel with you – and, I trust, you'll have no more quarrel with me when I'm gone from Gaul." He nods towards Andecawa. "The Saxons are still there, if you wish to deal with them. As are the Armoricans."

"He's right," I say to Ursula in Iutish. "We gain nothing by keeping him here."

"I don't even care anymore," Ursula replies. She waves her hand with a sigh. "He's harmless now, and despite all his bluster, I can tell he's afraid of whatever, or whoever, is coming tomorrow. Who knows, maybe one day he will find a way to show how grateful he is to us for his release."

I summon Audulf again.

"Give these men back their weapons and horses," I order to his surprise. "Make sure that they're well away before you leave them."

Even Odowakr is taken aback by my lenience. "I almost feel insulted. Am I not even worth anything to you as a prisoner?"

"If you had anything you thought you could bribe me with, you'd have presented it at the start," I reply. "And there's no one whom I could ask for your ransom – the men you've abandoned will think you a traitor, and your master in Rome will consider you an expendable failure."

He nods with a chuckle. "It is not my best moment, I admit – skulking away in the darkness. But I survived worse." He takes his sword from Audulf, fastens the belt, and bows before me and Ursula.

"Don't take this the wrong way, but I hope we will never meet again," he says as he bids us farewell.

"Stay in Rome, Skir," I tell him. "You seem to be doing better there than you ever did in Gaul."

"Likewise, I'd advise you to stay in Britannia, Iute. Let us both leave Gaul to her own devices. There are already too many who want to rule it – there's no place left for outsiders like us."

"Finally, you said something we all can agree with," says Ursula. "Now go, before we change our minds."

He salutes and bows once again, then turns to leave. When he reaches his horse, he turns away one last time.

"A word of advice, Iute," he says. "Tomorrow, when you finally discover what drove me to this flight – consider your alliances well. Because everyone else will."

The Crown of the Iutes

CHAPTER XV
THE LAY OF TAMMO

Nothing much happens in the morning, except more rain, more wind and, a few hours after dawn angry shouts coming from the city as the men inside discover their warchief had abandoned them. I order the Iutes to stay armed and be wary – and advise Eishild to tell her Bacauds the same; angry and disappointed, the Saxons are likely to lash out against the nearest enemy.

By mid-day, the rain stops; by afternoon, the clouds part, letting in pillars of blazing sunlight, as if announcing the arrival of a host of archangels, come to vanquish the heathens before them.

They are not archangels – but they might as well be. They ride in from the north, trotting down the Cenomans road. Five hundred Frankish riders: all clad in bright mail from head to waist, each donning a polished helmet of riveted steel, each with a war-axe slung over his back, a *seax* dangling at his belt, and a bundle of leaf-bladed javelins at his saddle. Behind them roll wagons filled with provisions, surrounded by a swarm of camp followers.

"Is this what you were hoping for?" asks Ursula when *Rex* Hildrik and his queen reach the perimeter of our camp at the head of the column of the riders. The guards part to let them in.

"This is what I *prayed* for," I say. "But I never actually thought to see."

I reach for my helmet, and hesitate before putting it on. It's battered and dull, covered in muck. My clothes are tattered and bloodied, damp with sweat; my hands are calloused from holding

The Crown of the Iutes

the lance shaft. I feel embarrassed showing like this before the mighty Frankish riders, who all look as if they'd just put on their armours for the first time after this morning's bath.

"You live!" Basina cries out in joy, dismounting. "I feared we'd be too late!"

She embraces Ursula first, before reaching out to me. "You took your time," I tell her when she squeezes me between her breasts. Breathless, I add: "We were just about to pack up and go home."

"Go home?" Hildrik laughs. "But we've only just arrived. We were told there's a battle to be had! Or did Basina drag me from my palace for nothing?"

"There is – if you enjoy your sieges," says Ursula. She gazes admiringly at the long line of riders behind Hildrik. The Frankish king turns around and gives his men a wave – a signal for them to dismount and accept gifts of food and water from the grateful Iutes, while the servants proceed to set up a camp of their own.

Hildrik glances to Andecawa. "This little old thing?" He sniggers. "We won't need a siege to take it."

"Careful," I tell him, and point to the *ballistae* on the walls – the few the Saxons left behind – and the Armorican soldiers lining the battlements; they all came out in force to watch the arriving Franks, to jeer and shake their javelins at them. "Those walls bite. Do you have anything to take them with?"

"*I* don't," says Hildrik. He looks to the sky with an impatient grimace. "I thought they'd be here by now – they were supposed to march out ahead of us…"

"*They?*" asks Ursula.

The lookouts on the Turonum road cry in alarm. Coming from the east, slow and lumbering, is another column of men: light riders in front, and footmen behind them. They are fewer in number than the Franks, and not as finely garbed; the riders in front are Alan horse archers, wearing drab tunics and woollen hats instead of mail and helmets. The footmen at the back wear blue and black cloaks, and carry heavy, roughly made spears, and large, oblong shields. In front of this troop rides a bronze-plated travelling coach, bearing banners of the Roman eagle surrounded by a golden wreath and the letters *A* and *S*, which I don't recognise at first, before remembering seeing them on the ramparts on Aurelianum.

"Is that… Patrician Syagrius?" I ask. "Did he come himself all this way?"

"He'd better," says Hildrik. "I made him promise he would bring his *bucellarii*, as my condition of being here. I don't trust him enough to have him at our backs when we fight the Saxons."

"If you don't hurry, you may have no Saxons left to fight," says Audulf, having just arrived from a patrol to the riverside.

"What do you mean?" asks Basina.

"As soon as they saw you all coming, they rushed to their ships," he says. "With Odowakr gone, it seems they have no heart left to fight – I'd wager they'll all be gone before sundown."

"Then we have no time to rest!" Hildrik grins. He whistles at his riders again. "Leave the tents to the servants, men, and mount back up! Octa, Ursula – will you join us in sending those filthy pirates to the Halls of the Slain?"

"I would want nothing more," I reply. "Audulf, Seawine, gather everyone. Call Eishild and Saphrax, all the horsemen who can ride.

The Crown of the Iutes

This time, we won't let ourselves be ambushed. For victory, and vengeance!"

It is the strangest feeling, to walk the streets of a city emptied of nearly all its inhabitants. Though we are many, there's not enough warriors in the combined allied armies to fill out the devastated avenues and ash-filled squares of Andecawa. The few citizens who haven't been taken to slavery or fled into the woods, are huddling around the cathedral, where the bishop's men are handing out bowls of meagre soup, brewed from whatever food is left in the town's stores after the Saxon depredations. Just as Victurius said, the church itself was spared the Saxon plunder, but the rest of the city centre, around the *basilica* and the *Praetorium*, having burned for days, has been all but reduced to smouldering cinder and charred rubble. Thankfully, the storm helped smother the flames before they spread throughout the rest of the town.

I pass through the Forum, the empty space slowly filling with returning refugees, lamenting the loss of their homes, but rejoicing in their survival. The grey stones beneath my feet are still splattered with the blood of Paulus's men, who made their last stand before the *basilica*. I stride a carpet of arrows, discarded shields and shattered spears, careful not to slip on pools of silvery ash mixed with rainwater that fill out the cracks in the pavement. As I come near the eastern wall, I hear the sounds of song, music and bawdy cries: the victory feast of the Franks.

Hildrik forbade his men from entering the city; whether he thought the sight of the death and destruction would dampen their moods, or that he wouldn't be able to stop them from plundering what was left, I couldn't tell. The feast is not as full of merriment as one would expect from a victory celebration – the songs are solemn, rather than cheerful, and though the ale flows in streams, it does little to brighten the eyes and voices of the Franks. But then, the victory itself wasn't as glorious as Hildrik had expected when he decided to bring his finest warriors across half of Gaul.

Budic's Armoricans, seeing their Saxon allies abandon them – and, consequently, getting over half of their number slaughtered in a Frankish charge before most of the ships managed to set sail – surrendered to the bishop before we even reached the city walls. Only Budic himself and his closest retinue fled across the bridge, back towards whatever Armorican wilderness they had come from. His soldiers hoped to win lenience, citing the defence of the church from plunder; their hopes were not in vain. At the bishop's vouching, Syagrius agreed to let most of them go free. We retained only the officers in custody – but their punishment was left to Marcus, since in theory, at least, they were his rebellious subjects.

I find Ursula waiting for me at the eastern gate.

"Is the feast not to your liking?" I ask.

She scoffs. "I don't see you drinking and singing with the Franks."

"I had matters to deal with in the city," I say. "Captives. Provisions. Quarters for us and our men."

"There are still rooms left in the city?" She raises her eyebrow.

"The bishop granted us the use of his guesthouse for a few nights."

"I thought Syagrius would take it all for his retinue."

"The bishop seems to appreciate us coming to the city's help long before Syagrius bothered to." I glance towards the camp. "It sure took them long enough to get here…"

Ursula scratches her nose and leans against the gate.

The Crown of the Iutes

"You don't trust them."

"The only people I trust in this city are you, Eishild and our riders."

"You think Odowakr was right to warn you about our allies?"

I turn to her. "Tell me, does Hildrik's army look to you like that of a people ravaged by plague?"

She shrugs. "Not particularly, no. But then, we both suspected Hildrik was lying when giving a reason for his absence."

"And then he decided to come after all."

"Wouldn't be the first time your powers of persuasion worked on Basina and her husband…"

I snort. "I don't believe it for a moment. You don't assemble a force like that on a whim. He was going to come here, whether I talked to Basina or not."

"They didn't seem to be in a great hurry when they arrived."

"No, they didn't." I nod. "If they had arrived just a couple days earlier, Paulus and his soldiers would yet be alive."

"It could just be a coincidence. Or a stroke of bad fortune. Maybe something slowed them down. You don't think Hildrik and Syagrius deliberately waited for the slaughter to end?"

"I don't know what to believe – but I know neither of them was fond of Paulus, and both profited from his demise. More than Odowakr could have benefitted himself."

I notice a man leaving the Frank camp and heading towards us, holding a wine-skin in one hand, and waving at us with the other. I shield my eyes from the sun and strain to see who it might be.

"Is that – Hildrik?"

"I think he wants us to join him," says Ursula.

"Fine," I say. "I did want to ask him a few questions, and it might be easier to get some answers out of him after a few flasks of wine."

With an exaggerated stagger, I approach the rack upon which Hildrik and his officers display their armour and weapons. I run the ringlets of his mail tunic between my fingers.

"This is a fine work," I say with authentic admiration. "Might be the best I've ever seen."

The steel rings are riveted together in a perfect mesh, tight yet flexible, able to withstand a blow from a war-axe just as well as a spear thrust. The edges, on the sleeves and around the neck, are trimmed with golden rings, and embedded into the mail on the chest are little jewelled bees, Hildrik's clan emblem.

"Fresh from the forges of the Legions," Hildrik replies. "The Gauls are unmatched weaponsmiths."

He's slurring as he speaks – we already drank all the good wine we commandeered from Syagrius's own stock, and moved on to simple ale, brought in barrels on the Frankian wagons in expectation of victory. The feast is slowly coming to an end; it never reached the heights of what I knew the Franks are capable of

The Crown of the Iutes

when celebrating, even when they were eventually joined by my Iutes. Everyone shares the sense of unease, the feeling that something odd and confusing has happened here. This wasn't a battle that will be written about in the chronicles – and if it is, I imagine the chroniclers will have to fill in the confusing bits themselves. Could it truly count as a victory if *Comes* Paulus and a large part of the armies of northern Gaul have been destroyed? If most of the Saxon fleet got away? If the city that was the target of the pirate expedition was ravaged, its people taken, its wealth plundered? If the supposedly victorious warriors of Frankia had nothing to show for their valour except for a wagon full of captured Saxon gear, a few ships stuck in the shallows, and the gratitude of the handful of survivors?

"It must have cost a fortune," says Ursula. She sits on the other side of the campfire, sipping a mug of *Sicera*, an intact *amphora* of which she found in the ruins of some torched tavern.

"It wasn't cheap." Hildrik nods. "The work of the finest armour smith in Turonum."

"And all your men are clad in steel, too…" I shake my head in disbelief. "I never would have guessed the campaigns against your Alemann and Saxon neighbours were so profitable."

Hildrik chuckles. "I lose more silver fighting these poor wretches than I gain from their chests. Why do you think the Saxons have turned to piracy? There's nothing in their land worth taking except slaves and furs."

"Then how can you afford all this?" I wave my hands around. "Is Toxandria such a fertile province?"

"Toxandria is but sand and marsh." Hildrik scowls. "I have half a mind to give it all to Friesian pirates. My real wealth comes from Belgica."

"I didn't know you also ruled Belgica," says Ursula.

"Aegidius granted us parts of it for my help at Aurelianum, and Syagrius was too weak to take it back. My uncles and I are *Comites* of all the *pagi* from Ambiacum in the west to Remi in the east – and the River Franks of Coln pay us tribute, too."

"My father would appreciate if you shared your secrets with us," I say. "Our chests run empty, and there's nowhere to expand in Britannia without provoking the wrath of the *wealas*."

He points to the log beside him, invitingly. "Sit down, *aetheling*. You too, Ursula, come closer. Let me tell you how a barbarian king can afford to feed his people and arm his men without constant campaigning."

I sit down and reach for my goblet, but the smell of ale makes me retch. I tell a servant to fill it with cold water, instead.

"I understand you're now a Councillor in the Cantian Magistrate, is that right?" Hildrik asks Ursula.

She nods. "Since my mother's death."

"My condolences. But that means there's still a *Pagus* Council in Cantia, in the manner of the Roman administration. What, then, is your father's position in it?" he asks me. "I'm guessing he, too, is a *Comes*?"

"He's the *Rex* of the Iutes – but he holds no title that the Britons would recognise."

"You're telling me he doesn't control Cantia's treasury?"

The Crown of the Iutes

He seems genuinely astonished – which, in turn, surprises me and Ursula.

"No – he's a heathen king, why would he?" Ursula asks. "The taxes and customs, such as they are, all come through the Council in Dorowern. It's the same in every other *pagus*."

"Except in the Regin country," I remind her. "Aelle disbanded the Council there and took over as *Comes*, against his father's advice."

"And he's been having trouble running the place ever since," says Ursula. "He tried to force the merchants into paying their dues instead of relying on the old networks of clients and officials. And he's been bleeding them dry, giving nothing in return. The Britons don't take kindly to that sort of thing – they've been leaving his domain in droves. Have you seen how empty and poor New Port is?"

Hildrik rubs his eye with his thumb and belches. "There's your problem."

"What do you mean?" I ask.

"You don't slaughter a milk cow," he says. "But you don't let it run free, either. As the *Magister* of Belgica Secunda, I control all the *walhas* taxes. Of course, I leave the actual collecting to the magistrates – but I make sure that my share of it is just and proper. That way, the merchants and the townsfolk don't even know anything's changed."

"The Council of Cantia would never agree to this," says Ursula. "They wouldn't even reimburse the Iutes for their war with the pirates. They say they already gave the heathens all they could."

"They gave us land." I nod. "But you can't fight the Saxons with clumps of dirt. We need silver."

"Taking over the taxes is the only way for a barbarian ruler to survive and thrive on Roman soil," says Hildrik. "The Goths were the first to do this in Tolosa, and Burgundians did the same in Lugdunum. Everyone profits from such arrangements: the *walhas* can go about their business as they always have, and we can afford to defend them without having to constantly raid the neighbouring provinces. If you had a *Dux* as wise as Aegidius, he would've forced the local Councils into compliance."

"There is no *Dux* in Londin," I explain, "and the only man who tried to take the diadem is now lost somewhere in Gaul, fighting the Goths."

"Then I have no more advice to give you." Hildrik shakes his head and pours the final drop of ale out on the ground. "But if your chests are really this empty, have your father send me an official request. I may be able to divert some of the tax gold his way as aid after the plague."

I stand up and approach the fire. I spread out my hands to warm them. There's a chill in the air, from grass, still wet with rain and evening dew, and from the sky, as the storm clouds gather once again over our heads.

"Are you sure you really have enough gold to spare? Even after equipping your entire army with the finest armour and weapons?"

"What are you getting at, Octa?"

I turn back to him, and notice the mist fading away from his eyes. Just like me, he was only pretending to be drunk – or at least, more drunk than he really was.

"Basina said the reason you couldn't come to Paulus's aid was the devastation of pox," I say. "And yet, here you are, with five hundred of your best warriors bound in silver and steel. If this is

The Crown of the Iutes

what your army looks like after a plague, I can't imagine it when in more prosperous times!"

He wipes the ale from his mouth and snickers.

"I knew we wouldn't fool you for long."

"Then I was right. You used the Saxons to rid you of Paulus. Even if it meant destruction of his troops and the city of Andecawa. Now, yours is the most powerful army in the North."

Hildrik winces and smacks his lips. "It was never my intention for poor Paulus to die. I swear on my ancestors. This wasn't the plan."

"And yet, his ashes are strewn in the river," says Ursula.

"A plan? What plan?" I ask.

Hildrik pauses and swipes his hand across his face. Just then, Basina emerges from one of the nearby tents, her face flushed. She ties up the laces on her tunic and runs her fingers through her dishevelled hair.

"Come here, my love!" Hildrik calls her. "Our friends don't believe my honesty."

"Did Octa finally see through your deceit?" She laughs. "I told you it wouldn't last long."

She sits beside her husband; he pulls her tight, then sniffs her hair.

"Mahthild? Again?" he asks.

"Who else?" she replies, licking her lips. "There is no one better than her – except Ursula, of course."

"We asked you a question," replies Ursula, suddenly irritated.

"It was all Syagrius's idea at the start," Hildrik says. "But I agreed to it, so I can't make excuses for myself. Paulus wanted to cross the Liger in answer to the same Imperial summons that brought your Britons here. We had to stop him. Neither of us wanted to get embroiled in some new Imperial expedition against the Goths, or support a Bacaud rebellion doomed to failure. On this, I agreed with Syagrius – it is much better to have Aiwarik as good neighbour than an enemy, at least for the time being."

"And you couldn't just refuse the Imperial summons?" I ask.

"Remember, we *are* both Roman officials," he says. "And while there are many advantages of my position, one disadvantage is that when Rome demands that I march to its defence, I can't simply tell them I have better things to do…"

"A gilded cage," says Ursula. She glances at me. "Your arrangement suddenly doesn't sound so appealing."

"I keep to it as long as it suits me," Hildrik replies. "Unlike you Britons, I know how to deal with Rome without her infringing on my freedom."

"So you used the plague as pretence for your inaction, hoping that Paulus would turn to an easier target," I say. "But then, why are you here at all?"

"I had my spies amongst the Saxons," Hildrik says. "I knew that they were planning something big, that Paulus's force alone wouldn't be enough to defeat them. We planned to let Paulus stew a little behind Andecawa's walls, and then come to his relief. A defeat would've weakened his position among his loyal troops. I would support Syagrius as *Magister Militum* in exchange for command of Gaul's armies. Half the soldiers are Franks already, and I am a better commander than Paulus ever was. If I weren't a barbarian — and the Romans didn't guard their titles so jealously…" He palms his fist in anger. "The plan was to wait for two weeks. Andecawa should've held out for a lot more than that."

"But you haven't accounted for Odowakr having traitors inside the city and capturing it in a day," I guess.

"Two weeks haven't passed yet," notes Ursula.

Hildrik looks to Basina. The queen smiles.

"When my beloved Basina told me of your taunting, and of your Iutes marching to Paulus's relief, I understood that what I was doing did not behove a Frankish warchief. I became too involved in the petty intrigues of the *walh*. Surrounded myself with too many Gaulish advisors. Betraying allies, avoiding a fight — this was not a warrior's way. And I knew my men were feeling the same. They cheered when I told them to march out."

"We would've been even sooner," says Basina, "if we hadn't had to deal with Hildrik's various uncles and cousins. Meroweg gave them half the land in his will — every time we gather the *fyrd*, we have to ask them for permission."

"Chlodebaud is the worst," says Hildrik. "Chlodebaud of Camarac."

"Sigemer's son," I guess, remembering the town's name and its previous ruler from the days of our fighting at Trever.

Hildrik nods. "He blames me for his father's death — and suspects me of other crimes, too." He grins, knowing we share some of his dark secrets. "It's not that he bears a grudge — but he uses this blame to be a thorn in my side. You're fortunate not to have brothers, Octa. Family means chaos. It means weakness. Just look at Tolosa." He nods south, in the direction of the River Liger flowing somewhere beyond the horizon. "Brothers killing brothers —"

"Sons killing fathers," I say.

He fall abruptly silent and stares into the campfire. We all sit quietly for a while, chewing on dark, heavy Frankish bread.

"If you don't want to march on Goths, where will you take your army now?" I ask. "What happened here can't satisfy you or your men. It was barely a skirmish. What would your uncles say? This couldn't have been worth the bother of riding all this way."

"No, I don't suppose it was…" He sighs and leans back. "Still, it's not all bad. Syagrius now owes me doubly – for getting rid of Paulus, and for coming to Andecawa's help. And the Goths will think twice before sending their warbands anywhere near the border, once they've dealt with your Briton expedition."

"Riotham!" I cry out. "I almost forgot about him." I stand up. "I should go see Syagrius. He must have heard some news about the Briton army."

"Oh, do sit down." Basina pulls me down by the sleeve. "Syagrius will be busy with some local whore by now. You'll see him in the morning. There's still some ale left – and wine. All this talk of politics made my throat parched."

In the morning, I awake to the sound of chariot wheels tumbling on the cobbles of the Turonum road. It passes through Andecawa's gate and heads in our direction, followed by a detachment of horsemen– all wearing the red cloaks of the *equites*.

The Crown of the Iutes

The detachment splits after leaving the city; some, led by Ahes's chariot, ride straight towards us, while what has to be Drustan and his wing – though I can't tell for certain from a distance – hurries south, towards the Bacaud camp.

The first thing I notice when Ahes halts in front of Ursula and myself is the body strapped to the side of her chariot. Stripped of his armour and tunic, and with his face disfigured by an axe blow, the dead man is difficult to recognise at first.

"Who's that?" I ask, after exchanging greetings and expressing my relief at seeing the *equites* – most of them, at least – alive.

"Patrician Budic," replies Marcus. "We chased after him and his guard for two days, before finally catching up to them as they were trying to cross the Liger at Namnetes."

"The traitors are all dead," Ahes adds with a weary, but proud smile. "It's all over."

"And what of Namnetes itself?"

"The Saxons only burned the harbour on the way here; the town itself is safe."

"But we didn't hurry back just to tell you of our victory," says Marcus. "Well, maybe Drustan did…" He glances towards the Bacaud camp. "We found someone else at Namnetes – someone I thought you'd like to meet as soon as possible."

One of the *equites* rides up. There's another man on the back of his mount – this one's alive, clutching on to the rider's back in terror. It takes some effort to convince him to let go and dismount. His eyes are wild and bloodshot, his clothes are torn to shreds and his skin is covered in a mesh of thorn scratches. He's a young boy – barely of age, with only a patchy stubble of a beard.

"I know him," whispers Ursula. "He's a Briton. One of the Cantian recruits."

"Did he tell you anything?" I ask Marcus.

"Other than Riotham's name, he barely said a word," Marcus replies. "But I have seen this look in men's eyes before. He must have witnessed a massacre."

"For a moment there, I really thought we were going home," says Ursula, looking wistfully across the river.

The *ceol* disgorges its load of Iutish riders on the opposite shore and wobbles back precariously across the strong current. The storms swelled the Liger into an even greater obstacle than before. Fortunately, the Saxons have abandoned a number of their ships in their flight, and though they managed to scuttle some before the Franks got to them, we still found a few river-worthy vessels to carry us and the thirty ponies south again – back to the land of Goths.

There are a few new faces among the riders; seven warriors, chosen by Seawine from among his men to replace those of my bear-shirts who died or bore wounds too harsh to accompany us on this new mission. For the rest of the surviving Iutes, the war in Gaul was over. They have fought enough; to them, the victory at Andecawa had been neither quick nor easy – they gained their practice and glory, but little else from their expedition, and they deserved rest; indeed, from what I managed to overhear, many were beginning to wonder what they came to Gaul for in the first place. And so I sent them all away to Armorica with Marcus, ordering Seawine to take them back to Cantia at the nearest opportunity.

The Crown of the Iutes

"You didn't *really* want to go home, did you?" I ask Ursula. "We only just got here." I force a chuckle.

I don't need to remind her what we left back in Britannia; it was she who insisted on coming to Gaul, to forget about the pain and suffering that the plague brought on our family, and on her people.

It did, however, take some effort to convince her — and myself, first, for I was filled with just as many doubts — that it was worth us returning to the Gothic kingdom and embarking on the new mission of rescue, even as Aiwarik's armies roamed close to the border, seeking the same handful of Cantian survivors as we were.

The boy's name, coaxed out of him only after the bath, long rest and a few mugfuls of ale, was Tammo. He hailed from a farmstead west of Dorowern, bordering the highway to Londin; other than the walled cities, it was these small clusters of huts near the main roads that suffered the worst of the plague. Tammo's entire family, including his little sister, perished in a few winter days. When Riotham's recruiters passed through his desolate village, he joined them without a thought.

As a simple farmer, with only a fire-hardened club and his father's hunting knife to fight, he knew nothing of where they were going and why — and he didn't care; but Riotham, to his credit, made sure to keep even the lowliest of his soldiers informed of the great cause in which they took part: defeating the great Gothic scourge and saving the Empire.

"We knew not of those matters when we left Britannia," Tammo said. "I barely knew what Rome was, and that only because sometimes passing merchants or priests would stop in our village to wait out a storm or fix a wagon wheel, and entertain us with tales of distant lands. But hearing Riotham's heralds, you'd think we were marching to storm the Gates of Hell themselves, to aid the angels in their fight against the lords of evil."

And it was all going well, too. The city of Bituriges fell without a fight, as the Gothic garrison retreated on sight of the four cohorts heading their way. For days, the victorious army feasted on the spoils. Tammo, and many of his comrades, at first believed that the city – the largest they'd ever seen outside Londin – was Rome itself, and that their campaign was over just as it began, with their foes vanquished and the Empire rescued. The only thing that disturbed him was how little gratitude the locals showed to the liberating army.

"I could barely understand what they were saying, with their strange accents and even stranger words," he said, "but I knew when they were insulting us. The tavern doors shut when we approached them, and even the whores wouldn't serve us."

Eventually, an order came to march out again. The heralds announced that the Imperator himself was coming to meet them at the head of a great army, and that they would join forces at a place called Lemowices, from where they'd march on the barbarian capital itself, Tolosa. Tammo's head spun from all the new names and places, but one thing was certain: Bituriges wasn't Rome, and the world was much greater than he could ever have guessed.

They never reached Lemowices. They barely marched a day beyond Bituriges. When they were crossing a river in a small town called Dol, the Goths pounced upon them from all sides. They fought bravely, and Riotham led them well – at least, so Tammo heard later from those who knew about such matters – but not even Hannibal himself could have won this battle. The Goths split them in two. The main host got surrounded on the Dol bridge. The rearguard, where Tammo fought, and where most of the Briton nobles found themselves thinking it a safer place during the march, cut off from the rest, struggled for survival, slowly pushed upriver, away from the others – and from a way home. This was the last Tammo saw of Riotham and any of the Briton warriors that went with him.

The Crown of the Iutes

A man called Atrect – a *praefect* of the Dorowern *vigiles*, as Ursula remembered – took over command of the fleeing rearguard and rallied them to a last stand. To everyone's surprise, the army made up mostly of serfs with clubs, a few fat noblemen and a handful of *vigiles*, prevailed – whether through divine help, or because the Goths saw that they weren't worth losing men over. As the Britons retreated, by what could only be ascribed to the Lord's miracle, they found another forgotten ford, further up the river, and an overgrown road which led them into a deep, dark marsh.

"They are still hiding in that marsh now, Lord willing," Tammo said. "Three hundred men, maybe more. Most of them Cants, like myself. But with no food and only swamp water to drink, I don't know how long they will last. Atrect sent out several messengers to seek help. I don't know what happened to the others – I all but lost my wits fleeing the Goths and the pirates alike, before the red cloaks found me."

It was a dreadful tale, but it wasn't enough on its own to convince Ursula and me to ride to the help of the trapped Britons. It wasn't just that the task seemed impossible. The Gothic kingdom was now like a nest of angry wasps, disturbed by a bear. While a few weeks ago we could have snuck past Aiwarik's patrols on our way to Pictawis and Andecawa with ease, those same roads were now, according to Tammo, heaving with warriors, searching for any refugees from Riotham's army. If three hundred men couldn't break out of the marsh on their own, what good would thirty Iutish riders do?

But this wasn't the only reason for our hesitation. I was more inclined to march to the trapped army's help than Ursula. The Iute warriors were obliged to defend the Cantian citizens in accordance with the treaties my father and his predecessor signed with Wortigern and the Council at Dorowern – though one might argue just how far beyond Britannia that obligation applied. If it was at all possible for us to save them from annihilation, I believed we had to try. It was Ursula who protested the loudest.

"Why should we risk our lives to save these fools?" she fumed. "Those nobles let Riotham lead them into a trap in a vain pursuit of glory. They thought a war would be easy! None of them ever so much as struck another man in anger, except when a slave didn't bring them their morning potage with enough haste. I say, let them rot in that marsh."

"They are your people, Ursula. Cants. You helped recruit them yourself. Not all of them of noble blood. Many are simple farmers, like Tammo."

"They are all destined to perish sooner or later," she replied gloomily. "We would just needlessly prolong their futile existence. The sooner they fade away, the sooner they make space for those more deserving to live. The Iutes. The Saxons. The Angles."

"All this may well be true," I said, not wanting to argue with Ursula while she suffered one of her intermittent bouts of melancholy, "but nobody deserves to be left to starve in a marsh, far from home."

"Even so, how do you propose we achieve anything useful? You've heard what the boy said – there are whole warbands of Goths roaming the border, searching for anyone who even looks like a Briton…"

"I think I know how to reach the marsh unnoticed, at least. We'll need some of those ships the Saxons left behind – and a little help from Eishild and Hildrik…"

The *ceol* grinds onto the gravel. Eolh and Deora grab onto the ropes and draw it further in; Ubba throws down a ramp for the

The Crown of the Iutes

ponies. Ursula, hesitant to the last, smacks her lips and pulls her mount's reins, to lead it onto the deck.

A few miles east from where we are, Eishild and her Bacauds should have, according to the plan, already crossed the river, and marched southwards, down one of the minor roads towards Pictawis, making as much noise and commotion as they can to attract the Goths' attention. Some distance to the west, meanwhile, Hildrik's Franks will approach the border in their pursuit of Saxon pirates. Hildrik refused to cross the border in force, despite my pleas, still not wishing to start a war with Aiwarik on my account; but we hope his march, and a few diversions he promised along the way, will confuse the Gothic commanders into anticipating a two-pronged invasion across the Liger, to avenge the disaster at Bituriges. It is this confusion that the success of my plan depends on.

"This might be the most foolish adventure you've ever convinced me to embark on," Ursula says, when I join her on deck.

"You can still catch up to Seawine."

Ursula's stare hits me like a punch. "Don't push your fortune, *aetheling*. And better pray that your ruse worked and there isn't an entire Gothic warband waiting for us on the other side."

CHAPTER XVI
THE LAY OF ATRECT

Tammo's dubious description of the uncountable Gothic hordes roaming the countryside south of the Liger proved, understandably, inflated by fear and lack of experience – or maybe Hildrik's and Eishild's feints worked a little *too* well, for on our way towards the marshes we encounter merely regular patrols, of the same sort we had to avoid the first time we marched through here. What did change in the aftermath of recent events was the frequency of patrols – and their size. They now count eight riders, sometimes more; no longer can we hope to overcome them in a fight, not without losses we can ill afford. We can only sneak past them, riding mostly at dusk and dawn, by day finding shelter in ruined farms and abandoned *mansios* at a distance from the main roads.

The boy is a poor guide. He can hardly be blamed – this is all a new land for him, and he's only been here the once, fleeing for his life and hiding from anyone who seemed even remotely dangerous. It was a miracle that he got as far as he did. All he knew for certain was that he was following rivers, heading roughly north-west for many days until finally reaching the impassable Liger, which led him to the still functioning ferry at Namnetes; judging from the description of his route, he may even have passed Caino along the way, somehow avoiding the Bacaud watchmen. At times, he tells me that a nearby hill or grove looks familiar, but all hills and groves in this part of Gaul look the same, so I don't know how much his word can be trusted.

I have with me a military map, taken from Paulus's archives, but the singed scroll only shows what is of interest to an army commander: the stone highways, major forts and cities, river crossings and mountain passes. Since no army ever needed to march into the marsh, there's no mention of it anywhere on the map. With no other clues, we too are forced to simply make our way up the main rivers. We reach Vigenna, and follow it up to where another river meets it. Tammo studies the fork for a long time, before finally deciding we should follow this new branch.

"Are you sure?" I ask.

He stares at me with fearful eyes. "I'm not, *Domnus*. I don't remember this place well…"

"It must be," says Ursula. "If we go any further south, we'll reach Pictawis, and that has to be the wrong direction."

"How did you find your way across?" I ask the boy. Both rivers flow wide here, bound by golden crescents of beaches at the bends, and with a thick, dark wood covering the angle between, like the hair between a woman's legs. The only way to reach the other side is a broad ford, running over the ruins of an ancient bridge, linking two sides of a Roman highway – the road from Turonum to Pictawis, as the moss-covered milestone tells us. Both approaches to the ford are barred by recently fortified blockades, each manned by a small contingent of guards.

"These weren't here before," says Tammo. "I just caught a ride on a passing merchant's wagon. Nobody checked us."

I study the ford and the barricades. I count maybe a dozen men on our side; the barricade on the eastern shore is at least twice as large. We could wait for the night and try to swim across – the current doesn't look much stronger here than in Mosella at Trever, where our ponies managed to carry us over with little trouble. But we've been skulking, hiding and sneaking for too long, and I can see my warriors itching for a fight. A dozen warriors should pose us no problem — as for the other side, we'll deal with them when we get there…

"Test your weapons," I order the Iutes. I slide my sword out of its sheath to make sure the movement is smooth, and weigh the lance in my hand — a new weapon, taken from the Saxon stores, heavier and shorter than my old one, with a narrow, thrusting blade. Many of my men have armed themselves with blades and shields taken from the Saxons and Budic's soldiers; we have not yet had a chance to try their worth in battle. "We're hiding no more."

I raise my sword — but the war cry falters in my throat.

They storm from the north, in a thunderous tumult of horse hooves, in a flash of blades and armour, fifty heavy riders under the blue dragon banner, unstoppable, unbreakable. The Goths manning the eastern barricade rush out to face them. I see now that they were too numerous for us to have ever hoped to defeat them in a charge. But the Taifals smash through them like wild boar through wheat, halting only when they reach the palisade itself, where they dismount and launch into an assault on foot.

"Let's go," I call to my men. "Show them how the Iutes fight!"

The Goths on our side of the river fight poorly, terrified and confused of the two-pronged assault. I leap from the pony onto the palisade, vault over and land on top of a guard on the other side. There are a few more warriors here, uncertain whether they should rush to aid their brethren across the river or stand against us. One of them raises his shield and a spear at me; I shove him aside as I scramble up — his feet can't catch hold on the wet sand. I thrust my sword into the stomach of another enemy, then spin and hack at the first one's shield with both hands, once — twice — until his battered hand drops the shield. The third blow splits his skull.

The Crown of the Iutes

I wipe blood and brain from my blade. Around me, the brief fight is over. Audulf's men pull down the gate in the barricade, to let the ponies in. I mount up. We splash into the ford and reach the eastern blockade just when the Taifals break through on the southern flank. Between us, we make short work of destroying the Goths – almost disappointingly so, for I still feel the battle rush boiling in my veins when the remaining few warriors drop their weapons and raise their hands.

I take too long to contemplate whether to accept their surrender. The Taifals don't wait – they mercilessly cut the captives down and throw their bodies into the river.

I understand their decision – we can't afford the other Goths finding out what happened here; but I notice Ursula grow pale and turn away from the atrocity.

"Saphrax!" I call the Taifal chieftain. "Don't think I'm not grateful for your help, but – what are you doing here? Didn't Eishild tell you all to go to your homes after the ruse is done?"

"Pictawis *is* our home," he replies.

"You want to fight the entire garrison with just the fifty of you?" Ursula asks doubtfully.

He grins. "There will be more, Lord willing. The Goths haven't dared to take the entire city over yet – if we hurry we may make them think twice before trying."

I bow. "We won't hold you any longer, then. Whatever Fates brought you our way, we thank them. May the Lord assist you as you assisted us today!"

"Ask them about the marsh," says Croha when I turn back to my mount.

I blink. "Of course! If this is their home, they're bound to know the lay of the land! Saphrax!" I halt the warchief just as he's about to ride away and explain our quest.

He scratches his cheek. "You must be talking of the Bredanna Marsh," he says. "It's not far." He waves at one of his soldiers. "Senoc will take you there. He knows the short way."

"That was quick thinking," I tell Croha, as we watch the Taifals wade into the river. "Saved us a lot of wandering."

I put a hand on her arm in an approving gesture. She beams, her eyes gleaming, and nods. "I am your servant, *aetheling*."

My hand lingers gently on her shoulder. I feel the warmth of her neck. She doesn't stir from my touch, and her gaze softens. "I am your servant, *aetheling*," she repeats, quietly this time. Over her shoulder I glance Ursula staring at us both with a puzzlingly amused expression.

Bowls of cold nettle soup and some freshly picked cherries. It's not the hearty meal we expected after the long march, but as I sit on the sun-bleached grass in the shadow of the hut's eaves, spitting stones and wincing when I taste the sour fruit, I can't imagine eating anything more suitable to our surroundings.

The farmstead lies on the outskirts of the great marsh, so near in fact that the wind wafts swamp stench inside the huts, and the ground under my feet wobbles from moisture. Little if anything grows on such soil. Our good hosts serve us nettle soup not because they have some special fondness for the dish, but because at this time of the year that's all they've got, as they wait for the meagre oats to grow tall enough for harvest. The houses are built of mud and reed, and are as damp inside as outside; any attempt to

The Crown of the Iutes

light a fire fills the entire hut with thick, black smoke. A few bony goats bleat inside an enclosure – we were served some cheese of their milk in the morning, alongside flat, burnt oat cakes. It tasted of dung and mould.

Just beyond the drystone wall that marks the edge of the low rise upon which the farmstead was built spills the first of many shallow, silvery pools scattered to the horizon. Tufts of tall grass and reeds poke out in tiny islands. Groves of hazel and willow dot the landscape where there's enough dry land to support them. A great flock of geese somewhere makes an immense racket, but their meeting place is hidden from sight behind one of the grassy rises. I spot a low sandbank – or a causeway – which stretches eastwards from the farmstead, dividing the pool into two and disappearing in a small forest; it's the only way across the water that I can see. The locals must be using it to wade deeper into the marsh to hunt for waterfowl and pick herbs and roots that grow only in damp areas like this. There are drier patches, too, to the north and south, outcrops of soft, grey rock overgrown with heather and wild flowers. Further still, these rises grow into undulating hills, adding yet another dimension to this maze of pools, streams, sandbanks, causeways and wooded ridges. No wonder the Goths don't even try to penetrate the swamp in search of the Briton fugitives, content with surrounding it with a ring of steel. An entire *Legion* could hide here forever – if they had enough supplies.

"Look at the ponies," says Ursula. She spits a stone into her hand. "They've never seemed merrier."

"This moor must feel like home to them."

"They were all born in Cantia. They must have a memory of their homeland in their blood."

The woman who prepared our meal comes out of the hut, carrying a small basket covered with cloth. She approaches us with a conspiratorial smile and reveals a few rashers of dried, black meat.

"For the *centurions*," she says. "*Anas*. Duck."

I smile back and thank her, reaching for the meat. It's hard like oak wood.

"Is this all the Bredanna Marsh?" I ask her, pointing at the moor with the piece of duck.

"The locals called it such," she replies. "But we just call it the Stink."

"And… you're *not* a local?" asks Ursula.

The woman straightens her back. "My ancestor got this land from the Imperator when he retired from the Legions. We are Romans."

I look around in surprise. There isn't anything even remotely Roman about the place. I imagine the ancient Gauls must have lived in just such huts, with just such bleating goats, eating just such nettle soup, long before Caesar declared this land as belonging to the Empire. The woman's accent is harsh, rural, difficult at times to understand. I stare at her face trying to discern any distinct Roman features, but of course, I don't see any. Whatever old history she's talking about must have happened generations ago.

"You don't believe me?" she scoffs. "Come, I show you."

She leads us back to her hut. In the back, by the beddings, stands a small chest – I recognise it with surprise as one of those war chests that I've seen in the *Praetor*'s rooms in the old Imperial forts from Mona to Icorig. This one is covered with a layer of grime and soot

The Crown of the Iutes

an inch thick. The woman reaches inside and holds out gingerly some ancient heirloom, over a foot long and weighing some two pounds, bundled in faded red cloth.

Carefully, she unravels it to reveal a short, straight, double-edged blade, with no hilt, rusted almost beyond recognition. It is a sword of the sort I've only seen hanging on walls of noble houses, or used as a rusty farm tool, but one which for centuries was the symbol of the Empire's far-reaching fist: a legionnaire's *gladius*. The piece of cloth in which it is wrapped is still marked with a faint sign of a bull, and the barely legible letters: 'LEC VIII AVGVSTA'.

"Unbelievable," I whisper. "You really are the scion of a legionnaire. How old is this thing?"

The woman puts the *gladius* back in the chest. "Old," she replies, meaning she herself has no idea how many generations have passed since the soldier first settled in the marsh. Was this still a fertile land, then? Settlement would have been a reward for long years of service – I can't imagine a legionnaire being sentenced to a midge-infested marsh.

I'm struck by how, after all the uncounted years, these people still think of themselves as Romans. Is this how things were in Britannia, too, before the island separated from the Empire? Nowadays, if the peasants and townsfolk ever bother to think of such matters, they only count themselves as members of local tribes – Cants, Regins or Trinowaunts; few but the nobles and learned priests would even call themselves 'Britons'. If they felt like having to differentiate between themselves and the encroaching barbarians, they'd sometimes use the simple term *combrogi* – "countrymen" – but I've heard this word more in the West, in Ambrosius's domain. In the East, in the absence of a collective identity, I even heard some refer to themselves as *wealas*, the heathen word the only way for them to feel as though they belong to some greater whole.

But here in this remotest, poorest corner of Gaul, hundreds of miles from Rome, and decades since last seeing a Roman soldier, the people still believed themselves loyal subjects of the Empire. It was a sentiment that I hoped to use to our fullest advantage. The woman and her family were only vaguely familiar with their new Gothic overlords, but they loathed the idea of being ruled by a barbarian *rex* in place of a provincial magistrate, once again revealing an extent of knowledge beyond anything I could expect from a few peasants lost in the marsh: I was surprised they were at all aware of any change in the way Gaul was governed since their ancestor first set foot on this sandy knoll.

"Our Legions once kept the Goths and their likes far beyond the *limes*," the woman grunts. "Everything went downhill once we started making deals with the barbarians. First we gave them our land, then our gold. Now they think they can rule us!"

I prefer not to ask what she thinks of my men, very much 'the likes' of the Goths. As soon as I found out how deeply patriotic she felt, I told her we were a detachment of Imperial *auxilia*, searching for an allied cohort lost in the marshes. She accepted me and Ursula as the *centurions* of the detachment, since we both look suitably "Roman", but her words leave a nasty aftertaste in my mouth, reminding me of the fear and hatred the Britons like Wortimer and Riotham spewed against my people.

"Do the Goths give you a lot of grief, then?" Ursula asks.

"They came here once, years ago," the woman replies. "We hid in the marsh. They took our fattest goat." She spits.

"How do you even know –" I start, but I stop myself. She clearly wouldn't be able to tell the Goth warriors from any other barbarian raiding party. She thought our Taifal guide one of them, before we explained who he was. To her, all fair-hairs look the same. "Goth" is just the latest word to describe them.

The Crown of the Iutes

"About the lost cohort…" I return to the main reason for our conversation.

Finding the marsh itself seemed like the truly difficult part of our rescue mission, but now that we're here, Tammo's confused memory of his arduous journey is of little help again. Besides, *praefect* Atrect would have kept his men constantly on the move, if he wanted to avoid capture; they could be anywhere by now. We will not be able to find them – and not get lost ourselves – without local help.

"You'll want to find old Luto," she tells me. "He lives in the deepest marsh, and knows of everything that's happening there. He's the one who's bringing us these ducks." She waves the rasher with pride, as if it was the finest, sweetest piece of fowl. "Now, I'm sure he saw your missing soldiers – though he didn't know who they were at the time. He complained about some strange men scaring the birds and the fish the last time he was here."

"And how do we find him?"

"You won't – not on your own. But my son knows the way. He will take you in the morning. Do you want any more duck?"

"Please –" I raise my hands in protest. "We don't deserve such generosity. We've had more than enough."

"There they be," mumbles Luto proudly. "What'd I tell ye?"

He licks his lips and grins a toothless grin, pointing to a small camp set up in a scrap of heather moor on the edge of a rotting pool. I count maybe twenty men there, half of them on horseback – all under the black crow banner of Aiwarik's cavalry.

"Oh, by the Lord's bloody wounds," Ursula swears. "Can't you tell a Goth from a Briton?"

Luto's eyes widen in surprise. It's clear he's never seen either, and has no idea what we're talking about. We asked him to find the men who disturbed his fish, and he did his best to lead us to them. It's not his fault they turned out to be the exact opposite of who we wanted to find.

"Be these not the warriors ye're looking for?"

"We're looking for a whole Briton army, not a Goth patrol lost in the swamp. Haven't you seen anyone else?"

"Only more men like these ones, but they left a few days ago."

Ursula sighs. "We've wasted our time. Not only do we not know where the Britons are – we don't even know where *we* are now."

"Wait." I hold her hand. "These Goths are not here by accident. Perhaps they know something we don't know. Let's watch them for a while."

We lie in wait for some time – an hour, maybe two, time passes here like a lazy, meandering river. I suffer from the heat and the clouds of midges that somehow decided we are a tastier treat than the Goths' horses. I feel as if they drained half the blood from my body. At length, I'm fed up with this plague and I decide it's time for us to move on – when an alarm call rouses the Goths from their tents.

A new band of warriors appears on the heath, some two dozen of them; though they're only armed with cudgels, knives and hatchets, they charge at the Goth camp with fearlessness that betrays desperation. A chaotic brawl erupts on the camp's edge, as the Goths, overwhelmed by the surprise assault at first, quickly form a

The Crown of the Iutes

rough crescent around their horses; this allows a few of them to mount up, even as the attackers push against the line of defence.

I leap on the pony and blow on the warhorn. Ursula and Croha join me in the first charge; it takes a moment for the rest of the Iutes to mount and follow, but I can't afford to wait for them: the Goth riders are already flanking the enemy's rear. With their heavy lances, they cut a wide swathe in the enemy line. The assault breaks; the attackers pull back – in a few moments, they will be routed.

I charge at the nearest Goth. He turns around to face me only to have the Saxon lance thrust in his chest. The impact throws him off the saddle, but he manages to grab at the shaft and tear it from my hand as he falls. With the weapon gone, I draw my trusty *spatha*. Croha passes me by and engages another rider. Ursula swerves to avoid the third one; instead of fighting the horsemen, she chooses to ride in between the Goths and their enemies, separating the two. The Goths pause, uncertain what to make of our arrival. We don't look like any army they know – and with our Saxon weapons and fair hair we appear more as some barbarian allies than friends of the Britons. This is their mistake: by the time they realise we're here to destroy them, the rest of my Iutes reaches the battlefield.

"Don't let any of them get away!" I cry: the only order my men need. After we deal with the few horsemen, the remaining Goths don't even try to defend themselves, knowing they stand little chance against mounted warriors. They seek salvation in the marsh, wading and swimming across the pond, but they don't know the skill of our ponies in finding footing in the moor where there's none to see. Some of the warriors, those who had the misfortune to put on armour when the fight started, drown in the swamp before we get to them. Others are mowed down by our swords and trampled by our mounts. The last one, climbing out on the other side of the pool, falls to Croha's flying axe, striking him straight between the shoulders.

When I'm certain that no Goth managed to escape, I return to the heath, to meet the leader of the attacking band. He, like all his men, is a *wealh*, and wears the mud-caked black cloak of a town *vigil*; in the few patches not covered by mud and dirt, I spot the embroidered outline of a white horse. He's the only one of his band carrying a proper sword.

"Are you Atrect?" I ask.

"Yes," the *praefect* replies. "I know who you are," he says, nodding towards Ursula. "Councillor." He bows. He wipes blood and sweat from his face, and sheathes his sword. He seems exhausted – far more than he should be after the short skirmish – and famished. "Have you come to save us? Are the Gauls finally coming to our help?"

"Yes – and no…" I answer evasively. "Are you all that's left? We were told there'd be three hundred of you."

"There's more," he replies. "Though I doubt there's as many of us left as you hoped. I had them scattered throughout the marsh – it's easier to forage and avoid detection that way. It will take some time to gather us all together again."

"We don't have time," says Ursula. "Those Goths wouldn't have come alone."

"The Councillor is right. We need to march out in…" I look to the sky. "Two days, at the latest. We'll lend you our ponies if you need them to get your men, but anyone we can't find before then will be left behind."

"I understand." Atrect leans against my pony's flank and takes a few deep breaths. He's holding his side and winces – I spot a fresh scar in the tear in his tunic. "It's good to see familiar faces again,"

The Crown of the Iutes

he says, forcing a smile through pain. "I thought our prayers would never be answered."

"Save your prayers," I tell him. "We're not out of the marsh yet."

I don't think anyone has ever been more disappointed in me saving their life than *praefect* Atrect. Understandably so; trapped for days in the inhospitable marsh, he accepted there could only be two outcomes to his men's ordeal: to perish, either from hunger or by Gothic swords, or be rescued by a relief army sent from Gaul. What he did not predict – or looked forward to – was the arrival of thirty Iute riders, all alone and almost as lost and weary as himself.

What we couldn't bring him in numbers, however, we brought in knowledge – and the speed of our ponies. We knew Gaul better than him, we knew how to get around it; some parts of it we now knew almost as well as Cantia. For Atrect, this was a new, strange land, a dense network of roads leading to cities he's never heard about, inhabited by people he could barely understand. All he ever saw of it was the single highway leading from Rotomag, through Aurelianum, to Bituriges – and then the stretch of hostile land between the final battlefield and the marsh. Even if he could break through the Gothic blockade, he didn't know where he was, or how to get back home from there.

What Atrect soon learned to appreciate was that not only did we know the way home, we could spy it out for him – and that, more than any of our swords and lances, could help save his men from oblivion. Twice already we spotted a Gothic blockade on one of the narrow paths leading out of the marsh, and warned the Britons about it. In this way, we discovered that the shortest route to Syagrius's domain, through Turonum, was also the one most heavily guarded – not only against us, but against the Taifal rebels gathering at Pictawis.

By evening on the third day since our arrival to the marsh, Croha's shieldmaidens return from a patrol with news that the last path out we were hoping to take ends at a stone watchtower, manned by dozens of warriors.

"They know what they're doing," I tell the *praefect* and Ursula. "We will have to march around them."

I unroll Paulus's map on the flat stone. Atrect stares at it, scratching his chin, but the names and the markings mean nothing to him. As a captain of the local guard in a small Briton town, he never had to learn to read a Roman military map like this.

"It's not easy to tell, but we're somewhere in this triangle between Turonum, Pictawis and Bituriges," I say, pointing to the marked cities. "If getting to Turonum is out of the question, the road to Aurelianum will be doubly guarded."

"What do you propose?" asks Ursula. "We can't march across fields and forests all the way back to Andecawa."

"Why not?" I ask with a grin. "In fact, I think we should go even further." I search for the name on the map; I find it barely legible on the far edge, blackened and torn. I put my finger on it. Ursula leans over to decipher it.

"*Namnetes?* You want to go to Namnetes?"

"Tammo reached it on his own. It's a long way, yes – but it's the last thing the Goths would expect us to do."

"Because it's madness," says Ursula. "One boy may have avoided detection along the way, through Lord's providence – but we have three hundred men to guide across... What can it be, a four, five days of forced march?"

The Crown of the Iutes

"More than that, if the measurements given here are correct."

"Three hundred tired men. *Starving* men. Men who aren't soldiers and don't know how to march such distances even on stone roads, much less over rough ground. And all that with an entire Gothic army on our backs."

"Not if we do it right." I look up to Atrect. "I need you to pick fifty of your best men for a battle most of them will have no chance of surviving."

"Octa!" Ursula stares at me with shock.

"I'm sorry. I was thinking about this all night, and for the first time, I could not come up with a plan that doesn't involve great casualties. We need to lure the Goths in another direction – and they're too clever to fall for just a handful of Iutes riding about."

"I understand." The *praefect* nods. "Sacrificing fifty men to save the rest may sound harsh, but if there really is no alternative – it must be done. I would've prayed for such odds when we were stuck in that marsh."

"We will, of course, join these fifty in battle," Ursula volunteers, though this wasn't part of my plan. "And try to save as many of them as we can."

"I will expect you to catch up to us before we reach this 'Namnetes'," Atrect replies. He taps the map. "And someone will have to explain to me how to read this damn thing, if we are to get anywhere at all."

CHAPTER XVII
THE LAY OF CAIT

"**T**his is wrong," Ursula says firmly – for about the tenth time tonight.

We ride up and down the front line of the fifty Briton warriors. The volunteers stand proud, their weapons by their sides, even if I can still see the hunger and weariness in their sallow, sunken faces and eyes dulled by pain and worry. We took some food from the farms we passed along the way, but it wasn't enough to stave off the famine completely, and for now, honour and sense of duty must suffice to power them through the battle.

"I don't see you coming up with a better plan," I snarl, but seeing the look in her eyes, I mumble a swift apology. I'm as frustrated as she is with what I will require of these men, but as their commander, I cannot show it.

"Just because I can't think of a better idea, doesn't mean this one's any good. There must be a way to win without throwing away so many lives. Look at them – they're all common folk," she says. "They didn't come here to seek glorious death in battle. They all thought Riotham's campaign would just be a way to forget about their troubles for a few months, to earn some silver, to see some strange lands beyond their own. They had no idea what war is like."

No noble volunteered to join the forlorn force; they've all gone with Atrect. I'm fine with that. From my father's tales I know how difficult it is to command *wealh* nobles in a fight – especially for someone like me, a heathen.

The Crown of the Iutes

"They would've learned by now," I say. "And they all knew what they were volunteering for. Or have you forgotten what we *all* fled from? None of these men have any family to go back to in Britannia."

The pain flashing in her eyes makes the familiar bile of guilt come up in my throat, but I know I have to be brutal to make my point.

"I'm sure the *aetheling* knows what he's doing, Councillor," interjects Croha. She and Audulf are helping us form the Britons into something resembling a Roman muster line, three rows deep and sixteen abreast. "If he says there's no other way, there can be no other way. Better them than us, right?"

Ursula's stare turns icy. "Know your place, shieldmaiden," she tells Croha. "Do not come between me and my husband."

Croha's cheeks burn red. She bows and rides hurriedly away, to help Audulf with the rearguard.

"What was that all about?" I ask.

"Have you lain with her yet?"

"You know I haven't. And I don't plan to. Why are you envious? Not long ago you were practically pushing me into her breeches yourself."

"But you do agree with her."

"About what?"

"That it's better that these Britons die than your own warriors."

[332]

I roll my eyes. "I don't send anyone to their deaths with light heart, Ursula. But yes, if I have to choose, I choose thirty trained horsemen over fifty common spearmen. It's a calculation every commander must make in the field. Besides, weren't you the one who was telling me just a few days ago how they must perish, to make way for the barbarians?"

"Don't throw my words back at me. You have no idea what it's like to…" She shakes her head and calms down. "I shouldn't have snapped at Croha like that. None of this is her fault, and we need her to be at her best today. I'll go tell her I didn't mean –"

"No –" I take her hand. "She'll be fine. We don't have time for this. They're about to move out."

We ride to the front of the muster line. If I had weeks to train them instead of hours, I know I could forge these fifty Britons into a fine warband. They're not much different to our Iutes – most of them, too, were common folk once; farmers, fishermen, village craftsmen… If there's anything I've learned since the first warband I ever led, formed of slaves freed in Epatiac, it's that once they're treated as soldiers, all men *become* soldiers, at least in their minds. I have no illusion that they're yet a worthy fighting force – and certainly not right after days of starving in the marsh – but for what I have planned for them, strong minds might prove more important than strong arms.

"We, Iutes, believe that it is a man's greatest glory to die in battle," I tell them. "That it is enough to perish with a sword in your hand to gain entrance to Wodan's Mead Hall, where the feast never stops. I know I cannot offer this comfort to you, Christians. But I know you understand the value of sacrifice, better perhaps than any heathen. Like your Lord, many of you will die today, to save your people. Maybe even all of you. But each one of you will die a martyr. The God you believe will recognise your heroism and

The Crown of the Iutes

sacrifice, like He recognised that of the Thebans and of Albanus. Your deaths will not be in vain – neither in this world or the next."

It is not a rousing speech, but then it's hard to raise enthusiasm for a battle which is destined to be a defeat. The only thing that I require from these Britons is to hold out for as long as they manage – and try to take as many enemy with them as they can when they inevitably fall.

My Iutes need no such motivation. To them, the glory of death is reward enough; besides, I'm sure they haven't failed to notice that I don't require the sacrifice from them. They trust me – they know I will do my utmost to lead them to victory, just as I have countless times before.

There's nothing more for me to say. I nod at my men. We gather in a loose wedge and ride out onto the road leading to the ruined village of Dol and its infamous bridge. Some distance behind us, fifty Britons follow, in solemn silence, to their deaths.

Everything about Dol matches Atrect's description of the place when he last saw it – except for the recent destruction. In the fierce battle with Riotham's main host, most of the small town - more an oversized *mansio*, really, with a chapel on one end and an already long-ruined bath house on the other – was razed almost to the foundations, leaving only rectangles of charred stone with blackened timber stakes sticking out like dark crosses. It is a grim sight, but it makes for perfect, ready-made fortification.

Unlike most other towns and hamlets along this river, Dol lies on its right, western bank. This, too, is to our advantage. The Gothic garrison, what little of it remains, is stationed across the water, with the exception of a flimsy, symbolic barricade set up on the bridge's western end, more to control the traffic than to prevent any attack.

Not that the Goths here anticipate much trouble. The road through Dol is a minor one, and ends at Bituriges, where a strong garrison now awaits anyone foolish enough to try to repeat Riotham's short-lived occupation of the city. There are better crossings to the north and south of it, for an army that is in a hurry to reach Gaul and wants to avoid enemy fortresses; and returning to the place of our defeat is the last thing the enemy expects us to do.

Since the entire battle is one great ruse, it is only fitting that it starts with a series of smaller feints. We smash through the barricade with ease and send the Goths flying across the bridge; but when we reach the palisades of their camp, we halt and turn tail, as if in fear of the garrison's greater numbers.

As we turn around, Ursula glances at the palisade with barely hidden contempt. The fence is poorly set up, with plenty of gaps for infantry to exploit. Even the place where we met the Taifals was better defended. If this was a real attempt at a crossing, we would have no trouble forcing our way through. Clearly, the Goths sent here are far from the finest of Aiwarik's warriors.

"Fortune favours us," I tell the Britons when we get back on the left shore. Not all of the fifty are here yet; I ordered them to come in ragged waves, to make an impression of a routed army on a desperate run.

"How so?" asks one of the soldiers, Cait; I knew the Britons would need a commander from their own ranks, to lead them in the final stand when we were no longer here. I chose this man at first simply because he bore the most scars. Others later confirmed that he was among the fiercest fighters in the retreat from Dol, almost losing an eye and an arm in the process. In Cantia, he was a member of what was left of the tribal militia. He even managed to convince several other former militiamen to follow him to their deaths, proving he had what I needed from him – valour and skill in command.

"The Goths here are cowards," I reply. "They will exaggerate our numbers when they report our arrival. If we make enough noise, they will think a whole cohort is coming to fight them. Now get to work, we have a few long days ahead of us."

As the Britons build a fence around the town's ruins – tall enough to hide our true numbers, and broad enough for a camp that could house several hundred men – I set up the watch post in the small church overlooking the river, the only stone building still standing on this side of the town. We're in no hurry. It takes a day for the Goths to send a messenger out to Bituriges and for the city's garrison to march out in full force against us. Before that happens, I watch as various smaller detachments arrive at the Gothic palisade, brought in from other crossing points, as the news of our arrival slowly spreads along the river. Every day of delay works to our advantage. By now, hopefully, Atrect should have moved out of the marsh, following the hidden paths and secret causeways, shown to them by the loyal guide recruited from the legionnaire's family's farmstead. The more Goths we can draw away from the route of his march, the better.

When the Bituriges garrison finally arrives, the result of our ruse exceeds all my expectations. There must be a full cohort of warriors facing us on the other side of the river, if not more; are the Gothic commanders really that worried about the Briton breakout? Half of that number would've been enough to stop any attempt at crossing the bridge, even if our force was the size of Riotham's original army.

"Something must have frightened them more than just us," notes Audulf, joining me in the church.

"Perhaps Hildrik decided to cross the border after all," I guess. "Or maybe Saphrax was more successful with his revolt at Pictawis than we expected."

"What if they come at us from the rear?" Audulf asks.

"They will, eventually. If their officers have any sense. We'll just have to get the men out of here before they do."

"By men, you mean us."

I nod. "The Britons volunteered to die here. We didn't."

The sound of warhorns shatters the sky; a frightened flock of ducks launches into the air, quacking irritably at the disturbance. The first Goths enter the bridge tentatively: a line of shieldsmen, followed by some javelin-throwers, to test our defences and our resolve.

"Here they come," I say. "Get the riders. You know what to do."

"What about you?"

"The Britons need to at least put up a pretence of resistance in that first skirmish. They will need someone to show them how."

The night is a time for burials.

We dig eleven shallow graves in the church's hallowed ground; all of them for the Britons. Ursula recites a solemn prayer for the dead. Tears of real grief flow down her cheeks when she's finished. I have never seen her shed tears like these, not even after Pascent's death.

The Crown of the Iutes

"We will not hold out long with these kinds of casualties," she remarks grimly after the ceremony. She helps Croha and her shieldmaidens to take care of the wounded, but there's little any of us can do to ease their suffering, except give them copious amounts of bark from the marsh willows to chew. We have no other ointments or balms, and we have to tear the tunics taken from the dead to use as wrappings.

"This first day would always have been the toughest," I say. "We had to give the Goths a bloody nose, to have them bring up more men to fight us from elsewhere."

I rub my weary eyes, and stretch the right shoulder, strained from the sword work. All day I have been leading the Britons and the Iutes in a long, exhausting battle. The Britons fought better than I could ever have hoped; they quickly learned how to keep formation, how to advance and pull back in good order, to make way for the Iute charges and turns. Three times the Goths thought they succeeded in pushing us away from the bridge, and three times the well-timed Iute charge threw them back, until at last, the enemy gave up and retreated beyond their palisade to lick their wounds.

"And are you still sure this plan of yours will work?" she asks. "That we won't all just die here, in vain?"

"I'm never *sure* any of my plans will work," I reply. "I'm only human, after all. I try my best, but I can only keep us alive for as long as the gods allow."

"Then I can only hope I prayed enough for the both of us."

I hold her hand. "This is far from the most dangerous situation we've ever been in, you know. All we have to do is ride back into the marsh. The Goths will never catch up to our ponies once we're in the moor."

"If we had enough ponies to save everyone," she asks, "would you have tried?"

"We don't have enough ponies," I reply.

She purses her lips and stands up. "I must go back. I have my wounded kin to attend to."

The pale red light of dawn ignites the eastern horizon. I yawn and stretch again. The pain in the right arm radiates all over my side and back, but I must ignore it, for now. A distant sound of warhorns announces the Goths launching another assault.

Two days later, I gather what's left of the Britons in a depressingly small circle. Less than a half of them remains. I lost two of my men, too – Bidda and Wehthelm, from Ubba's "blade", thrown off the bridge by a desperate charge of Gothic spearmen at the end of the third day's last assault. It's clear to everyone what's coming – especially now that the Goths have finally decided to send two of their warbands across the river, to surround us and cut us off from the marsh. They finally realised how few we are, and that no other reinforcements are coming. Judging by the movements I observed from the church, the Gothic commander must have grasped our ruse, for I saw him send half of his men away yesterday, including most of his horsemen, no doubt in search of Atrect's real army of fugitives.

"You have all done your ancestors and your kin proud," I tell the Britons. "You fought better than I could have ever hoped – and put the fear of a Briton soldier in Gothic hearts. But it will soon be all over. We've done what we can. There's no more point defending these ruins. Today, when the Goths attack, we break out. Those who wish to try their fortune, are free to flee with us – those who wish to stay behind to cover our retreat, must do so on their own."

"I will lead the last stand," says Cait. He finally lost the eye – and a chunk of his left foot – but he lost no will to fight. I lay a hand on his arm.

"You'd have made a fine officer in the Legions," I tell him. "And a worthy warrior in my father's guard."

"Maybe we will all meet in that Mead Hall of yours," he says with a chuckle. "Or in Lord's Heaven. Who can tell?"

"Who indeed." I nod.

"They're coming!" Audulf calls from the lookout. "From both sides!"

I mount up. "Open the gate," I order. The "gate" is just an opening in the camp's fence, barricaded with logs, which the Briton soldiers pull down to let us out. "Cait, I will need you and your men back on that bridge. Make every strike count. The rest of you – it's every man for himself."

We storm out of the camp, and head straight at the Gothic band approaching us from the rear. Our counter-attack catches them by surprise – they expected us to make another stand on the bridge, just as we have so many times before in the last three days. But the surprise doesn't last long. We are a tiny force, after all, and a weary one, a mere single arrowhead aimed at a great wall of spears and shields. I glance over my shoulder. Only ten Britons decided to try fleeing with us; the rest of them set up a thin defensive line on the bridge. I notice Cait turning back to me and raising his sword in salute.

"Left!" I cry, just before we hit the Goths. The Iutes swerve as one. The Goths throw their javelins – and, in the confusion, miss us all. The enemy commander hesitates, unsure whether to chase after us, or focus on Cait and his defenders. The hesitation costs him the only chance he got to catch up to us. What happens next is something even I hadn't planned for: when I look back once again, I see the ten Britons running after us turn and throw themselves on the Gothic spears in a suicidal charge.

Their brutal, bloody deaths shock even the Goths. Their advance wavers. My men slow down, too, staring at the still twitching corpses in a daze.

"Don't stop now!" I cry, desperate to rally them back to a gallop. "Just a few miles more! If we make it to those willows, we'll be safe from any pursuit. Don't let their deaths be in vain!"

I spur the pony for one final spurt of speed. Behind us, the Goths raise a great war howl and rush again – not at us, but at the bridge, at the lonely line of the Briton last stand.

"I dreamt about them again today," Ursula tells me. "I watched their bodies bleeding out on the Gothic spears. Then one of them turned to me, and I saw Pascent, as an adult."

"How did you know it was Pascent?"

"The way you know things only in dreams."

I can't see her face clearly in the darkness; I can't even tell if she's crying. We ride by night, and sleep by day, in farms and villages, passing through small, friendly towns where the Goths haven't yet bothered to set up guard. From what the locals tell us, we're following Atrect's trail closely, just as he follows the route marked

The Crown of the Iutes

out on the map I gave him: as straight towards Namnetes as possible, but still staying a good distance away from the Roman roads. The Britons are keeping a surprisingly good pace, and have marched further than I expected, but we should catch up to them in the morning, near the town of Segora. The keeper of the remote *mansio* where we stayed yesterday told us of a long column of weary strangers passing by his place only the day before; they seemed hungry and exhausted, but they didn't stop at his place for rest.

We have had no trouble with the Goths yet – which means that either our ruse at Dol worked too well, or they have sent their warriors ahead of us, to intercept us when we inevitably try to cross the Liger back into Gaul. The latter is more likely. The locals in the farmsteads and villages know only rumours, but they talk of armoured riders going back and forth along the stone highways, in numbers which remind them of what they call "the great war of six years ago".

"Our son would've made a great warrior one day, I'm sure," I say. "And an even finer *Rex*."

"Especially with the blood of Cants in his veins," she replies with a sad chuckle.

"Who could've guessed the *wealas* would fight so well? One wonders why they need our help defending their borders at all."

"Those *wealas* kept you barbarians at bay for generations," Ursula says. "Who do you think served in the Briton Legions?"

"I suppose you're right." I nod. The pony halts before a ditch – an old irrigation canal, now barely visible under the lush growth. I tut at it to carefully go forward, and pass the word about the obstacle back to the rest of the troop.

"What happened to your people, then?" I ask when we're all safely on the other side, and back on the wide, slightly sunken path, used by generations of local cattle drovers to move their herds from one pasture to another. "I used to think the Britons just weren't as warlike as the Iutes or Saxons – that fighting wasn't in their blood. But you're right, they *used to* be masters of war, a long time ago. Rome's Legions took longer to conquer Britannia than Gaul – and even they were halted in the mountains of the North. They didn't always need barbarians to fight their battles for them."

"They grew lazy," Ursula replies. "And rich. It's become easier to pay off the barbarians than to fight them, and so they have forgotten they ever knew how to do it. Now they, too, believe that it's something only the heathens have skill and keenness for. And they have no great warchiefs to lead them, not since Wortigern. Riotham may think himself a fine commander trained in the ancient ways, but he's a laughing stock compared to the *tribunes* and *duces* of old."

"Perhaps my father should consider recruiting the Cants into our ranks."

"I doubt your father would ever trust us enough. And he'd be right not to. You never know when a next Wortimer or Riotham will spawn, and convince us to stab your people in the back with their own *seaxes*."

"Then I will do it, once I'm the *rex*," I say firmly. "Now that I've seen what your people can do, it would be too much of a waste to let them wither in the farms and *villas* while we bleed out on the beaches."

"You just want more spear fodder for your Iute warriors to shield behind."

The Crown of the Iutes

"*You* are a Iute warrior," I remind her. "And a future Queen of the Iutes."

"I am also a Dorowern Councillor. And I have *my* people's well-being to care for."

"In our kingdom, the Cants will be treated no different to the Iutes. And *we* will make sure to forge them into warriors as good as we are, the sons and daughters of Donar. Together."

It is only a day's march from Segora to Namnetes, according to the Roman map – if one follows the stone road. We're not hiding anymore; there's no point. If the Goths have guessed where we're going, they will be waiting for us at the river crossing anyway. Speed is more of the essence now than stealth, as Atrect and I lead the two hundred and fifty Britons in the final march to what we hope to be salvation.

The Britons welcomed the grim news from Dol with silent acceptance. They may have hoped – and prayed – for some of their comrades to survive, but deep down they all knew none who came with us would return. And, having crossed hundreds of miles of Gaul without encountering so much as a Goth patrol, they knew how much their sacrifice was worth.

The town of Segora, where we found them, may have once been an important post on the road to Armorica, but since the Roman rule in Gaul collapsed and the provinces fell apart, the town shrank both in size and significance, until all that remained was an old *mansio*, a chapel, and a cluster of huts around them, all in the midst of abandoned, half-ruined tenements and public buildings, the use of which not even the locals remember. A short section of a wall bound the city from the north, but the construction was abandoned long ago, when it became clear that no enemy will bother marching from the direction of the marshes spreading around the mouth of the Liger, and even if they did – they would find nothing worth taking in this miserable memory of a town.

Though we were in a hurry, we agreed to stay in the town for one day. If a Goth detachment was indeed waiting for us at the Liger crossing, we needed to be fed and rested to face them. Surprisingly, an old priest still resided in Segora's chapel, serving the surrounding farmsteads and the rare traveller; he agreed to perform a mourning Mass for the fallen Britons – and even recited a short prayer for the Iutes we lost in all the battles since coming to Gaul.

"I prayed for the Goths when they marched against the Huns," he told me. "And I prayed for the Alans when they marched against the Goths. Whether you worship Wodan, Mars or the Sun, you all merely follow the Lord's great and mysterious plans."

"Aren't you worried we might be following the Adversary's plan instead?"

He smiled as if he was talking to a child. "Bless you, son. Even the Adversary can only act out what the Lord has written for him."

The Crown of the Iutes

CHAPTER XVIII
THE LAY OF HATHUGAUT

I remember the old priest's words when we reach the shores of the Liger. This near to the mouth the river is more like a gulf of the sea, flowing wider than the Rhenum in a weave of broad streams, among a myriad of islands, islets, sandbanks and clumps of reed. It's impossible to tell where the river ends and where the marsh begins. The engorged currents encroach on the abandoned farms and pastures, submerge the forests and sink the ancient stones scattered randomly in this land. The span of water is too great to have been bridged, even by the Roman engineers of old; ferries serve the crossing, such as it is, linking Namnetes on Armorica's side with a smaller town on the southern shore, where the Roman road ends.

The town is not marked on my map, so I don't know its name – I didn't even expect it to be here. There's no wall around the town itself, and most of it is a ruin, shattered and plundered by the years of pirate raids; but there are remains of an ancient stone rampart thrown around its church, guarding it from the landward side, and a watchtower over the harbour. We dare not get close to it, seeing the banners of a Gothic garrison flying from the watchtower and the heavily fortified camp around it.

We're not the only ones trying to cross the Liger here. We arrive just in time to witness the end of a skirmish in the town: a failed attempt of a small band assaulting the harbour in a handful of row boats.

"They must be Hildrik's men," I tell Ursula. "He's keeping his promise, trying to draw the Goths' attention away from us."

The Crown of the Iutes

"It's a pity he's doing the exact opposite," she replies.

"He can't know we're here. Maybe if we send a few men across…"

"It's not going to help us," she says, studying the river. "We can't ferry three hundred men in row boats."

"There has to be some other way."

Before we start setting up camp, I send Ubba's riders upstream, and Croha's shieldmaidens downstream. Croha is the first to return.

"You'll want to see this yourself, *aetheling*," she tells me.

I mount up and follow her shieldmaidens to the west of the harbour town, where the fields and pastures dissolve into more marshes, criss-crossed by shallow streams and dotted with muddy ponds. With every step we rouse some dozing creature – ducks, quails, otters, all leaping from under the hooves of our ponies. A flock of some giant, grey, long-necked birds I've never seen before, rising to four feet on stilt-like legs, watches us pass by with raucous unease.

Before long, we climb a low ridge and descend it again, to reach the Liger shore on the other side. The river bends into a sort of cove here, a horseshoe of white sand bound by tall, rustling reeds which serve well to hide it from view of any ships sailing past.

Hiding in this cove, dragged out onto the beach, is a fleet of twenty *ceols*, most of them bearing heavy damage from some recent fierce battle. Bustling all around them, working hard to make the ships seaworthy again, is a Saxon warband, by my count at least sixty-men strong.

Watching the cove from our hiding place in the roots of an ancient, dark oak tree, I spot what must be the fleet's flagship, a large *ceol* with its sails striped red and white, and painted with a figure of a wild boar: the crest of Sigegaut's clan. A *ballista* is mounted on its aft – I'm certain it's one of the machines hauled away from Andecawa's walls. Another is being repaired on a neighbouring ship.

"And you're sure they haven't spotted you?" I ask Croha.

"No, *aetheling* – I don't think they expect anyone looking for them here."

"No, it doesn't seem so." I scratch my chin. "You may have saved us all," I tell her.

"I only did what you ordered, *aetheling*. Anyone could've stumbled on this cove."

"And yet, what we needed was your good fortune that once again showed us the way. Who knows, maybe the gods are looking after you, guilty for what they allowed to happen to your family," I say, remembering how Croha came to live with us in Cantia in the first place – after the Saxon raiders killed her parents in the Meon Valley, many years ago.

"Many families perished in that war, *aetheling*," she says, turning away. The light in her eyes dies down. "The gods don't owe me anything."

"Well then, maybe they just like you for who you are," I say with a smile. "You deserve their good will."

She's so close I can smell her sweat even through the mud caked to her skin. I reach to brush some poplar fluff, stuck to her hair in

The Crown of the Iutes

white tufts – it's floating everywhere in the marsh today, like summer snow.

She wipes the mud from her face and stares back at me. I'm suddenly struck by the soft beauty of her features, and the bold light burning in her eyes, unusually dark for a full-blooded Iute. Ursula was right – she *is* a fine woman. I imagine myself kissing her bow-shaped lips, biting her neck, cupping those shapely breasts she keeps bound under her mail shirt – and I grow suddenly envious of any man who had her. Is she still lying with Deora, I wonder? Or some other warrior, back in Cantia? A woman like her should not be spending her nights alone…

A bittersweet memory flashes before my eyes, a vision of poor young Odilia, moaning sweetly under me; many years ago, we lay together in just such a thicket, while spying on Odowakr's other army in Trever. I had no qualms taking what she offered me that day. Why am I so reluctant now? Is it only because I am now wedded to Ursula? Because I'm older and more responsible? I know most Iute men wouldn't hesitate in my place, even if they didn't have their wives' overt permission to do so. Or maybe it's precisely *because* Ursula wants me to do this…?

"*Hlaford?*" she whispers. There's a bemused, challenging glint in her eyes, as if she's sensing my turmoil.

"It's nothing." My voice comes out hoarse, breathless. I clear my throat. Now is not the time, I tell myself. "Stay here and watch," I say. "If anything changes, ride back – don't be a hero. I'll soon return with the others."

"I'll be waiting for you, my *Hlaford*." Her whisper brings heat to my loins.

"I don't want a battle," I explain to the Britons. "We're all tired, and we're too close to safety to risk even one of your lives. The Saxons seem tired, too, and they're also running away from something. I will try talking to their warchief first – but be prepared for a fight. We have more than twice their number, and we hold the higher ground. There's no chance for us to lose. I hope the Saxons will see this, too."

"What do you need us to do while you're down there?" asks Atrect.

The entire Briton army has gathered in a hollow on the far side of the low ridge, just out of sight of the Saxons. Our flight across Gaul taught us how to keep stealthy in any circumstances; the pirates still haven't the slightest inkling that nearly three hundred men are preparing to fight them less than half a mile away.

"Spread out in the dunes, stay ready, and wait – either for my signal, or for Audulf's orders, if I'm no longer able to give them."

The Saxons, busy with the repairs, don't even notice Ursula and me at first, as we ride down into the cove. They, too, must be tired from all the fleeing and fighting. When one of them finally spots us, the news of our arrival spreads like fire in dry grass. The warriors drop their tools and pick up their weapons. As we ride on towards Sigegaut's flagship, they surround us in silence, brandishing their bloodied *seaxes* and battle axes. They seem in no better shape than Atrect's Britons: weary, hungry, and covered in scars and bruises, their clothes turned to rags, the blades of their weapons chipped and blunted.

I call for Sigegaut three times. At last, the warchief emerges onto the deck, wearing only a loincloth and a helmet, holding a great axe in his hand.

"Who wants to see me?"

The Crown of the Iutes

"Have you forgotten me already?"

He looks down, shielding his eyes from the sun. "*Aetheling* of the Iutes? How is it that you're here? Are we all dead, and on our way to Wodan's Mead Hall?"

"As strange as it may seem, we are both alive – and I would wish for it to remain so, at least for a while yet. Come down and talk with me, warchief. I have a proposition to make."

"A proposition?" He leaps heavily onto the white sand and presses the axe's edge to my sternum. "If you came to join us, I fear you're too late. We're leaving this land. If you wish to surrender your men, however, I can see to it that they fetch a good price in the Burdigalan market."

"Neither, warchief. I come to demand that *you* surrender to *me*."

Sigegaut laughs. "You? And your two dozen Iutes? Or have you sprouted a *real* army since we last met?"

"Curious you should ask."

I raise my hand, holding a white flag. All around the cove, the scrubs on the dune tops rustle, and two hundred Britons – with my Iutes scattered between them – emerge tumultuously, weapons drawn, howling and jeering, making it seem as if there were twice as many of them as their real number.

Sigegaut's face turns sour.

"The Saxons do not fear death in battle," he declares.

"Neither do the Iutes, I assure you. Wodan welcomes all of us." I glance to his ships. "But if you wanted your men to die in battle, you wouldn't have tried to flee Gaul on those wrecks. Who was it that forced you to run in such an ignominious manner – Hildrik?"

"The Frank, aye." He nods, resigned, and lowers his axe. "Ever since Odowakr betrayed us, we have only been retreating. In every battle I lost ships and men. Now all I want is to sail back home. At least for the winter."

"But you have to fix the *ceols* first," I note. "And if I know anything about boatwrighting, you still need a few days to be able to brave the open sea."

He gives me a sharp look. "You don't want my men. You want my ships."

"You have the vessels," says Ursula. "We have to get to Armorica. We are both fleeing – you're chased by the Franks, we're running from the Goths. It only makes sense for us to work together."

"Then why the talk of surrender?" He scoffs. "Just pay us, and we will ferry you over. I may not be able to sail out to sea just yet, but I still have a few ships that can take you across the river."

"I have nothing to pay you," I say. "And I need you to take us further than just Namnetes. This frontier is on fire, and I can't risk my men getting trapped between the Franks, the Goths, and what Bacauds are still out there, fighting."

I tell him about the Taifal revolt in Pictawis, and of the Goth army in our pursuit.

"As our captives, you'll be able to pass through Armorican waters without trouble," says Ursula. "And land in Armorican harbours for the night. Just get us to Gesocribate, and you'll be free to go from there wherever you want."

The Crown of the Iutes

Sigegaut rubs his chin in thought.

"And you won't betray us to the Franks or the Armoricans the moment you get the chance?"

I hold out my naked knife. "We swore a blood *ath* once before. We can do it again, if you want. We are both Wodan's sons – you and I are kin, unlike all those *wealas* that surround us."

He pushes my hand away. "That won't be necessary, Iute. An *ath* should not be thrown lightly like this. Sometimes you just have to trust one another."

He glances to the Briton army on the dune ridge. I can see he calculates something in his mind.

"I will need three days to fit the ships enough to take you all on," he says, at last. "The Goths from Ratiates will have discovered us by then – especially with so many of you roaming around the marsh."

"Don't worry about the Goths," I say, guessing that Ratiates must be the name of the ferry town we just passed. "We'll take care of them when they come. Just get those *ceols* fixed."

I dismiss Sigegaut's fears at first. For the Goths, this is still a strange, new land. They would have been given this *pagus*, along with its capital Pictawis, after the Battle of Maurica, with *Rex* Thaurismod, Eishild's father, claiming it as reward for their service against the Huns – but they only started manning the garrisons two years ago, after peace with Syagrius. If Ratiates was of any importance, beyond the rarely used ferry, more Goths would have been tasked with defending it from the pirates; but the remnant of the town was these days clearly only a poor relative to the greater city on the Armorican side, and there was nothing left here for the Saxons and other sea bandits to plunder. I doubted what few warriors there were guarding it, wary of the Frankish army still looming in Namnetes, would dare enter the Liger's impenetrable swamps in our pursuit, just as their kin feared entering the marshes of Bredanna.

I am soon proven wrong.

The first to come are single riders, followed by small patrols, prodding ever deeper and bolder into the marsh. By the second day, they start coming dangerously close to the cove, though they don't know it yet. None of them live long enough to report back; we have, by now, become skilled in fighting in the swamp, and making the enemy "disappear" in it without a trace. But the fact that they're heading our way in the first place is worrying in itself.

"They know we're here somewhere," says Audulf, wiping the sword from the Goth's blood. "Someone must have told them."

I glance to the ships. Some two-thirds of them appear ready to sail. The Saxons have already begun gathering provisions for the long journey home, coiling the ropes, slotting the oars, letting the sails dry in the breeze. Seeing the vessels being prepared like this makes me anxious. Should Sigegaut decide to abandon us and sail away on his own with just the repaired ships, there would be little I could do to stop him. I put all my trust in his word, but what worth is the word of a pirate chief? Could he really have betrayed us to the Goths, in exchange for safe passage? But then, I'm sure he must be wondering the same about me and the Armoricans…

"If someone told them where we were, the Goths would already be here in full force," I say. "They must have tracked us into the marsh somehow, but then lost the trail."

The Crown of the Iutes

"It won't be long before they find it again," says Ursula. "What a stubborn mule that commander is!"

I look around and realise that being sent to this inhospitable, remote frontier, must have been some kind of punishment for Ratiates's commander. If he wished to ever return to more civilised provinces, he had to prove himself to his superiors, and what better way than to trap the famous contingent of runaway Britons, pursued by now by everyone in the kingdom?

"I don't think we need to worry about the garrison," I say. "How many men can there be in that camp, fifty? A hundred? We're only in trouble if they send for reinforcements. The *ceols* are almost ready. We'll be out of here in no time."

"If Sigegaut keeps to his word," says Ursula.

"He knows what it's like to be betrayed," I say. "I have a feeling we can trust him more than we can trust anyone else in Gaul."

"Hold the line!" I cry. "Whatever happens, even if it means you'll be slain, don't break! Your death will buy others their lives. Remember the sacrifice of those who perished at Dol!"

As I watch the Goths rush up the dune, I regret having sent Seawine back to Britannia. The Britons are not trained in the art of shield wall, and even if they were, we have only a few long shields and spears between us. I have them stand in a line two-men deep, the first row ready to take on the full impact of the Gothic charge, the row behind them, their arms locked, is to serve as a living rampart to support their comrades from falling and retreating.

Even my Iutes have dismounted for this battle. I put them into the front line at intervals, like keystones in a wall; each of them a commander of the men fighting nearby. Only they are allowed to make their own decisions when I'm too busy to give orders: I know my warriors well enough to trust them when they decide to advance and when to pull back, something I trust no Briton militiaman with, not even Atrect, and certainly none of the haughty nobles that are with him.

It was so much easier to command Cait's detachment of commoners. The nobles grunt at my every order, and mumble at having to lock arms with the simple serfs as equals. I put most of them in the centre of the line, hoping that the pressure from both sides will keep them in check – and I position my best warriors on their flanks, to keep an eye on them and make sure to fill in the gap when they falter. That they *will* falter if the Gothic assault turns too strong to withstand, I'm almost certain; Atrect shares my poor opinion of the nobles' fighting prowess, remembering how much effort it took him to keep them from routing in the retreat from Dol.

Given all these difficulties, it's fortunate that there's no place for complex manoeuvres in the dunes surrounding the cove. I have no reserve – I threw all the men under my command into the frontline. They will either hold, or they won't, and there's little I can do to affect the outcome either way, except raising rallying cries. We have the high ground: the Goths need to wade in wet sand and mud, through ferns and over tree roots to get at us. If I had any skirmishers, I could pick them out one by one. But we have no javelins, and though we have some hunting bows, normally used for foraging, I couldn't spare any men out of the line to wield them. All we can do is watch, and thank the gods that the Goths can't throw missiles up the steep slope with any accuracy, either.

Behind us, down in the cove, the Saxons push the first of the *ceols* out from the beach. Not all the ships are ready yet, but we have no time to worry about those anymore. Whatever can stay afloat, must be put to water; the rest of it we'll have to abandon. I don't yet

The Crown of the Iutes

know how we're going to execute a retreat to the ships once they're ready to set sail. I hope we can hold out long enough for the Goths to grow weary and give us some respite. If we can last until nightfall, we should be safe…

They march towards us in an imposing mass, but I know there could have been more of them. When the first *centuria* of reinforcements arrived at Ratiates, I decided I couldn't wait for the enemy army to build up to a size that we certainly wouldn't be able to handle. I sent Audulf out to provoke the Goth patrols into chasing after him, and leading them to "discover" our hidden cove. The ruse worked. The commander of Ratiates was all too eager to destroy us before any of his superiors could arrive to take the credit for the victory. That he had a chance to capture a remnant of the pirate fleet in the bargain – now that the Saxons were fleeing and leaderless, the Goths did not bother keeping to their alliance with Odowakr – only further added to his motivation.

With their fresh reinforcements, the originally hundred-strong garrison almost doubled in size. The Goths are still fewer in number than us, but they are all seasoned warriors, and well rested. They know it, too; I see no trace of hesitation as they climb towards us, aware that their enemy is just a band of lightly armed commoners, whose only experience of warfare until today is one lost battle, followed by a long retreat.

"Hold!" I cry out one last time, as the first of the Goths reach the line. I thrust my sword into the belly of a young warrior. He stares at my blade in surprise, his hand, holding a small, Frankish-style axe, still raised over his head, before I draw the sword back and kick him down.

"Good sign," I tell Ursula, fighting at my side. She, too, fells her first enemy with ease. "They didn't think we would seriously fight back."

"Did *you*?" she asks, digging her *spatha* in the shoulder of another foe.

I parry a spear thrust, pull on the shaft and stab the Goth under the armpit, where his mail shirt ends. Bright blood splatters my hand.

"I do now."

The line is no more. Broken and scattered by the relentless assault, we're grouped into clusters on the dune tops, each formed of the surviving Britons gathered around their Iute commanders. It's as if each of my riders has grown a dozen sword arms. Audulf, on the dune to my left, rallies his men to a counter-charge one more time, and pushes the Goths down slope, before pulling back. To my right, Eolh and Croha spread their line wider, trying to fill in the gap between them and Deora, surrounded on a rocky outcrop. Ubba, on the far flank, fights the fiercest; the slope of his dune is grey with the blood and guts of the fallen. His Britons seem impervious to enemy blows, as if they had drunk henbane.

I did not expect the Iutes to show such skill in command. I did not expect the Britons to fight so well. I did not expect us to hold out this long. And I did not expect that the Goths would keep on fighting, well into evening, despite the losses, despite the weariness. Now, as the dusk creeps in from across the Liger, their assaults grow even more desperate. They know that if we can hold until dark, it's all over: we'll be able to board the *ceols* and sail away under cover of the night. My men know it, too, and though we're all exhausted beyond reason, in that last stage of the battle the fighting grows fiercer than ever before – and bloodier.

I never agreed with the *scops*, the war poets, singing of the beauty of battle; there is glory in a fight, yes, but all war is ugly business, and this gruesome, tired brawl is as ugly as any I've seen. The sword

The Crown of the Iutes

blows miss, the hatchet strikes slip, the spear thrusts glance on the mail and helmets. Hacked limbs fly, guts are spilt, gouged out eyes dangle on stems. Either way, the battle is not going to last until night. Neither side has the will to stop – but neither has the strength left to continue for long, either.

I can't see into the cove anymore – the Goths cut us off and pushed away from the beach, higher up the dune ridge; catching glances between the waves of attackers, I see the masts of the *ceols* bobbing on the river, and this gives me hope. Sigegaut had plenty of time to sail away while we defended his ships. By now, the pirates must be fighting the Goths themselves. Pity the enemy who, having broken through our line, rushed too hastily to the beach hoping for easy victory. Every single one of Sigegaut's men is a battle-hardened veteran of countless raids and sieges; they must be, to have survived with him to the end. The question is, will they fight as fiercely as the Britons and the Iutes, or will they, when faced with the Goth onslaught, break their warchief's vow and flee the cove on their swift *ceols*?

I grab the *spatha*'s hilt with both hands. The blade has chipped to a nub, but the tip is still sharp, a testament to the skill of whatever legionnaire craftsman forged it in the smithies of Trever. A Goth appears before me, carrying a club and a shield with markings I haven't seen before. Some new reinforcements must have arrived to the field while we fought; this explains how they were able to keep the battle going for so long. I let the club fall on my shoulder, too weary to dodge. The blow is mercifully weak; the enemy is as exhausted as I am. I thrust in the gap between the man's shield and his club arm, but I miss, and draw only a deep scratch in his side.

I can't even see what kills him at first. One moment, he stands there, raising the club to land another blow – the other, he's thrown aside by some great force, leaving only a bloody mist in his place.

I wipe blood from my eyes and search for what saved me. A *ballista* bolt lies a few feet away from the Goth's mutilated body. While I contemplate this sight, someone grabs me by the tunic and pulls – away from the path of another missile.

Sigegaut gives me a quick nod and turns to face another enemy. The Saxon's *seax* makes quick work of the Goth. All around me, his warriors rush into a charge. The two *ballistae* launch bolt after bolt. The enemy pulls back in droves, as frightened of the siege machines as all barbarians are.

"Get your men to the beach, Iute!" Sigegaut cries. "We won't hold them back for long."

"What about you?"

"There's not enough places on the ships for all of us."

"They're *your* ships."

"Not anymore – we surrendered them to you, remember?" He grins tersely. "Come now. We couldn't let the *wealas* have all the glory of the battle. We are warriors, not shipwrights. Everything is ready. I ordered my captains to take you wherever you ask."

I pause, overwhelmed by the nobility of his spirit. I feel a sudden kinship with this man, greater than I ever felt with any of the Gauls or Britons. He and I may have been mortal enemies through the years of Saxon raids on Cantia – but we both come from the same world, a world where a warrior's honour and glorious death count for more than gold or a promise of salvation in some other life.

"You will be forever remembered in the songs of the Iutes, warchief," I tell him.

The Crown of the Iutes

"It is a rare honour," he replies, beaming, then, as he dispatches another enemy with a swift blow to the temple; he grows serious once again. "I left a son somewhere in your country," he says. "Hathugaut. He's only a mewling child now, but if you can one day find a way to tell him about me – Sigegaut of Treva…"

"I understand. I promise, he will know all about his father's deeds."

We bind our hands in a warriors' farewell, and then he pushes me away and picks up a Gothic shield from the ground.

"Then go, Iute," he bellows, "save yourself and your men, while there are still some left alive to tell that tale!"

PART 3: BRITANNIA, 469 AD

CHAPTER XIX
THE LAY OF MANDUBRAC

Somewhere out there, beyond the field of campfire stars, beyond the rustling darkness of the sea, is home.

It is our last day on this side of the Narrow Sea. A farewell feast, out on the wide beaches of Alet, a small, friendly harbour on Armorica's northern coast. The townsfolk have all come out to make merry with us, too – it is a rare occasion for mirth in these troubled times. The short, brutal campaign season is over. Andecawa and the villages downstream have been retaken; the Saxon pirates have abandoned their hidden harbours at the Liger Mouth and sailed to their winter harbours in Frisia; and the Goths, weakened by all the fighting in the North and battered by Hildrik's raids, eagerly renewed their peace treaties with Syagrius so that they could focus on repelling the rumoured Imperial invasion to their South.

The town itself bears scars of recent Saxon raids, and the few locals I talked to tell me they're ready to abandon its often-breached walls and move further inland. To them, too, this is a sort of a farewell feast, and so the beach is filled with dozens of blazing fires, and hundreds of people drinking and singing; many of the locals are Britons themselves, refugees from the southern provinces, and they all know the same songs and dances as the men who came with us.

Though we fled the cove with heavy losses, there are now more Briton soldiers ready to set sail back home than set out with us from the Bredanna Marsh. Dozens of them managed to successfully retreat from the first defeat at Dol on their own and, knowing that Armorica is ruled by their kindred, one way or another made their way to Marcus's kingdom. Some of them were helped along by Eishild – she is here, too, having brought some of the Bacauds with her, including a handful of Saphrax's riders fleeing the brief, doomed revolt at Pictawis. Many of those gathered at Alet decided to stay in Armorica and help Marcus

The Crown of the Iutes

defend his borders from the Goths – or anyone else who would wish to threaten them. To my surprise, I hear them mention Hildrik's name with the same distrust and apprehension as that of Aiwarik's.

Some of the arriving Britons bring news from Riotham, trapped in Lugdunum, a great southern city now ruled in the Empire's name by the Burgundians. Though the Goths did not yet dare – or care – to send a force to besiege the mighty fortress, they surrounded all roads leading north and west from it so effectively that only lonely, brave messengers managed to get past the blockade.

"He's still sending out orders, as if there's still an army to command," Atrect told me. "He wants us to send him reinforcements. He claims the Imperator is on his way with a great army to relieve him. He offers reward to those who aid him, and threatens us with retribution to those who don't, once he's out of Lugdunum."

"I hope you ignored all that foolishness."

"It's not up to me anymore," he replied with a shrug. "I'm back to being a mere *praefect* of the *vigiles* again. Here, it's the nobles who rule. The surviving Councillors chose a leader among themselves, some man called Mandubrac."

"I know him." I nodded. "*Comes* of the Trinowaunts. One of Riotham's fiercest loyalists on the Council."

"He doesn't seem loyal to anyone but himself. But what do I know, I'm only a town guard."

"You'd make a better *Dux* than any of these nobles, *praefect*," I told him. "But, then, how did Mandubrac decide to respond to Riotham's orders?"

"He paid for a Mass to mourn the fallen of Lugdunum, that's how," Atrect replied with a bitter chuckle. "Riotham may well be dead to them. It would be better for everyone if he was."

As night grows darker, the singing and dancing slowly gives way to a more usual, primeval nightly pursuit. This is how the Iute and Saxon feasts always end, but tonight even the Christian Britons have reasons to succumb to their urges. Tonight, the warriors of Dol celebrate having survived the tribulations of Riotham's failed campaign. Tonight, the whores of Alet offer discounts as they bid farewell to their favourite patrons. Tonight, life and love triumph over death and destruction.

I wrap my arm around Ursula and close my eyes. The darkness around us heaves and grunts, but she remains cold and stiff under my touch.

"It was on a night like this that we conceived our son," I say. "What was it, a harvest feast?"

"*Hlafmastide*," she replies. "Before the harvest begun."

"Ah, of course, he was a May child."

I reach to her breast over her shoulder. I feel the heat and sweat of the night slowly overcome my senses. She takes my hand and moves it away.

"I haven't touched a woman since Basina," I complain.

"Then go find yourself some wench," she says, pointing at the gleaming campfires. "I'm sure any girl here will gladly open herself to the great *aetheling* of the Iutes."

The Crown of the Iutes

"I don't want *any* girl," I say. "I want *you*. I love *you*. I want *you* to bear my children."

"I'm sorry, Octa, but all I see when I think of having another child is Pascent's body, shrivelled with pox." She shakes her head. "I'm not ready yet. I don't know that I'll ever be."

In my heart and mind I understand her troubled state; but my body, hot and sweaty from the strong mulled Sicera rushing through my veins, no longer heeds their command. I turn to her and grab her forcefully in my arms.

"Then let us not speak of children," I say. "You are my wife. Think of it as your duty."

"Octa!" she exclaims; I should notice the fear in her voice and in her eyes, but the Sicera – and lust – make me deaf and blind to her protestations. I push her to the ground and tear off her tunic. "No!" she cries. I reach to her breeches and start pulling them down – when I feel a cold blade at my crotch.

"Go away, Octa," she orders. Her boot knife – a weapon every Iute shieldmaiden carries with her for just such an occasion – trembles in her hands. "Go away and cool your drunken head before you do something you'll regret for the rest of your life."

She gathers her torn clothes and runs off into the night, leaving me suddenly cold, sober and filled with shame – but my manhood remains stiff and demanding.

In a drunken daze, I climb down from the dunes and walk slowly to the harbour. The streets of Alet are all but deserted, with most of the townsfolk out celebrating.

The ships that are to take us back to Britannia are all here, bobbing gently in the waves. Four great galleys, the largest vessels Marcus could have spared from the fleet he inherited from Graelon. One look at their hefty bulks tells me these aren't warships, but merchant transports, each capable of carrying hundreds of *amphorae* of wine, olive oil or butter to whoever would be willing to pay for it. Ships this size rarely visit Britannia's coast; I've only seen them a few times in my life, and always in Londin, never in any of the smaller harbours. We're fortunate that these have all gathered in Armorica's ports to wait out the brewing war. Now that it's all over, they're all ready to return to their more profitable routes, between Aquitania and Hispania, as soon as they take us all back home.

Such a gathering of large, slow merchant ships would have been a perfect bait for the pirates only a few months ago. But the pirates are gone. Having brought us to Gesocribate, the Saxon captains bid us farewell and sailed back to their distant northern havens, to mourn their warchief and their fallen in the ancient manner. I demanded that Marcus leave them alone as they passed along the coast of his domain and, in turn, they declared they would send word to anyone who could threaten us on the Narrow Sea to stay away.

"The name of Sigegaut of Treva still means something in these waters," one of the Saxon captains assured me. "Even the Scots won't dare touch you – not this season, anyway. And next year, we will go north for plunder. I lost my taste for the southern waters."

I wonder how much of that is true, as I watch the galleys. Despite their imposing size, they are nearly defenceless, should any pirates decide to attack us after all. Perhaps if my Iutes were to…

I shake my head. Tonight is not the night for plans and strategies. All the fighting is over. I have other worries to think about. How will I ever apologise to Ursula? In all the years we've been together

The Crown of the Iutes

I never once tried to force myself on her. What was I thinking? Could I really have blamed it all on the heady Armorican Sicera?

I notice a silhouette at the end of the quay, someone small, slim, short-haired. I approach quietly, only to realise it's Croha, staring gloomily at the four ships.

"*Aetheling.*" She bows. She doesn't seem as surprised to see me as I am to see her.

"What are you doing here? Shouldn't you be feasting with the others?"

"Shouldn't *you*, *Hlaford*?" she replies with unusual boldness.

"I had enough feasting for one night. Everyone I passed insisted that I drink a horn of ale or Sicera with them. I'd be dead by the morning if I stayed there."

"You're the reason they have anything to celebrate in the first place."

"The men owe their survival to nobody but themselves. Each one of them bought his life with his own sweat and blood. I only showed them the way."

"A fine speech, *aetheling*, but we both know none of them would reach Armorica without us."

I come closer, and smell strong ale on her breath. The lights of the ships' lanterns dance in her eyes like sprites. She looks around.

"Is the Councillor with you?"

"Ursula? No, she… She's not feeling well. What about Deora?"

She scoffs. "That coarse goat? I lost interest in him a long time ago. All he cares about is humping. Men like him just never grow up."

"Is that why you're here? To stay away from men who act like horny goats?" I ask, and step away, remembering my own shame.

She looks to the quay, and for a while we watch the sea in silence.

"I don't think I want to go back," she replies.

"I know what you mean… But the fighting here is over, and there's no more reason for us to stay in Gaul."

"That's not my reason."

"Then what is it?"

She turns back to me. In the light of the lanterns, I see her cheeks flush red. "When we return to Cantia, you'll be the *aetheling* again. The king's son, giving counsel in the great mead halls and discussing grave matters with the nobles and the elders, with your wife, the Councillor, at your side… And I'll just be the guard at the gates, hoping to be humped by some eager young warrior. I will never get another chance to…"

She's stunned by her own sudden confession. She turns away.

I touch her shoulder. "You'll never be a guard at the gates again," I tell her. "And any young warrior would be fortunate to have you."

"But I don't *want* any other warrior," she blurts.

She turns to me and looks me straight in the eyes, her face inches from mine. Her breath quickens, her lips part.

The Crown of the Iutes

Find yourself some wench, Ursula told me. Maybe if I had listened to her in the first place, none of it would have happened...

"You want me," she whispers. "I've seen it in your eyes. I can give you what your wife could never have given you."

I feel the familiar tingle of ale and Sicera in my head, drowning all reason, and I lean in to kiss her.

She yields to my touch with the eagerness of one who's waited for it for too long. When my hand rests on her breast, her legs tremble and buckle. We lie down right there on the cold stone of the quay. Her skin is soft and supple; her youthful beauty, unspoiled yet by time, reminds me of that first, clumsy time I lay with Ursula, when we were both barely out of our childhoods. Except Croha is not as clumsy and inexperienced as we were back then. She slips out of her tunic; I feel the scars on her sides and shoulders under my fingers, each a mark of a victory in battle. She moans aloud when I take her breast into my mouth and runs her fingernails along my back. She kicks the breeches off me and wraps her thighs around me.

"My *Hlaford*..." she moans, just as I'm about to enter her. "My king!"

The tingle of Sicera suddenly disappears and my mind is clear again. My manhood shrivels. I pull away.

"I am not your king yet," I grumble. "And you are not my queen."

"What's wrong, *Hlaford*?" she groans, as she slowly realises what happened.

"*This*," I reply. "*This* is wrong."

I'm only doing this because Ursula spurned me tonight, I think – but I cannot tell her this.

"You're too young to be bound to me as the *aetheling*'s concubine," I say, knowing it's a poor excuse. "You have your whole life to decide what you want to be, and who you want to be with."

"It's only for one night." She runs her finger down my chest. "Everyone is doing it tonight. No one needs to know."

"I doubt I'd be satisfied with only one night." I pull the breeches back on. "And Ursula already knows. She was the one who tried to convince me to do this."

"The Councillor?" Croha sits back up with a frown. "Why?"

I rub my eyes and sigh. "She and I… We have an understanding."

I explain to her briefly how my relationship with Ursula works – and how we were looking for a solution to the problem of finding an heir to my father's diadem. As I speak, I see the expression on her face turn from that of slight confusion to outright fury.

"Then I was to be just a child-bearing whore?" she exclaims when I finish. She pulls away and covers her breasts with her arm in shame. "A belly to spawn your bastards? And to think I almost fell for your misty eyes and soft touch."

"No – no, it's not like that…" I say, but my protest is feeble. That's the second time I have angered a woman I wanted to lie with. What is *wrong* with me tonight? I need to lie down – or find some harbour whore who will care only about the amount of coin I leave her.

"You're right to be angry," I say. "This – is not what either of us would have wanted."

"How do you know what *I* want? Do you even know what *you* want? Do you want *me* for who I am, or do you just need a convenient fertile hole for you to spill your royal seed into?"

"Of course I *want* you, Croha. You are a beautiful young woman, and a brave shieldmaiden. Lately, you… you've been haunting my dreams. And if you ever decide that you wish to bear my heir, I would be more than grateful to take you. But I want you to live your life to the full before you make this decision. There's still time. I'm not even a *rex* yet."

"I'm not *that* young, anymore, *aetheling*," she replies. "I would have born Deora's children a long time ago, if I had wanted to. Still…" She gathers her clothes from the quay. "I appreciate your honesty. Lesser men would just take me without any hesitation, and let me worry about the bastard they spawned."

"An *aetheling*'s child is not like any other. Even if I did burden you with it, you wouldn't have been left alone."

She grunts. "I wouldn't need your charity. I can take care of myself." She puts on her tunic and stands up. "I see you still see me as that helpless child your father brought from the moors. Come back when you think of me as a grown woman, and one equal to your wife in your heart. I *will* bear you an heir, and I'll be honoured to do so – but on my own terms."

The ships move slowly, and at an uneven pace, heaving forward like a pregnant seal. We're so overburdened that the tall waves lick the deck and each strong gust of wind threatens to capsize the galleys. The men pray to any gods that would listen, Christian or heathen, hoping at least one of them will heed our pleas and grant us a safe passage.

The only way to fit us all on the four heavy galleys was to turn some of the Britons into oarsmen. Having done this myself, if only briefly and a long time ago, I know how hard work it is, especially for someone unused to such heavy, repetitive toil. The farmers take to the oars as if it was just another of their daily burdens; but the townsfolk and the *villa* servants – the shop owners, the bakers or the bath attendants – groan under this new strain, as the muscles they didn't know they had tear and burn with each stroke.

"I would've been better off in thrall of the Goths," I hear one of them grumble as I pass through the oars deck on the second day of the journey.

"Stop your whingeing," his neighbour scolds him. Judging by his rough, ruddy demeanour and bear-like hands, the man is either a farmhand or a fisherman. "We're alive, and we're almost home. Think how many of our comrades wish they could say the same."

"Oh, why did I let Cait convince me to join the army!" the first one continues. "I have nothing to show for it but scars and blisters."

"You've seen the world outside your little town," the second replies. "And you've learned how to hold a spear. That must count for something. Maybe next time the pirates come, we won't have to depend on those filthy heathens for our defence so much."

"Shh," the grumpy one says, fearfully, and glances towards me. "They're listening."

"Oh, I don't mean like the ones who fought with us," the second one replies. "These riders are fine people. We need more like them, and less of those lazy serfs who took all our best land. I tell you, when I was a lad, my family worked the whole slope of the valley,

The Crown of the Iutes

all the way down to the river. Now, the Iutes live by the river, and we have to toil the dry stones up the hill. How is that fair? Just because these heathens –"

"Be quiet, man!" the first one raises his voice. "The Iutes may be heathens, but without them our churches would be stripped of everything but the rafters, and our streets would flow with blood instead of ale."

"Pox!" The farmer scoffs. "You townsfolk will never understand us. Wait till you run out of barley for your ale, when we have nowhere to grow it."

"The Iutes brew decent enough ale," the townsman replies. "And cheaper. Maybe we don't need you and your barley anymore."

They fall silent, except for the grunts accompanying each heave of the oar. With a quiet chuckle, I climb to the open deck. A few hours ago we departed from Coriowall, a small fortified harbour at the tip of Armorica's northernmost peninsula. The late summer sun burns bright golden, like a *solidus* hanging high in the sky; the only clouds float on the southern horizon, where we just came from. The wind is good, not too strong, but enough to occasionally swell the galley's one striped sail. I take a deep breath. The farmer was right – not in his moaning about the Iute farms, but in his gratitude for being alive and finally coming home.

I look at the sail again. It flutters in the breeze, though the wind hasn't changed. I check the sun's position, then search the southern horizon for the black dots of the distant Lenur Islands.

"What's wrong?" asks Ursula, noticing my concern.

The wreath of wildflowers in her hair has dried up and shrivelled. I picked the flowers on the dunes of Alet, after the feast, and wove the wreath myself; Ursula accepted it, and my apology, but I wonder if she continues to wear it as a sign of reconciliation, or as a reminder of my transgression. Her words are soft again, but her touch remains cold.

"The ship's going due north," I reply.

"And that's a problem?"

"That's not how the wind blows. I may not be a mariner, but I have sailed these seas enough to know a southwester when I see one. We should be going straight for Leman or Dubris. The captain's giving the oarsmen twice the work."

"I'm sure he knows what he's doing."

"Maybe. Or maybe somebody's given him orders to take us to New Port, instead of Cantia."

I find Atrect among the oarsmen on the stern; ever a good commander, he wouldn't let his men do all the hard labour without himself taking some of the burden.

"Find Mandubrac," he tells us. "If anyone's giving the orders to the captains, it's him and his fellow nobles. I'm sure he's got his reasons."

"And I'm sure they're all the *wrong* reasons," I mumble.

Up on the open deck, Mandubrac lounges lazily in the sun, fanned by a half-naked female slave whom he managed to somehow procure between our arrival in Armorica and setting sail for Britannia. Once again, it amazes me how quickly these people fall back into their old lives, as if nothing had happened, as if they were simply returning from a vacation in Gaul.

[377]

The Crown of the Iutes

"New Port is closer," he replies when I confront him. He's only got one eye open when he talks to us. "We'll get there faster. I don't like the sea."

"We'll only get there faster if you force your men to row harder," says Ursula. "The wind is taking us to Cantia."

He closes the one eye and shrugs.

"In Cantia, we'll be protected by my father's warriors," I say. "In New Port, we'll be at the mercy of Aelle. And need I remind you, we're no longer the four cohorts that marched from Londin – we're barely four *centuriae*, of weary and injured men."

"Aelle wouldn't dare threaten us," Mandubrac replies. "We are the sole remaining representatives of the Londin Council."

"And that's supposed to impress him?" Ursula scoffs. "That only means he'll get a better ransom for you."

He opens both eyes. "We have a treaty. Bound with blood."

"Signed by Riotham. Where is Riotham now?" I look around. "Where are his cohorts? The only language Aelle understands is force."

The noble shrugs again. "I have made my decision. You can stay on the ship and sail on to Cantia after we've landed, if you're so afraid of a few Saxons."

"Or is it *you* who's afraid – of your own people?" asks Ursula.

"I don't know what you mean."

I glance at her – I, too, am not sure of what she's accusing the Councillor, but then, I'm not as versed in Briton politics as she is.

"You can't just enter Londin with this sorry handful of men remaining of the hundreds you took to Gaul, and with your leader gone," she says. "You'd be laughed out of the city. You hope to prepare a triumphant return, using your contacts among the Regin nobles."

Mandubrac grunts something and turns on his side, proving that Ursula's guess was correct.

"What are we going to do?" she asks when we retreat to the shadow of the cloth roof stretched over the aft part of the deck.

I shrug. "He *is* in command here. There's nothing we can do, other than what he said – stay on the ships and sail on to Cantia, hoping Aelle will be too busy with the Britons to bother with us."

"Remember, there are many Cants among these men. I can't just let Aelle slaughter them after we led them safely through so many perils."

"I doubt Aelle will *slaughter* the commoners – more likely he'll just capture the nobles for ransom and let everyone else go."

"Unless the nobles order them to fight him."

I glance towards Mandubrac; the Councillor scrambles from the deck and orders his slave to bring him more wine.

"Why would anyone want to fight for the sake of this lot?"

The Crown of the Iutes

CHAPTER XX
THE LAY OF HILLA

"I remember when this harbour was as loud and bright at night as it was during the day," says the captain, staring at silent, sleepy New Port.

His is the last of the four galleys that remain in the harbour. The other three sailed off a few days ago, having filled their holds with what little their captains thought worth buying in Britannia to sell in Gaul – barley and wheat, freshly harvested from the Regin fields, and lead and iron from Andreda. The captain agreed to take us to Dubris – but we have to wait for him to find enough recruits in the town and the surrounding villages to replace the Briton oarsmen; the winds have changed since our arrival, and without a full complement of rowers we could be stuck here for days.

"You've sailed the Narrow Sea before?" I ask.

"In my youth," he replies. "When there was still gold to be made on this route." He looks about sixty – a ring of white hair surrounds his bald, wrinkled head like a silver diadem. He would remember Britannia just before the arrival of the Iutes, before the Saxons took over the *pagus* of the Regins; Gaul before the ravages of the Huns and the worst excesses of the Goths. An Empire with still enough interest in the lost province to send Bishop Germanus to Britannia to deal with the Pelagian heresy and support loyal nobles against the rebels.

There is nothing in Britannia anymore that would interest a veteran captain, one who had plied the waters of the great ocean from Burdigala to the Pillars of Hercules, and beyond. It's scarcely believable how much could have changed in one man's lifetime.

The Crown of the Iutes

And few places on the island changed more in that time than New Port.

It's changed even since I last saw it, only a few months ago. The hope that sprouted in the spring was quashed with the coming of autumn. When Riotham's cohorts sailed, triumphant, to Gaul, the mood in the town was full of jubilation; now, as the townsfolk slowly come to terms with the terrible news of what happened to their kin at Dol, a deathly silence falls on New Port, as if the plague had returned – except for the songs and shouts of the Saxon warriors, celebrating the demise of *wealas* in the harbour taverns.

"Do you think you'll find the rowers soon?" I ask.

"I only need a dozen more. I sent a man to Mutuanton today, or what's left of it, that should be enough to end the matter." He gives me a puzzled look. "Why won't you just ride back to Cantia? It can't be more than a few days from here."

"The king of the Saxons who rules this place and I aren't exactly friends," I tell him. "A small group of riders like us might easily suffer some… accident along the way. I'm my father's only heir; I have to take care of myself. This ship is the only safe place for us in all of the Regin *pagus*."

The captain rubs his chin. "I was wondering why you wouldn't even come down to the harbour." He slams me on the back. "This Saxon king might think himself powerful on this fog-shrouded, pox-ridden, rain-soaked island, but my friends in Gaul and Rome are more powerful still. He won't dare do anything when I'm with you. Come with me to the tavern, and have a drink on me."

The inside of New Port's largest and oldest tavern still resembles an ancient Roman establishment, such as could have been seen in any harbour of the Empire, in the days when a ship that sailed from here could end up in Syria or Sicilia. The walls are painted with ancient, faded murals – great ships land in a harbour, amply bosomed mermaids leap over the waves; Neptune, his bearded face all but gone under layers of dust and time, threatens sailors with his golden trident; and there's still the L-shaped counter with holes for *amphorae* and hollows for bowls of small dishes to eat with wine. But these few vestiges are all that remain of the old glory. It is now a mead hall in all but shape. Saxons, and those who wish to imitate them, now rule this place, instead of Briton sailors and merchants. Gone are the lounging chairs and small dining stands, replaced by oaken benches and long, heavy tables, soaked in meat grease. Dirty hides are thrown over the counter, turning it into just another table, as no one here has need for *amphorae* of wine and small, dainty meals when ale flows freely from the barrels, to help wash down haunches of boar and bowls of stew.

The Saxons fall silent when the captain, Ursula and I enter the hall. There are about a dozen of them, and they are all warriors, judging by their scarred, muscular arms and a pile of weapons by the door. They have the long table and all the benches to themselves; the innkeeper rushes to lead us to a dark, damp corner, where we find a small table roughly hewn out of an oak trunk.

"Wine, if you have any," the captain demands, and when the innkeeper skulks off, he turns to the Saxons and stares at them defiantly.

One of the warriors stands up and comes over, swaying.

"You –" He points to me. "Why are you still here?"

"We're waiting for good winds," the captain says. "Don't worry, I'm as eager to leave as you are to see us gone."

The Crown of the Iutes

"You should've gone with the other *wealas*," the Saxon slurs, ignoring the captain.

"Why should we?" I reply. "We're not *wealas*. We're Iutes."

"Iutes?" He frowns, confused. "You don't look like no Iutes to me."

"Did he just say they're *Iutes*?" another man shouts from the table. "What are the Iutes doing here?"

Two more Saxons stand up and stagger dangerously towards us. I have no wish to die in a tavern brawl, and though they're all drunk and unarmed — like Ursula, I have my *spatha* at my side, re-forged to brilliant sharpness by an Armorican weapon-smith — I don't want to take my chances with a dozen warriors in the inn's cramped quarters.

"We're only passing through, that's all," I say, raising my hands. "We want no trouble."

"I saw you come with those *wealas* on the big *ceols*," the first Saxon says. "Are you spies for Aeric?"

He looms over me. The captain stands between him and me. "You would do well to leave my friends alone, Saxon," he says. "If you want another merchant ship to land in your master's ports ever again."

"Oh, leave them be, Hundfeald, and finish your mead," someone cries from the long table. "Once our *Rex* gets what he wants from the *wealas*, it won't matter what Aeric does — all Iutes will be our slaves."

[384]

The Saxons guffaw. I give Ursula a quick glance. She shakes her head to stop me from asking any more questions. The innkeeper returns, manoeuvring between the Saxon warriors, with a jug of wine and mugs. The one called Hundfeald grabs the jug and takes a sniff. He winces in disgust.

"Figures a Iute would drink this *wealh* swill," he says. "This isn't a drink fit for a warrior."

He slams the jug on our table and takes his comrades away, still laughing at the thought of having a Iute slave.

The captain pours the wine and also winces at the smell. "What is this swill?" he asks the innkeeper.

"It's all I have," the poor man replies. "It's from Cantia's best vineyard. I thought —"

"It will do," says Ursula, and sends the innkeeper away. "Apologies, captain," she says. "We try our best, but there's only so much one can do with all the best *vinetarii* having left long ago for Gaul, and the weather being so foul these past few springs."

"How do you know so much about wine making?" the captain asks her.

"Because, if I'm not mistaken," she replies, giving the mug another sniff, "this wine came from my family *villa*'s southern slopes."

Mutuanton — the name I've only heard of, never having a reason to visit this place before — presents what might be the final stage of a Briton town's decline into oblivion. Though it still lies on a crossroad of Roman highways — one running north, to Londin, the

The Crown of the Iutes

other parallel to the coast, from Regentium in the west to Anderitum in the east – and would once have been a bustling hub, with a couple of *mansios* and a bath house, it is now a place inhabited mostly by wraiths and wild dogs. Barely anyone lives here, and with good reason: nearly half of the town has been submerged under the waters of an inlet of the Narrow Sea, which long ago burst its banks and swallowed the whole of the marshy valley its waters cut through the Downs. The harbour is gone completely. The Forum is now a beach. The jagged teeth of the bath house peek from the muddy waves, slowly succumbing to the greedy currents. The road to Anderitum, running for the most part along a low sandstone ridge, is still passable, but only just. What remains of the highway to Londin is a muddy tract, narrow and winding, piled from the ancient paving stones into a rough causeway over the murky brine.

A handful of Regins cling to their half-ruined, single-storey stone houses in the western part, rising above the rest of the town on a spur of rock, though what it is that they do here and how they make their living, I can't guess. A few Saxon fishermen have their huts and muddy vegetable plots by the water, in the grounds of the old Forum and further north, where the sea recedes to make a place for always damp fields and groves of willow and hazel. Goats and ducks are the only inhabitants in the narrow streets of the *castrum* – the oldest part of the town, where the Romans once built a small fort to guard the crossroad from which the rest of the settlement sprouted.

There is little reason for anyone to be here; New Port, with its taverns, is only a few hours' ride away. There is no industry here, no guest houses, no chapel, no craftsmen shops, not even a blacksmith to help with lost horseshoes and broken wagon wheels. And yet here we are, staring at the sunken ruins as the midges from the marsh descend upon us and our ponies in great clouds of buzzing irritation.

James Calbraith

When the captain's messengers first brought the news from Mutuanton – along with the last few rowers the galley needed to finally take us to Cantia and then sail back to Gaul – we could scarcely believe it. *Comes* Mandubrac left New Port four days earlier, leading the four hundred Britons towards Londin. We always knew their march would be slow, as the nobles needed time to gauge the moods in the capital, gather all the support they could and prepare the heralds to announce their arrival and somehow present Riotham's expedition to the city folk as something other than the ignominious, costly retreat that it was. They couldn't, as originally planned, have done it all from New Port; even Mandubrac must have accepted that four *centuriae* of weary, injured men were not the same as four cohorts of triumphantly marching soldiers, and that the Saxons' firm grasp on the harbour town threatened to cut them off from Londin with each passing day.

We may have known they'd be slow, but we never expected the Britons to come to a stop at Mutuanton. It took the captain's men less than half a day to return to New Port, and that only because they had to find a way around a stretch of the old road blocked by a recent landslide.

"Looks like we won't be needing your services anymore," I told the captain. "We'll have to ride to Mutuanton ourselves, to find out what happened."

"Are you sure?" he asked. "Even after seeing how hostile these Saxons are to you?"

"I have to try. I feel responsible for the fate of those Britons, even in their own land. Besides, there's a chance that with Aelle's warbands distracted, we may be able to sneak past them now – and Mutuanton is on the way to Cantia… More or less."

I have no clue yet as to how Mandubrac managed to waste four days covering this short distance and lead his men to this forsaken

The Crown of the Iutes

place in the middle of a marsh, especially since this isn't even the right route back to Londin – it's some way away from the main road that I know so well, the one that runs past Saffron Road and my father's old *villa* at Ariminum.

"I swear, this is the last time we have to chase after these Britons into some marsh," I say.

"I've heard that before," says Ursula. "I told you we'd have to save them from their own incompetence again."

"Only this time it's for our own good."

The news that Mandubrac only managed to reach Mutuanton wasn't the only indication that something went terribly wrong with the Briton attempt at return to Londin. The boasts of the Saxons at the harbour tavern were another. And then, in the morning, as I watched a detachment of Aelle's warriors march out of town in the direction of Mutuanton, singing of victory and glorious conquest, I understood that I could not let the Britons simply perish in a battle with the Saxons. This was about more than just punishing the nobles' arrogant, destructive pride. Whatever *Rex* Aelle had planned, him breaking the peace treaty could affect the balance of power in the entire island, threaten my father's rule and the safety of my people. Wearily, I resolved that we should at least try to find out what was happening at Mutuanton, though I had little hope of actually stopping Aelle's designs with just our handful of riders.

Ursula nods to the east, where Ubba's "blade" descends the slope of the Downs on the other side of the river in a hurry. "Looks like they found something."

"Yes, the *wealas* are here," Ubba confirms, once he reaches us over the causeway. "In an ancient hillfort on the southern ridge. At least, we think that's them."

"What do you mean?" I ask. "Why aren't you sure?"

"We couldn't get close enough," says Ubba. "There's hundreds of Saxon warriors in those hills. It looks like Aelle's entire army has come here."

"Then you were right, Octa," Ursula admits. "He did break the *ath*, as we feared. But what are we going to do about it? Even you can't think we can wage war on an entire Saxon warband with thirty bear-shirts."

"If Aelle wanted a fight, he'd have no trouble capturing that hillfort," I say. "But that wouldn't give him what he needs. He must be negotiating something with the nobles – and he won't be doing that on a windswept hilltop."

I look around. To the east and west, the Downs rise in a green, undulating wall; to the south, the brackish marsh glistens in the setting sun. To the north, beyond the gap in the hills, spreads a flat plain, covered in a grid of fields and pastures, most now laid fallow and overgrown with weeds, but with still discernible borders.

"What's that?" I point to some gleaming white rising in the middle of the plain. "An outcrop of chalk?"

"Could be a *domus*," says Ursula, straining her eyes. "If it is, it's a large one. More like a palace."

"A palace fit for a *Rex*, perhaps. I'll go check it out."

"On your own?"

"If it's Aelle, he's not going to hurt me."

"Octa, be…" Her voice breaks. "Be careful."

The Crown of the Iutes

The *domus* is even more enormous than it seemed from a distance, sprawling as far as the low rise of chalk allows, in two tall wings of whitewashed, half-timbered stone, linked by a long central corridor. The east wing spreads further along the courtyard, ending with an annex that is itself the size of a large farmhouse. The west wing is shorter, and ends abruptly on what looks like an ancient burial mound. This place has been inhabited by countless generations, before the owners finally abandoned it – at least a century ago, and in a hurry, judging by the amount of waste and debris they left behind. I'm guessing the noble Regin family who controlled this area must have fallen victim to the Martinian rebels, but I have no way of knowing for sure.

The Saxon who drags me across the *villa's* yard stands before the door and calls for the guard to open it for us. Astoundingly, the iron lock still works, and the guard inside still has the key to it, though he struggles a while with the rusted mechanism. The Saxon shoves me into the dark corridor.

"He wants to see the *Rex*," the Saxon tells the guard.

"The *Rex* is busy," the guard replies grumpily. "And why in *Hel* would he want to see some nameless cur, anyway?"

"This one claims to be the Iute *aetheling*," says the Saxon. "Though I'm sure he's lying."

"*Aetheling?*" the guard raises his eyebrow. "I'll let the *Hlaford* know. You, wait here."

He returns in a hurry. "Come with me," he orders. He leads me to the west wing. Along the way, I pass rooms with sunken roofs and doors leading nowhere; old shoes and farm tools lie rotting in the corridor, tiles and scraps of red and black mosaic scatter the floor.

What should be the dining room, overlooking the garden at the back, is an empty hole, facing a blind fence and a forest of ferns.

We reach the last room in the west wing, the only one that still somewhat resembles its original purpose – the master's study. The burial mound looms outside the window. A wooden library still stands by the wall, though all that's left of its contents are a few lead seal weights still hanging from their chains, marking a place where a scroll whose secrets they held has rotted away into nothingness.

There's a desk here, and some chairs, not the original ones, but brought in from somewhere, since they're of a much more crude design than what would be in use in such a magnificent place. Sitting on the chairs, with grumpy, doomed expressions on their faces, are Mandubrac and a couple other nobles, whose names I never bothered to remember. Opposite them, squatting on an iron-bound chest and studying some old map, is Aelle, *Rex* of the Saxons. His wife, Hilla, sits on the floor beside him, picking at her nails with a dagger.

"Young Octa." He welcomes me with a broad grin.

"Hlaford." I bow. "Hlaefdige."

He dismisses the guard. "It's alright. Bring us another chair. Octa is always a welcome guest in my house."

"And… this is your house?" I ask, looking around the dilapidated room. "Since when?"

"It might be, when this is all over. I haven't decided yet."

The Crown of the Iutes

"I was wondering when you'd come," says Aelle. "You and your father are never far whenever history happens."

Hilla pours me some mead. I notice the cups and plates of the Briton nobles are empty. The three men look haggard and famished. They must have been besieged in the hillfort for days before finally agreeing to come down to negotiate their release with Aelle. The *rex* hasn't yet deemed it necessary to feed them, possibly believing they would be more eager to agree to whatever terms he wanted to impose on them when they were hungry.

"And what history is happening today?" I ask.

Aelle nods at Mandubrac. "Tell him, *Comes*."

The Briton looks up from the table and clears his throat. "We've agreed to make Aelle the new *Dux* of Britannia Prima."

"Him?" I splutter. "A *Dux*? Are you out of your minds?"

I look to Aelle – he's beaming, enjoying my shock. Mandubrac shrugs. "We don't have a choice," he says. His voice is shattered with the sense of defeat.

"You swore an *ath*," I tell Aelle.

"And I am keeping to it," he says. "No Briton warrior was harmed by my men – yet. But my treaty was with Riotham. When it's confirmed he's not coming back from Gaul, I will no longer be bound to it. My Regin lawmen confirmed it – as did they," he nods at the nobles.

"You'd sell the title just to save your own skins?" I ask Mandubrac. "Is it worth so little to you?"

"It's not about us," one of the other two nobles replies, indignantly. "I would gladly give my life if it could save Britannia." I don't believe him for a moment.

"The four hundred men surrounded on the hilltop are all that is left of our army," says the third noble. "All the *vigiles*. All the tribal militias. All the surviving veterans and old officers. We have no one to train the new recruits. No one left to defend our cities."

"Your *villas*, you mean," I scoff. But I have to admit he's right. Like Constantine sixty years ago, Riotham took with him to Gaul everyone who knew how to hold a weapon – and then lost them all on his hapless adventure. There's only a handful of *vigiles* left in Londin, and none at all in smaller towns like Dorowern. And while my father's warriors would continue to defend Cantia, there would be nobody left to guard the rest of the province from barbarian attacks – including those of Aelle's Saxons themselves.

Despite my loathing for Mandubrac, I understand his dilemma well. Having destroyed the remnant of Riotham's army, it would only be a matter of time before Aelle marched on defenceless Londin. Nobody could stop him from taking the diadem by force – except, perhaps, *Comes* Albanus, still lurking in the North with his *Gewisse* mercenaries. A battle between two hordes of barbarian warriors raging in the city would have been a disaster which would overshadow even my father's razing. There was little chance for what was still left of the capital to survive such an ordeal. It was far better to nominate Aelle the city's ruler and protector, and in this way, ensure peace.

"Is the deed done?" I ask. "Then why are the Britons still besieged in the hillfort?"

"We've sent envoys to Londin," says Aelle. "Asking the Council to confirm the title – and to bring me *Domna* Madron."

The Crown of the Iutes

"Whatever do you want with Madron?"

"She's still bound to wed a *Dux*'s son," he says calmly. "And my Cissa is about to come of age."

"You would need to baptise him."

"Of course." He nods. "I will have everything done according to the *wealh* laws."

"Otherwise, you'd have Ambrosius to deal with."

"And your father, I imagine," he says. "He won't take kindly to the changes."

"No, I don't believe he will. He is still the girl's legal guardian."

"Don't worry," Aelle laughs. "Contrary to what you may have heard my warriors boast, I don't plan to turn Iutes into slaves. I'd rather keep them as allies. I will be a merciful *Dux* – I will be satisfied with an annual tribute and with your father yielding to me as the *Bretwealda*."

I wince. "He'd sooner die."

"Then I will have to take my tribute from yourself. Unless…"

"Unless?"

He leans over the table. "I know why you came here, Octa," he says. "You thought you could somehow stop me from achieving my ambition."

"If I did, do you think I would just march into your *villa* and let myself be captured like this?"

He smiles. "You and I are more alike than you might wish to believe. Arrogant pride is our greatest failing. The same arrogant pride that makes me want to do this –"

He waits for me to finish the mead and calls the guard back.

"Escort the *aetheling* back to the gate, and give him his sword back."

"You're letting me go?" I ask. "After everything I've just learned?"

He chuckles. "My *Hellruna* told me that you would one day be all that stands between me and my destiny. I can't wait to prove her wrong. If I were so easy to defeat, how could I deserve the *Dux*'s diadem?"

As I crawl through the parched grass, dragging a boiled goat bladder behind me, I reflect on Aelle's words, and how right they were; for what, if not arrogant pride made me conceive and execute all of my increasingly complex and dangerous plans, with decreasingly little chance for success other than what little hope Fate and the gods deemed to grant us for their entertainment? And tonight's plan might just be one of the most complex and dangerous I've ever attempted. It is sheer foolishness to hope it will succeed at all – but a fool's hope is all I have left.

So far, everything is proceeding smoothly – surprisingly so. The chief concern of the Saxon warriors, surrounding the hill spur from the north in a tight half-ring of watch camps, is to prevent the *wealas* from leaving the peak, rather than stop anyone coming in. In the pitch darkness, the watchmen fail to notice our passage; we crawl right under their noses, over the wet grass and chalk outcrops, through thick fen and brambles, through dung-smeared pastures and ancient fallow fields. The bladder catches on thorns, the ferns rustle like the sea, the mud – and worse, since there are still sheep

The Crown of the Iutes

and goats grazing in these meadows – gets in my eyes and ears; still, the Saxons see nothing. The first men to spot us are the Briton guards, watching intently, and wearily, for any sign of the enemy assault. They catch us just as we reach a deep ditch and a low earthen wall, a crumbling line of defence cutting the fort off from the northern, most vulnerable side.

One of the guards recognises us before the other two raise alarm.

"They're the Iutes who saved us from Bredanna Marsh," he explains to the others.

"Is Atrect still with you?" I ask.

"He is – but he's not the commander anymore…"

"I don't care. Take us to him, and hurry, before the Saxons notice."

There are no tents here – the Britons sleep under the stars, wrapped in blankets and cloaks, huddling around a few meagre campfires. They must have been caught completely by surprise by Aelle's army. It was a miracle that they even found the shelter of this ancient, crumbling fort, though it would only have bought them a few days respite at most. Just like when they were trapped in the marsh, they are already running out of food and fuel. At least they have water – the fort has its own spring, crystal-pure, seeping through chalk and flowing out of a small cave in the north-east corner.

It is in that cave that we find Atrect and a few other officers, asleep on some travel sacks and dirty sheep skins. We wait for them to wake up as we dry ourselves by the fire.

"Are we still in that damn marsh?" Atrect asks, rubbing his eyes and yawning. "Were the last few weeks just a dream? How is it that you are here?"

"I knew you'd get in trouble the moment I left you alone," I say with a chuckle.

"How did you find us? Or did Mandubrac send you?"

"We're in Britannia now – this land has no secrets from us. And no, Mandubrac did not send us – though I did see him only a couple of nights ago."

"You spoke to him?" asks another, a nobleman, judging by his manner and a thick golden ring on his finger. "Then you spoke to the Saxon king, too? What does he want from us? Why aren't they attacking us?"

I nod and raise my hand. "There will be time to explain. For now, I need you to gather your men. We're leaving this place."

"Leaving?" The nobleman scoffs. "Have the dozen of you defeated the Saxon army while we were asleep?"

"A dozen?" Atrect looks at the Iutes and only now notices I brought only half of my men with me. "What happened to Audulf and the others?" he asks with concern.

"They're fine – they have other tasks to fulfil. And no, I did not defeat the Saxon army, nor did I need to. Come, we don't have much time. We need to be out of here before the tide's out."

"Tide? What tide? We're on top of a hill!"

"Trust me –" I tap the side of my head. "I have it all figured out."

The Crown of the Iutes

The spur of the Downs on top of which the ancient Britons have built their fort extends deep into the surrounding flood plain. At low tide, it's bound to the south by a stretch of brackish marshland, with another ridge rising a mile or so away. At high tide the marsh turns into a strait of the Narrow Sea, deep, dark and ominous in the moonless night. The sea flows further to the east, spilling out onto a vast gulf, criss-crossed with drystone walls and old causeways peeking from the oozing black waters.

Halfway across the strait the land rises again, briefly, in an eruption of mounds and knolls. I can't see it right now, but Atrect tells me that in daylight one can see there the ruins of a *villa* and several barrow mounds. At high tide it turns into an island. The Saxons have set up another watch camp there, to guard what they believe to be the only way across the salt marsh. A few campfires flicker there now, like spirits lost in the swamp.

"This is your great idea?" Atrect asks. "I lost nine men trying to get across this stretch. We tried to wade it at low tide, but it's only shallow enough near that *villa*. If we go by day, the Saxons shoot at us. If we go by night, we get tangled in the reeds and gorse, or dragged under by the hidden mud pits."

"This is why you need to wait for the high tide."

"Most of us can barely swim, much less in waters that treacherous."

"You won't need to know how to swim if you use these."

I present him with the goat bladder. I struggle to show enough confidence to convince him; the truth is, I have no idea if these will work. I came up with these by remembering various scraps of ancient chronicles and military manuals, mixing my Pliny with my Vegetius, and recalling some half-forgotten bits of Herodotus; all of them mentioned ways of staying underwater for a limited time, and from what I remembered, most of them involved breathing reeds and animal bladders of some sort.

We spent a whole ignoble day catching goats in the rubble-strewn streets of Mutuanton, gutting them, boiling out their innards and sewing them up again until we produced a dozen leather bladders, filled with air. My men fulfilled my orders without a grumble, though until I tested the first bladder in the shallow, murky waters on the town's edge, they couldn't even guess at what I was making them do. It didn't seem to help me much, but then I was already a decent swimmer without it. I can only hope it will be of more assistance to those who don't have my training and endurance.

"I can't promise all your men will get to the other side," I tell Atrect, having explained how to use the bladders. "But it will greatly increase their chances."

He frowns. "I see now that you don't value the lives of my men as much as your own," he says. "It was one thing to risk death when we were trapped in a marsh in Gaul, about to be slaughtered or taken into slavery by the Goths. But we're almost home now. These Saxons haven't brought us any harm, except when we tried to flee – all they did was bar our way north. All we have to do is wait for Mandubrac to end his negotiations with the Saxon king. Why should we face these dark waters when we can be free in a couple of days?"

"Do you know what Mandubrac is negotiating? Do you know what prize Aelle bought with your lives?"

"I don't know, and I don't care," says Atrect. "I just want to go home to Dorowern."

"I care," interjects the nobleman with the golden ring. "What's going on in that *villa*?"

The Crown of the Iutes

When I explain Aelle's demands, the noblemen gasp at the news, but the revelation makes no difference to Atrect. In his weariness, he can't see how having a new *Dux* be a Saxon would change anything for him and his men. He saw parts of Gaul ruled by barbarian kings, and saw how little they differed from those ruled by Syagrius and his Roman adjutants. The cities under Hildrik and Aiwarik remain as Gaulish as they ever were. The heathens have settled the countryside, and the farmland they took over was already largely abandoned and fallow long before they came. The barbarian warlords and chieftains took their share of the taxes and customs, but in exchange they defended the land from other barbarians. It all seemed to work just fine. Little wonder that the Arwernians plotted to join the Gothic kingdom rather than remain part of the increasingly powerless Empire. The ones who lost out the most on the change were the Gaulish nobles, their power replaced by that of the Franks, Burgundians and the Goths, their *villas* turned into mead halls and hay barns; but what did a Cantian commoner care for the fate of Londin's nobles?

"You may wish to be enslaved by the heathens, *vigil*," one of the noblemen sneers at Atrect. He wasn't with us at Bredanna – he must have travelled to Armorica some other way. "But I have no intention of paying them tributes or sharing my land with them, like those Regin cowards. If the *aetheling* believes he has found a way to save us, and save Britannia, I say we give it a chance."

Atrect shrugs. "Suit yourself, Abulius – but I don't know how many of us you'll be able to convince to throw themselves into this black, cold abyss just to save your *villas*."

"We don't have time for your quarrels," says Ursula. "Those of you who wish to stay behind to cover our retreat, may do so. I don't believe Aelle will harm you, but he *will* keep you in that fort until he's satisfied with the outcome of the talks, and that might take days. Everyone else must come with us *now*. We only have a dozen of those contraptions; it will take ages to get everyone across."

"I'll gather the men," says Abulius. "Wait here. I'll be back in no time."

The Crown of the Iutes

CHAPTER XXI
THE LAY OF ABULIUS

The only point of reference in the surrounding darkness is a red dot of a torch held by one of my men on the other side of the channel. Beyond it, everything is as black as it must have been at the making of the world, before the sun and the stars came to be. I don't even feel wet anymore, just the all-numbing cold and misery. All I know is that I must plod ahead. The rope around my waist chafes my bare skin. The weeds tangle at my feet. The rough goat's bladder is more a hindrance than help, except when I have to stop for rest. I discarded the soggy breathing reed a long time ago – it was a foolish idea to try to dive in these shallow, brackish, sludge-murky waters in the first place. The distance I have to cover is less than a mile – I could swim more in my sleep – but this is the fourth time I have made my way across, each time with ten other men tied behind me, slowing and dragging me down.

"Why do we keep stopping?" I hear someone mumble behind me. His comrades silence him with whispers. It's unlikely that any Saxon guards at the island *villa* would hear us, but we can't risk being noticed. Not when we're so near the end of this long, exhausting night. This is my last trip across the valley – I doubt I'll be able to walk far after this, much less swim. Ubba and Deora are the next to go after me, to bring the last twenty of Abulius's men, before dawn illuminates the channel and presents us as clear targets to the Saxon archers.

A hundred or so Britons decided to stay with Atrect, rather than try their fortune in the brine; common folk who, like the *vigil* captain, could see no threat to themselves in Aelle's schemes. Indeed, without the nobles to command them, they decided to surrender to

The Crown of the Iutes

the Saxons in the morning, figuring it was the fastest way for them to return to their towns and farmsteads – and hoping that it would distract Aelle from pursuing us: one last favour Atrect agreed to for the sake of our friendship.

Ursula was as unconvinced of the need of our nightly escapade as Atrect. Not wishing to undermine my authority, she kept her doubts to herself, until I pressed her for an answer, sensing her unease when the first of the nobles waded into the shallow sea.

"I never thought I'd see you side with the Briton nobles against the common folk," she said.

"I never thought you'd side with Saxons against your own people," I retorted.

"You're not doing this to save the *wealas*," she said. "You're only doing this to save your father's kingdom."

"Do you think the Iutes would be the only ones to suffer under *Dux* Aelle?"

"I doubt he'd care about the Britons enough to bother them. I've seen how he 'rules' the Regins – they're mostly left to their own devices."

"And the entire *pagus* suffers for it. Everything here is falling apart. The poor grow poorer, the rich run away, only the Saxon chiefs grow fat. There's more to being a *Dux* than wearing a diadem."

"And you think Riotham would be any better? Or any other of those old nobles? Mandubrac? Albanus?" She nodded at the Briton, shuffling nervously in line, waiting for his turn at the goat bladder. "Britannia is lost, no matter who rules it. All any of these men care about is the power and glory that comes with the title – and a chance to plunder the last of the gold in Londin's treasure chests. Just like Aelle. Just like your father."

"My father?"

"Don't tell me Aeric wouldn't take the diadem if he had the chance. He needs that gold just like everyone else."

"If he wanted, he could've been a *Dux* a long time ago," I said.

"If you say so." She shrugged. "Don't get me wrong. There's nothing wrong about an *aetheling* doing what he thinks is best for his own people. I would've done the same in your place. And maybe you're right, maybe Aelle *will* sell all those Cants into slavery when they surrender to him tomorrow."

"Let's hope he'll have other things on his mind by then."

My feet reach the bottom. I struggle to untangle from the dense seaweed and wade for a couple hundred feet more, until I spit and splutter out onto the muddy shore. Ubba helps me out, the other Iutes pick up the exhausted Britons, and prepare the ropes and bladders for the next journey.

I spot Croha and her riders standing beside the torch-bearer. I summon her to me – my limbs are too stiff to move.

"Have you seen it?" I ask.

"Yes, *aetheling*. Anderitum is still held by the treaty garrison, and its gates are closed shut – but there's a Saxon camp at its gates."

"How big?"

"Some thirty men, maybe forty."

The Crown of the Iutes

I stand up, heavily, and stretch my sore muscles. I dream of a campfire by which I could dry myself out, but we can't afford being spotted, not when we're so near the end.

"Shouldn't be too much of a problem," I say. "We just have to –"

A flaming arrow flies with a whistle and lands with a sizzle in the water, just a few feet away from us. Croha cries out and pushes me to the ground as another missile whooshes past us.

"They found us!" I shout. I scramble up; in the darkness, I can't yet see where the arrows are coming from, but a flaming arrow can't travel far. "Gather the warriors! Mount up! Guard the Britons, we're moving out!"

"What about the ones still on the other side?" asks Ursula.

"They'll have to fend for themselves."

She frowns. "You're abandoning them again."

"We freed as many as we could. We're too tired to fight – we need to reach shelter before the rest of Aelle's army gets here." Another arrow hits the sand inches from one of the Britons. I see the silhouettes of the approaching Saxons in the faint light of dawn. There are a couple dozen of them at least, moving carefully, uncertain yet what to make of us.

"We have to go," I press. "Or we risk losing the ones we've already saved."

"Hurry! We're almost there!"

The great circular wall of the Anderitum fortress looms across the flooded plain, half a mile away, with the morning sun rising right above them, surrounded by concentric rings of earthen banks and ditches. I remember it from the stories as a once-great fortress and naval harbour, where Aelle's father, Pefen, first made his seat as mercenary captain, and from which he launched his slow conquest of the Regen country. Aelle was a fool to give it away, even if his hand was forced by the peace treaty. It would take less than a hundred men to defend the mighty walls against any force we could muster; indeed, no army has ever taken it by force when the Legions were still here.

We're on the final stretch of our flight across the Downs; the men are exhausted, soaked-through, shivering with cold and yet drenched with sweat at the same time. We've been force-marching them for the ten or so miles separating the hillfort from Anderitum. I can't imagine how they're still finding strength to march, but somehow, seeing the fortress so close seems to have given them renewed energy.

"Can we really take it?" asks Abulius, gazing towards the Saxon guard camp, set up within one of Pefen's old defensive enclosures, before the fort's tall western gate.

"They are few, and on foot," says Croha.

"And we are tired, cold and hungry men," says Abulius. "Many will perish trying to break through." He glances back and his eyes narrow. "And they don't need to hold us for long."

I can't tell how many Saxons are pursuing us; all I see is a dark mass, moving up and down the ridge of the Downs in a cloud of dust, a few miles behind us. It can't be Aelle's entire army – he wouldn't have time to gather all his men together, and some of them would have stayed to check on Atrect and those who stayed with him at the hillfort. But even a hundred warriors would

The Crown of the Iutes

massacre us if we let them catch up to us. The Britons are on their last legs, heaving with effort, barely able to hold on to what few weapons some of them managed to bring over the sea passage.

I call to my riders. "Follow me," I tell them. "Abulius, stay back. Don't come too close to that camp until I give you a signal."

The camp guards watch us approach down the Roman road, at first with curiosity. They can't expect a dozen riders to try to fight them. If they fear a trick at all, they're not showing it. From a distance, we're indistinguishable from a mounted Saxon patrol – and even up close, it would take a keen eye and ear to tell my Iutes from Aelle's warriors.

"What's going on?" one of them asks us. "Where are you going in such a hurry?"

"Woe!" I cry. I don't look up, hiding my red hair under a hood. "Death! We were ambushed by a *wealh* warband in the Downs – they're chasing after us. Look, they're coming over the marsh!"

The guards stare at the approaching Britons for a moment, mulling their options, before finally deciding to let us inside the earth bank.

"Rest a while," says the captain of the guard, "then we'll send you into Anderitum. You'll be safe there."

I look around. "Is there only the twenty of you?" I ask, fearfully. My hands and my voice tremble – not with pretend fear, but with the power of the henbane coursing through my veins.

Returning to Britannia meant going back to the familiar forest and herbs of our homeland. During our stay in Gaul I did not dare to experiment with the weeds we could find in its woods and marshes, however familiar they may have looked, but as soon as we departed New Port, Ursula pointed out the unmistakable berries of the nightshade growing on the side of the road; the likes of Saxons and Franks used the berries themselves, mixed with some mushrooms, to brew a potent wine that induced in them a shield-biting frenzy, but I knew it was only one of the many components mixed with the henbane ale to make the secret Iutish potion.

We had little time to gather the necessary ingredients on our way to Mutuanton, but there was enough of it to prepare a few mouthfuls for each of us. I had the men drink it as we rode towards Anderitum, just in time for it to start working as the Saxons let us into the fortress.

"Thirty – but the others are out on patrol."

"Good," I say. I draw the *spatha*, close my eyes and feel the fire flow into my limbs. It's been a while since I last made the brew, and I wasn't sure if I remembered the proportions correctly; my eyes burn brighter than they should, my ears ring louder. I can barely hear the Saxon's concerned cries over the din in my head. I'm certain he's asking why I have my weapon drawn – and, as the hood falls from our heads, he realises we may not be the mounted patrol he's been expecting, but something more terrifying altogether.

The realisation comes too late. Grasping my sword with two hands, I hack at his neck. His mouth and eyes still open in shock, his head rolls off his shoulders and onto the sand. With time slowed down to a blurry crawl, I rush to the next Saxon and thrust the sword through his chest. I only feel his blood on my hand when I slash at the third enemy; he, too, is too slow to react – or maybe my world moves too fast for me to notice his attempt at a parry. His call for help is cut short by my blade slicing his throat.

All around me, the Iutes dance the deathly dance of blades and blood. It is rare that Iute warriors can so freely make use of the henbane trance; it's usually a device of last resort, taken to break

The Crown of the Iutes

out of an encirclement, or to make a last stand against overwhelming enemy numbers. Here, the Saxons are few and surprised by our sudden outburst. Within moments, half of them lie dead in the mud. The remainder runs off towards Anderitum, calling for the garrison's help.

For some of the younger warriors, and those who joined us after Andecawa, this is the first time they ever tried henbane. Croha is among those youths – I see her, cheeks red with excitement, eyes wide and shining, lips apart. She throws one axe, then another, after the fleeing Saxons. Each lands in the back of one enemy, splitting them open. She picks up a knife from one of the fallen warriors and throws that, too, striking a third Saxon just as he reaches the fort's gate. He hangs, limply, on the latch.

I sense the brew evaporating slowly from my body. The portion was small, and its effects short. The blur in my vision clears, the world returns to its normal speed. Not all Saxons are yet dead; the survivors clustered at the gate, pleading with the men of the garrison, but the Iutes and Britons stare at them and us in confused hesitation. I call my men away and look up at the guards on the gatehouse.

"Hleo?" I cry out in astonishment. "Is that you?"

"*Aetheling*!" the warrior shouts back. "What are you doing here?"

"Open that gate," I tell him. "There's not much time."

"My *Hlaford* – the Saxons…"

I mumble a curse. I forgot there are also some Saxons inside the fortress.

"Deal with them, Hleo. Just like I taught you. We'll hold, but not for long."

[410]

I look around. The trance recedes from the men. A few are bleeding, but these are only scratches; it takes more than a frightened Saxon guard to wound a bear-shirt. I turn to Croha. A rivulet of bloody spittle trickles from her mouth. Her nostrils are still flared, her eyes dark with dilated pupils. She's trembling, her teeth are chattering. Her hands are twitching, squeezing the air as if she was still holding a weapon. She's still searching for another enemy to slay. Her eyes fall on Ursula. She picks up a hatchet from the ground and lunges at her with a howl. Just when she's about to strike, I leap on her and grapple her to the ground.

I, too, still feel the effects of the henbane, though not what I'd expect in this dangerous moment. Croha's grunting and writhing under me makes the blood, still hot in my veins, rush to my nethers. I focus and at length, both she and I calm down. She starts shivering, her eyes dance. Ursula pushes me off her, covers Croha with her cloak and holds her until the shivering subdues.

"Will she be alright?" I ask, crouching down beside them.

"You gave her too much," says Ursula. She alone took no henbane, preferring to depend on her skill and prayer. "She's smaller than most of your men, and she's unused to it. You've poisoned her." She rubs Croha's arms and back. "Bring us some water!" She calls on one of Croha's shieldmaidens. "And give me my saddlebag, I have some tincture of hellebore there."

I step away, to give them air and peace as Ursula prepares a brew to draw the toxin from Croha's now somehow frail-looking, body. Inside the fortress, the screams of dying men, one by one, fall silent.

"Go get the Britons," I order Ubba. "Before Aelle catches up to them. And you –" I turn to the Saxons still huddling at the gate. "I'm too tired to fight you. Throw down your weapons and go join your king," I say, pointing at the enemy army heading our way.

The Crown of the Iutes

Abulius is the last to pass through the gate; we shut and lock it behind him with a thud. On the opposite side, by the harbour, my men finish tying up the surviving Saxons, who gave themselves up – and, more importantly, the storage barn they were defending – as soon as they saw the three-hundred strong Briton army enter the fort.

"Was this your plan all along?" the nobleman asks me, glancing at the ramparts. "To exchange one wall for another? We're as trapped here as we were on that hill."

"Except here you have food, fuel and other provisions," I explain. "We took the fort's stocks, untouched. They can last us for weeks. And these walls are impervious to anything Aelle can bring against it," I add, tapping the cold stone. "He would need siege machines to break through. We have javelins, we have arrows – we even have some *plumbata* darts, though most are rusted through."

"What we don't have, is time," he says. "The Council in Londin will not have heard of our escape. They will yield to the Saxon's demands before long."

"Not if my men have anything to do with it," I reply with a grin.

This is what I sent the other half of my riders to deal with, I tell him. Audulf's task is to intercept any envoys sent between Londin and Mutuanton, to make sure that the negotiations in the *villa* are delayed – or, hopefully, broken, once Mandubrac and the other noblemen learn of our flight to Anderitum. "We should gain at least a few days this way," I say. "Audulf knows how to do this sort of thing."

"What good is a few more days?"

"In a few days, I'll be able to reach my father," I reply.

The answer seems to satisfy him – for now. One of his men brings him a pitcher of water, taken from the fort's well. He quaffs it in four great gulps, wipes his mouth and takes a solemn look around.

"My grandfather once stood on those ramparts," he says mournfully. "A centurion in the last *numerus* stationed here. I was named after the town they came from – Abulia, in Hispania."

Looking at the nobleman, I can see the traces of foreign blood in his veins. His skin is the shade of olive; his hair is raven black, though splattered with grey. His eyes are as dark as two bits of charcoal; his nose is sharp like a hawk's beak.

"Our gravest mistake was to give this place to the barbarians," he says, misty-eyed. "They were supposed to defend our shores, not take them for themselves."

"The Iutes still honour the treaties," I remind him.

"Indeed – and we remain grateful for your father's loyalty." He looks back down to me, as if remembering who he's talking to. "Did you say you're going to bring him here?"

"I will… try." I scratch my head. I haven't yet had a chance to think about what I will tell my father when I finally see him. Is the threat of Aelle becoming a *Dux* going to be enough to convince him to risk his warriors in open battle, just to save some Briton nobles?

"Did your grandfather share with you some lessons on how to defend a fortress?" I ask.

The Crown of the Iutes

Abulius shakes his head. "He left with Constantine, like everyone else, leaving my grandmother behind with a child... But if we have enough men and provisions, as you say – how hard can it be?"

I glance to the gatehouse. Deora waves his hand three times, indicating he's spotted the Saxon warband heading our way.

"Looks like you're about to find out."

Croha kneels down on one knee, bows down and offers me her sword.

"What I did yesterday was unforgivable," she declares. "I am not fit to count myself among your warriors."

"Don't be a fool," I say. "It was my fault. We're fortunate it's all that happened – a poorly made brew can kill a man twice your size. And you still managed to kill three Saxons while fighting the effects of the poison. I'd like to see any other of my warriors do that!"

I pull her up from the ground, take her chin in my hand and look into her eyes to make sure the toxic brew is all gone from her body.

"Looks like you're alright," I say. "Try to get some rest. Drink plenty of water. Purge, if you can."

"Yes, my *Hlaford*."

I brush hair from her brow; my fingers linger on her cheek for a moment.

"When you're rested, go down to the beach and find us a decent boat," I tell her. "Hleo and Haering – I still can't believe they're both here! – will help you pick the right one."

"A boat?" she asks. "We're sailing again?"

"Rowing. It's the only way out of here. It doesn't have to be big, but make sure it's seaworthy!"

"You were really worried about her," says Ursula, approaching from the direction of the storehouse with a new spear blade she found in one of the Legion's chests.

"I'm concerned about all my warriors."

"And do you caress all your warriors like that, or just those you plan to spawn bastards with?"

"That was *your* plan, remember?" I sigh and rub my eyes. I hear one of the Britons call us from the gate. I wave back at him to let him know we're coming.

"I don't have time for this now, Ursula," I say. "There will be no spawning, bastards or otherwise, if I can't get us out of here alive."

"I'm not being spiteful, Octa. I'm glad you've grown fond of her. She deserves to be more than just an object of your lust."

"First, you wanted her to replace you in my bed – now you want her in my heart, too?" I snap. "What, exactly, is your plan? If you want a *dissolutio*, just say so. Don't drag poor Croha into our family trouble."

She steps back in fright. "A *dissolutio*? Why would you say that? I never –"

[415]

The Crown of the Iutes

"Forgive me." I take her hand. "I keep saying and doing things I don't mean. It's this damn war – I feel like I'm losing my mind, trying to keep all the threads together, and it's only just begun."

"Don't lose focus, my husband," she says, and strokes my palm gently. "Don't let politics and strife get in the way of what's *really* important."

"I'll try – but it's not easy when you're the son of a king."

"It's not easy for a Councillor, either." She smiles sadly. "Let's go see what that guard wants from us, before he tears his throat from shouting."

"There's someone here asking to talk to you, *aetheling*," the Briton guard tells us.

I climb up a wobbly ladder; there used to be a staircase inside each of the two round towers, but the stairs crumbled to a pile of stone and rotten wood a long time ago. A wooden platform, patched up in Pefen's times, supports the guards on what remains of the gatehouse, allowing me to look over the jagged, dusty parapet.

There are maybe four hundred warriors gathered on the muddy plain below, amid the earthworks raised by Aelle's father, at a javelin's throw from the ramparts. More are still trickling in from the north and west, in small bands, to join the siege. They are wary of the Briton and Iute soldiers, who line the northern wall with darts and bows in their hands, looking imposing in the tattered, faded red cloaks, a chest of which we found in the fortress's storehouse, buried under straw and dirt. What the Saxons can't know is how few of the *wealas* are in fighting shape. Only a day has passed since we arrived in Anderitum, not enough to feed and heal all the weary, injured warriors. All through the day and night we've been lighting fires to warm and dry ourselves after our escape under the sea, and to boil the simple potage of dried oats and lentils. What the rats and worms didn't gnaw through should suffice to sustain us for however many days Aelle would want to besiege us, but it's scarcely food fit enough for a warrior.

If Aelle decided to assault the fortress today, the battle would be bloody, but short. With each day he hesitates, we will grow stronger: our wounds healed, our bellies filled, our blades sharpened. I wonder how much of this he is aware as I watch him and Hilla ride up to the gate with the banner of truce.

"I knew you'd cause me grief," he says, after Ursula and I climb down to meet them. "But I didn't think you'd take my father's *burh* from me."

"You know, I gave birth to my son in these walls," says Hilla. "And Pefen's ashes are buried not that far from here." She nods to a dune ridge in the distance.

"You shouldn't have given it away so easily, then," I say. "If it means so much to you."

Aelle laughs. "It's only a pile of *wealh* stones now. The great Wall of Londin will be my fortress soon." He scratches his nose and takes a deep breath. "Listen, Octa. We've all had our merriment, and I appreciate how much trouble you've gone through to disrupt my plans – I still don't know how you got all those Britons out of that hillfort unnoticed – but now might be a good time to end it. What is it that you want from me? I'm willing to consider your father's position in my new kingdom. The Iutes don't want to be ruled by Saxons – I understand it! I was at Eobbasfleot. I saw many of your people die fighting for their new homeland." He waves his hand. "Fine, you can have it. With Londin and everything else in my hands, I will have no need for Cantia."

The Crown of the Iutes

"We are bound by treaties to defend the Britons, including from the likes of you," I say. "We do not break our oaths as easily as you and your father."

"The Britons don't want to defend *themselves*," he scoffs. "Those noblemen would have given me their entire island just to save their skins. They're not worth a single drop of your warriors' blood."

"I don't fight for the noblemen; I fight for all the *wealas*. My mother was a *wealh*. So is my wife." I lay my hand on Ursula's shoulder. "And so was our son. The *wealas* are our families, friends, neighbours. They are all worth shedding our blood for." I shake my head. "Besides, I have no authority to make such a decision. Maybe if you'd let me speak to my father…"

"I'm afraid I don't have that much time, *aetheling*. You need to start making your own decisions, without waiting for your father's permission – like I once did." He looks to the ramparts again. I can see he's uncertain of the worth of the Briton defenders. How much has he heard about what went on in Gaul? He'd know Riotham lost the campaign and most of his army perished – but he'd also know that the men who reached Anderitum are the ones who *survived* the disaster at Dol, and fought their way back across the Gothic kingdom. They are now battle-hardened warriors, probably more so than many of Aelle's own men, who would've had little war experience beyond chasing after pirates or forest bandits.

And then there's the wall itself, an impenetrable barrier of stone that had thwarted so many of his kindred over the centuries since the fort was first built…

"You have until tomorrow," he says, at last. "Choose wisely."

My arse is cold and damp. I sit in a shallow puddle of seawater, seeping through the boards of the boat with my every heave. The boat is small and cramped with the six of us, but it was the best we could find in the harbour; the Saxons kept no *ceols* in the fortress, and only a few row boats they would have used to supplement their diet with some fish. The current and waves of the coming tide push us onto the cliffs, and it takes all of our effort to steer our shell out to sea and further along the coast. Ursula operates another oar beside me, and Hleo and Haering row on the bow; Croha and Deora sit in the middle, watching the shore pass by and fighting the sea sickness.

"Are you sure –" *Heave!* "– we shouldn't have –" *Heave!* "– accepted Aelle's terms?" Ursula asks. "Would it have been so terrible to be his ally when he's the *Dux* of Londin?"

"He's not a *Dux* yet," I reply. "Have you seen how anxious he's grown? Audulf must be doing a good job keeping those messengers away. Aelle hadn't heard back from Londin yet. This must be why he hasn't attacked the fortress. He's not as sure of his position as he pretends to be."

We set off in the morning – rowing at night in the turbulent waters of the Narrow Sea would've been tantamount to suicide – when it became clear that Aelle's threat was empty, and that his Saxons were not any more keen on assaulting Anderitum than they had been the day before. I'm certain they spotted us leaving, but could not be bothered to chase after a single row boat. I left the fort under the combined command of Abulius and Ubba; neither of them had much experience defending from a siege, and I hoped they wouldn't have to learn it before I returned.

"Even if my father yielded to Aelle as *Dux* and *Bretwealda*, how long do you think we'd be able to stay independent from the great Saxon kingdom?" I say. "Starved of iron and silver, imprisoned within the borders of Cantia, how long before we'd be forced to

The Crown of the Iutes

pay tribute just to survive – in men, when the silver runs out? We'd be nothing but a source of slaves and plunder to the Saxon hordes."

"I wonder if your father will see it the same way."

"I don't know. He's always been wary of Aelle – but he's been preparing for a different kind of war, one where the Saxons invade us from the South. If Aelle takes Londin, if he recruits more warriors from the North and the West, if the *wealas* join him – we have no earthworks out there, except the walls of Robriwis. We wouldn't be able to defend ourselves."

"The Cants will never join a war against those who defended them for so long," Ursula says.

"Maybe. But there are others who have little reason to stay loyal to us. Whether to avenge the memory of Eobbasfleot, or to simply share in the plunder, I fear there will be many Britons who will not hesitate to follow their new *Dux* into battle, even if he is a filthy heathen."

"*Rex* Aeric is no coward," says Croha, overhearing our conversation. Her face is no longer green, but it's still pale and sunken. "He will fight them all if need be."

"He's no coward," I agree. "But my father is a cunning leader, and he loathes wasting lives if there's a chance to solve a quarrel in a peaceful way. Perhaps he will see some other solution that yet evades me."

A strong wave throws us a few feet in the air. The hull creaks dangerously, but still holds, though for how long, I can't say.

"How far are we going, anyway?" asks Ursula, spluttering and rubbing the seawater from her eyes. "You can't hope for us to reach Leman in this eggshell. I can't go on like this for much longer."

I look to the shore. A while ago, the sandstone cliffs and tall dunes to our port receded, making way for a broad beach of pink and yellow shingle. Since then, a unit of riders has been following us along the dune ridge. As I watch them, they ride down onto the beach and hail us, though their cries are lost in the wind. In the distance, to the east, I spot the blurry outline of a harbour village and, above it, on a hilltop, a black finger of a Roman watchtower. A menacing dot of a sailing boat departs from the beach and heads our way on the easterly wind.

"Looks like we're here," I say. "Or at least, as near 'here' as he'll let us."

"Here?" Croha notices the riders on the shore. "Where is 'here'? And who is this *he*?"

"An old friend," I tell her. "At least, I hope I can still call him that."

The Crown of the Iutes

CHAPTER XXII
THE LAY OF HAESTA

The mead hall is built into an ancient bath house, its rafters rising in place of the bent vaults of the *caldarium*. The hollow sound that my steps make tells me that the wooden floor was built straight over the red bricks of the hypocaust.

Instinctively, I search for the brass door of the cauldron; I find only a hollow where it once was, now used to store a chest of riches.

The bath house, when still in use, would have been a simple building, serving the workers of the nearby iron mine. All that remains of the long abandoned mine are heaps of slag scattered everywhere, and shaft holes scarring the ground like pock marks. We're some two miles inland from the old harbour which would've once been used to haul the iron out to the markets. It, too, is abandoned – what little is left of it; the rest was buried under silt and sand brought on by the storms. The new village was built a few hundred feet to the south, but now only fishing *ceols* depart from its shingle beach.

I have never visited Haesta's tiny domain before, and I'm surprised how well kept it is, despite the small size. I can see his people are proud of what they managed to accomplish with the few resources at their disposal. They are too few to bring life back to the iron mine, but a large forge is still working through the remains of ore dug up from the abandoned heaps – the main source of the Haestingas prosperity when they can't count on mercenary pay. The huts, though most are made of mud and wicker, are tidy and airy. Not much grows in the sand, peat and heath that cover most of the land, but the pigs the Haestingas keep are fat and their sheep are heaving with wool.

The Crown of the Iutes

I congratulate Haesta on the state of his little kingdom, but the flattery gets me nowhere. He frowns, eyeing Ursula, Croha and the others; his bushy, grey-speckled brows meet over his sharp nose.

"Why shouldn't I give you straight back to Aelle?" he asks me.

"I invoke the ancient laws of hospitality," I say. "And friendship."

He winces. "You're a trespasser here, not a guest. And friendship counts for little when the future of my people is at stake."

"Do you fear Aelle?"

"I *know* him. Better than you or your father do. For most of the time my people lived here, we were under his… 'protection'." He grimaces when he says the word. "Now that he's about to go to war against the Britons, it would be foolish to make an enemy of him."

"You know about his plans?"

He scoffs. "His border is just a few miles away from here. I have to know everything that goes on in his domain. I even know where *you* just came from," he says, pointing at me. "How long do you think that *wealh* fortress can hold out?"

"Long enough," I reply. "If you lend me your help."

"I'm not going to fight the Saxons for your sake, if that's what you're asking."

"I'd never ask this of you. All I need is a few of your horses, and we'll be on our way. It will be like we were never even here."

Haesta swipes his hand down his face. "Aelle's got his spies among my men just like I have among his. He likely already knows you're here."

"Then we have even less time," says Ursula. "Only your horses can take us to Rutubi swiftly enough."

"Rutubi?" Haesta raises his eyebrow. "If you want to reach your father, you won't find him there."

"That's where he should be at this time of year," I say.

"You didn't think he'd just wait for Aelle behind the walls of his fortress?" He chuckles. "You need to give your father some credit. He's been gathering the *fyrd* ever since we got news of what happened in Gaul, expecting some trouble."

"Where is he, then?"

"Somewhere on the upper Medu, I bet. On the border. By Catigern's Tomb, or maybe on one of the dykes." He scratches his nose. "I could stop all of this right now," he says. "I could hold you here until your father surrenders to Aelle. That would be certain to win me his gratitude."

"I'm well aware of that," I say. "And still, I came to you."

"And what did you think you could achieve by coming here? What are you hoping to achieve by talking to your father? If he believed the Iute *fyrd* alone could win against the Saxons, he would've launched an invasion already."

"My father is a cautious leader. He doesn't waste his men's lives at whim. But he doesn't know everything. He thinks he can still reason with Aelle. I have to convince him otherwise."

The Crown of the Iutes

"You *want* a war?"

"There may be no other way to quell Aelle's ambition. Once and for all."

He frowns. "You're not giving me much reason to let you go. If there's a war between the Saxons and the Iutes, their armies will march straight through my lands."

"There are other roads."

"Not as suitable for a *fyrd*."

"If you help me, I'll make sure your people are left alone."

"And if you win, what then?"

"I…" I hesitate. I glance around the mead hall. Several of Haesta's warriors stare at me intently, but their warchief understands my hesitation.

"Leave us alone," he orders his men, then looks back at me, expectantly.

"You too," I tell the others, sensing he, too, has some secrets to share. "All of you." Ursula raises her eyebrow, but she, too, leaves without a word.

Haesta walks up to the hall's door, to make sure we're not being eavesdropped, before returning to his seat.

"She's as fine a woman as ever," he notes. "I hope you treat her well."

"I didn't come here to discuss my marriage," I reply.

"Then I was right to sense some trouble between you." His eyes dim. "I heard what happened in winter. No parent should live through something like that."

"We weren't the only ones," I say. "How did your people fare?"

"We are far away from anywhere here. In winter it's as if we're on an island of our own. One of my sons was briefly ill, but we had few losses otherwise, thank Friga."

"Then you still have all your heirs."

"It must pain you to see others' fortune."

"Not at all." I shake my head. "I just… Did my father ever talk to you about what would happen to his kingdom if I die heirless?"

"You know I rarely speak with *Rex* Aeric… with Ash. Why?"

"He mentioned *you* and your clan would inherit it."

Haesta laughs, then sees I'm serious and stops abruptly.

"Then you'd better get to work spawning those sons, Octa."

"I don't think it would be such a terrible idea, seeing how well you've ruled your own domain."

"Everything I know about ruling I've learned from your father," he says. The confession surprises me.

"Weren't you always trying to overthrow him?"

"In the past, yes." He nods. "I was certain I would rule the Iutes better than some clan-less, half-*wealh* upstart. That I deserved to rule them because of the blood of Wodan's line in my veins." He smiles mysteriously. "There was a time I could have overthrown him without a single sword blow."

"How?"

"By revealing his darkest secret."

My mouth falls open. "You – you knew?"

"He told you, too, then?"

"If it's the same secret… Yes, though not before I learned it myself from Wortigern."

Haesta nods. "I was there at Eobbasfleot when Ash told Hengist about him and Rhedwyn. I brought him before the *Drihten* myself – and then hid to listen to their conversation, thinking to learn something I could use against either of them one day."

"Then… why didn't you?"

He scowls. "It didn't seem right. I am a Iute warrior. I fight with a sword and shield, not with words and intrigue, like some *wealh* noble. Besides, revealing the secret would have meant telling everyone that Ash *did* come from Wodan's line – and one nobler than my own. As long as he ruled well, as long as he kept the Iutes on his side, there was a risk that they would turn against *me*, instead." He shakes his head. "I watched him all those years. Hoping he would make a mistake that would cause him to lose face before his warriors, that would prove that I was better suited to rule the Iutes than him. But the tribe grew from strength to strength, and he never failed at any of his endeavours. I understood I could never be as fine a *Drihten* or *Rex* as him."

"And what did you think about Aelle?" I ask, after the long pause that I need to take in his revelations.

He snorts a loud, scornful scoff. "Aelle is a child in a grown man's body. He's a warrior, nothing else. He's bored of peace. If he could, he would plunge this entire island in a war, not caring even for victory, only for the glory of fighting."

"Then you would rather not see him become a *Dux*."

"A *Dux*? Is that why he's doing all this?" He laughs. "And here I thought he was just stirring trouble for no reason. I may have underestimated him, after all. But… he won't last a year in Londin. Those nobles will eat him alive."

"There aren't enough nobles left. Many perished in Gaul. The others are weak and cowardly, thinking only of preserving their precious *villas*. They all but surrendered to him. Aelle may have a child's mind, but it's a cruel child, and one who knows how to hold the *wealas* with an iron fist."

"And I suppose the Iutes will fight him out of the good of their own hearts, and to keep the peace and freedom in the *wealas* land," Haesta says scornfully. "We're wasting time. You still haven't told me what you and your father will get out of this war."

"You said my father is a good *Rex*. Do you think he'd make a good *Dux*?"

"Ah."

Haesta rubs his chin, and drinks his ale. I try to add more to my explanation, but he hushes me with a raised hand. Nothing more needs to be said. We both know that in this moment, he's holding the future of Britannia in his hands.

The Crown of the Iutes

The silence that follows is long and uncomfortable. Whatever he's thinking about, he's not sharing any of it with me.

"Hel take you, *and* your father," he says at last, slamming the table. "But if there has to be a heathen *Dux* in Londin, I'd rather it be one of my own kin." He stands up and calls for one of his men. "If anyone asks, you stole my horses and fought your way out," he tells me when the servant arrives. "Aelle already thinks me a coward and my warriors a jest, so this will hardly surprise him."

I bow deeply. "Thank you, warchief. You will not regret this act of mercy."

"I already am. Remember what you promised. Now get out of my sight and let me return to my brooding, before you convince me to do something even more rash."

I haven't seen the great *fyrd* levied since the Battle of Eobbasfleot, when the Iutes fought for their survival against the forces of the Briton tribes united under Wortimer. I was a young boy then, witnessing only the battle's final act: my father, defeating the Briton general in a duel that decided the outcome of the conflict. I did not know then how rare an event the calling of the *fyrd* was. In the eighteen years that passed since, no threat was deemed so great as to warrant my father once again ordering all Iutes capable of holding a weapon to gather into one mighty force – until now.

There must be at least a thousand people here: warriors, shieldmaidens and camp followers. This is only a fraction of the several thousands of free men and slaves that call my father their king; he would have chosen only those he could trust to hold their own in a battle. It must be costing a fortune to feed and equip even this small number, though most of the warriors carry only clubs, farming tools and woodsmen hatchets.

The camp – if this loose sea of tents, lean-tos, shelters, folk sleeping under the stars on furs and blankets, or in the farmhouses and shepherds' huts can be called that – lies scattered throughout the flood plain of the upper Medu River, just as it flows down the escarpment into the dark fastness of the Andreda Forest; it's centred roughly around an old *villa*, one of several built along the river shore, overlooking the old Roman road that brought us from Haesta's coast. It's not an obvious place to stave off an enemy invasion – there are no fortresses here – the great dyke in the fields around Mealla's Farm starts a few miles to the west, and only the line of the Medu presents a barrier to the coming army; but after the summer droughts the river is shallow and slow-moving.

As I ride up the Roman road, however, I begin to discern my father's reasoning. This is his land in more than one way. He personally owns a stretch of the shore on both sides of the river; not far from here is a river crossing called Aelle's Ford, and the ancient standing stones where Catigern, Wortigern's eldest son, and Horsa, a Iute warchief, are buried. My father bought all of it a long time ago, to preserve the memory of this place. This is where Aeric and Aelle had their first fateful meeting: the first, a slave in the service of an old nobleman, Master Pascent; the other, a young commander of a forest band.

My appreciation of the location's strategic value grows when I note the old pilgrim track to Dorowern running along the southern slope of the Downs, providing one of the three good passages between Cantia and the lands further west. The other two run along the coasts – through Robriwis in the north, and through Haesta's territory in the south; both can be reached by the old Roman road from here, and both require only a small force to hold any invaders in check. The *fyrd* is a slow-moving, cumbersome creature, and it's best to keep it here, halfway between the two approaches. The pilgrim track, with its many crossroads, might also provide a good route for a counter-attack on Aelle's flank, should an opportunity arise. All of this tells me how serious my father is

The Crown of the Iutes

about waging a war on his Saxon neighbours; and yet, he is not willing to make the first strike.

We reach the border of the *villa*; a low wall of white stone surrounds its grounds. Beyond it, I spot the warriors of the *Hiréd*, some training, some resting. I hear cries of Betula, the old *Gesith*, ordering her men into some mock battle. I'm struck by a sudden pang of nostalgia. We may not be at one of my father's usual courts, but it all looks and sounds familiar, as if we never left Cantia. I glance to Ursula and see tears in her eyes. The painful memories, held at bay by the distance and thrill of our expedition to Gaul, all come flooding down.

I hear another familiar, hoarse voice, calling our names. It's coming from the ruins of a smithy; white tents cluster to its brick walls like mushrooms to a tree trunk. I recognise some of the men bustling about those tents before I spot the man who's calling us. They are the Iutes who went with us to Gaul, and fought Odowakr at Andecawa – and the hoarse voice is that of Seawine himself.

"*Aetheling!*" he cries one more time. "Over here! We have mead!"

"I must see my father at once," I call back.

"*Rex* Aeric is away on patrol," Seawine replies. "He won't be back until dusk. Come, tell us what happened to you after Andecawa. I hope the six of you are not all that's left of the bear-shirts?"

"Not at all – though we have lost a few more since you last saw us." I look at Ursula again; she wipes her eyes.

"Bring out the barrels," she tells Seawine. "There's sand in my throat that needs washing away – and memories that need drowning."

[432]

"Are you sure it behoves a *rex* to be going on patrols on his own, Father?"

I bite into the hard, dark bread and wash it down with water. On an expedition like this, with a thousand hungry mouths to feed, a king must eat like his own people, and so the meal prepared in the *villa*'s largest remaining room is a simple one: apart from the bread, there's only a thin stew with some groats, and a few pieces of some game bird caught in the hunters' snares. It is a gloomy meal, not least because the windows are all overgrown with ivy and weeds. The room has an odd, octagonal shape, with seven of its eight walls opening out onto the fields outside. Through holes in the tessellated pavement I can see the hypocaust, carved straight into the chalk below. The masters of the *villa*, like so many others in this part of Britannia, would have abandoned it during the civil war – if they survived the uprising of the Martinians first; sixty years have passed since anyone repaired the roof or cleaned the weeds from the garden. It's enough for a large apple tree to have grown out of the floor in the northern corner, its roots and branches crashing through the walls and the roof: someone must have dropped an apple core here just before they left.

We all sit on the cracked floor, leaning against the walls, with the stew cauldron between us: Ursula on my right, Seawine on my left, and Betula, the chief of my father's household guard, next to him. The two of them have just returned to the camp.

"I wasn't on patrol," my father replies. He winces at the taste of the stew. "We went to Wealingatun, to meet with my brother's messengers."

"*Wealingatun?*" I ask. "Oh, you mean your old *villa*, Ariminum. You're in contact with Bishop Fastidius? Then you know all about Aelle's designs."

[433]

"It wasn't Aelle we talked about today – at least, not just him. A letter arrived in Londin a few days ago – from Lugdunum."

"Lugdunum?" I scratch my head, trying to remember who in Lugdunum could be sending letters to the Council. "Riotham?"

My father nods. "He's still alive, and so are a few hundred of his soldiers, sheltering among the Burgundians. But you'd think he's already the *Dux* by the way he carries on in the letter." He chuckles.

"Let me guess – he demands the Council send a force to relieve him."

My father nods.

"He asked the same of us when we were still in Armorica. So the Imperator didn't come to his aid, after all… What did the Council have to say about it?"

"They have little time for Riotham's posturing. As far as they're concerned, he and all those who went with him can rot in Lugdunum. They're only worried about Aelle and his Saxons – but they can't do anything about him, either, so they're just stewing in their own helplessness."

"What of Albanus?"

"Busy with the fighting in the North, as always. He's been providing men to keep peace on Londin's streets in Riotham's absence, but he's not keen to face the Saxons in the field. He would rather wait for Aelle to waste his strength trying to rule the capital, before trying to oust him through some political intrigue."

"Then you agree that it's up to us to stop Aelle."

"Is it?" The king scratches his chin, covered in a thin stubble. "Are you telling me to start the war myself? Why would I want to do that?"

He slurps more of the stew.

"You can't possibly think Aelle being the *Dux* will be good for the future of our kingdom," I say.

"It doesn't matter," says Betula. "The *fyrd* is not an army. We may have more than a thousand men here, but they're just a militia of farmers and fishermen. They will hold the enemy from crossing the Medu and the dykes well enough, but if we march them on Aelle's fortresses, they will soon perish."

"Why have you gathered them, then, if not to keep the diadem from Aelle?"

"When I heard the news of Riotham's disaster in Gaul, I knew instantly there'd be trouble, one way or another," my father says. "I wasn't sure if it would be Aelle who made the first move, Albanus, or some other Councillor who waited for Riotham to fail. Either way, the balance of power on the island has been disrupted, and whenever that happens, it's not long before everyone is at each other's throats. The Iutes needed to show they won't be an easy prey in the chaos."

"So it's all just a show of force, against anyone who'd try to invade us?"

"It is not Aelle that I worry about," he says. "He's never shown any ambition of becoming a *Dux* before. This is just another of his childish whims, a vengeance for the humiliation he suffered in spring, when we forced him to sign the treaty. My concern is how the Britons will react to his ascension. Those Londin nobles may sell him the title for a promise of safety, but before long they will claim they were forced to do this, and ask their kindred from the North and the West for help against the barbarians. It will be like Wortimer's War all over again, only this time they'd know they're all fighting for their very survival. They'd have to prove to us, and anyone else who might think to try the same, that no heathen could ever again humiliate them like Aelle."

"We won once, when they were stronger," says Seawine. "We'll beat them again."

"We might, but at what cost?" My father shakes his head. "You're old enough to remember how many good men we lost at Eobbasfleot, Seawine. No ruler would risk such a tragedy for his people again, if it could be avoided."

"And if the Saxons win that conflict on their own?" I ask. "We'd be at Aelle's mercy."

"Aelle will not stay a *Dux* for long," he says, repeating Haesta's prediction. "He doesn't know what he's getting into. He hasn't prepared any support for his power. Running a province is nothing like being a *rex* of a heathen tribe. Managing the Council, dealing with the tribes, trade, taxes… Even the Briton noblemen know how demanding a role it is, this is why no Councillor before Riotham even tried to win the diadem for himself."

"Could *you* do it, if you were offered the title?" I ask.

He scoffs. "Yes, of course. For a few years I was practically running the place at Wortigern's side. I know how to run the Council better than anyone. If I had to –" He looks at me sharply. "This will never happen."

"Why not? You being a *Dux* would solve so many of our problems. It wouldn't just resolve this current conundrum. Remember how you complained about there not being a strong ruler in Londin

[436]

with whom you could make deals? What if that strong ruler was yourself? When I was in Gaul –"

"The Britons are not Gauls."

"They're not *that* different, Father. And they've been letting barbarians rule them for generations. Hildrik is a *Rex* of the Franks, and a *Magister* in Belgica. The kings of the Goths are the *duces* in Aquitania. Ricimer, a barbarian, all but rules the Empire and decides for himself who sits on the throne."

"I have heard all this," my father says. "And so did Aelle – where do you think he got the idea in the first place?"

"But you're not a barbarian, like Aelle. You were raised as one of the *wealas*, a Christian, son of a nobleman, a Councillor, Wortigern's right hand. And you're the one to whom Wortigern gave –" I stop myself. I don't know if Betula knows about Wortigern's diadem in my father's chest – and Seawine certainly doesn't. "You are better suited to rule Londin than anyone," I finish. "If the Council is willing to accept Aelle, they'd have no reason not to accept you."

He frowns. "I already have one kingdom to look after."

"I'm with you, *Rex*," says Seawine. "We don't need to involve ourselves in the matters of the *wealas*. Our people are already becoming more like them every day – we dress like them, fight like them, we drink wine instead of mead –" He raises the mug with disgust. My father brought a flask of good Gaulish wine from his trip to Ariminum, no doubt a gift from the bishop. "Before you know it, we'll be paying *taxes*…"

My father gives him a quick glance at the mention of taxes. Seawine nods in satisfaction. He must be thinking he just gave the king a good reason for staying away from Londin's politics – but I know

The Crown of the Iutes

it only helped my case. I'm surprised at his words; I never thought the warrior had any strong opinions on such matters, either way.

"It is all a moot point," my father says, with an impatient wave of his hand. "Whatever we do, the diadem is as good as Aelle's. As long as he's keeping those Britons hostage inside that hillfort, the Council will do his bidding."

"But that's just the thing, *Rex* Aeric," Ursula interrupts him. "The Briton army is no longer trapped in the hillfort. This is what we came here to tell you."

My father and Betula both look at us in surprise. "What do you mean? Fastidius assured me he has all the latest news."

"If that's what they still think in Londin, then Audulf has done a better job than we hoped," says Ursula.

A cold wind penetrates through the cracks in the garden room's walls. An owl hoots nearby – it must be hiding in the boughs of the old apple tree. The sky outside is dull grey. It's almost dawn.

Ursula stirs in her furs. The little pebbles of the tessellated floor rustle under her. I pull her close.

"Can't sleep?" I ask. "Are you cold?"

"It's being back home," she says. "In Cantia. It plays on my mind."

"You're thinking about Pascent?"

She stirs again and turns on her back.

"I wasn't until now – and I didn't need you reminding me of him. No, I'm thinking of what's going to happen after this war is over."

"We might all be dead by then."

"You don't believe it. Between you and your father you'll find some mad way to save us all from Aelle. Aeric will be a *Dux*, and your child, whoever bears it, will be the heir to Britannia's throne."

"I don't know about that. My father didn't seem so keen on my idea."

"He didn't say 'no' outright, either. He said he'll have to think about it. You know what it means."

I chuckle. "Yes – it means he's calculating how to improve what I proposed. But… why does it worry you so?"

"I know what power does to men."

"My father is different."

She turns around. I feel her breath on my face. "But are *you*?"

"You don't trust me?"

"I haven't seen you wield power, except in war – and I haven't always liked what I saw. You use men's lives for your own means. *Especially* when they're not of your own kin. How will I know you won't use Cants or other Britons for some nefarious reasons once you're on Londin's throne?"

"You'll be there to stop me," I say.

"I'm serious."

The Crown of the Iutes

I slide my hands under her tunic, for warmth. "Come on, Ursula. My father is still strong. He will live for decades yet. What's the point worrying about it now? If there's anything that truly worries you about how I may rule Britannia –" I laugh at the thought "– you'll have plenty of time to rid me of those vices. Just stay near me, and everything will be alright."

The moist heat of her skin so close to mine inevitably causes my manhood to harden. I inch away, to make her more comfortable, but Ursula moves closer and reaches between my legs.

"Ursula…" I moan.

"Have you really not humped anyone since Basina?" she asks.

"I haven't," I admit. "I… tried it with Croha at Alet, but it didn't feel right…"

"Then this won't last long," she says as her hand starts moving up and down my shaft. "I'm sorry that's all I can give you."

"It's – hngh – it's all I need," I gasp. I pull up her tunic and bury my face in her soft, round flesh. "I love you," I whisper. "Please don't ever leave me alone."

CHAPTER XXIII
THE LAY OF LAURENTIUS

It still sometimes surprises me how fast a horse can travel a long distance on the stone Roman road, when it's pushed to its limits. It only takes us a day to cross the forty miles between the Medu flood plain and the gates of Londin, though by the end of the journey, the mounts we borrowed from Haesta have their flanks and mouths covered in thick foam. My horse sways from side to side when I give it to the stable boy at the cathedral.

"Haesta will never give us his beasts again," notes Ursula.

"I'll pay him double what they were worth when this is all over," my father says. "They served you well – and in this, they may have saved my kingdom. But you'll be riding ponies from now on – I keep a few spares in Londin, just for such an occasion."

There's only the three of us here; my father didn't trust any of his warriors enough to accompany him to Londin. We rode out in secret, at dawn, packed lightly, with father insisting in particular that I tell nothing to Seawine or any of my bear-shirts. "There may be others who think like Seawine," he said. "I don't want them to be getting any ideas in our absence." The only other person who knew where we were going was Betula, but she was given another task: to prepare the *fyrd* for a march.

I look around the courtyard. I haven't seen the cathedral since Riotham's siege. It still sits roofless and charred in the sea of ruin. There's been no effort to rebuild what was razed during the battle. The guesthouses are gone, so is the market place. Only the stables have returned, in the form of a simple wooden construction, fit only to accommodate a handful of horses. The soot and blood have been washed from the cathedral's walls, but the holes in the wall, patches of fallen render and other scars of war remain as if the battle had ended only a couple weeks ago. Puddles of rainwater gather on the main hall's floor and flow down the aisles, mixed with dust and ash. Stretches of sailcloth spread between the walls shield the altar and its immediate surroundings from the elements – making the once glorious cathedral look no different to Wulf's "court" in the Poor Town.

On the way to the cathedral we passed several of Aelle's men; they didn't recognise us, but their presence in the very heart of the city speaks volumes of the Saxons' sudden importance. The guards at the city gate let us through without questioning. They must have thought we were yet another group of Saxon envoys, coming from the South with new demands from their king. Nobody here would have any reason to suspect my father's arrival, accompanied only by two other riders, when last they heard he was leading the Iute *fyrd* towards the Regin border. Bishop Fastidius is the only one to recognise us, when he comes down into the courtyard to welcome the strange visitors.

Within moments of greeting us at his home, Fastidius sends out urgent messengers to all the Councillors present in the city. He doesn't need convincing that the matter with which we came is of the utmost significance – it's enough that both my father and I arrived in Londin together, and with no notice.

One does not refuse a bishop's summon of such importance, even as the day comes to an end, not after said bishop had only a few months ago humiliated the mightiest of them and showed to all of Britannia that God is on his side. And so, after a couple of hours, they start arriving, sweating and huffing grumpily, poorly disguising their annoyance at having been torn away from their duties and pleasures. By nightfall there are more than twenty of them gathered under the sailcloth canopy – this must be all that remains of the Great Council these days.

"What's going on, Fastidius?" asks one of the nobles, showing no respect to the bishop's rank and title. He is a grumpy, fat, old man, dressed in a fine tunic of Serican weave, bound by an old Roman army belt. He wipes sweat from his forehead with embroidered cloth. His fingers jangle with golden rings. "Why did you call us all at this ungodly hour? Does this forsaken heathen warlord have any more demands? We gave him everything he asked for already, even *Domna* Madron's hand!"

"You will not be needing to succumb to *Rex* Aelle's demands for much longer," my father speaks, "if you listen to what I have to say."

He emerges from the shadows like an actor entering the scene. A murmur of displeased recognition spreads through the Councillors.

"Fraxinus," the fat nobleman says, referring to my father by the name he was known when he served at Wortigern's Council. "I knew you'd be back to your meddling ways as soon as you smelled our blood. What do you want this time? Can't you see we are busy enough without you?"

"I come to bring you a choice, Laurentius," my father replies. "A flicker of hope to light up your darkness."

He still hasn't explained which of my arguments – if any – swayed him to even consider my proposal, and then to present it to the nobles of Londin. His silence on the matter was as mysterious as it was disturbing. What plan did he come up with that needed to be kept secret even from me?

The Crown of the Iutes

"I'm the only one who can protect you from Aelle," he tells the Councillors. "I have enough men, and skill, to lead them. But it will be a costly war, and I will not wage it just to save your skins."

"We've given you all the land you could possibly need," one of the noblemen says. "If we give you any more, there'll be no difference between surrendering to you or the Saxons."

"Isn't it your duty to defends us?" asks another. "Are you not bound by Wortigern's treaties?"

"My duty is to my Iutes, and to the people of Cantia – and as Councillor Ursula will attest, I have been fulfilling this duty to the best of my abilities. To guard Londin itself, to protect the entire province from enemies – that sounds like something you should demand from a *Dux*."

The gasp is now more audible, and it echoes under the vaulted roof of the cathedral hall. "The audacity…" "Now it is clear!" "Did the bishop know?"

"You want the diadem for yourself, then?" asks Laurentius. "Have you planned this with Aelle – to force us into thinking that we have no other choice?"

"You *have* no other choice," my father replies, "unless you wish to wait for Riotham's return, or for Albanus to pick up the pieces after Aelle's done with you. But I don't need your approval to take Wortigern's diadem for myself – for I already have it."

He nods at me. I step forward, unravel the bundle with the diadem and raise it into the light. It's surprisingly heavy when I hold it high in one hand, a band of gold bound with precious, gleaming jewels. The Councillors welcome the sight with stunned silence, as they ponder the significance of what just happened. There isn't one man among them who doesn't recognise the insignia, if only from tales.

[444]

"Ten years ago, my son returned from the West, with *Domna* Madron and with this trinket," my father continues, "both given to him by *Dux* Wortigern just before his death."

"Lies," the Councillors at the back seethe. "You stole it from him on his deathbed!"

My father ignores them. "Some of you will remember what happened at Sorbiodun, twenty years ago," he says. "But what none of you, except the bishop here, knows, is what happened soon after. Just before Wortimer's coup, *Dux* Wortigern planned to adopt me as his heir. The papers were already laid at the registrar in Londin."

Another murmur, and more accusations of lies – but one look at the bishop's stern face silences the Councillors. Fastidius would never allow my father to lie on such matters in the House of the Lord.

"Wortigern had predicted what would happen to Britannia. He knew that one day, one of barbarian blood would be needed to lead you all into the new future. Back then, he thought it could've been me; alas, Fate and the gods intervened otherwise. A lot has happened since then, but at long last, today we can finish what Wortigern started."

"So you want us to swap one barbarian for another," Laurentius scoffs. "Aelle for Aeric. A Saxon for a Iute. What choice is this to us?"

"No, that is not the choice I give you," my father says to the surprise of everyone, myself included. "As I told Octa when he proposed the same thing, I already have a kingdom to rule. My hands are full. And, as you rightly note, I *am* a barbarian, despite my upbringing. Gods know you lot have been reminding me of this since I first set foot in Londin. I would only succumb to the same

The Crown of the Iutes

problems as Aelle. Sooner or later, you would rebel and ask Albanus and Ambrosius to save you from the heathen yoke."

"Then who?" The Councillor grows impatient.

"Octa. My son."

"*Me?*" I almost drop the diadem.

"His mother was a Briton, as is his wife," my father says, ignoring my astonishment. "He was educated by Bishop Fastidius, and is as capable in all matters political and religious as any of you. He is the second best commander I know, right after me." He smiles. "And he's got powerful friends on the continent – from Armorica to Frankia, which is more than can be said about Aelle, or even myself. The more you think about it, the more obvious it becomes. There isn't anyone better than him to rule Londin."

"Father – I don't…"

"I know – you don't want it. Didn't you tell Wortigern to throw it away, all those years ago? And still, he chose *you* to carry it. How long can you refuse your destiny?"

"What about the Iutes? What about our kingdom?"

"I still have many years in me," he says. "We will have time to discuss this. For now, there are more urgent matters to deal with."

The Councillors look to each other in confusion. Laurentius retreats to discuss the news with the others. There are more mumbles and whispers, but not as many as I'd expect. Most of them must realise how little choice they have, at least for the moment. Some must think I'm not as bad a choice as the alternatives – not just Aelle, but even Riotham; others hope I will be easy to manipulate, a barbarian youth with little skill in intrigue and diplomacy. Others still are willing to swallow the humiliation for now, to then cast me down as soon as the more immediate danger passes.

Laurentius steps forward again. He turns to Fastidius this time.

"Your Grace," he says, "you have gathered us all here to hear out this heathen king – but we haven't yet heard from you on this matter. We pray for your guidance."

The bishop, sitting on a carved oaken chair by the altar, leans forward with a thoughtful expression.

"I am not part of your Council," he replies, "and I cannot decide for you. I do not know if *aetheling* Octa will be a good *Dux* – though the fact that he hesitates to take the diadem shows he is more worthy of it than most here. But I do know my brother, Fraxinus. And I knew Wortigern, as did many of you. Great sinners, both of them –" He smiles. "But also, great leaders of men. Greater than anyone else I've ever met. And both of them chose Octa." He spreads his hands. "Make of that what you will."

I look to my left, where my father stands. He looks back to me and nods with an encouraging smile. I look to my right, to Ursula. She frowns, her lips pursed. I know this is everything she feared, me getting such power over her people, and at such a young age. *I fear this.* One word from her, one show of resistance from anyone right now, would make me refuse the diadem. But she keeps silent – as do the Councillors, who have now finished their bickering and anxiously wait to see what happens next.

Laurentius, with a miserable expression, turns back to my father.

The Crown of the Iutes

"We put our hopes and prayers with you, Fraxinus," he says. "If you can truly defeat Aelle and release our kin from his thrall, you will be granted what you ask for."

"Know that we risk all by even considering your demand," the other one adds. "If you lose, we will be at the mercy of the Saxons' vengeance."

"If I lose, my people will perish," my father replies grimly. "That is my warranty. What warranty will you give me that you will keep your word while my men bleed for you?"

"Do you still believe in the power of the Holy Scriptures?" Laurentius asks.

"I do not – but I know that you do."

At these words, Fastidius rises from his seat and waves at an acolyte, who rushes up to us with the heavy tome of the Scripture, wrapped in white cloth. I see some of the Councillors are taken aback at the speed with which the events of the night proceed, but Laurentius himself shows no surprise. He already suspected the bishop of concocting tonight's plot with King Aeric, but in his eyes it is not a bad thing – it is exactly the kind of efficiency that made my father an exemplary Councillor back in the day.

"I know you think we are weak and have no power to punish you, Bishop," he says, ominously, his hand hanging above the tome, "but if it does turn out you two planned this whole thing together with the Saxons, you will find the Lord's justice is swift and terrible – especially for those who claim to preach in his name."

"I'm not a *wealh*," my father replies. "I don't deal in treason."

[448]

"Why didn't you say anything?" I ask Ursula. "Why didn't you stop me?"

We abandon the ruined splendour of Saint Paul's and climb down the cathedral hill, leaving my father to what he does best – negotiating minor details of his agreement with the Councillors.

I'm still reeling from what happened. There wasn't a man in the cathedral more surprised than I was at what my father proposed – and how swiftly the Councillors accepted his proposition. But I had little time for mulling my new, peculiar situation. As soon as Laurentius removed his hand from the Scripture, I was taken aside by Bishop Fastidius, and we sat down to discuss the more immediate matter – of defeating Aelle and relieving the Britons besieged at Anderitum. It was with the bishop's help that I came up with an unexpected plan for victory.

"I wouldn't be stopping *you*," Ursula replies. "I'd be stopping your father and standing against his carefully planned scheme. I had no right to do that."

"What about your fears? What about all this power driving me mad?"

She shrugs. "It's too late now. You'll just have to try to prove me wrong. And at least this way, you'll have your father to advise you – and to hopefully restrain you."

"But you don't trust him, either."

"There aren't many people I trust these days."

"Considering how many betrayals we've witnessed in recent years, yours seems like the only reasonable approach."

The Crown of the Iutes

She pauses and looks around, astonished by the filth, squalor and heaps of waste surrounding us.

"Where are we?" she asks. "Where have you taken me?"

Of course – she doesn't know the city as well as I do.

"Poor Town," I say.

"So *this* is Poor Town," she whispers. "I should've guessed."

Like the cathedral precinct, the Poor Town hasn't changed much since I last saw it. There might be some more rubble and dust, but I couldn't tell. There are certainly fewer people than last time around; many have perished from the pox, others fled the city, expecting that the other townsfolk will turn against them, blaming them for the plague, as they had in the years past. The once crowded narrow alleyways are eerily silent now; the cries of children and the noises of families at work have been cut short by death's sickle. I haven't felt the impact of the disease this strongly since the passing of winter.

"Maybe you should go back to the cathedral," I tell Ursula. I fear the morbid mood will only further remind her of our loss. "They don't take kindly to strangers here," I add, nodding at a dusty alleyway, barred with an overthrown pillar. A sullen guard stares at us from the top of the barricade, making no effort to stop us.

"These people must still be in deep mourning," she says, eyeing the guard. "I think I'll feel right at home."

Where once they'd leap out on me from every corner, now the guards of the Poor Town pay little attention to two lonely travellers coming down from the cathedral hill. Only as we approach the site of Wulf's mead hall, do I sense some eyes upon me. Some men are following us at a distance. They see I know the way, so I must have visited their chieftain before, they reason – and lived.

Alerted by the guards, Wulf comes out to meet us before the walls of the *curia* that is his hall, accompanied by several warriors of his retinue. His face is scarred deep with pockmarks, as are those of his men, another reminder of how harsh the plague has struck this unfortunate place.

"*Aetheling.*" He gives me a slight nod. When I come close, he stops me and studies my face. "I see the plague has spared you," he notes.

"The gods saw it fit to protect me. This time. Will you not invite us in?" I ask.

He glances to Ursula and bows, recognising her nobility, though he can't guess who she is.

"What trouble do you bring this time, *aetheling*?" he asks, after I introduce her.

"War," I say simply.

His eyes narrow. He scratches a scarred cheek and orders his men to clear out the hall. A flock of noisy hens, a panicking goat and a few crying children emerge from the ruined *curia*, pursued by Wulf's warriors. He winces at the unbecoming sight. At length, one of his shieldmaidens announces that the hall is ready.

The inside is dark and smells of dung and piss. Gone are the trinkets adorning the walls – even the bishop's candlestick and the golden crucifix. I look for a place to sit down, and the chieftain shows me a pile of hides in the corner, damp with fat and soot. I don't need to ask what happened to all the furniture – a stack of

The Crown of the Iutes

hard timber hewn into firewood lies by the hearth. The same shieldmaiden who invited us in earlier throws a log on the fire.

"War?" he asks when the three of us sit down to share a jug of thin ale between us. "Which one?"

"My father has summoned the *fyrd* of all Iutes," I say.

"We do not answer to his summons," Wulf replies, but the news intrigues him. He, too, would remember the last time the Iute army gathered, and knows how rare an event it is. "Who is he marching against this time?"

"Aelle of the Saxons."

He scoffs. "And why should I care about this? I have both Iutes and Saxons among my people. Neither are willing to die for these self-proclaimed 'kings'."

"This war is about something more than just deciding which tribe is stronger," I tell him. "Its result might affect even your little corner of the world."

"I find that unlikely. The Iutes and the Saxons live far beyond the Walls of Londin. Unless they find a way to move their battles inside the city, I can't see how…"

"Aelle wants to be the *Dux* of Londin," Ursula interrupts him.

He ponders this for a moment, then laughs. "So that's why there are so many Saxons in Londin lately. Good for him!" he says. "He can't be any worse for us than any of the previous lot. A fair-hair *Dux*? What is there to worry about?" He tilts his head. "And I suppose your father would like the title for himself."

"No," I say. "He wants it for *me*."

His eyebrows go up. "You? Yes, I suppose that does make more sense... You *are* a half-Briton. I still don't see why I should prefer one of you over another – and what would you want me to do about it?"

"If I become a *Dux*, I swear to make your life and that of your people easier," I say. "You took care of my mother, and took in my father when they both lost everything. My family owes you a great debt – and I would repay it with interest. You will not get such a promise from Aelle. He couldn't care less about Londin – he just wants the title, and to plunder it for its gold."

"And what would you want in exchange?"

"As many men as you can spare. Especially the ones from Andreda, if any still live."

"You'll have no trouble finding the forest folk here – they proved the toughest of us all. But why would you need my warriors? If your father's *fyrd* is not enough to deal with the Saxons, then why is he waging this war in the first place?"

"My father's *fyrd* is his and Betula's to command. It's their war. I need my own army, to prove that I am worthy of the *Dux*'s diadem – if only to myself. I only have my bear-shirt riders, and they won't be enough for what I have planned."

"Haven't you seen what this place looks like outside?" He waves his hand towards the entrance. "Do you think I have *any* warriors to give you?"

"I just spoke with the bishop. He knows how many still come from Poor Town for their daily bread and stew. You have plenty men to spare, even after the plague, but you no longer have a way to

The Crown of the Iutes

provide for their needs. I will pay you silver for each of them, and I will feed and arm them at my own expense. Surely it's a better fate than staying here, among the shadows of the dead."

He rubs his chin in thought. "And how many of them do you hope to bring back?"

"A few, if we win. None if we lose."

"A fair answer." He nods in satisfaction. "Ash would try to tell me everything would be fine – but I see you took honesty after your mother." He stands up. "Very well – come back here in the morning, and you will have your army."

He escorts me outside. "But know this, *aetheling*," he says, when we reach the edge of the *curia*'s courtyard, "if Aelle's men came to me with the same offer, I would give them the exact same answer."

"But they did not come."

"No, they didn't."

"I would also have a war task for yourself," I tell Ursula when we reach the Bull's Head; with the cathedral's guesthouses razed to the ground, there aren't many places in the city where we can stay the night. "If you're willing to help."

The innkeeper gave us the same room I stayed in last winter. Everything is just as I left it. I'm not even sure if he bothered to change the bedsheets; they still carry the same musty smell they had the night I let Lucia satisfy me.

"Me? What can I do? I don't have any men to command."

"You have the respect of your people."

"My mother had their respect, won by years of hard work and dutiful service. Few Cants outside Dorowern are even aware I exist."

"I don't need false modesty. You helped recruit Cants to Riotham's army. I will need you to do it again."

"Any man who knew how to hold a weapon went to Gaul," she replies. "There isn't anyone left."

"There are women. Younglings. Old veterans. I don't need many – a couple of hundred would suffice."

"Just more spear fodder."

"No – a diversion. We need to strike at Aelle from as many sides as possible. The Saxons are masters of shield wall, this is why my father was so loath to attack them in pitched battle. But their rear will be exposed. I will be bringing a force of my own from the west – I need someone to strike from the east."

"Haesta's in the east."

"And if I could count on Haesta's help, I wouldn't need to ask you."

"How would even I convince anyone to join me? Some of their husbands and fathers would have by now returned home from the hillfort. Now is a time for healing, not fighting."

"Not all of them came back – there are still many trapped at Anderitum. Are they not worth fighting for?"

The Crown of the Iutes

She sits down on the bed, leaning on her hands, then looks at the hands and wipes them on her tunic with disgust. "I don't know, Octa." She shakes her head. "Sending women and youths against Aelle's warriors sounds like a recipe for disaster. It's going to be hard for the *pagus* to recover after the plague and Riotham's war as it is – much less if we lose even those who were left behind."

"All I ask for is a momentary distraction. Trust me, if all goes well, your losses will be insignificant."

"That's just the problem, Octa. I *don't* trust you."

Her words cut like a *seax*. I reel from the impact, but I'm not shocked. I have given her enough reason not to trust my word.

"You asked me never to leave your side," she continues. "And now you want me to go to Dorowern, while you march to war on your own – with all the power of a *Dux* at your disposal. How do I know you're not planning some other scheme you're not telling me about?"

"I told you what I need Wulf for, and what I require of you. I don't have any more plans."

"For now."

I don't know what more I can tell her to reassure her of my honest intentions. We both know that when the battle starts, even the best plans must be discarded, and a skilled commander needs to react to the situation as best as he can. I don't know what I will find at Anderitum. I don't know how many men I will have to sacrifice in the name of victory when things go wrong.

"One last time," I plead. "Trust me this one last time."

She leans against the wall. She pulls her knees to her chin and wraps her arms around them with a thoughtful pout.

"Even if I somehow do everything you ask me to, how ever will I bring these women and younglings to Anderitum on time? It must be at least fifty miles, some of it across hostile land. Most of these people would barely have travelled outside Dorowern."

"I've planned for that, too."

She rolls her eyes. "Of course you have."

"When you said you wanted my men, I thought you needed warriors, not dray oxen," Wulf says, swiping a horse fly from his face.

"I assure you, chieftain, you will have your great battle yet."

I was puzzled to see him lead the Poor Town army, two-hundred strong, for the first time marching down Londin's main streets openly during the day. The city folk of the wealthier districts watched us keenly and with considerable distress, only now realising the true, hidden strength of the Poor Town bands; for each of the two hundred carried a weapon, an axe or a long knife, and some even wore helmets and shirts of padded cloth for armour; Wulf himself wore a mail shirt and a steel helmet and wielded a rusty *spatha*. Many must have wondered what the handful of *vigiles* still left in the city could do to stop these warriors from plundering their palaces and storehouses – and breathed a deep sigh of relief when we all turned to the Bridge Gate.

I did not ask why Wulf decided to march with us, but I wondered if, in his old age, he wasn't feeling ready to finally die a warrior's death, to ensure his spirit's passing to Wodan's Mead Hall, like any

The Crown of the Iutes

good Iute should. I preferred not to think what that said of his hope for our chances of victory.

By the time the start of the long, unruly column reached the Bridge Gate, its end emerged from the winding, narrow streets of Poor Town onto the main avenue, and the crowd gathered to watch us released a loud gasp seeing what the warriors dragged behind: a Wall *ballista*, a giant siege machine, pulled by two dozen strong men on a platform made of two market wagons lashed together to form a broad enough vehicle.

This was the very same *ballista* used by Bishop Fastidius's soldiers in the defence of the cathedral. Repaired from the damage sustained in the winter siege, it had since been refitted with new bow ropes and equipped with freshly forged bolts, to guard the bishop's home once again. I asked him if he could give it to me for the war with Aelle. The request surprised him – he wasn't even sure if it was possible to carry the machine such a great distance. After all, it wasn't a *carroballista* of the sort he and my father once used against the Picts, but a great engine of war designed to stand on top of a wall tower. It was only when I told him of the carts the Saxons used at Andecawa and showed him the drawings of similar vehicles in one of the war manuals I brought from Gaul, that he yielded to my request.

It took us five long days, with the men changing every few hours at the ropes, to drag the machine, with its wheeled platform and a cart full of bolts and spare parts, first down the New Port highway, and then past the crossroad marking the end of Londin's domain along the secret forest paths and old droveways of Andreda, far from the prying eyes of the Saxon spies. Our guides were the Free Folk of the forest. I was certain there were no men alive who knew these dark woods better than these woodsmen. Some of the guides were old enough to have fought alongside young Aelle in his days as a chief of the forest bandits. Though the woods have grown even darker and denser since their youth, the secret paths were still there, past the walls of thorn and bramble, still trodden by those of their kin who remained behind.

At long last, we've reached the tall, steep, wooded chalk ridge overlooking a narrow valley. Here, halfway between New Port and Mutuanton, the stone road linking Regentium with Anderitum crosses over a broad stream the Saxons call Mearcraedes, the Treaty Border, for it once marked the border of their first settlement as the *foedes* of the Regins. The location, discovered a few days earlier by Croha and Deora – whom I summoned to my side from the Medu camp – with its full, unobstructed view of the crossing below and our own position obscured by the dense forest, is even more suitable to an ambush than I had hoped from the shieldmaiden's description.

"What do you think?" I ask one of the soldiers working to remove the *ballista* from the platform and preparing to set it up in the firing position. They were as uneasy about the mission as the bishop himself – if not for their sense of pious duty, and the kinship they felt towards me as their comrade in arms from the winter siege, I doubt I could have convinced them to accompany us all this way.

I notice Wulf's men observe their preparations with a superstitious apprehension, even those who dragged the machine through the woods staying at some distance and staring at the *ballista* as if it was some mythical monster, a dragon spewing fire and steel, released from its binds. It confirms what I've already learned about the barbarians' fear of the siege engines. Just as they aren't keen on living within stone walls, so do all fair-hairs loathe the machines that help conquer them. Ten years ago my father made good use of this fear, defeating Aelle's first, half-hearted attempt at an assault on Robriwis. Apart from King Aeric, Odowacr was the only heathen chieftain I knew who managed to convince his warriors to use the war machines, and that only because most of his army had fought with the Huns before, where they would have learned their usefulness.

The Crown of the Iutes

"It's almost as if we were shooting down from the Wall," the soldier tells me with an approving nod. "I could scarcely ask for a better site. But surely the enemy will know of this place, too?"

"Aelle has my father's army to deal with," I say. "He and his best commanders will be focused on the main battle at Anderitum. The others will have no idea what a siege machine like this can do."

"Then who are we waiting for here?" asks Wulf, frowning.

"Reinforcements," replies Audulf.

We picked him and his riders up along the way, not far from Saffron Valley. Their swords were still wet with the blood of the latest of Aelle's couriers, sent with increasingly urgent messages to the Saxon delegates negotiating with the Londin Council. Having intercepted a number of these missives, Audulf gained a detailed understanding of Aelle's latest war plans.

"While you were in Londin, Betula and her *Hiréd* have been harassing the rear of the Saxon force besieging Anderitum," he tells us. "Aelle knows the *fyrd* is coming, and requested the western warband to march to his aid from Port Adurn."

"And that warband will be passing right through here," I say.

"Can we really take a full Saxon warband on our own?" asks Wulf.

"We only have to delay them for a few days," I reply. "I will need to ride to Anderitum after that, anyway – and you'll be free to return to Londin with the machine."

"If there's anything left of it – or of us," Wulf remarks grimly. "So, Birch, Ash and I will all be fighting in the same battle," he adds with a wry smile. His eyes grow misty at the memory of his old comrades. "Just like the old times. A pity Raven and Eadgith didn't live to see it."

He draws his *spatha*, whirls it in the air and hacks at a nearby beech with the force and speed that belies his age. The blade digs halfway into the trunk. Red resin oozes from the wound like fresh blood.

The Crown of the Iutes

CHAPTER XXIV
THE LAY OF WULF

We don't have to wait long for the warband to arrive. The morning after we set up camp, the forward watch reports a large column heading our way. They fill out the entire breadth of the stone road, showing no sign of expecting an ambush even as they enter the valley of the Mearcraedes. There's a good reason for their recklessness. We're deep inside the Regin territory. Not knowing about the secret forest paths, nobody can suspect that a significant enough force was able pass by the Saxon border guards without being noticed.

The column grows narrower as the warriors reach the water. When the Romans first built this road, the bourn was small enough to have been put into a culvert under the highway's surface. Since then, the current has grown into a river, pushing the stones out of its way and forming a muddy, weed-grown ford, spilling out into a mill lade further downstream. The Saxon vanguard moves forward to test if the crossing is safe. I glance to the *ballista* crew. They nod, indicating their readiness. I raise my hand. Behind me, two hundred Poor Town warriors make ready to charge downhill. Further still, beyond a line of willows, looms the shapes of nine riders, waiting my orders.

As the first of the Saxons wade to the other side of the ford, I study the column behind them. I can't see its end, disappearing behind a bend in the ridge; there are maybe three hundred warriors here, if not more. There couldn't have been more than a hundred in Port Adurn itself – this must be the entire western half of Aelle's *fyrd*, meaning the western and northern borders of the Saxon kingdom have been left unguarded to deal with the Iute threat. It's a great gamble; nothing now stops Aelle's western neighbours from

The Crown of the Iutes

invading and taking swathes of the Saxon kingdom for themselves while Aelle's warriors bleed out against my father's army. I can't decide if it's a mark of recklessness or confidence in his skill and that of his warriors.

At the front of the column, on the far shore of the stream, I spot a man in a tall steel helmet, with some kind of beast figure on top. I point him out to the *ballista* crew. I know it's not a precise weapon, but they manage to move it a few inches to the right and aim a little bit lower, and nod at me again. I give them the signal. The *ballista* twangs, the bolt flies down, gleaming like lightning in the autumn sun, and hits two warriors next to the chieftain. It skewers the first one, flies through and hacks off a leg off the other. The force of the impact blows the helmet off the chieftain's head.

The rest of the Saxons are frozen in place. The chieftain looks frantically around for the source of the missile. I imagine him thinking some giant warrior must have thrown the javelin down; he can't possibly guess that a siege engine might be hiding in the forest above. The *ballista* crewmen use the pause to draw the weapon and aim it again. It seems to take an excruciatingly long time, but at last, they're ready to shoot once more. This time, the bolt strikes one of the vanguard warriors standing in the river, raising a fountain of water and dust mixed with blood. The red mist soon fades, revealing the man howling, and holding a stump of a torn-off arm. To the more superstitious of the Saxons it must seem as if Donar himself is casting thunderbolts from the sky. Still they're not sure how to react to the sudden attack. The third bolt hits two more warriors, killing them both in an instant.

Only now do the Saxons have enough sense to scatter, as far and wide as the narrow valley allows them. The chieftain shouts an order, and a group of his men start climbing up the slope towards the *ballista*'s emplacement. They still don't think it part of a greater ambush – they can't comprehend how it could have possibly got there, but they know they must get rid of it before it kills any more of them: just like now, when the fourth bolt pierces one Saxon, then bounces off a rock and cuts the head of the one running behind him.

I blow my warhorn. Wulf's warriors rush down the hill and strike the Saxon flank like a landslide, pushing them into the river. A bloody chaos erupts all along the bourn. With the Saxons scattered and disordered, the men of Poor Town have a momentary advantage and, despite insufficient training and meagre weapons, they seem to be inflicting great damage to the warriors of Aelle's western *fyrd*; but I know the confusion will not last long.

I rush through the willows and join the nine Iute riders. Following a small ravine, we draw a wide arc around the Saxon column and strike in a vengeful wedge of steel at its rear. I whirl my lance like a bloody sickle, cutting a swathe through the rearguard, a warrior falling with each strike of the blade. We don't let the Saxons realise who and how few we are – we break away, then charge again, at a different angle. The valley is broader here, allowing us some space for manoeuvres, while further down the Saxon column is trapped in the ford's choke point.

Not knowing yet what's happening at the ford, the Saxons in the rear, fearful of our baneful blades, press at their brethren at the front. In the chaos, their pushing and shouting makes it seem as if a third mysterious force was attacking the column, trapping the *fyrd* from all sides. Surrounded by an incomprehensible enemy, who by some magic transported siege machines and cavalry into the middle of what was supposed to be a safe, familiar territory, the Saxon chieftain loses the remains of his courage. He blows his warhorn and cries a panicked retreat, calling his men back from the hill. From what I can tell, they were just about to finally reach the *ballista*'s emplacement and engage its crew in what would have been a short and deadly battle.

The Crown of the Iutes

Moments later, as the last of the fleeing Saxons runs past me, I sheathe the lance and blow my horn again, to call off the pursuit. Wulf's warriors halt, obediently, at the edge of the valley; their warchief trained them well. Beyond the ravine, the plain spreads flat and wide, all the way to the sea, and the Saxons could make good use of their greater numbers, once they realise how few we really are.

"Get your men back up on that ridge," I tell Wulf. "Pack the *ballista* back onto the wagons."

"Again?"

"We won't surprise them here a second time. We're moving further east. Hurry, before they notice we're not chasing them after all!"

It takes me a while to realise that the murky plain we wade across between one spur of the Downs and another, is the same inlet of the Narrow Sea we swam across just a couple of weeks ago. At low tide, it is a dark, deep marsh, with only a few paths marked by stones heavy enough not to be washed away by the rising sea.

We pass the *villa* island – now a cluster of grassy hills – undisturbed. As I foresaw, Aelle pulled all his forces towards the familiar marshy plains of Anderitum, leaving no one to guard the roads to the battlefield. Like the men we fought at Mearcraedes, he has no reason to suspect anyone would be able to pass unnoticed from this direction, from inside his own domain, and threaten his rear.

We left Wulf and his warriors some five miles behind, on another convenient spur of chalk, where they waited for the Saxon warband to find them. I ordered him to harass the enemy only briefly, if he deemed it at all possible. We've delayed the Saxons enough already, and there is no need to waste any more lives on this mission, especially now that the *ballista*'s string finally broke after shooting more than a dozen missiles, and we were forced to abandon it in the forest, covered with leaves and vines. But I could see in Wulf's eyes that he wasn't planning on ever returning to Londin, other than as a corpse on a bier.

"Give Birch my love," he told me when we parted. "She was always the best of us all – in spirit and in flesh."

No matter how bravely Wulf and his men fought, they couldn't hold the western *fyrd* back anymore, and despite the casualties we inflicted in our skirmishes, the Saxons remained a mighty force. I could only hope my father knew how to make use of their delay on the battlefield.

Late in the afternoon, we reach the final ridge of the Downs before Anderitum, and climb to the top, to see the siege from above. Here, we finally find the first of the Saxon warriors, guarding the way to the lookout point. Their surprise at our arrival lasts only as long as we need to thrust our lances into their throats and chests. Once again, simply fighting mounted gives us an unstoppable advantage over Aelle's foot warriors. If only the Iutes had as large a cavalry force as the Goths or the Franks, we would never need to fear the Saxon invasions…

From the top of the hill I can see for miles across the tidal plain stretching to the east, almost all the way to the sand-locked borders of Haesta's domain. We must have come during a lull in the battle. I see the Iute camps to the north, on the edge of Andreda Forest, the Saxons to their south, separated by a marshy plain of a river that winds its way around the fortress – and a sea of corpses between them. The Iutes have taken the outer fortifications of Anderitum at least once already, judging by the destroyed barricades and bodies strewn over the earthen banks, but the Saxons have managed to repel the attacks and throw my father's forces back to the camps.

The Crown of the Iutes

"The *wealas* are still in Anderitum," notes Croha.

I can't tell from a distance how many Briton and Iute defenders are left on the ramparts, but the gates of the fort remain firmly shut. Aelle is more focused on repelling the Iute *fyrd*, which leaves dealing with the Britons for later – he knows they are too few to mount a coordinated attack on his rear. Only a thin screen of warriors is needed to keep the Britons in check for the time being.

As before, a small camp of Saxon watchmen stands in the middle of the great sand spit at the tip of which stands Anderitum, separating us from the fortress and the rest of the battlefield. They're not part of the main force – they're only there to guard the approach to the western gate from any subterfuge; they would be expecting the western *fyrd* to be coming their way already. I can't see a way around them – the river flows to the north, and the sea gnaws on the shore to the south. I'm not keen on finding another boat to try to get to the fort the same way we left it, either.

"We'll just have to make a run for it," I tell the men. "It doesn't look more than a couple of miles."

"We've survived worse," says Audulf with a grin and rears his pony.

We charge down the slope and ride straight towards the Saxon camp in a scattered wedge, Croha to my left, Audulf to my right, the remaining riders behind us. I lean down to my mount's neck, draw the lance and lay it down and to my right as we approach the camps' guards. A Saxon watchman raises an axe in defence; I cut right through the shaft and through his neck, without stopping. I close my eyes and breathe in the salty wind. We've ridden such charges so many times before, on beaches just like these, that it's become my second nature – and Aelle's men are nowhere near as good fighters as Sigegaut's pirates. I am one with my pony, my lance is an extension of my arm; I barely feel anything when I cut through another warrior's shoulder.

We storm through the enemy camp, weaving between tents and leaping over sizzling campfires and stacks of equipment. The Saxons are, at first, too surprised to stop us – and once we're halfway through their lines, they realise we are not a threat to them unless they try to get in our way, and most of them decide to move out of our path.

Most – but not all. A well-aimed javelin hits one of Audulf's riders and throws him off his mount; he disappears in a crowd of Saxons, who club him to death in an instant. Worse still, moments later, a group of spearmen emboldened by their first victim, surround Deora and cut him off from the rest of us. I swerve around to see if there's any way to help him – but Croha bars my way.

"There's nothing we can do, *aetheling*," she says with a determined frown.

"But it's Deora!"

"You must save yourself."

"The girl's right!" cries Audulf. "There's dozens of them now – and they're all coming our way!"

Two Saxons run at us with war axes. I slash one – Audulf joins me in slaying the other, whacking his sword about with both hands like a great axe. I lose sight of Deora. Croha urges me to run once more. Cursing, I turn towards Anderitum, trampling another Saxon guard in my way. Moments later, we leap out into the open plain. Only a few more rows of tents and two low earth banks separate us from the fort's ramparts.

I hear Abulius himself cry at the men to unbolt the gate – and the Iute guards shouting back in reply. The Saxons camping at the northern embankment spot us too, now, but they're too late; creaking, the western gate of Anderitum opens, and then shuts with

The Crown of the Iutes

a loud thud behind us, just as the first of Aelle's warriors rush towards it.

"You've stirred them up now," Abulius shouts from the top of the gatehouse, looking at the field to the north. "Looks like the whole Saxon army is coming after you. Britons, take up your arms! Today we finally get to measure the worth of our lives!"

In the end, Aelle moves only about a third of his force against the fortress, leaving the rest to face the renewed Iutish assault from across the river. I can't see how this can result in anything other than the Saxons bleeding themselves out against the walls of Anderitum. With the entire garrison mustered to the ramparts, I count almost as many men as there were when I left them; Aelle made little attempt to take the fort while the threat of my father's *fyrd* remained, and it looks like he's not going to try in earnest this time, either.

Abulius sends most of his men to the northern wall, to face the main prong of the assault. A few of Ubba's Iutes line the eastern rampart, overlooking the harbour and the marshy plain. We ignore the western side, where the Saxon watch we roused with our passing is too weak to be a threat to the mighty gatehouse.

"Why have you returned to us, *aetheling*?" he asks as we watch the approaching enemy. "Why not join your father over there?" He points at the Iute line, also heading our way, far in the distance, in a single, long wall of shields.

"I left my men here," I reply. "I came back for them."

I search for Betula's banner in the Iute wall. The *Hiréd* approach far on the right flank, in a rigid boar's head formation; I'm guessing my father's plan is for them to drive a wedge between the two wings of

Aelle's army. Of course, he's chosen the best possible tactics for the situation; I couldn't have come up with a better plan myself. I wish I could just watch the manoeuvres of the Iute army with the detachment of a neutral observer. Is this how Wodan and the fallen warriors watch us from the Mead Hall? I imagine the gods placing bets on the warring sides and cheering at their favourites. Who will gain Donar's blessing today?

"That's very noble, but I'm sure the life of a king's heir is worth more than these few riders," says Abulius.

"Not to me. Besides, I knew you'd need some help from a competent commander to get you through this mess."

"And you think you can find a way to save us?"

"We'll see who it is that needs saving," I reply with a wry smile, and turn back to the approaching enemy. The Saxons outnumber us at least two to one. According to military manuals, there would need to be at least twice more of them to threaten a legionary fortress the size of Anderitum. Some of them carry ladders, others ropes, but Aelle's hasty orders didn't allow them to gather most of their equipment. When the first warriors reach the steep, thirty-feet-tall walls, it becomes clear that they plan to simply scale them using their hands and feet, seeking out holes and protrusions in the weathered stones.

I watch for an hour, then another, as the Saxons climb and fall, reaching the edge of the ramparts at great effort, only for the Briton and Iute soldiers to push and kick them away. It's easy for us to simply shower the enemy with missiles, and when these run out, pelt them with loose stones and bricks picked from the crumbling battlements... too easy.

The Crown of the Iutes

I didn't come here to defend an impregnable fortress from a half-hearted assault. I came here to help my father defeat the Saxons in the field. And I'm not going to do that hiding behind a stone wall.

"Ursula should already be here," I say, staring anxiously towards the eastern horizon. A long, broad, muddy beach spreads from the remains of the harbour to the steeply rising hills that mark Haesta's domain. Few Saxons guard it from anyone who would try to strike from this side — they know that the Iutes have no fleet to speak of, and their king assured them that Haesta will prefer to remain neutral in the conflict.

In the north, the Iute and Saxon shield walls push against each other along the river's edge. My father's army is in an unenviable position — like in the Battle of Crei, the attackers climbing out of the water are being easily forced back into the current. The *Hiréd*, having crashed through the eastern flank, is in danger of being surrounded and cut off from the rest of the *fyrd*, as neither of the enemy wings is budging any further.

"What happens if she doesn't come?" asks Croha.

A Saxon's head pops up over the battlement right in front of me. I hit him across the head with my sword, Croha kicks him off; he flies down with a blood-curdling shriek. Like hydra's heads, two more take his place at the foot of the wall and start climbing towards us.

"The *fyrd* will soon break," I say. "And with that, all hope for victory will perish."

"Surely you must've thought of another way for us to prevail, *aetheling*."

"I have," I say. "But it's… It's the wrong way."

"How can there be a wrong way to win a battle?"

I bite my lips and say nothing. Yes, I thought of a way to break the back of Aelle's shield wall without Ursula's help – but if I do it, I will be breaking the promise I gave her. If this is my first act as a *Dux*, it will confirm all her worst fears and doubts. I may win the war, but I am certain to lose her heart…

I look to the northern rampart. The Britons are all tired and there's not one of them who hasn't suffered an injury. With every passing moment, new wounded pour into the makeshift infirmary in the courtyard. Some of them don't go back into the fray. Beside the infirmary's tent grows a small heap of bodies waiting for burial. But there's still enough of us left to hold the Saxons at bay for a few more hours – by which time, I'm sure, Aelle will have decided it's not worth wasting any more men and will throw his remaining reserves against my father's flank, sealing the Iute *fyrd*'s fate.

I still have a choice. But it is a terrible choice. If I do nothing, the Iutes will be pushed back one last time, my father will be forced to retreat to prevent a rout; Aelle will march on Londin to be crowned a *Dux* and take Madron's hand for his son. But the Britons in Anderitum – in whose name we came to fight here, after all – will live. We've heard by now what happened to Atrect and his people after their surrender at the hillfort – except for a few officers, retained for ransom, all were allowed to return to their homes safely. It's likely that those in the fortress would meet the same fate. At length, there would be peace again in Britannia, except not on my father's terms.

I stare at the horizon once again, trying to wish into existence the reinforcements that would spare me having to make the choice. But the coast and the sea beyond it are shrouded in an evening mist. Even if there is a fleet coming to our aid, I wouldn't be able to see it in the murky shadow – and I can't wait for it any longer.

[473]

The Crown of the Iutes

"I'm sorry about Deora," I say.

Croha shrugs. "Such is a warrior's fate. We follow you even unto death, *aetheling*."

"Then you would do all I ask of you?" I ask.

"Of course. And so will every single one of us."

"Even if it seems wrong, or foolish?"

Croha takes my hand. "I trust you, *aetheling*. I know you'll do what is best."

"I wish I could share your faith in me, Croha."

"What's so terrible about this plan?"

"It would mean the death of most of the Britons in this fortress."

"But *we* would live? And win this battle?"

"Donar willing."

"Then what is the problem?"

I wince at her indifference to the Britons' fate. "My father made a deal with the *wealas* of Londin, for the lives of those trapped at Anderitum. If we fail to save them, why did we even bother to come here?"

She stares at the ramparts. "I don't know anything about deals and politics," she says. "But I know we owe nothing to these *wealas*. *They* never came to our aid. When my kin asked their help at Meon, they locked themselves behind the walls of their cities, letting Aelle kill us and plunder our farms." She speaks with bitterness which takes me aback, before I remember her family's history – her parents slain by Haesta's mercenaries acting on Aelle's orders when she was only a child.

"These men are not at fault for what happened to your family," I say.

"*Wealas* are *wealas*," she says firmly. "How many times do we have to save their skin? The marshes, the Liger Mouth, the hillfort, and now here… Not to mention all the countless battles we fought for them on Cantia's shores. And for what? So that they could roll over and show their bellies to the Saxon wolves at the first opportunity?"

"You don't understand. They are my responsibility now, too."

"Your responsibility is to your kin and blood. To your father, the king. To the gods."

I shake my head. Croha's world is incomparably different to the one I and Ursula inhabit. Hers is a straightforward one, a world of war and love, of drunken songs and bawdy, violent heathen gods. How could I even start to explain to her the intricacies of the Council intrigues, of my father's secret dealings with Londin nobles, of the delicate power play between warchiefs and Briton officials?

But sometimes, the straightforward solution is the only possible one. Yes, letting the Britons of Anderitum die would go against my father's deal with the Council – but with Aelle's army destroyed, who would dare oppose him? Oppose *me*?

"You make it all sound so simple," I say. "If Ursula was here, she'd –"

"But she isn't. Isn't that the whole reason why we're having to do this in the first place? You put your trust in her – and she failed you. Now it's up to us, your Iutes, to clean the Briton mess up. As always."

"And yet –"

"Enough!" she cries forcefully. "Do not doubt yourself now, *Hlaford!*" she says, looking into my eyes. "You've saved us so many times before. You will do it again. I'm certain of it. Pox on the *wealas*. Forget what your wife would want you to do. Tell me what *I* must do."

I close my eyes and take a deep breath. I wish there was a God to whom I could pray for guidance – but in my heart, I feel as alone as ever.

"Tell Ubba to relieve the Briton guards at the northern gate," I say. "I need every man on the gatehouse to respond to me only. And send for Abulius to meet me up there, urgently."

"You asked to see me, *aetheling?*"

Abulius breathes heavily, having climbed up the creaking stairs to the top of the northern gatehouse. Blood trickles from the scar above his eye, and his left arm is wrapped tight. He hasn't been saving himself, unlike most Briton commanders would in his place.

"What is it?" he asks. "Trouble?"

"How are your men faring?"

"Tired," he says, "But we will hold, as long as it takes." He glances north, to where the Iute and Saxon shield walls wrestle in a deadly clinch. "Not so sure about your father's army, though."

"Tell me, Abulius, what is it that you think we're fighting for here?"

He looks at me in wonder. "For survival."

"But you and other Britons would live if you surrendered to Aelle. Just like the men who stayed behind with Atrect."

He rubs the back of his head. "I don't mean my own survival. I mean Britannia as we know it. We cannot let a heathen king be the *Dux* in Londin – that would be our end."

I haven't told him yet of the deal struck with the Council. He is, after all, just another Briton who fears the passing of his people.

"My wife would tell you your old Britannia is dying already. That the tides of time cannot be stopped, and that all we do is just prolonging its agony. *Dux* Wortigern believed that, too."

"Perhaps they're right," he replies. "But I would hate to be the one who helps deal my land the mortal blow."

"You would die for this Britannia, then?"

His eyes narrow.

"What are you getting at, Iute?"

"Do you know the story of Cait's fifty warriors?"

The Crown of the Iutes

"The ones who sacrificed themselves to save Atrect's men at Dol?" He nods. "Yes, I have heard about them. A worthy end to the lives of commoners."

"Not to the lives of nobles."

"We came here to fight, but not fight to the end. Unlike those poor serfs, we still have much to live for."

"Then you would surrender to the Saxons?"

"If it came to that, yes. But they're never going to breach these walls –" He steps back, his eyes now wide in realisation. "What are you planning?"

"Your valiant deaths will buy us victory over Aelle," I tell him. "It is better if you die willingly."

"*Us?*" he asks, his voice rising mockingly, then breaking, as fear takes him over. "Who is this '*us*' you speak of? You are merely a Iute *aetheling*. You and I have nothing in common."

"I am a *Dux* of Londin, and your supreme commander," I tell him. "As of last Sunday."

He takes a moment to compose himself, then shakes his head. "Pointless," he whispers. "It's all pointless."

"You *do* believe me?"

"Why not?" He shrugs. "It makes as much sense as anything else that's happened this year."

"Then you and your men will obey my command?"

He straightens himself and brushes dust off his tunic. "I am a free man of Britannia, not a Roman subject," he declares proudly. "I will not take orders from a heathen. And neither will anyone else here. Now let me through. I will tell my men not to throw away their lives for you or any other barbarian warchief, no matter how many stolen diadems he wears."

"In that case… I am sorry, Abulius."

Rex Aeric must win this battle, no matter the cost. It is the fulfilment of all the plans Wortigern seeded so long ago, and thought lost; of Master Pascent, who raised my father from depths of slavery to one fit to one day rule a kingdom… No, it is more than that. It is our destiny, nobleman. The same destiny which saved my father from the disaster of Eobba's ship, which caused him to grow up not in the squalor of Tanet, but in the splendour of a Roman villa; that made me, born of a Briton mother and a Iute father, live through Wortimer's War, even when so many around me perished; that made me meet Wortigern and bring his diadem back from the West; that brought us all here, for this final battle, to decide the fate of the province; the same destiny, at last, which caused the tragic, inexplicable delay to Ursula's fleet – and forced me to do what I'm about to do…

I step up to him, lay a hand on his shoulder, then swiftly draw a knife and thrust it into his chest. In the chaos of battle around us, the only ones who see my foul deed are my Iutes – and a few Saxons who got close to the top of the battlements, baffled by what they're witnessing.

"I wish there was another way, nobleman," I tell him. "But the future of Britannia was chosen for us a long time ago."

"So this is how it ends…" Abulius croaks, blood spilling from his mouth. I hold him up from falling, as his legs buckle under him. "Tell the Council… they chose well…"

The Crown of the Iutes

"How come?" I ask, surprised.

"To fight the demons… it takes… a demon."

None of Abulius's soldiers have yet realised what we've done — and for a brief moment, not many of the attacking Saxons, either. They've been avoiding the northern gatehouse, knowing it's the strongest and best defended part of the fortress, and so, they fail to even notice at first that we've removed the heavy iron bars and flung the mighty Roman gate open.

They only spot us when my bear-shirts and I ride out of the gate in a broad column and charge across the battlefield, heading north towards the rear of Aelle's line by the river. Behind them, the Iutes of the fort's garrison fan out across the marsh into a broad front.

With a roar, the Saxon attackers pour towards the open gate, not stopping to wonder what accident or treachery gifted them the unexpected boon. Too late, the Briton guards return to try to shut it down. The overwhelming wave of enemy warriors sweeps them aside. The triumphant shout spreads through the battlefield. By the time we reach the river, so does the great cry of victory: Anderitum has fallen!

I dare not look back towards the fortress, and the slaughter that unravels within. I keep telling myself it was the only way. It was certainly the swiftest way, one that would result in fewer casualties altogether than letting Aelle and my father slog it out for a few hours more on the river shore. Already I can see the plan work around me, and I can tell victory is at hand. Breaking the enemy's line by making him think he's won, letting him inside the shield wall, or within the ramparts, was one of the oldest ruses I trained for with the bear-shirts. Fastidius taught this trick to my father, and my father taught it to me. I saw how well it worked at Segont, ten years ago, when the Hibernian assault faltered after breaching the fort's gates, and I knew it would work here; with their chieftains far on the front line, the Saxons at the rear would have no one to stop them from falling into the obvious trap.

I focus on the battle before me. As the news of the conquest spreads through the Saxon ranks, the mighty shield wall unravels from flank to flank. Every warrior wants to take part in winning back *Rex* Aelle's ancestral home from the *wealas*. Before long, only Aelle's own *Híréd* remains in place – everywhere else, the lines break up and scatter. My father's chieftains notice this quickly, and they push the *fyrd* through the breaches. Betula arrives at our side with her warriors – no longer surrounded and cut off from the main army, but now a threat to Aelle's dispersing rear.

The battle is not won yet. There still remain enough of the Saxon army at the riverside to hold us all in check. For a moment I fear that I've miscalculated, that even the unwilling sacrifice of the Briton defenders was in vain. Aelle rallies his men on the eastern flank, and reforms the shield wall, shorter now, but more compact, formed only of his best, most reliable warriors. Soon, the slaughter at Anderitum will end, and those who rushed into the fortress will be returning into the fray. The Iute *fyrd* made some great advances in the north and the east, crossing the river and reaching in places almost to Anderitum's ramparts – but now a new enemy force appears on the battlefield, with a roar and blowing of horns.

At last, the western *fyrd* of the Saxons has broken through the last of Wulf's defiant blockades, and marched onto the sand spits. Two, maybe three hundred fresh, eager men ready to join Aelle's ranks. If they reach us before we can make the final breakthrough, the battle is as good as lost. I look around, seeking a way out, but can't find any. There's nothing I can do anymore. I'm now part of the greater Iute army, commanded by my father – the finest warchief the tribe ever had; if he can't think how to turn the battle around, nobody can…

The Crown of the Iutes

"Who's that?" I hear Audulf's concerned question. "Have the pirates come to Aelle's help?"

I stare to where he's pointing – the beach to the east. Half a dozen *ceols* emerge from the fog like a fleet of wraiths and grind onto the gravel. Audulf is right to recognise them as pirate ships: these are the *ceols* we took from the Saxon pirates over the years, and which my father had repaired in secret in Dubris's boatyards. An army pours forth from their decks. No, not an army: a horde, a throng of people, shouting, shrieking, waving primitive weapons – clubs, tools, kitchen knives. A horde made up mostly of women, younglings, and old ones who can barely hold a stick in their hand.

"That's Ursula, with the Dorowernians," I tell him. "She made it! Just in time!"

And yet, too late... I feel suddenly cold, as I imagine trying to explain to her what I did at Anderitum.

"I didn't know Dorowernians had cavalry," Audulf notes.

Further to the east, the mass of the Cantian militia is flanked by a wing of riders, charging down the broad beach towards Anderitum's harbour on great warhorses.

"They don't," I say. I strain my gaze in the falling dusk. "Those must be... the Haestingas!"

"Ha!" Audulf claps his hands. "Haesta's coming to our aid? Now the victory is ours for sure!"

"I hope so – but we still have to live long enough to see it. Look out," I say, wearily raising my sword, "those spearmen are coming back!"

James Calbraith

She slaps me in the face and then, for good measure, knees me in the groin. When I collapse, two Iutes grab her by the arms and pull her away, despite her protests. They're my father's men, so they don't know who this strange *wealh* woman is, or why she's attacking their *aetheling*.

"Let her go!" I order them. "Ursula – there was no other way."

"There's always another way," she says coldly. "All you had to do was wait for us."

"You took too long. I couldn't have known you were coming. By the time you arrived, we would –"

"Many of your precious Iute kin would have died. I know. Instead, you decided the lives of the *wealas* were worth less than those of your brethren. As always."

"It's not that – it was the only possible strategy…"

"Tell *them* of your strategy," she cries out, pointing accusingly towards her army of women and younglings. "Tell the wives and daughters who sailed here to save their husbands and fathers! You ask me to bring them here – no, you begged me to, and for what? So that they witnessed your first act as their *Dux*, sending their kindred to slaughter, just so your father could have his triumph! And you didn't even have the guts to ask them to volunteer this time."

"I'm sorry – I truly am. But I couldn't do it any differently. There was no time."

The Crown of the Iutes

"You had time to get all your Iutes out – but none of the Britons. What happened to treating all your subjects equally? What happened to shedding blood for the *wealas* as if they were your own kin?"

I have no response. It's useless to point out that many of the Iute footmen also perished in the sally from the fort – and many more died fighting the shield wall at the river. I know she's right. I failed her – and I failed the Britons who trusted me to keep them from harm.

"I knew this would've happened. I warned you. The moment I turned my back on you, the moment I left you alone, you found a way to break all the oaths and use my people for your own means," Ursula says. "I can't do it anymore. I can no longer be your conscience. If this is who you really are, if that is how you want to rule, so be it – but you'll have to do it without me."

"Wait – what do you mean?"

"It's over, Octa. We're done. I can't be wedded to a murderer."

She turns around and storms away; I move after her, but someone grabs my hand and stops me.

"Leave her be, *Hlaford*," says Croha. "She will calm down and see how right you were. Those *wealas* fought well and their wives and mothers should be proud of how their sacrifice brought us victory. They will all join our warriors in Wodan's Mead Hall. Nobody could have done it better."

"I have to be with Ursula now."

"You have to be with your people. We have a great victory to celebrate and many good men to bury. The warriors need their *aetheling* tonight." She pulls me to her. "You need rest, *Hlaford*. It

[484]

was a long day, and it's going to be an even longer night," she says, and then whispers in my ear: "Did she just say you're a *Dux* now?"

"Yes – that was the deal my father agreed in Londin…"

She licks her lips.

"*The* Dux's *concubine* – I have to admit, that does sound better than *an* aetheling's *wench*…"

The Crown of the Iutes

James Calbraith

EPILOGUE
THE LAY OF ADELHEID, 470 AD

The wind shakes the boughs of a young apple tree. The white petals scatter, whirl in the breeze and fall onto the freshly swept pave stones of Dorowern's Forum.

A great crowd has gathered once again on the city's sole open space, cleared for the occasion of waste, refuse and makeshift huts that had grown back on it since my last triumph, almost two years ago. Today, the crowds are even greater, formed not just of the townsfolk and visitors from nearby countryside, but huge numbers of Iutes, who've been arriving to Dorowern for the past month to take part in the celebration.

Today's feast is not about me and my titles. Bishop Fastidius put the heavy diadem on my brow late last autumn, at a subdued ceremony in the ruins of the cathedral. It was nothing like the grand rituals of old, when Wortigern and his predecessors were taking power over the Britannia Maxima province. Out of the five *pagi* that in theory still fall under my authority, only two sent representatives to pay tribute: the Cants and the tiny tribe of Trinowaunts in the east. The others snubbed me, the way they've been snubbing the Council itself since Wortimer's death. The Atrebs, at least, under the aging Masuna, sent a message of congratulation, though it was clear from the tone that they didn't think much of a half-heathen forcing himself onto the *Dux*'s throne. *Comes* Albanus said nothing, haughtily ignoring my ascension, and biding his time – and the Regins, of course, had no power to say anything anymore.

Aelle may have been defeated at Anderitum, but he was far from crushed, and my father and I saw little point in humiliating him

The Crown of the Iutes

further by demanding that he subjects his Saxons to Londin rule. The South was lost to the Britons for good, and I had no plans to waste men and silver recapturing it for them. I was content with Aelle acknowledging my title as the heathen *Bretwealda*, retreating his warriors to the Regin borders and officially ceding all his claims to Wortigern's diadem. Today, however, is different, and I see him with his wife, eldest son and his household guard out in front of the crowd, next to the Cantian nobles on one side, and the chieftains of the Saxon clans of Trinowauntia on the other. Today, Aelle is forced to pay tribute to the man who vanquished his ambitions and ruined his hopes of ever becoming anything more than what he is now: the king of the Southern Saxons in the former *pagus* of the Regins.

Even Haesta is here – for the first time in Cantia in many years. He is as much a hero today as my father. The charge of his cavalry on Aelle's eastern flank sealed the fate of the Saxon army at Anderitum. He never told me why seeing Ursula's ships struggle with the tides and winds as they passed by his domain's shores ultimately convinced him to rally his riders and join the battle on my father's side – and I didn't prod, knowing how much turmoil the decision must have caused him. For his part in the victory, the grateful *Rex* Aeric granted him and his people, at long last, a pardon for their rebellion, and he granted them a swathe of fertile, box tree-covered hills to the west of his domain, carved out of what was once the Regin frontier.

My father is not yet present on the Forum. He makes the crowd wait for his arrival, shiver in the cool spring breeze. I tighten my coat of black fox fur. My riders are all with me – those who survived the wars in Gaul and Britannia; they are now the *Dux*'s personal guard – my very own *bucellarii*, led by Audulf, all clad in their red cloaks thrown over the bear-skin capes and wielding silver gleaming spears; they wear no tunics under the furs,to show off their scarred, muscular torsos, pale and rosy in the cool air.

James Calbraith

The riders may all be by my side, but Ursula stands across the Forum, with other Dorowern Councillors, and not just because she is the city's new *Praetor*. She hasn't forgiven me for what she perceives as the betrayal of her kin at Anderitum. She alone voted against my becoming a *Dux* when the Council gathered in Londin after the war – all other nobles were too terrified of my father's victorious armies, and too weary of the devastating conflict, to dare make such a stand. Since the row after the battle, through the whole of autumn and winter, she has barely spoken to me, and never once visited me in Londin, communicating with me only through official messages sent by the Dorowern Council – or through my father, with whom she continued to maintain some relations. In Ursula's place, Croha stands by my right, her belly already swollen with our first child. She may have hesitated to give herself to me when I was a mere *aetheling* – but once I became a *Dux*, the most powerful man in Britannia, her resistance melted away like spring ice. I was clear that she would never be anything more than a concubine – Ursula was my wife then, and would remain forever, unless she herself demanded a dissolution. But though we lived separately for such a long time, Ursula still hasn't yet given me the formal request of dissolution. By law, we remain wedded. Now she stares at me from across the Forum with eyes as cold as the wind – though once in a while I spot a glimpse of the old warmth, and hope for a reunion springs in my heart anew.

The great *villa* where I live and rule from, in the city's northern palace district, was granted to me by the Council; it was the same one which only a few months earlier belonged to Riotham, but the news we received from Gaul on the first ship that came after winter storms made clear that the Councillor would not be returning home anytime soon. Imperator Anthemius's grand campaign against the Goths failed horribly. In a battle at Arelate – another of many fought around that strategically placed southern city – Aiwarik's generals defeated Rome in alliance with the Arwernians, slaying the Imperator's son, dispersing his armies and shattering all hope of breaking through to Lugdunum to relieve the

[489]

The Crown of the Iutes

Briton army trapped there. We received no more letters from Riotham, except one, sent through one of his Arwernian contacts. It read like a farewell, and ended with a call to Britons to remain steadfast against the relentless onslaught of barbarians. Ironically, it was the first official letter I read out to the Council in my capacity as the new *Dux* of Britannia Maxima. The words of Riotham's appeal rang hollow within the walls of his own house.

The consequences of Anthemius's defeat were far-reaching and not all of them adverse; with the demise of the southern armies, Syagrius became the most powerful remaining Roman leader in all of Gaul, and finally could call himself a *Dux* – making *Rex* Aeric, his ally, the most influential of kings of the fair-hairs settled on Britannia. Between this, thwarting Aelle's ambitions and putting his son on Londin's throne, my father's achievements required recognition through a new title, one that reflected what he really became over the years: not only a protector of Cantia's borders, but also the man in whom the Britons put their hopes and to whom they referred for guidance when the Council at Dorowern faltered.

The trumpets blast a triumphant call; a murder of crows flees from the roof of Dorowern's church. The crowd stirs, and then freezes in place, expectantly. The first to enter the Forum are Betula and the *Hiréd*, clad in cloaks of boar-skin. After them, my father is brought in, standing on a great round shield painted with the design of the white horse, carried by four Saxons, captives of the war with Aelle. The Saxon king winces at the sight, but he kneels like everyone else when my father climbs down from the lowered shield and approaches the Councillors, huddling around Ursula.

I glance to the right, where the city's lone priest stands, frowning, surrounded by a handful of acolytes. This is not a pagan ceremony, but it's not one condoned by the Church, either; unlike Bishop Fastidius, who blessed Wortigern's diadem before putting it on my head and signed the Council's decree that gave me the power, the Dorowern priest was neither asked nor agreed to have the ceremony in his city. He is merely powerless to stop it. He should be glad that the Iutes haven't brought their own priests into Dorowern; my father's victories are proof enough of the might of the heathen gods.

Ursula steps forward. *Rex* Aeric kneels on one knee and gives her his circlet. She raises it to the sun. The rays glint off the silver thread. It is a modest trinket compared to the heavy, gem-studded jewel that I carry on my head, but it bears a certain dignity. My father had it forged from *Drihten* Hengist's diadem, one of the few objects brought over from the Old Country on those first three *ceols*. Hengist won it in his youth in Frisia, and wore it whenever he commanded the Iute armies, before my father replaced him and claimed the new title of the *Rex*. All this happened many years ago – an entire age in this fast-changing world. The circle of history has turned again, and once again, my father is re-forging his destiny like none before him, with a new title and a new diadem to add to his collection.

"You'd be surprised how capacious men's heads can be." The words of *Dux* Wortigern ring out in my head as Ursula lowers the silver circlet onto my father's brow, and then adds another, golden one, prepared by Cantian smiths with metal taken from the Saxon dead at Anderitum. A grimace mars her face momentarily as she remembers the other men who died in that battle: the Britons slaughtered within the fort's wall to bring my father his triumph. The Cants paid dearly for my father's victory, and if it was up to her only, I know she'd never agree to honour *Rex* Aeric like this. But her people, as weary and frightened as the Londin nobles, decided otherwise, and she had to yield to their choice, however wrong and unwise it might seem to her.

She soon composes herself and continues with the ceremony.

"You have guarded us well as the *Rex* of the Iutes, Aeric of Ariminum," she says through clenched teeth. "We hope – and pray

The Crown of the Iutes

to our Lord – that you will do the same as… our own kings of old."

This is the breakthrough; this is the innovation. No roaming barbarian tribe's ruler before my father has ever proclaimed himself the king of both his own heathen tribe, and the Christian, Roman people in whose lands they settled. Aiwarik is the king of the Goths, but rules the Gauls as a *Dux*; Hildrik, king of the Franks, is a mere *Comes* to his Latin-speaking subjects. Even Aelle bears only the circlet of the Saxons, leaving Regins in his land to rule themselves as best they can. All those monarchs were sometimes conquerors, sometimes allies, sometimes enemies of the Gauls, Romans and Britons in whose midst they lived, those strange men they called the *wealas*; but no *wealh* and barbarian tribe ever accepted each other simply as equals, the same men before law and God. Until today.

"I swear before your God and mine," my father declares, "that I will treat the Cants as I would treat my own subjects, and obey your laws as I obey the laws of the Iutes. No Cantish man or woman shall suffer under my rule where a Iute wouldn't suffer, and each will be rewarded for his service to me just as a Iute would be rewarded in his place. My sword is your sword. My shield is your shield."

His lofty vows, so similar to the promises I once made her, must ring hollow in Ursula's ears, but she presses on.

"Then rise, Aeric, take up your sword and your shield, and present them to your people," she commands, and when my father does so, she continues, her voice at once sweet and noble: "In the name of the Council of Dorowern and all free men of the *pagus*, I grant you the ancient title of the King of the Cants. May you bring us the fortune and prosperity that the kings of old brought us, before Rome – for Rome is gone, yet we are still here."

[492]

James Calbraith

There is a silent pause as the gathered crowd seems to be pondering the significance of what they're witnessing – until, at last, Betula raises a loud cheer, and we all join in a thundering cascade of triumphant roars.

Ursula sits at the foot of the carved timber bed and gazes gently at the child sucking softly at Croha's breast.

"She looks… strong," she says, at last. "And healthy." The sadness in her voice breaks my heart.

"Adelheid will grow into a mighty shieldmaiden," says Croha, proudly. "And a great support to her brother."

"Brother?" Ursula looks up. "You are with child again?"

"Not yet," Croha chuckles and glances to me. "But I'm sure I will soon be. The *Dux* needs an heir, doesn't he?"

My daughter gurgles and stirs in Croha's embrace. I wrap my arm around Ursula's shoulder, expecting to be rebuked, but she strokes my hand briefly. It is the first time she's touched me since Anderitum. I feel a great weight lifting slowly from my chest.

"They look like they both need rest," I say, nodding at Croha and my daughter. "Why don't we move to the dining room?"

There isn't a speck of dust on the marble floor, or on the citrus wood table in the middle of the sigma-shaped recliner. I made sure that everything was perfect in the *villa* for Ursula's arrival. The precious furniture, like everything else in the house, belonged once to Riotham – and it is by far the most luxurious in Londin; he must have imported it at great expense from the continent.

The Crown of the Iutes

A dark-haired youth sits on the edge of the recliner, staring at a speckled starling in the garden; the first of the season. He startles when we enter, but I calm him down. "It's alright, Weroc, you can stay," I tell him. "This is your house too, after all."

"You let Riotham's son stay with you?" Ursula asks.

"He lives with his mother – at least until Riotham returns from Gothic captivity. They have their own wing and separate entrance; we rarely even see each other. This place is big enough for several families – enough for you to move in, too, should you decide…"

"I only came to see the child, Octa," she replies. She sits down beside Weroc and stares at the starling in silence. The bird bursts into a complex, triumphant trill.

"This… is a nice place," she says, stroking the fine leather. "I might be coming here more often."

"You *will* stay the night?"

"I'm staying at the cathedral. I'm sorry."

I wince. "The cathedral is a windswept ruin. I have many empty bedrooms. Each more lavish than the other."

"Maybe next time." She smiles, softly. "Your father sent me to discuss some matters with the bishop…"

"You are my father's messenger now?"

"He *is* my king," she replies with an incredulous chuckle. Like most Cantian nobles, she too has a hard time accepting Aeric as a ruler not just of the Iute warbands, but of everyone living to the east of the Medu border.

"I can go with you," I offer eagerly. "I also need to speak with Fastidius, and I haven't seen him in several weeks. It's funny, really – when I moved here, I thought I'd be visiting the cathedral every other day, but I've been so busy these days…"

"You just had a child born," she replies. "It's understandable. Even a *Dux* needs some time for himself."

The starling flies away. Weroc, bored with our conversation, bids us farewell. I sit in his place, my shoulder touching Ursula's. I'm moved by an odd feeling, as if sensing the wheel of time turn a full circle. I am back at the beginning of my friendship with her, having to work my way back to her heart. Whether she's forgiven me for Anderitum, or if she decided I have suffered enough for my sins, I cannot say – and I dare not ask. All that matters is that she's here, now, her voice as warm and her eyes as bright as the spring sun that brings life to the *villa*'s gardens.

"I saw the chapel you started building on Dorowern's graveyard," she says quietly. "A fitting memorial to the fallen."

"It will not bring them back to life."

"They live life eternal with the Lord now." She pauses. "His Grace mentioned you also paid for the Mass in their memory."

"It was the least I could do."

"You *could* swear you're never going to send men needlessly to their deaths."

"Their deaths weren't…" I protest, but stop, seeing her scowl. "Anyway, I doubt I will ever lead an army to battle again. A *Dux*'s job is far more tedious than that. Right now, for example, I spend most of my days preparing for the great revels of Easter…"

The Crown of the Iutes

"Why, what happens at Easter?"

"*Dux* Ambrosius is coming, at long last," I say. "It will be the first time that two *duces* meet since Wortigern. And likely the last – Ambrosius is an old man now…"

"Is he going to finally wed Madron to his son?"

"I would assume so. Though it hasn't been confirmed yet. You can ask Fastidius tonight."

"Londin will be empty without her," she notes wistfully. "She is a bright spark at the cathedral."

"I doubt she'll be able to stay away for long. Londin is all she knows – and the city has a way of carving itself on one's heart forever."

"Do you think Honorius will let her come here?"

"She's too strong-willed to be commanded by the likes of Honorius. And all she has to do is write me. I will always be able to come up with some official reason for her visit. These aren't Wortigern's days – we're not in conflict with the West anymore."

"Maybe one day we'll even be able to go see her in Corin."

We. The weight on my chest melts away completely. I take her hand in mine.

"I'm so glad you came," I say. "It's been so lonely here without you."

"Lonely?" She laughs. "In Londin? With Croha and the child? With Riotham's family next door? With all those servants and supplicants crowding the corridors?"

I grimace. "You know what I mean. Other than Fastidius, there isn't anyone here with whom I could just… talk. And we're both too busy to meet regularly. I don't want to turn into my father, bitter and alone in his mead hall."

"You have a good friend in the bishop," she says. "It was he who told me I should come here today."

"Then I must remember to donate a few more gold rings to the rebuilding effort next time I see him," I say with a forced chuckle. "How did he achieve this miracle?"

"His Grace truly believes in the power of forgiveness… He said he had to absolve your father of far worse sins than you could ever have committed – so that they could stay brothers and friends."

"Did he tell you what those sins were?"

"No – but he didn't need to. I can guess what kinds of things a man had to do to rise from slave to a king. And I can guess what being raised by such a man might do to a young boy."

"I was raised more by the bishop than by my father," I say. "And before that, the hermits in the monastery in the West."

"Then perhaps, Lord willing, there is still hope for you."

"For us both."

She turns to me and stares into my eyes.

The Crown of the Iutes

"Have you grown to love her?" she asks.

"She bears my child."

"That's not what I asked."

"I… yes, I suppose. But never as much as I love you."

She lowers her eyes. "My *villa* also gets lonely sometimes," she says quietly. "Wraiths roam its empty hallways. On moonless nights, I feel the demons prowling in the darkness, encroaching from all sides, and I weep in fright."

Demons…

I see the accusing stare of Abulius, dying in my arms, and close my eyes to get rid of the sight.

"This is a dark age," I say. "None of us should be facing it alone."

"I… perhaps I could stay one more night in the city, after all."

"I would like that." I gently stroke her hand. "I would like that very much."

The starling returns to the garden and lands on the branch – with another, a female, summoned next to him by his romantic warbling.

James Calbraith

HISTORICAL NOTE

The tragic tale of the Briton leader Riothamus and his failed expedition against the Goths is the last, tantalising glimpse into the post-Roman Britain we have until the muddy, apocalyptic ravings of monk Gildas, seventy years later – and the last time anyone on the continent seems to have anything concrete to say about the situation in Britannia until Augustine's mission. It is all the more curious that even at this late date, the Briton aristocracy is clearly involved with the highest level of the Western Empire's politics and diplomacy: Riothamus is in contact with Emperor Anthemius in Mediolanum, with Burgundians in Lugdunum, and with the famed man of letters, Sidonius Apollinaris in Clermont (Arvernis). These few scattered mentions paint a picture of late fifth century Britannia very different from the remote, barbarian-swamped backwater often imagined. No wonder that a few historians want to see in Riothamus yet another source for the myth of King Arthur.

That something very important – and very confusing – has happened in the late 460s around the River Loire, there is no doubt. Various chroniclers describe battles between Saxons, Franks and Gauls in Angers and on the islands of the Loire, though it is not always easy to tell from their reports who's fighting whom. A certain Odovacrius is mentioned, leading the Saxons, and though most historians now think he is a different man than the later known Odoacer, King of Italy, it is simply too attractive a coincidence for me to pass on.

With the Battle of Pevensey (Anderitum) I finally tie the fictional chronology of these books with that of the Anglo-Saxon Chronicle: Aelle's legendary "invasion" of Sussex and his subsequent conquest of the *civitas* of the Regnenses. Though the Chronicle puts the massacre of Britons at Pevensey as late as 491 AD, the confused lunar dating used for these early entries means it may have happened – if it was at all historical – 19 years earlier.

Printed in Great Britain
by Amazon

21298277R00285